I0788578

Requited Rivalry

also by Chelsey Blue Spicer

Paramour Promise
Optimistic Oath

The 2nd Collection of Colorful Choices

Requited Rivalry

Chelsey Blue Spicer

To the teenager without shoes
sitting outside Starbucks in December.

And the pink haired girl
with the sign on the median.

Also, the one sleeping in that car
outside of the grocery store.

Oh, and the one at the 24 hour
school library who accidently
fell asleep on her book.

1

Zoe killed Vincent Gibson so many times, but not once did she do it correctly. The downtown lights of Phoenix cast a yellowish glow on the city below the prosecutor's seventh-floor office. Sighing at the window where the sun had long set, she admonished herself for having lost track of time.

With a deep breath, Zoe closed her eyes and tried to kill the prison guard correctly.

She pictures Gibson near a small table with his back to her. The scene is paused like a DVD, waiting for her to hit play.

"Something's wrong," she whispers, feeling her stomach trying to tie itself in a knot.

She scans the kitchen, cataloging the pans piled up in the sink and surrounding counter. A fly crawls around the edge of one filled with molding water.

Her tongue scraped against her teeth at the idea of the stench.

Mail is thrown over the table with the envelopes sliced along the tops. The small knife is under the electric bill. She steps from the back door to the knife and picks it up. Only four inches, but it would get the job done.

Zoe exhales slowly, and Vincent Gibson comes to life. He doesn't know she's there, and the laminate floor doesn't make a sound as she closes the distance between them.

She raises her arm, bringing it down on the top of his shoulder.
"Shit!"
The blade hit the wrong place on his back.

She'd imagined it wrong, again. She'd forgotten to consider she was bigger than the girl that had stabbed Gibson.

The kitchen vanished as Zoe's eyes popped open. She held her breath, adjusting to reality. The tension faded as she relaxed in the leather office chair. Her toes rubbed against the familiar rough carpet below her desk. She scanned the wall of legal texts across the room until she separated herself from the murderous teenager she'd been impersonating.

Zoe knew she had to go back to the kitchen for what felt like the one thousandth time. She knew if she tried to go home now, Gibson would show up in her dreams covered in blood. Just like he had every night since she'd been assigned this case. It didn't matter how many times it took; Zoe wouldn't be able to sleep until she got it right.

She closed her eyes again.

The off-white walls and yellow floor are waiting for her. She stands by the back door silently with the knife already in her hand when Vincent Gibson appears. She imagines him taller, then wider. She focuses on getting him right this time— cropped hair balding from the guard's cap, sweaty white shirt still tucked into his work issued khakis, and a cell phone in his hand.

She raises her arm again, bringing it down through his shoulder. First through the left trapezius, then slices the levator scapulae. The blade knicks the C6 vertebrae, and he falls into the table.

Gibson's knees crack, fracturing under his weight, and she hears him cry out.

Zoe retreats a step towards the grotesque sink to continue this time as a spectator, instead of the murderer. The oily haired teenager, Olivia Moore pulls the blade from Gibson's flesh. His white shirt turns red with blood flowing from the first strike as she delivers another blow. This time into the top of his shoulder, stopping at the clavicle. Four inches isn't enough, or the teenager doesn't have the force to do much damage here. Moore thrusts the knife into his back for the third time. All strikes to the left side of the man's body.

His phone falls to the floor. He can't call for help. Gibson tries to push himself up from the table, but the fractured patella stops him from being able to get up.

Zoe pauses the characters in her head. She moves to the other side of the room, where both the victim and the murderer face her. Moore's cold eyes glare in fury; her teeth bare like a feral cat. Gibson looks terrified and seems to be searching for someone to help him through the kitchen window.

Comfortable with all the details, Zoe breathes them back to life.

Moore pulls the knife out of Gibson's back. She looks at the door because Zoe feels this would be the point any normal person would try to leave. She didn't leave though. Instead, she comes around the front of him.

Gibson goes for the knife because it's his only chance of surviving this. His bigger frame launches toward the girl. He played football in high school, so he would use his size to his advantage.

The imaginary people travel through Zoe, leaving a blood trail that isn't in any of the crime scene photos.

Zoe opened her eyes again. She yanked at the roots of her hair. Pulled until real pain distracted her from the frustration causing her muscles to twist into knots.

The whiteboard across from her desk had been filled with the photos from the kitchen. Gibson lay in the center of the room with numbered crime tags surrounding his corpse. Notes were jotted in expo marker and Post-its were stuck to several photos. She'd constructed the scene that morning, finally bringing the images back from her own apartment. The board was another reminder of how long she'd been sitting there failing. Something she wasn't accustomed to, which was why this case was hers.

The other prosecutors on her floor annoyed her with their socializing throughout the day. There was a camaraderie the others on the floor shared while she worked on cases, they could only dream of being assigned. Their constant chatter repeatedly broke her concentration, so she'd looked forward to the mass exit between 4 and 5PM. They would go out for drinks or home to families while she walked through the scene over and over again. But the quiet halls provided the blank-faced people in the photos the peace they required to properly haunt her office with their equally silent stares.

"Just get it right so you can go home," she told herself.

She didn't remind herself Gibson's ghost would follow her back to the one-bedroom apartment if she didn't get it right. The yawn that escaped was enough of a warning to get her version of events to align with the evidence. Failure to do so would give Gibson's ghost an excuse to disrupt her sleep, like he had every night for the past year. A year of trying to figure out how the fifteen-year-old murdered him with a four-inch blade and walked away with only a cut on her arm and bruises around her wrists.

"Just choreograph it right so he'll leave you alone."

Another yawn hit her, and she knew she was running out of time. Closing her eyes, she started again.

Three strikes before Moore comes around to the front of him. He pleads with her to stop, so she kicks him back.

"Still doesn't make sense." Zoe hit her hand on the desk. "Even with one arm, he would have had the ability to block her kick. Stop making them do the same thing."

But she couldn't think of another way to explain how Gibson ended up on his back and stabbed in the groin.

Zoe's head rolled against the back of the chair, followed by another yawn. This time her whole body expelled the minimal energy she had left.

Her eyes drooped. She tried to keep them open, but her chin fell with her eyelids. That's all it took for Gibson to stand in front of her, the crotch and leg of his khakis soaked with blood from the final blow Zoe can't explain.

The disgusting kitchen immediately dissipates until only Olivia Moore stands in the doorway at the back of the house. She's looking down at what she'd done. Her mouth moves, telling Zoe what she needs to know, but no sound comes out.

"I can't hear you," Zoe says to the teen who was in the middle of a silent explanation.

Olivia's mouth closes as she looks once more at the man covered in blood. She turns from them both. Her fingers leave a trail across the back door as she walks away. That was another imaginary trail of blood, not in a single photo.

Zoe shot up in her chair. Fingers dug into the leather arm rests. Her chest was heaving because the kid was still alive. She wasn't supposed to be in Zoe's dream because she was the killer. Zoe knew she was the killer. There was no way she couldn't be the killer. And killers didn't haunt Zoe.

Victims haunted her until she found answers. But Moore wasn't a victim. There was no evidence that the bruises on the girl's wrists came from Gibson. The female DNA on his penis hadn't belonged to the teen, so there was no reason to believe he raped her, which Zoe might have struggled with the decision to prosecute Moore if that had been the case.

The fifteen-year-old with brown hair plastered to the sides of her face and vacant eyes stared out from the mug shot on Zoe's desk. The girl wasn't sad, angry, or even smiling at what she had done. The teen simply looked at Zoe like she couldn't understand.

At first, Zoe tried to imagine the shadowed path of Moore's life before she picked up the knife. The kid didn't have a record, and no one could be sure Olivia Moore was even her real name because on paper she didn't seem to exist. So, Zoe walked the downtown alley Moore had used to flee the crime scene. Spoken to hookers, crackheads, and the college students who traveled the same path. No one had seen the girl before, so Zoe searched crevices and along dumpsters for the words 'Olivia was here,' like had been carved into the collapsing apartment above Gibson's garage.

Zoe had asked questions the night Moore was arrested. Used every trick she'd learned, but Moore didn't answer questions. She didn't speak. Not once in the year since she'd told the arresting officer she couldn't go back and that her name was Olivia Moore.

So many questions still needed answers. Zoe needed answers because someone like Olivia Moore didn't make since to her. A kid didn't just disappear without a paper trail in 2023.

Zoe's own mother had sent her six TikTok videos and called twice just that afternoon. She ignored both calls, but asked the photo, 'Where is your mother?'

When her brother text her to remind Zoe that they were going fishing that weekend, she asked, 'Do you have any brothers or sisters?'

After Zoe ran into her ex-girlfriend at Starbucks, she asked the photo, 'How did you just drop into Phoenix without a trace?'

Taping up the photos on the whiteboard gave her more questions to ask the photo of the girl. The first was 'Why were you staying in that shitty apartment?' She asked next, 'Did the drugs you took make you forget killing a person was wrong?' Then, 'Did you ever care about anything at all?'

Even now Zoe wanted to ask Moore the questions. Wanted to interview her like she'd done with the serial murderer's wife, Janice Carter during law school. Take notes as she tried to understand how someone could murder a person or watch as a person was murdered. Maybe then she could stop second guessing locking the kid up in the same prison as Janice Carter.

A kid in the same cell as that woman who'd stood by as her husband killed twelve women was something Zoe wasn't completely okay. Not when she didn't understand why Moore murdered Gibson.

"Nothing justifies murdering another person," Zoe reminded herself, just like her father would.

She closed her eyes once more. Went through the visualization strategy her father had taught her, even though he'd been a corporate lawyer, not a criminal prosecutor. It was the same tactic he'd used when working with DA Nia Williams, Zoe's current boss. As a child, she'd sat outside the office and listened to her father coach Nia through the Carter Serial Killer case when Zoe was seventeen. That was the case that made her want to be Nia, only better.

First, she had to bring the scene to life once more.

'Close your eyes,' he'd said to Nia.

The kitchen is exactly the same. Gibson leans against the table with three wounds on his back. Moore comes to the front with the knife because she's not afraid of him. She kicks him back as he tries to get up. He's down, but Moore doesn't leave. She kneels over him, twisting the blade into his groin.

"You're still here," the very real voice in the very real office said.

Zoe's eyes popped open as she held her chest. Nia Williams stood in the doorway with jacket and purse in hand. In all the years Zoe had known Nia, the woman's style had never changed. Her blouse even had shoulder pads, something Zoe didn't think came in shirts since before she was born.

The office didn't sound quiet with Zoe's brain shooting out a hundred commands in her father's tone to fix herself for Nia. Her feet immediately slid back into the Jimmy Choo heels under her desk. They pinched her toes, but she couldn't handle the idea of Nia considering her unprofessional. Not when the woman had known her since preschool and watched her grow up beside Nia's own daughter.

Working under Nia's sharp eye and quick tongue left Zoe constantly worried she'd lose her boss's favor she'd acquired when the woman's daughter, Ari had left for the army right after graduation. Nia hadn't cared that Zoe broke Ari's heart by pretending to be straight, in fact, Nia commended her for it. She'd shaken Zoe's hand that day for protecting both their families from a homosexual scandal during an election year. She'd also promised to mentor Zoe when the time came. Something she desperately needed now.

"Ms. Williams. I was... ahmm... walking through the specifics. Jury selection is next week."

Nia's authority pulled Zoe to her feet. She fumbled with file folders, sliding Olivia's picture within one. Zoe picked up the folders and returned them to the white box on the table in front of the window. She hoped Nia didn't notice the way her ankle twisted when she stepped wrong in the high heel.

The District Attorney walked to the whiteboard and analyzed the crime scene photos. She tapped on Olivia Moore's mug shot with a nail that was missing a chip of polish.

"I heard Judge Miller released the girl to Greyson Academy."

Zoe rolled her eyes at the mention of Judge Miller. He hated her and she couldn't help but feel it was because she was a woman. Every chance he had the man would call her by that stupid nickname Nia once overheard when Zoe was on the phone in law school. It had spread like fire through the office and courthouse, and Judge Miller used it to burn her when he said it in the condescending tone he reserved for Zoe.

"He *felt* she didn't pose a threat there. Some social worker woman named Dilynn showed up to plead the girl's case. Miller took one look at her and signed the papers."

"That wasn't some social worker. That was Dilynn Greyson." Nia turned to Zoe, shaking her head. "Myopic Miller is an old fool. He only has his seat thanks to Sylvia Winters and Dilynn Greyson, and that school for delinquents is just Greyson's project to pad their family's bank account. Her family has their hands in everything. If it isn't Greyson-the-Do-Gooder, it's The Winters Group. And don't even think for a second you can separate the two because Greyson and Winters were together for years, and I wouldn't doubt that they are still sleeping together, even though Greyson is married to one of those 'gender doesn't exist' freaks."

Zoe hadn't considered the woman who showed up in court as a threat to her case, let alone The Winters Group. The thirty-something blonde in her bulky cardigan didn't look like someone with the type of money capable of buying judges. She didn't even wear nice shoes.

"I was having dinner with the mayor when they arrested the girl," Nia explained. "It surprises me Greyson intervened since Moore broke her daughter's nose trying to resist arrest. I was expecting assault on an officer to be added."

Zoe held up a hand.

"Wait, Greyson's daughter is a cop? How? The woman looks barely older than me."

"Greyson adopted the girl when Evie was in high school. I think there's maybe ten years between the two. She has three. All adopted as teenagers. Maybe two. I'm not sure the last one was actually adopted because no one really talks about that one." Nis turned to Zoe. "Do you care to guess who was the judge for each of those adoptions?"

Zoe narrowed her eyes at the yellow pad of witnesses on her desk.

"Miller."

She hadn't thought about the arresting officer, and it irked her that she'd failed to connect Officer Everleigh Greyson with the woman who'd came to court to speak on Moore's behalf.

Nia dismissively waved her hand in the air. "Doesn't matter honestly. This is not juvenile court, so Miller's opinion holds minimal influence on the jury."

"Landon Woods has convinced Moore to plead not guilty due to self-defense."

"Did he put Greyson's daughter on the witness list?" Nia asked.

Zoe flipped to the defense's list. She ran her finger down the names until it landed on Everleigh Greyson. Tapping it, she made a mental note to speak to the woman's commanding officer about being on the wrong side.

Then she said, "He did."

"Figures."

"Why?"

"On Monday, I will send you over the file I've kept on the Greysons since the woman started collecting violent offenders. And just so you know, Evie Greyson was the first violent offender she brought home. The kid took a baseball bat to a friend of mine's car when she was fourteen. She was a drunk and a drug addict, and she ruined his name with her bullshit."

Zoe looked out the window. She'd spoken to Officer Greyson briefly before she questioned Moore. Had worked with the woman often enough to know the officer wasn't still a drug addict. In fact, she was a witness on a lot of Zoe's cases because the officer tended to take any call where a female was being assaulted.

"Just know when I say that family has their hands in everything, I am not joking. Woods is Greyson's personal attorney, and..." Nia lauded dramatically, "her daughter's high school sweetheart. Then, there's the homeless one Greyson picked up from the literal street who's a state's prosecutor for family court, and the third is related to the freak Greyson is married to. That one is an intern with the Department of Child Services."

Nia chuckled wickedly before she continued.

"Woods looks like a giant fat baby, and he's gained so much notoriety so quickly because he's been fucking the cop since high school and Dilynn will do anything to keep her poisonous princess happy. But just be happy you're facing Woods and not my snake of an ex-husband who handles all Sylvia Winters's cases. Dilynn is keeping this in house it seems. Just watch out because where Dilynn is, Sylvia Winters is lurking in the shadows behind her. Pretty sure Winters owns half of the state because she funds anyone who will back her homosexual agenda. She definitely owns Miller. And Winters would definitely pay off a jury if Dilynn asked her too."

Zoe rubbed her hand over her eyes. She was too tired to process all the ways this whole thing had to breach some form of ethical code. It didn't stop her mind from trying though.

"So, what's the motive?" Nia asked, pulling Zoe back to the bigger problem in her hands.

Nia set her purse and jacket down before lowering herself into a leather armchair. This was an opportunity to work with the woman she'd known since childhood. The woman who's poise in the courtroom was worshiped by her father. She needed to learn everything she could to efficiently replace Nia someday as District Attorney. The only problem was Zoe's inability to effectively participate in these sorts of situations.

'Just act human,' she told herself. But she wasn't even sure what she meant.

Zoe gripped the edge of the table and supported her weight to alleviate some of the pressure on her feet. She tried to appear relaxed, but her heart drumming in her ears made it difficult to come up with anything that seemed halfway intelligent.

She could feel Nia studying her until Zoe confessed, "Without any statement from Moore, I am just playing it over and over again in my head trying to find a reason this happened. I keep walking through the scene like my father taught me, but I can't explain why she stabbed him in the groin."

"What do you know?"

"Last name she gave hasn't turned up any hits. No police reports about her as a runaway. Couldn't get her to say what school she went to. It's like this girl dropped into Phoenix from the sky," Zoe explained. She glanced out the window, seeing one of the regular junkies moving down the street as he searched trash bins. "I know no one is looking for her, so definitely homeless."

She handed Nia a photo of the scene.

"Police found evidence she had been staying in the apartment over Gibson's garage."

Nia looked over the photograph of the dilapidated dwelling. The only thing there was a mat made from old couch cushions with a tattered blanket. A bucket filled with urine and feces. And scratched into the wall, the words: Olivia was here.

"So, she's living on the street and finds the apartment vacant. Gibson finds her squatting on his property. She is a runaway, under the influence, and she snaps. Kills him so she doesn't get locked up."

Zoe holds up her hand, "Except she killed him in the kitchen of the house."

"So, she followed him inside. Maybe tried to bargain with him. He doesn't want to deal with her. He deals with scum all day long; he shouldn't have to do it in his own home. Tells her he's calling the cops. She snaps."

Nia snapped her fingers, emphasizing the breaking point.

The older woman made the whole event sound so simple. Zoe went back to the scene, but this time started in the apartment. There was a confrontation. Olivia was strung out and tried to reason with him, but he wouldn't listen. Gibson left to call the police and Moore followed him. She fixed Moore's face with one of paranoia, then stood her in front of Gibson. She couldn't get arrested because drug charges had mandatory sentences, so she picked up the knife from the table and the murder took place again.

It didn't feel right, though. Running away made more sense than following someone. And if Moore was just trying to get away from Gibson, one stab in the back would have been enough. Unless she was a cold-blooded murderer. Zoe glanced at the mugshot once more. She searched for any humanity in the girl's face as she had when she'd written her case study on the serial murderers, James and Janice Carter. Moore looked like a ghost compared to Janice Carter, whose fake smile had left Zoe feeling like she was next to be murdered.

"Here's what I don't get." Zoe took a deep breath, and collected her thoughts so they would run in a straight line. "Moore's small, malnourished even. A rear attack would be safest. But she comes at him from the front, and he doesn't defend himself almost like he was holding something, but there was nothing there. And you said it, he worked with prisoners all day. But he couldn't take on a fourteen-year-old girl half his size?"

Nia clicked her tongue and waved her index finger back and forth. "Not something you should dwell on."

The older woman smiled wickedly. Her red lipstick had smeared across the front of her teeth, making her appear like the Twilight casting call reject the woman's daughter always claimed her to be.

"But—"

"You have a drugged-out teenage girl found with the victim's blood on her clothes. You have her blood on the victim. He fought back enough to cut her. Thanks to *CSI*, this is an easy conviction."

Zoe tried to swallow the honey coming from Nia's fly trap of a mouth, but a part of her was sickened at how easy Nia made it all sound. It was like when Nia's daughter Ari came out and Nia sent the girl to live with her father. Throwing away her daughter during an election year seemed as easy as convicting a fifteen-year-old girl in criminal court as an adult. It was just acceptable and necessary.

The vacant green eyes stared back at Zoe from a photo on the evidence board. She briefly wondered if Ari had looked at her mother the same way when she'd learned she was disposable. Zoe cast away the thoughts of her childhood friend and first girlfriend to focus on Nia.

Her boss was here and important, while Ari was just one of many real estate lawyers representing The Winters Group. What happened between Ari and Nia didn't matter anymore because Nia was going to help Zoe be important like she was. She'd always favored Zoe over Ari, and this was why. Zoe would do what it took to win and make the woman proud.

Nia stood up and headed to the door before commanding, "Go home, Zoe. Get some rest."

The kid's eyes challenged Zoe to figure out what was missing while Nia's presence lingered in the office. She kicked her shoes off and slouched into the leather armchair that still smelled like her boss's perfume. She hated the perfume because to her it smelled like Raid.

Vincent Gibson in his prison guard uniform stared at the camera for his ID photo. He didn't smile, and the photo had the same empty expression as Moore's. When Zoe had taped up his photo alongside Moore's, she'd meant it to help her recreate the scene. But together, their lack of emotion made everything blurry.

Zoe moved Gibson to the other side of the board. He was a victim. Olivia Moore murdered him in his home and the semen found on her clothes wasn't a DNA match for Gibson. He hadn't raped her like Zoe had at first thought, but she'd stabbed him four times and left him lying in a pool of his own blood.

If she wanted to replace Nia someday, Zoe would have to start acting like her. Whatever happened to Moore to make her lose her sense of right and wrong didn't matter. It couldn't matter because Gibson was dead.

2

Plastic tipped darts *thunked* in sets of three. Women cheered and groaned over the country music playing in the oldest lesbian bar in the Phoenix Metro area. The points tallied around Parker as she stood at the line posed to throw her third dart.

"Oh, come on! We gotta get to zero first. Stop shooting at the fucking one mark! 20s or 19s!" Echo called out over the bar noise.

Parker lost focus as the electronic dart board seemed to inch farther away. She glanced around her and saw the other players in the league watching her suck. She dropped her hand and rolled the borrowed dart between her thumb and index finger. She had tried holding the dart closer to the plastic tip during the first round of throws, but it didn't even hit the board. Apparently, what she was doing now wasn't working either.

"Twenty. Twenty and she'll shut up," Parker muttered to herself.

She tried to loosen the tension in her shoulder, placed her foot along the edge of the tape line, and aimed at the largest portion of the twenty mark.

"Just focus on the number you want to hit. And make sure it's not the fucking one again!" Echo yelled at her.

Parker snapped around. "How the fuck am I supposed to focus with you yelling at me every time I try to shoot?!"

Echo's response was a laugh and a raised Coors Lite.

Her eyes had no problem shooting imaginary darts at her best friend's head, but even those didn't stick. Turning back to the board, Parker quickly released the last dart in her hand before Echo could interrupt her again.

This time the dart missed the one mark the other two had at least stuck in. Heat spread up Parker's chest and settled in her cheeks as the third dart sailed just over the eighteen mark. The tip bounced off the outside of the board, then smacked against the ground.

She took the short walk of shame back to the high-top table.

A woman on the other team staggered up to the line, while Parker and Echo sat quietly. The dart machine sang praises for the other woman's skill as she quickly hit three triples, ending the fourteenth game. With only one game left, Parker and Echo's team was destined to lose the match.

Echo finished her fifth beer and fished a sixth from the dented tin bucket. Her dark eyebrows knitted together when they ran over Parker's folded arms.

"Still no job?" Echo asked.

Parker's brown eyes studied the beer in her hand. "Yep."

Echo pressed the faded NWBA cap on her head. Then, she asked, "What happened at ArtReach? I thought it was going well."

"It was."

Parker stared at the patio door, praying the other team would come back from smoking so she could avoid this conversation. The music was barely audible over her own heart beating in her ears. She didn't have the courage to look at Echo. With each drink, Parker tried to ignore the way her skin burned from the laser focus Echo had on her.

Parker sighed as a second song ended on the digital jukebox.

"They googled me," Parker grumbled.

Slowly, Parker shook her head, trying to brush away the pitiful look the director of ArtReach had given her when he'd said they wouldn't be hiring her after her internship ended. She did not want pity, but it was what she would find in Echo's dark eyes if she looked up.

Parker set the beer bottle down, then picked it back up. Twirled it some, considering how good it would feel to throw it. But she would not throw it. Especially in Echo's bar. She may be unemployable trash, but she had manners. She set it back down again and stared at it.

"It just sucks." Parker looked at the wooden rafters, shaking her head once more. "I completed my master's in half the time as anyone else... and... and... and it means nothing. I'm a fucking good therapist, and no one is going to give me the time of day because of who my parents are."

She took another drink to wash away the bitter taste the word 'parents' left in her mouth. James and Janice Carter had been in prison since she was fifteen, but they were still fucking up the life of their only daughter. Even with years of practice, it took a lot of effort to stop years of bottled-up tears from escaping before they started the last round.

"It just takes time."

"Yeah, well... time takes money. And since there ain't any left, I'm going to have to dig out my fancy thong, pheromone spray, and body glitter."

Echo set her beer down. "You're not going back to stripping."

"I'm gonna have to do something. And if it means dancing, then it is what it is." Parker choked out a laugh. "I made good money at least. Paid for these tits."

She looked down at the second biggest financial investment she made in herself besides two college degrees. Two degrees that sat in a box because no one would hire her.

"No."

"Echo, I—"

Echo's voice turned to stone. "I said no."

Parker straightened her shoulders and set her eyes on Echo. She waited for the lecture to start, intentionally slowing her breathing so she didn't yell at the woman looking out for her. The only person who had ever treated her like family until Echo got married to a woman who hated her.

The sigh that came from Echo was worse than a lecture.

Parker leaned into the table, hoping if she closed the distance between them, she could reenter the protective bubble Echo had wrapped around her when they met in juvenile detention.

"I'm not trying to disappoint you," she promised.

Echo took another drink. She didn't look at Parker, but she spoke.

"You're not a disappointment. I just don't want you taking your clothes off for cash again. Yeah, it paid your tuition and bills in college, but I don't wanna worry about you getting raped or murdered or all the fucking drugs shoved in your face. And you can't forget how the only girl you ever were in a relationship with broke up with you because of it. You can't find someone if your taking your clothes off for cash."

Echo pushed her short dark hair from her forehead, then shoved the hat back on her head.

"You did better than all of us that got out. You didn't end up an addict like Henrietta. You managed to go to college and graduate instead of getting knocked up like Xio. You did things that I can only dream about. Got an education and that means something, so you shouldn't be rubbing your giant, gay, fake tits all over skeezy guys, no matter how much they pay you now that you're a D instead of an A. Not with a fucking college degree."

"You think I don't know that?" Parker stared at the table, only looking up when another bucket of beer was set down.

"Look, I know you don't want help—" Echo started.

"Then don't."

Echo shook her head. "Simone has this friend that owns this place—"

"I can get a job on my own," Parker growled.

Even if she couldn't, the last person she ever wanted to get help from was Echo's wife, Simone Wyatt. She'd already stolen her best friend when she was fresh out of juvie. And Echo was too loyal to see that Simone was a verbally abusive creep.

A wad of cash slapped against the table in front of Parker. A pile of twenties, crisp from an ATM that promised Parker a chance to breathe and eat.

"Simone said she saw you coming out of St. Vincent's with a food box. You should've asked..." The rest of Echo's sentence was lost in a mumbled breath. She rubbed her fingers against her temples and cleared her throat. "Just get yourself some groceries and put some on your electric box. And when you run out, you come to me. I'll put you to work with most of your clothes on."

The storm beating the fortified walls within Parker calmed just for a moment as she slid the bills into her bra. The paper against her breast gave her a momentary sense of relief because tomorrow she could eat something green. And she had at least one more week to land a job before she'd have to go back to the cabaret with her chin pressed against her chest.

The energy around the table changed as their opponents rejoined them. Parker watched Echo laugh with the two women, not even phased by the stench of cheap weed seeping from their clothes and hair. It never crossed her mind Echo would laugh with other people the way they had when the lights in their shared cell had been shut off. Parker never considered Echo had friends beside her and Xio, the barback, who had bed Parker well after Simone made it impossible to stay with Echo anymore.

Parker watched quietly, unable to insert herself into the conversation. Social situations weren't her forte, so she stayed still, hoping the others would forget she was there. Which they did, until Echo told them they had to get the next match going because Echo's kid was turning one tomorrow.

While one of the women set up the board and the other ordered another drink from the bar, Echo turned back to Parker.

She explained the game they'd already played three times. "Cricket is a strategy game. You have to hit all the numbers greater than 15 three times, and then you can..."

Spots flashed, blurring Echo's face as the music drowned out her words. Parker blinked several times, clearing the haze.

"Nineteen. I'll do the rest... I need you... This is strategy... losing too much."

A yawn escaped from Parker as Echo finished her explanation.

"Are you even listening?" Echo asked.

Parker rolled her eyes, and repeated the only thing that matter to Echo, "Nineteen."

"Your sister from another mister's up first," the skinnier opponent called to Echo.

Parker got up, and even with a cool head, the first dart landed in the one mark again. The one mark was literally on the complete opposite side of the board. Her chest filled with lead, pulling her to the ground as she studied the place she wanted to hit. When she could no longer hold the breath, she released the dart. It sailed through the air with just enough force to drop from the one to the eighteen.

"Better," Echo said. "But I said aim for the nineteen. It's literally the other side of the board."

Parker sucked her teeth. The momentary pride she'd felt at having hit a number to make the board sing vanished. She stared at the nineteen. Focused on the little strip that would give her triple the points. With a steady hand, she shot. This time hitting the bullseye.

Her hands shot up triumphantly. She turned, expecting to see Echo's eyes disappear into slits as she smiled in pride at Parker's accomplishment. Instead, she found Echo hunched over the table with a short lump of a human leaning against her. The beige flat hair hung thinly to the woman's shoulder, and Parker briefly wondered how a human walked out of their house not realizing they looked like a soggy loaf of bread.

Parker approached the table, eyes narrowed at the stranger touching her best friend. She looked up at Xio, clearing drinks from the table to find the hard masc shaking her head and her nose scrunched up like the woman smelled as bad as she looked.

The soggy bread's glassy eyes leered at Parker as she took her seat. Hairs on the back of Parker's neck rose. Her hand wrapped over the small space between her shirt and pants.

"This your wife?" the sourdough loaf asked.

"My sister." Echo nodded at the woman, "This is Andrea."

Andrea's whole body moved when she turned. Parker hated the way the woman's shit brown eyes raked over her.

"You two don't look alike. She's hot, one of those real redheads." She wrapped her arm over Echo's shoulder, then she let out a drunken cackle. "You're just an average dyke."

Parker tapped a finger to her lips. She could break the bottle over the trash talker's head. A palm thrust would break her nose. Slam her head into the table. Gouge out her eyes. Kill her. The news would say she had murder in her genes.

Parker tilted her head and studied the way the woman loudly whispered to Echo. She even saw some spittle fly out of Andrea's mouth in Echo's direction. The woman was clearly oblivious to how Echo had closed herself off, but Parker noticed.

She noticed, and she came up with a plan.

With a fresh beer in hand, Parker tilted her head at the woman. Her eyes softened, and she chewed softly on the bottom of her lip.

"Are you okay?" Parker asked.

Andrea looked up at her. "Uh," A smile spread across the lower half of her flat face as she side-eyed Echo. "Yeah, I'm great."

"Really?" Parker prodded.

The woman's eyes dropped to the front of her shirt. When she looked back up, she was obviously confused, but she said, "Yeah."

"Oh, I just thought..." Parker paused mid-sentence to take a drink. She held up her hand as she swallowed. "You know what? Never mind."

"What?"

Parker set her beer down and leaned in. She tilted her chin down, and then looked up at Andrea. She waited. Waited until the other woman leaned into the table.

"Well, I was just worried about you. I just thought... you know... I mean, you seem like a nice enough person, so there must be something going on that you had to call my sister a dyke. That's not a word we use in the community anymore."

Andrea's gaze from Parker in the direction of the other dart players standing by and hungerly watching the confrontation. She watched Andrea's mouth open, close, then open again. She started to say something, then swallowed it.

Parker waited like her clinical rotations had taught her. Waiting was harder than hitting. More effective too.

"I was just joking," Andrea spat out.

With a slight tilt to her head, Parker bit her lip innocently. Then shook her head, and leaned in closer to Andrea, who again matched her position.

"I'm sorry, I just don't understand. I mean, you're not stupid, so there clearly must be something else going on for you to be so mean to someone you're interested in. Do you want to talk about it?"

Andrea's shoulders rose, and a deep wrinkle set in her forehead. She stammered, "I just... I... I can say shit and she knows... it's just how we play around. Echo knows I just was joking around."

The glassy orbs fully focused on Parker for the first time as Andrea lashed out again, "Didn't mean to offend your princess ass."

Parker held up her bottle and shook her head 'no' once more. "And there it is again. You're trying to deflect your insecurities by calling me a princess."

"What the fuck is she talking about?" Andrea asked Echo.

Echo's eyes raised to the ceiling as she took a long drink of her beer. Then with a smile, she explained, "She's calling you a stupid, mean bitch in words you can't even understand."

Andrea blinked repeatedly as though Parker was out of focus. "You got a problem with me?"

Parker raised her chin and dropped her mask of imaginary concern. With an eyebrow cocked, she stared directly between Andrea's unsymmetrical eyebrows.

"Yes, I have a problem with you calling my sister a dyke. I have a problem with you hangin' on to her when you know she's married, then being rude because she has no interest in you. *And* I have a problem with you thinking a compliment from someone like you would actually make me feel good about myself."

"I—"

Parker held up her hand. "And just to be clear, she'll never be interested in you. Your tits are pointing in two different directions. And you clearly were never introduced to a fucking toothbrush."

"I just..." Andrea tried again but stopped.

They had drawn the attention of the other dart players from the All-Lesbian League and a small group of women enjoying a friends' night out. A circle of onlookers gathered around them. Parker heard someone chuckle and said, "pointy tits."

Andrea's stumpy body stepped towards Parker's half-starved form. The lump like human turned red as the blood rushed her soppy drunk face.

Parker gripped the bottle tightly. The alcohol flooding her system begged for Andrea to light a match, but Parker's mind wasn't completely lost in the need to hit something. This was still Echo's bar, and she had to respect the space.

She pointed the bottle at Andrea. "Let's just be clear, I'm not a fucking princess. I'm the devil's bastard daughter raised here in the center circle of hell. So, before you decide that since you can't keep up with me on an intellectual level, so you want to try and fight me, remember there's a reason a rottweiler bows to a fucking chihuahua."

Parker planted her feet with the bottle grasped so tightly her knuckles were white. Her hands did not shake for the first time all night.

"Because I'm a fucking alpha bitch."

The women surrounding them parted as Andrea stepped back from the table. The crowd laughed as Andrea waddled away.

Parker sat back down, her heart still rushing her boiling blood throughout her body. She didn't crack a smile as the rest of the dart players made jokes. She could hear them mimicking her words. Then the dart boards began to sing with the success of the other teams.

Her shoulders relaxed and the fire in her eyes smoldered by the time Echo returned from her turn. With the adrenaline wearing off, Parker felt the first wave of exhaustion setting in.

"So, the devil's bastard child?" When Parker didn't look up, Echo added, "Is that what you tell your trauma kids?"

She ignored Echo because it was not what she would tell traumatized children even if she had a job.

"I'm a fucking alpha," Echo mocked in an octave higher than Parker felt her voice sounded. But Parker had to smile at how ridiculous the words were.

Echo was always the alpha. Even beat out Xio in juvie for the title of top dog. Parker was trying to be a beta, hoping just to slide through life being a little more than invisible.

Echo pointed the mouth of the bottle at Parker. "You need to stop reading fanfiction about women with magic cocks. I shoulda never introduced you to my friend's dirty stories."

"She was a bitch," Parker snapped, ignoring the dig at her fascination with fantasy stories where she could imagine she lived in a world where being a juvenile delinquent turned stripper made her a badass instead of a liability.

"Yes, but I have to ask." Echo tilted her head at Parker. "Are you alright?"

Parker groaned at the second round of mockery.

"You know, you're a bitch too, right?"

A grin spread across Echo's face as she stated, "I love you too, Princess Lucy. Sounds way better than that time you decided to go by your middle name. Michelle made you sound so fucking basic."

Parker smacked the butt of her bottle to the top of Echo's beer. The liquid immediately turned to foam and began to rush through the mouth. Echo cried out in protest, but quickly wrapped her lips around the top and downed the soon to be ruined brew.

"You two going to play or what?" a member from the opposing team called out.

Parker raised her bottle in acknowledgement that it was her turn.

As Parker made her way to the dreaded line, Echo called out, "Hey, Lucifer's bastard, don't hit the fucking one!"

A smile grew as Parker looked up to see Andrea's dart bounce off the board a few machines down. The pride of having defended the asshole at the table made the dart between her fingers less scary. It was just plastic and metal she controlled.

She raised her arm and focused on the center of the board. Without blinking, she inhaled until she couldn't anymore, then released it with a flick of her wrist.

Parker imagined the *whoosh* as the dart sailed through the air, dropping from the fifty-point target into the nineteen.

"That's my sister!" Echo cried out.

Even though Parker's other two darts landed in the three mark, she felt lighter. Possibly even happy because their skinny opponent told her, "Great shot, Parker." And the other woman held up her hand for a high five.

Several of the other teams had gathered around Echo and Parker's table. They watched as Echo racked up points with each dart she hit and cheered each time Parker hit the board without the dart falling to the ground.

As the game drolled on, Parker felt the booze taking over her faculties. The dart board swayed as she tried to aim. Her hand dropped when the ground moved even though it didn't. She closed her eyes until the axis felt right again.

The board was where it was supposed to be when Parker opened her eyes. She raised her arm and tossed the dart at the board. As it hit the bullseye, the board sang and the crowd of Echo's friends cheered.

Parker staggered back to the table and plopped in her seat. She caught sight of Andrea staring at her from across the room. She let a smug grin spread across her tipsy face.

Echo came up alongside her.

"We're taking an Uber back to my place so you can earn that $300."

Parker rolled her head. After another sip, she said, "I am not sleeping with your wife. Or you. Or the two of you together. Or dancing for you two."

Echo choked. Beer dribbled off her lower lip, making her look like a slobbering pit bull.

Parker squinted and slammed the beer down to the table. With her finger's pointing out from her tits, Parker whined, "How could you not want all of this, you butch bitch?"

Echo spat beer over the table. The spray hit Parker's hands and chest before she could move.

She shook off the beer, while Echo held herself up on the table. Echo hacked, until her face was scarlet. Then they laughed like Parker was not unemployed and broke. Leaning over the table, each choked out their words, neither able to formulate sentences.

"Beer... spit... nasty ass," Parker said.

"Pointy tits!"

"You got me wet!"

"Drunkard."

"You fouled." Parker grabbed Xio and forced her chin in Echo's direction. "Foul. Tell foul. Call. Foul party."

The woman tugged her chin out of Parker's reach, then rolled her eyes.

"You two are trashed," Xio said before she walked away with her plastic bucket.

Parker laughed longer than Echo once they stopped trying to speak. She laughed until her chest hurt, and everything else threatened to break through. She could not let that happen, so she tried to get up. Tried and failed. She could not stand without stumbling, so she tried to sit back down. But the stool kept trying to walk away.

Echo pulled Parker's arm over her shoulders with their stuff already tucked under her other arm. She supported the younger woman's swaying form as they made their way out front to the Uber awaiting them.

When they were belted into the back seat, Echo explained the price of a week's worth of groceries and electricity.

"So, tomorrow, I'm going to need you to actually talk to people at Henrie's birthday party. It's going to be all of Simone's friends. But we are going to avoid Monica. You're my sister and she's Simone's cousin, and last time it made shit weird when you two left to fuck."

Parker sighed at the thought of Simone's floppy looking, goody-goody teacher friends. All at least ten years older than her and Echo. It would be worse because Simone's family would also be walking around in their unwrinkled pastels. All the people who had their shit together, and would ask her what she did, expecting her to be like an adult.

Her head fell back at the realization Xio wouldn't come to hide in the backyard with her or save her from Simone's cousin. She wished she didn't know Monica Rose more than she wished she hadn't slept with her after stupid Zoe had broken her heart. Sleeping with and seeing Xiò all the time wasn't an issue, but seeing Monica at each of Echo's family events sucked because Monica was a therapist who liked to play games with people, and Parker wasn't interested in giving her anything else in this lifetime to write an article about. She'd already been an unwilling participant in the woman's published case study.

"I have nothing to talk about," Parker tried.

"Tell them you got summoned for jury duty. They'll all have some way to help you get out of it."

3

Zoe's boat shoes kicked up gravel and dust with every exhausted step down the path to the Watson Lake boat ramp. She paused with slumped shoulders at the dock as she watched her older brothers, Zion and Zachery, shove each other aboard the pontoon boat. They hadn't noticed her yet.

'I could just go back home,' the voice in the back of her head said.

But it was the last weekend of the month. To fulfill the promise made to the old man, she'd have to go. Plus, she had the bait the overgrown boys needed.

Zion glared down at the younger brother he'd pushed into the seat at the bow. "I told you to drop it," he growled loud enough Zoe heard him on the ramp.

A tattered Diamondbacks hat came loose from Zachery's head and a gust blew it off the boat. Zoe made it just in time to snatch it from the dock before it was gone.

'You sure you want to be stuck with them when you could be home sleeping?'

She didn't want to, but the promise of sleep was a lie. The only thing waiting for her were crime scene photos and shit-talking online assholes playing Call of Duty.

Zoe climbed aboard the boat without acknowledgement from either. She held out the hat to Zachery as he climbed back on his feet. He jerked it from her without so much as a nod.

Zachery untied the lines and pushed off the dock. "You're clear," he called to Zion.

While Zoe settled into her side of the front of the boat, Zachery fiddled with the fishing poles. She quietly asked, "What are we *not* dropping?"

Zachery's voice was barely audible over the sound of the motor coming to life. "Got his medical discharge paperwork."

"Oh," was all she had the energy for.

Her subconscious had taken her back to Vincent Gibson's house more times than Zoe could count. She woke, without answers from the teen girl still talking in her dreams, too early to pretend she really cared Zion was never going to put on his Navy uniform again.

As the boat pulled away from the shore, wind tickled Zoe's arms and legs. She sprawled out over the bench across from Zachery, letting the movement lull her sleep deprived mind into a state of peace as it rose and fell over the water. Her arms and legs stretched out, and the yawn that followed made her head spin. But when she closed her eyes, Gibson's ghost wasn't waiting for her outside his grimy house.

Zoe's lips pulled up at the corners as her subconscious took her on a tour of the woods surrounding the lake. Waves slapped against the pontoons, rocking her as the electric motor hummed just loud enough to ease her into a murder-free sleep.

Her body jolted when the splash of the anchor tore her back from the dream walk to the boat waiting on the water. Both boy-men shuffled over the grainy blue carpet; fishing poles clacked together as they were removed from their holders.

She opened one eye to see the mouth of their family cove. Her bag smacked against her foot. She jumped to a seated position as Zion kicked the backpack at her a second time moving towards her end of the deck.

"Where's the bait?" Zion gruffed.

Zoe stretched again, ignoring her eldest brother. She didn't care about fishing today, she just wanted to enjoy the Gibson-free peace. She pulled a vape from the pocket of her cargo shorts and inhaled until her diaphragm refused to expand anymore, then she puffed out a series of vapor o's.

"Come on, Zoe," her eldest brother tried again. "Just give us the bait and you can sleep all you want."

When Zion asked again, Zoe leaned her head back against the cushion and closed her eyes. She slid the spaghetti straps of her tank top down, hoping if she moved them around enough, she'd avoid an unfortunate tan line. Not that anyone had seen her naked since she dumped her ex outside the strip club.

Zion kicked her foot to get her to acknowledge him. She didn't budge, knowing it was the most he would do to her.

He grabbed her backpack from beside her foot. "I'll just get it myself." He pulled the drawstring top, revealing a royal blue box of Superplus sized tampons. He dropped the bag as he cried out, "Jesus Christ!"

She fought back the smile, sustaining the mask of indifference while Zion yelled at Zachery. He apparently thought the box of tampons would establish her as the common enemy, but she knew better.

"Why does she always have to be difficult?" When Zachery didn't answer their brother, Zion barked at him. "Tell her to get the bait."

Zachery whistled a classic commercial jingle. She opened only one eye to find Zachery fiddling with his fishing hook. He smiled at the ground. When Zion pulled a ratty Cardinal's hat from his head looking at the sky, Zachery gave Zoe a silent nod of approval. The affirmation was all it took for her resolve to solidify Zion no longer existed.

Zion stood between them, even though it wouldn't make a difference if he was dancing a jig. They ignored his whining, and how his giant hands balled into fists.

She took another long inhale from the vape, before passing it across the boat to Zachery.

"How was your week?" she asked as he snatched it from her hands when Zion tried to swipe it.

"Eh," Zachery answered as he examined the thin tube. He took a drag, then asked with his exhale, "Yours?"

"Eh," she echoed.

She watched a bird flit across from one Ponderosa pine to the next. A seven-prong buck walked to the edge of the lake, shortly followed by several does.

"Fine, I'm sorry for shoving you," Zion growled Zachery's direction. He turned back to Zoe. "There. You happy?"

Zoe sucked her teeth, before sitting up to take the bag he'd retrieved from the ground. She opened it, pulling the box of unneeded tampons from the top.

Zion averted his eyes. "Put those away."

"What these?" Zoe held up the box and shook them.

"Seriously, this is why girls shouldn't be allowed on a boat," he whined again. "You should have said it was shark week. Fucking girls."

She rolled her eyes. "Says the one whining like a bitch over some cotton on a string. I guess the Navy got tired of all the whining too."

Content she'd won with her below the belt strike, Zoe rummaged to the bottom of the bag and pulled out the bait wrapped tightly in plastic. She tossed the bag to Zachery, but Zion caught it in midair by the unravelling plastic. He smiled at her, but the smile dropped as she reached for the blue box.

"Okay, okay," he said. He dropped the bag at Zachery's feet and pouted on his way to the back of the boat. The victory was small, but enough to remind Zion that even as the eldest, he held no power over them.

The siblings set their attention to rigging their poles the way their father had taught them before the dementia set in. This monthly trip to Prescott had been a homage to the man, and no matter how tired they were, they would fish until they each had something to take back to the old man in the assisted living facility. Their father no longer recognized them, but Zoe was the only Robinson kid to feel his loss.

"You talk to Mom this week?" Zion asked before letting out a wet belch.

Zoe added another layer of sunscreen to her face. "No. I've been busy with a case."

"Call her," he barked the order like she would listen to him.

"What for? She's just going to grill me about not having a girlfriend." She straightened her shoulders and flipped a hand in the air as she adjusted her voice to match her mother's. "How am I going to get grandbabies if you won't even bring a girl home to meet your mother? Your brother showed me this handsome girl on the tickytoky thingy with the sharp suits. You should wear a tie and suspenders like her, so the pretty lesbians know you like women."

Zachery snickered.

"Please stop showing her how to use social media," Zoe begged. "I got six TikToks that are lesbian thirst traps. Our mother is watching lesbian thirst traps, and she is fucking up my algorithm. And she thinks now I don't have a girlfriend because I don't dress masculine enough to get girls to recognize I'm gay."

"She's worried about you," Zachery said with a shrug. His eyes ran up and down her. "And you are pretty confusing. I mean, your shorts say you're packing a pecker, but your shirt says look at my boobies. You know what it's like knowing my sister is the one all my friends think about when they are jacking off?"

"She has nothing to worry about but the fact you still call imaginary people your friends," Zoe bit back.

"I thought lesbians were all about the U-Haul." Zion held his hands up like he was driving a car as he shuffled to the ice chest.

Zoe choked on the vapor she'd just begun to inhale. "Who told you about U-Hauling?"

"Sargent in my old unit. Said lesbians meet up for a beer and order a U-Haul before round two comes." Zion popped the top of his beer.

"That's just a ridiculous stereotype," Zoe groaned, but she felt Zachery's eyes on her.

"Is it though?" he asked, daring her to challenge him. "Your type definitely only cares about securing a sugar daddy."

The delicate fibers of peace Zoe had found quickly coiled in her shoulders first, then down her legs.

Zion called back at her, "Did that stripper call you daddy when she practiced sliding down your plastic pole?"

Zachery recast his line and stood reeling as Zoe tried to pretend, they weren't under her skin. He whistled the torturous tune as the empty hook came into view.

'Should've just gone back home,' her internal voice berated her.

Zion joined his brother's tune with off-key vocals. Zachery only stopped whistling to join Zion as they called out to the lake, "She's in love with a stripper!"

The boys continued their duet as Zoe felt the shame of her past prickle the hairs on her arms. Years of practice had only improved their ability to complete the entire song. Zoe ground her teeth just waiting for them to be done while Zion dropped his hatchet ass, grinding his crotch against his flimsy fishing pole.

'They would have sat here all miserable because they didn't have any fucking bait.'

As the song came to an end, Zoe struggled to fix her mask in place. She fumbled with the vape, regretting she'd lowered the nicotine percentage.

Zachery tossed his brother another beer, before slouching into his seat. A smug grin hung on his face as Zoe stared through him.

"We're just fuckin' with you," Zachery said.

"I don't know why you still even give a damn," Zion said. "You had your fun, and that's what strippers are for."

Zoe took another drag, exhaling quickly. When Zoe closed her eyes, she pictured the sparkly blonde spinning on the silver pole under the hot spotlight. She tried to slow her breathing as she forced back the memory of her ex, Michelle dancing on stage. The girl she'd planned on marrying. She held the pieces of her heart that she'd glued back together in place. Manicured nails dug into her palms to release the pressure, so she didn't combust.

"Hey." Zachery tossed an empty can at her feet.

She opened her eyes and met his matching set.

"I know you cared about her, and I wish I hadn't asked you to go with me that night." He exhaled slowly. "But it's better this way. She would have gotten in your way and broken your heart when someone threw enough money at her."

Zoe's hands ran up and down her face. Wiping away the tears before they ever had a chance to fall, she regained her composure.

"Yeah, I know," she said. "It's been years, and I just—"

"Just let it go," Zion called over his shoulder. "She was a whore."

"She wasn't a whore," Zoe snapped.

"She was a stripper. Same thing," Zion stated. "You're going to be the next District Attorney like Dad wanted. You were never going to settle down with a stripper."

Zachery grabbed the box of tampons from Zoe's bench and threw it at Zion. The cardboard split against the buzzed head. Wrapped floral packages rained down over Zion. He cried out, swiping at the tampon assault like murder hornets were threatening to send him to an early grave.

"Get it off! Get it off!" Zion cried out.

Zoe couldn't fight back the joy she got from Zion's distress. As the smile played on her lips, within she added another layer of super glue to her heart. Coating the entire thing until the toxic byproduct leached into her bloodstream, and she felt normal again.

A soft breeze blew away the lingering tune in her head. The birds chirped, and Zachery hooked the first fish of the day. A five-inch trout spun in the water against the pull of the line, fighting its fate.

Zachery set his pole in the holder after he reset his line and recast. He took a seat across from her, handing Zoe a beer before popping one open for himself.

"Haven't heard from you since Monday. Big case starts this week, right?" Zachery asked. He leaned back. His arms casually lay across the back of the seat.

Zoe took a sip of the cheap beer, smacking her lips at its grainy flavor. "Yeah."

"Nightmares like the last case?"

"Yeah. Worse." She swallowed the next sip, hoping it would get easier if she just kept drinking.

"You'll win. You're the best Robinson." Zachery's lips pulled up at the corners the way her father's used to when she brought home a report card with all A's.

While she appreciated his faith in her, she still wasn't at ease with not having a motive. She'd replayed the scene in her head until security kicked her out of the building the night before. Her kitchen counter became her new whiteboard, and she continued to go through the scene until her head slipped from the hand holding it up. She'd caught herself before cracking her skull into a granite countertop.

Zachery hit her foot with his. "What's wrong?"

She shook her head, and looked at her brother, the history teacher. She hadn't thought to ask him before. He worked with teenagers every day. He could have some insight.

"Maybe you can help me." She sucked her teeth and leaned forward. "The girl on trial is fifteen. She killed this guy in his house."

"You sure she killed him?" Zachery asked.

"No doubt. I could try this case in my sleep."

Zachery snorted. "Of course, you could. So, what's keeping you up at night?"

Pressing at her temples, Zoe explained, "She never gave a statement, and I can't figure out how she could just kill someone and walk away. She's fifteen. I just keep looking for what instigated the attack."

Zachery pulled his hat from his head. Twisting the bill in his hands. "Look, Zo, kids today are... desensitized."

"But stabbing someone multiple times, then walking out the door?"

"Was she on drugs?"

"Yeah. Look, I said I can win it easy." She took a breath. "She was on drugs and broke a cop's nose."

Zoe closed her eyes and gathered the courage to say what had been eating at her. "She stabbed this guy in the dick. And a part of me... part of me thinks... let's be real, I know that she was probably raped, but it wasn't by the victim. He was with someone else, so the bruises she had on her wrists were from something else. And she won't say a fucking word, so... I don't know if that's what just made her snap. And he didn't have... like his junk wasn't DNA free, but it wasn't hers either. But what if she is a psychopath and she doesn't actually give a damn about the fact she killed someone."

The tightness in her chest released. She'd said it, and the world hadn't collapsed. Zoe looked up to find her brother staring at her.

Zachery leaned forward, resting his arms on his knees. His eyes dropped to study the beer in his hand. He shook his head and took another drink.

"If you're asking for my opinion, I say it doesn't matter why she did it. She killed someone. Like Dad always said, don't matter what happened. God's the only one that gets to judge when someone has had their time on Earth. So, it doesn't matter why she did it."

He looked at her for a long moment. Then said what her father would have said. "Your job is to prosecute her. It's a big case that is going to make opportunities for you. Just put her away and move on. You got your whole career ahead of you and winning a case like this is what Nia would do. And you know Dad would be proud for you to be like her."

Zoe chewed on his words. It wasn't what she'd expected from the man who spent his day with kids. The words sounded like what Nia had said. When Nia said it, it felt wrong though. When Zachery said it, it was more palatable. She didn't like the taste of them, but Zachery was her brother, her best friend. And her father was the smartest person she'd ever known. Neither had led her astray before, and she had no reason to doubt them now.

"Would it matter why if she'd killed me?" he asked.

Her skin crawled at even the idea of someone hurting him. Nothing could justify her brother being ripped from this life.

"No."

Zachery got to his feet and picked up his fishing pole. He reminded her, "If she's locked up, she can't hurt anyone else."

The water slapped against a large stone. The doe was gone, but a butterfly found a resting place atop the rock. Her peace was disturbed by another wet belch.

She followed the sound of Zion pissing off the side of the boat. She'd forgotten he was there. The back of his buzzed head, and it made her think of Vincent Gibson. Her resolve settled, and she knew the safest option was to protect men like her brothers from Olivia Moore.

4

A child's birthday party should have streamers, banners, and balloons. All those things were missing from Echo's house. Parker had even tried to convince Echo to let her run to the Dollar Tree like they'd always talked about doing when they were still locked up. Planned their future celebrations to be filled with as many gaudy decorations as possible because birthdays just came and went in the detention center. Just like Echo's eighteenth birthday had come and she'd went out into the world without Parker.

Stuck-up Simone had scoffed at Dollar Tree decorations, and blamed Echo's poor planning on the house lacking any hint it was Henrie's first birthday. It hadn't sat right with Parker, but she'd already been kicked out of the house once before by the overbearing witch.

By one, the two living rooms of the house were packed with people Parker didn't want to talk to. She moved around the space on Echo's heels like a shadow because Echo wasn't lying about none of their people being there. That party would happen at Xio's house where all their birthdays had been celebrated after Parker left Echo with Simone.

She provided silent nods and cordial smiles to everyone Echo greeted, including Monica. The manipulative blonde was the only person she was forced to speak to because Monica addressed her by name when she asked Parker a question. A question about what she was going to do now she was certified. The one question Parker had no interest in answering, especially for the woman who'd learned about trauma by triggering her college peers.

Echo pulled Parker away before she had to provide anything juicy for the woman to store in her bank of shit to talk later with her cousin. It was more than Echo had done that first time. The time when Echo had pushed Parker towards the other woman as though getting under someone ever fixed a broken heart.

Once they were in the mostly vacant kitchen centered in the lower level of the house, Echo handed Parker the baby. The toddler felt like a feather even though her face had finally gained those chubby cheeks in place of the failure to thrive skeleton look Henrie came home with as she withdrew from more drugs than any woman should have consumed while pregnant. At least holding Henrie was a job. The only job Parker could do, and she felt good about giving Echo a break since the toddler had been in Echo's arms the whole day while Simone moved between their guests like this was her party instead of Henrie's.

"Strip her down," was Echo's only instruction when she shifted her attention to the birthday cake.

Parker shifted the birthday girl onto her hip and left the safety of the kitchen. She tried convincing herself this time would be different, but the wrestling match began once Henrie's back touched the cotton changing pad. Briefly, she wondered if stripping the kid included the corrective helmet Henrie wore all day, every day. That thought went out the window when Parker had to practically dive to keep the toddler from rolling off the edge of the changing table.

Parker looked around the room for judging eyes as she pinned the kid. No one paid her any mind except a petite blonde, who was trying her best to shrink away from the conversation between Simone and another parent holding a passive yet talkative toddler. The blonde's smile reached her eyes in tiny crinkles at the corners. She gave Parker a knowing nod but didn't turn away from Parker's wrestling match.

Focusing back on the baby, Parker hissed, "Hold still."

Henrie paused her wiggles only to giggle at her opponent. While she shook her hands in the air, Parker hooked her fingers between the material and diaper. She'd barely tugged when Henrie twisted from her back to her side. The snaps didn't come loose like Parker had hoped, and the mini wrestler managed to grab a red bottle of diaper rash cream from the basket of diapering essentials. Parker yanked the tube from the pudgy fingers and put it on the counter above Henrie's head.

'This shouldn't be this hard,' Parker chastised herself.

Henrie reached for the counter but couldn't get up with Parker's hand holding her chest down into the changing pad. When the toddler realized she couldn't move because of the hand, she looked Parker dead in the eye and growled like a feral cat.

Parker checked around again, hoping someone saw the wild child growling at her this time. But everyone was chatting amongst each other, like neither of them existed. Parker imagined an artist's hand adding a single stroke of paint down the middle of the room separating her and the baby from everyone else.

Henrie struggled and let out a whine, pulling Parker back to the task at hand.

Her eyes narrowed at the child, and she harnessed her inner grumpy auntie. "Look, little monster. These clothes are coming off."

While the toddler glared, Parker took the opportunity to yank the fabric unsnapped and tug it up the girl's body. It got stuck on Henrie's ears and helmet. The thick head of espresso curls poked out of the top, but Henrie was contained. The child grabbed for the material, screeching out for someone to tag in, but Parker managed to get it over the girl's head with an unheard pop.

With flushed cheeks from the match Parker couldn't claim to have won, Henrie revealed two deep dimples. Her tiny hands reached for Parker. A sweet and open-mouthed smile was huge on her round face, since the girl clearly didn't care who won or lost the battle.

A gravelly voice from Parker's past called from the front of the house, "Where's the future ball player?"

Parker scooped up the toddler and held her tightly to her chest. She stared at the small entryway between the kitchen and the dining room. Maybe she'd been wrong, because Echo would have told her if Evie Blake was someone Echo knew. Then she realized Echo didn't know Evie in juvie because Evie came the afternoon of Echo's eighteenth birthday. Moved into Echo's bed before Echo's mattress even had a chance to breathe.

"Baby Shark" started to play from the television speakers. The only other kid invited to the party began to sing and Henrie bounced in her arms. Chubby hands pressed into Parker's cheeks, but Parker couldn't tear her eyes from the doorway.

Her chest quaked at the possibility of her sanctuary being violated when she had just begun to paint herself back into the picture of Echo's life. The wet paint of her recently developed self-confidence was slowly dripping down the canvas of her self-painted family portrait. The one Simone had kicked her out of, only letting her back in when being a mom was hard on Echo.

She kept watching while her lungs screamed for her to take another breath. She was afraid if she looked away Evie would waltz through the doorway ready to finish what she had started all those years ago.

"I don't care she's only one. The kid needed a bat," came from the front of the house. There was no doubt in Parker's mind that the voice belonged to Evie.

She remembered the hatred in the turquoise eyes. Painted them in her head, then the scene where Evie had turned a bad situation worse.

Parker's pulse quickened, and she held the child tighter. A need to protect the little beast developed. A confusing concern for Echo's non-biological progeny wiped away Parker's denied jealousy Henrie.

Dark curls tickled Parker's nose as she pressed her face against Henrie's helmeted head. She tried to hold the sneeze and started a new count backwards.

Her nose scrunched at twelve.

Her muscles locked up at six.

She sneezed loudly before zero.

Parker opened her eyes to see Henrie staring at her in a mixture of fright and annoyance. Parker momentarily forgot about the voice and smiled at the girl.

"That's called Karma," Parker told the kid. "Think about that next time you spit peas in my face."

When Henrie sat back against Parker's hands, Parker saw *her* from around the child's head. Her raucous tone was louder than anyone else in the room. The now-woman pulled at the neck of a bullet proof vest with a silver police badge fixed to its left-hand side. She joked with Simone, smacking the older woman in the arm.

'Of course, the monsters flocked together.'

Henrie's little hand reached up, touching the scar across the bottom of Parker's chin. The toddler wasn't part cyborg, but her touch was as cold as the steel table that left the mark after Evie's right hook sent Parker spiraling downward nine years prior. Evie hadn't stopped with one punch. She'd hit Parker until Xio's gang crossed the boundary lines and pulled Evie off her. Everything was fuzzy at that point, and Parker vaguely remembered Xio's face blocking out the lights.

Parker made her way to Echo in the kitchen. She stood behind her protector, who fumbled with the one shaped candle. Echo had placed the candle directly above the cyclops's eye in the monster cake, but it leaned to the left. Parker could tell the lack of perfection due to the crookedness was causing Echo distress. There wasn't anything Parker could do to help Echo with her impending breakdown until she knew how Echo knew Evie.

Parker moved as close to Echo as possible so no one could hear her ask, "How do you know *her*?"

Echo tried to straighten the candle, but it leaned back to the side. Her nose crunched up as she asked, "Who?"

"The cop."

Echo glanced up and looked around, like she was unaware there was a cop in her house.

"Who are you talking about?"

"Over there." Parker nudged Echo in the direction of Simone and Evie.

The masc looked over her shoulder, this time in the actual direction where the woman stood in her police blues. "Evie? She's Simone's best friend's daughter."

Echo sighed heavily, giving up on adjusting the candle. Turning around, she almost hit Parker.

"Whoa. Close much?"

Parker hated how Evie was smiling and talking to people. She hated how Evie was more comfortable in Echo's home than she had ever been capable. This was her family, and Evie shouldn't have a place here.

Echo narrowed her eyes at Parker, and she leaned back against the counter. "What happened between you two? You hook up and she didn't call you back?"

"No." Parker growled.

The idea of her hooking up with Evie made her skin crawl. But her frustration turned on Echo, who was supposed to know her better than anyone, for even considering she would just hook up. That had only been that one time, and it was because Echo had said Monica would help her forget Zoe.

"I'm not a slut."

Echo's face tilted as her eyebrows raised at Parker. She pressed the hat down further on her head.

"Well, I am sensing a little tension. Did you want to be her slut then, but freaked when you found out she's a cop?" Echo held up her hand. "I know. The cop thing. I get it, but you gotta let the past rest. Not all people in uniform are bad guys or pervs. And the handcuffs can—"

"I'm literally holding your daughter like right here, you sicko."

Echo rolled her eyes. "She's one. How much do you remember from being one?"

The two watched as Simone stared daggers into the blonde still standing just far enough away from the conversation to hear but not partake. Parker understood that position all too well.

"So?" Echo asked. "How do *you* know Evie?"

"She was in after you left. With me and OG Henriette. Took your bed in the cell. She's the one."

With eyebrows raised again, Echo's smile turned into a smirk. "The one. Sounds a little kinky."

"The one that bashed my face in," Parker snapped.

"Oh. Wow."

Echo looked out the bay window, but Parker knew she wasn't looking at the pool. Echo had gotten her face broken a few times while in juvenile detention by the one spikey haired guard and occasionally Xio. Parker was pretty sure she had just triggered some unpleasant memories.

The larger woman ran her hands over her face. Then she blinked a few times, coming back from whatever memory she'd just walked through.

"I don't really know her well. The long story is basically Simone wanted to adopt her. Actually, I never told you this, but I met Simone the day I got out. She didn't know Evie couldn't have visitors yet, and she saw me waiting on the bus. She offered me a ride. Easy choice really. New SUV or getting robbed on the bus for my birthday."

Parker's upper lip curled, but she clenched her mouth shut to stop from calling Simone a predator to Echo's face. Her best friend wouldn't hear her anyways, and the last time she'd said anything negative about Simone ended in Parker moving out of that very house and spending months under Xio as she learned to be alone.

Unfazed by Parker's grimace, Echo returned to the point. "I only knew Evie as a softball player on Simone's team until Simone's best friend, Alex..." Echo pointed to the androgenous human whose matching toddler was cradled in Simone's arms. "That's Alex. So, Alex fell in love, like head over heels, for Evie's mom. But, next to babysitting, I don't know Evie well because Simone has this stupid rivalry with Dilynn Greyson. That's her right there." This time she pointed out the blonde, who was finally speaking as she stood sandwiched between her partner and daughter.

Parker chewed on the name, then glanced towards Echo. She tried the name out silently but couldn't place it in a sentence.

"Why do I know that name?"

"Dilynn opened the school I've been trying to tell you about. The one with a job opening. Alex is the AP there, but—"

"Greyson Academy?" Parker asked.

"Yeah. That's it."

Dilynn moved herself behind her partner, Alex. Her eyes searched the room for anywhere else to be as Simone glared at her.

"Why's your wife glaring at her?"

"She hates Dilynn for a variety of reasons. I think it's because Dilynn was popular." Echo sighed. "Sometimes though, I think she wanted Alex. She was with me already though."

Parker watched the woman with shoulders hunched inward. "For being Miss Popularity, she's really unsure of herself."

"Yeah, she is a lot like you. Unless it's about her kids, she just keeps to herself." Echo smiled, then added, "I should probably save her. It's kinda a deal we have when Simone and Dilynn have to be in the same room."

'No, don't do it,' Parker cried out silently.

"Hey Dilynn, come here. I have someone for you to meet!"

The honey waves bounced as the blue eyes searched for Echo eagerly. Her whole body shifted from a comma to an exclamation point when she locked in on their location. Dilynn smiled, waved slightly, and excused herself from the conversation she wasn't a part of. As the distance grew between her and Simone, Dilynn stood straighter.

"Hey, Marissa," Dilynn said as she got close enough not to have to yell.

Parker chuckled to herself at the weirdness of hearing someone call Echo by her government name.

"And happy birthday, Henrie." Dilynn held out her hands to the child, and the little traitor eagerly abandoned Parker.

"I'm so happy you could come."

Echo's eyes were soft when she looked at Dilynn. It was clear she liked Dilynn, and Echo didn't really like anyone. Ever. She played the role of friendly bartender, but Parker knew it was fake. Knew Echo was the person who showed up for everyone, but never needed anyone else.

"Yeah, me too. Feels like forever since I've seen you or this little ball of sunshine."

"Levi is turning three soon, right?" Echo asked.

Dilynn nodded towards Simone holding the calmer toddler. "Yeah. She's over there talking your wife's ear off. I have to warn you that two is the age they have so much to say and no words to say it with. I am dreading three though because I heard that terrible twos turn into terrorist threes."

Parker studied the ease in Simone's interactions with Dilynn and Alex's child. In the year since Henrie came home from the NICU, Parker couldn't remember Simone ever holding her own child for a prolonged amount of time. Parker assumed Simone didn't like kids, but maybe it was just the baby who'd cried constantly as she went through drug withdrawals. Or, knowing Simone was a shallow bitch, it was probably because Henrie looked nothing like her.

"I will be happy if we can ever get Henrie to speak." Echo ran her finger over Henrie's cheek. "I mean, with all the speech therapy and the occupational therapies, it just sometimes feels like we are so far behind in milestones."

Dilynn Greyson pulled Henrie in closer. She rubbed her nose against Henrie's, earning a giggle as a reward. With Dilynn's forehead still pressed to the baby's, she made Echo a promise she couldn't keep.

"She'll get there." Henrie's hands squished Dilynn's cheeks together as the woman added, "You are giving her all the support any parent can. Remember every kid is different and if she never speaks that will not make her any less amazing. And does not mean you're a bad parent."

This was why Echo liked the woman. Parker knew how much Henrie's special needs weighed on Echo. How the therapies kept her up during the day and she still had to go run the bar six nights a week. Parker decided she too liked the blonde with eyes that smiled. She'd probably even like coming to work for her, if it weren't for the fact Evie was her daughter.

"I don't think we've met." A small pale hand extended towards Parker. "I'm Dilynn Greyson."

Echo didn't leave Parker a chance to mess up. She nudged Parker lightly forward as she introduced her.

"This is Parker Carter. She just finished her master's in art therapy, and she is looking for a job."

Dilynn's eyes opened a little wider, and the corners of her mouth raised just slightly. "Oh, you're the friend Alex has heard so much about."

Parker tucked her hair behind her ear as she searched for something to say. Interviews weren't her specialty with her only job experience from a strip club. Something that would get her barred from the school.

"Well, Parker Carter, it's nice to meet you. I don't like to do business at celebrations. However, we are looking for an art teacher."

Parker looked over at Echo, deciding her friend must have lost her damn mind. She was not an artist, nor a teacher. She interpreted artwork and talked to kids. That was it.

Echo looked down at Parker from her height of superiority. Her eyes dared Parker to back out of the deal to talk to the guests. It was clearly a setup, since

Echo obviously knew Dilynn or Alex would be there. With a nod of her head towards Dilynn, Echo encouraged Parker to speak.

"Uh... sorry. I don't really teach."

"But you do art therapy?" Dilynn probed. "That's what Marissa said."

"Yeah. I... I mean, I finished my clinical internship at ArtReach a couple of weeks ago, and my license came in a few days ago."

Dilynn nodded eagerly. She started to wave the hand Parker never shook as she explained, "Well, Greyson Academy is a school focused on rehabilitating youth using trauma informed methods—"

"Stop reciting the mission statement."

The first thing Parker noticed about Alex the Interrupter was her need to look up. She wasn't short, but Alex was tall. Taller than Echo, with a face that was stoically composed yet interestingly calming.

A single kiss was pressed to the blonde waves before the arm wrapped around Dilynn's middle released her. Alex extended a long thin hand to Parker.

"Hi, I'm Alex and my pronouns are they and them," they said. Then Alex smiled down at their wife. "Dilynn usually tells people for me, but just in case."

"Parker." She offered, then took their hand. "She and her."

"Nice to meet you, Parker."

Alex pulled a wallet from their back pocket and retrieved a business card. "Simone and Marissa have told me a lot about you. Here's my card. Give me a call. Dilynn, or I, can show you around the school and see if our art position is something you'd be interested in."

Parker took the card and looked it over. Alex Trikru, not Greyson. She found it strange they had a different last name, but the school was only named after Dilynn.

"It's new." Dilynn's hands were waving like she could summon a viewing portal for whatever she was talking about. "The whole set up, and it's pretty incomplete so it's kinda a make your own—"

"Breathe, Dilynn," Alex said with a chuckle. "If she's interested, then she'll call."

Parker thought of her bank account. Thought of the first of the month coming up in a few weeks. She tried to swallow the lump of fear in her throat, and said, "Thank you. I'll—"

"Carter?" Evie asked.

'Never call in a million years,' Parker silently finished.

Evie, with her vest and her taser and her gun, approached Parker. She stepped into the one path of escape from where Echo had already backed her against the counter.

Her eyes darted around, looking for a way out. When she found none, she met Evie's intense stare. Same shape, same color, but after nine years they were different. The anger of childhood trauma had left her. The anger was replaced with shock and fear.

Grown up Evie still stood several inches taller than Parker. The height difference between them held the same element of control Echo's had on Parker.

"Blake," Parker half whispered with her chin tucked to her chest.

"It's Greyson now," Evie corrected.

Dilynn wrapped her free arm around Evie's mid back. "Oh, Evie, you know Parker?"

Voices from the other guests tried to break through the awkward bubble surrounding the two families juxtaposed by the younger women. Imagining the scene on a canvas, Parker pictured the brush smearing paint chaotically in the space between them. Both women's energy pushed away from each other as their families tried to push them towards each other.

"Evie?" Dilynn prodded. "Is this like the first time you met your sister, because Simone and Marissa don't have a house rules board hanging up for me to point at."

"We aren't going to fight. She probably thinks we are because..." Evie sighed heavily. "Carter and I were roommates. You know, before you got me out."

Echo cleared her throat, then pressed her hat back on her head. Parker knew Echo hated talking about those years. Parker didn't care as much, but Evie was clearly ashamed of where she'd ended up.

"That's how Parker and I met," Echo admitted. "I... uh... I got out but I guess, you took my bed."

Evie looked Echo up, then down. Her gaze wandered to Simone, then back to Echo. Parker watched Dilynn look back at Alex. She wondered if they were doing the same math she'd done when she'd met Simone for the first time.

There would be no answer to that question. Just like no one would say anything to the married couple, even though they were terrible together.

Evie's hand pulled at the vest's neckline again. She still had the detention ticks. Parker didn't wear t-shirts or anything with a button at her throat for the same reason. Even a sweatshirt had the ability to make Parker still feel like the top button of the state issued polo was choking her.

"Look. I... I don't even really know how to say it. It was so long ago, but I owe you an apology."

Parker stared at the wood grain of the floor. A line ran haphazardly in proximity to those around it but never touched the others. She followed it to its abrupt stop at the start of the next board. The next board didn't line up to the prior's grain, but she found a new line. This one twisted with the rest, coming to meet in a dark tangle with the other lines where for once it wasn't alone. Just like she was not alone in this space, where those years before she had been.

"It's in the past," she said, trying to force herself to believe it.

"Look can we—" Evie started, but a hand rested on Evie's shoulder.

"This isn't the place, E." Alex looked at Evie. "Another time, maybe."

Alex's long fingers squeezed; a signal of support Echo mirrored on Parker's shoulder. She wasn't sure if it made Evie feel better, but she was certain it didn't make her feel any safer.

Evie's head bobbed, and she held on to the top of the vest.

"Let's do the cake," Simone suggested, taking a position between Parker and the Greysons, a buffer Parker needed so she could breathe. "Cake makes things better. Plus, Alex, you actually like cake."

Parker's face scrunched up. She shifted her gaze from Simone to Dilynn. The potential employer was watching her with both her lips sucked into her mouth, surely trying to keep from laughing.

"Marissa, why is the candle crooked?" Simone asked.

Parker had to turn away to keep her shit together. Every single time she had to be near Simone, she just wanted to hit her.

"It won't stand up," Echo said, trying to fix it again.

"Monsters are crazy," Dilynn offered. "Would it really be a monster mash if the candles were as straight as the stick up Simone's ass?"

Simone whipped around like she was going to skin Dilynn Greyson alive. She'd have to go through Alex and Evie though, which looked painful. Parker decided she would stand in Simone's way too. She'd stand beside anyone who had the balls to tell Simone she had a stick up her ass.

"Cake time!" Echo called to the house full of people. She looked at Parker and with a nod of her head, she gave Parker an opportunity to escape.

Dilynn stole that moment with a hand reaching out to touch Parker's arm. A mother's tenderness Parker hadn't felt since before her parents' trial. An unexpected gesture Parker was unable to run away from.

"Call Alex. Okay?"

Parker forced a smile, and she received a similar one back.

'She knows I'm not going to call. I can't now. I'll have to explain, and I can't explain.'

5

Nia left the office door open where Zoe stood contemplating their conversation. The halls echoed with the constant clicking of heels and shuffling of oxfords against the marble floor as people made their way to the elevators after a long Monday. Zoe heard the "good nights" spoken between the other assistant district attorneys and staff.

At a quarter past five, Zoe knew she was one of the few people in the building and she found herself back at her desk. She placed index cards with each witness's name under the days she wanted to call them to testify. The blue cards held the name of her witnesses, while the pink were those Landon Woods submitted. She placed a yellow card below each of the blue cards with the evidence description on it, then weighed the impact the evidence would have on the jury.

A three-week trial meant the jury would be bored after the first two days. She'd need two witnesses to provide the most damning evidence. Moore's shirt was the best. The jury would always come back to the fact Moore had been covered in his DNA when she walked away from the scene.

Zoe considered the second piece of evidence to be presented before she let Woods take over. She needed the next heavy hitter. She picked up the yellow card labeled 'Moore's blood in the kitchen.' Tapping the card's corner against the desk, she placed it below her final witness. She set the yellow card down under the last detective on her witness list. Content with her plan, she checked her watch.

Everyone should be gone, but Zoe waited.

She picked up the pink card with Officer Greyson's name and the notes she had made about the woman's stent in juvenile detention. The officer was called by Woods, which meant Zoe couldn't expect a matter-of-fact statement regarding the arrest. She drew a star in the corner, because Woods and the little Greyson's relationship could get her removed as a witness.

The soft knock on the open-door broke Zoe's concentration.

Zoe looked up at the lithe Latina leaning against the frame. A fitted suit hugged perfectly to her body as her long hair dangled elegantly around the warm face. Her red lips were curled in the corners seductively when she asked, "You have a minute to discuss something?"

Zoe set the cards down, making her way around the desk barefooted. "Yes. Please, come in, Lyra."

By the time the door latched, Zoe had closed the space between Lyra and herself. Her hands gripped Lyra's hips as Zoe pressed the onyx-haired woman's back to the door. Lyra's head fell to rest against the dark wood, giving Zoe access to her throat. Zoe pressed her lips to the skin just below Lyra's ear.

"Miss me, Commander?" Lyra innocently asked.

Zoe bit Lyra's ear until she pulled a quiet gasp from the scarlet painted mouth for calling her by that dreaded name.

"You took forever," Zoe growled.

Her hands found a new grip on Lyra's ass as she lifted the lighter woman up. With her body pressed against the woman's core, Zoe ground her hips against Lyra's center just enough to alternate the amount of pressure she knew would draw a reaction.

"Some of us work on more than a handful of cases at once, Commander. Us lowly family court prosecutors handle—"

"Stop talking," Zoe interrupted. Her lips reattached to Lyra's throat.

"Why was Nia here anyways?" Lyra probed. A smug smile played on her lips as Zoe ignored her.

Zoe didn't care about Nia or the conversation anymore. She really didn't care about anything besides getting Lyra naked and hearing her real name sing from the red lips with gasps and moans of pleasure.

Adjusting her grip, Zoe took the woman's full weight and carried her to the desk. When she started to unbutton the pants in the way of her end of day treat, Lyra stopped her.

With a dramatic eye roll, Zoe fulfilled the woman's constant need for information. "She came to talk about the Olivia Moore case. She said she's stepping down, but let's talk about it later. Right now, I just want to be here with you." She fixed her courtroom glare in place. "Doing you."

Lyra placed a hand on Zoe's chest. Her bedroom eyes softened to apologetic. "I can't stay. My sister—"

"Okay, a little pressure but I can make quick magic. The record is five minutes, and I can beat it." Zoe raised her eyebrows a couple of times and reached for Lyra's pants again.

With a laugh, Lyra shook her head.

"You don't even have five minutes?" Zoe huffed, her head falling back. "You should have just texted me you couldn't come."

Lyra's fingers traveled delicately between Zoe's shoulder blades, sending electricity pulsing through Zoe's core.

"I could have texted you, but then I wouldn't get to see you. And I wanted to see you. I still want to see you. So..." Lyra pressed a kiss to Zoe's cheek. "I came here to ask if you would be willing to join my sister and I tonight. We could get something to eat at a real restaurant. I'll pay."

Zoe let go of her co-worker and slumped down in the leather chair. She'd known at some point it would come to this with Lyra, just didn't expect it to happen now.

"Look, Lyra. We already discussed—"

Lyra held up her hand. "You're the worst lesbian ever, you know? What type of woman just fucks someone on their desk without caring about anything else?"

The blade of Lyra's jab hit Zoe in the chest. She wasn't good at relationships because she didn't bother to try to be good at them. Being flamboyantly gay wasn't a look for the next District Attorney. And with Nia stepping down, she had to keep her priorities in order.

The number one thing she needed to focus on was work, which made Lyra convenient. She was fuckable and at work.

"I like what we have now without all the complications." Zoe gripped the armrests of the chair. She stared at the cards scattered all over her desk. "If focusing on my career makes me the worst girl ever, then so be it. Nia is retiring, and this is my chance to become the next District Attorney. It's my dream, and right now, I just need to win this case, so my face gets on the news."

"So, your face gets on the news? What the hell are you talking about?" Lyra bit back with her dark eyebrows scrunched in the middle.

Leaning back in the chair, Zoe looked up at the woman that apparently did have five minutes to spare. With a shake of her head, she explained, "Nia said the key to being elected was to get on the news by proving just how tough I will be on crime, especially high-profile murder trials."

Lyra's fingers tapped her lips. She removed them when her mouth opened, but then put them back like she was shoving the words back in. Her head cocked, and she stared at Zoe.

"So, you're actually arguing, counselor, that you can't try and see if this could be more than office fuckery because you have to go after your dream of being DA. And that the only thing that matters is sending a kid to prison for the rest of her life so you can win an election. A child, we both know, was probably being taken advantage of by a skeezy pervert. Am I hearing you correctly?"

Lyra made the whole thing sound dirty and wrong. Zoe had been able to adjust the words, so they were palatable when Zachery had said them. She hated that Lyra's anger with her made more sense than anything Nia and Zachery said.

Zoe's hands came up, pulling at the roots of her hair. She knew Lyra wouldn't understand because the woman was still in her first-year post law school and spent her days in kiddie court. She couldn't possibly comprehend all of what was at stake because she wanted to be in family court. Her aspirations were just lower than Zoe's. She couldn't say any of it without angering the Latina more, so she took a different approach.

With an open hand, Zoe pointed to Olivia's picture taped on the whiteboard. "When you look at the girl up there, you see a victim. Maybe she was. But you have to think about the reality that if the police had uncovered any evidence of it, then this would never have gotten to my desk. But they didn't. The 'child' killed a man. Brutally murdered him. I am not the bad guy here."

Zoe gestured to herself with her chest puffed. "I'm doing what's best for society. And if she's not a psycho, then she is so traumatized it's only a matter of time before she does something like this again. And maybe next time it won't be to someone you deem skeezy, but to someone decent. The best thing I can do is make sure she never has the opportunity to hurt someone else."

Lyra slid down from the top of the desk. She held on to the edge as she steadied herself, and Zoe looked her over to see if she was hurt.

"Look, Nia said it's about taking precautions." Zoe took a deep breath. "It's what we do as criminal attorneys for the state. We protect society from even little girls with a troubled past, so more people don't get hurt."

Lyra's arms folded over her chest. Her eyes narrowed at Zoe. "My mom once said, 'people will give up their strongest ideologies for the perception of safety.' I hadn't expected when we met six months ago or after Nia raged into you for giving a damn, you would ever want to be like her. Yet here you are standing on the precipice of something so important to you, and you're drawing lines between who gets to be a part of your society and who you can throw away."

"Look, Lyra—"

"Don't 'look, Lyra' me," Lyra snapped. "You can tell yourself I don't get it all you want. I'm sure it helps you convince yourself you're better than everyone else. The reality is though, I get it better than you could ever understand. I get things your privileged ass would never be able to even imagine in your worst nightmares. Must be nice to just sit on your pedestal and look down at everyone."

"Jesus Christ. You are completely jaded into thinking all juvenile delinquents are rehabilitatable?" Then, Zoe challenged her. "What don't I understand?"

Lyra looked down on her, and Zoe instantly regretted giving her the opportunity to hold the station of power.

"You are—" Lyra's mouth snapped shut. She shook her head, then held up a hand to create a barrier between them. "No, there's no point. This was a waste of time."

"What was?"

"You." Lyra closed her eyes, chin dropping to the ground as she shook her head so slowly. "You are... No. You were a waste of my time."

She'd invested no time in this because she and Lyra weren't in a relationship. It was supposed to be simple, and Lyra was lecturing her like they were fighting before going to meet her sister like the woman wanted.

Her eyes rose to Lyra as she decided on the real problem.

"You're just pissed I don't do relationships. But I'm not out whoring around."

She tried to stand up, but Lyra was too close. She took the calloused hand and laid down all her cards.

"I don't want what we have to get messed up by changing what works. I mean we eat together; we communicate. We have sex. I have sex with you and only you. Why can't this be enough?"

Lyra looked out the window at downtown Phoenix. Her body leaned against the frame as fingers clung to the window frame.

"I thought that if I gave you what you wanted, then you would meet me halfway. You'd see me and want me. All of me."

"I do see you," Zoe tried. "I see how beautiful and sexy you are."

"Yeah, you see me as an object." The laugh soaked in embarrassment broke free from Lyra's chest. Her eyes looked everywhere but at Zoe. "The reality is now I see you."

Lyra walked to the door. Her heavy steps made Zoe think Lyra would turn back to her.

"I don't know why I thought if I trusted you enough to fuck me that you would care about me." The woman sucked in a deep breath. Once more, she held herself up against the door like walking away hurt her. "I guess I didn't realize you think people are disposable."

"Lyra—"

"Save it, Commander." The dark head shook slowly. "You're going to need it for the war you're waging on a child to make a woman who threw her own kid away proud of you."

Lyra walked out of the office. The ballet flats on her feet masked the sound of her footfalls as though she'd never been there at all.

Zoe's head fell back. She traced the ceiling tiles, searching for a sign. But she knew there was nothing to save. There had been sex on her desk, the floor, the table, and against the door. But Lyra didn't know her, and she didn't even know Lyra's last name.

She sighed at the sight of the cards on her desk, all pushed out of order. Getting up from the chair, Zoe made her way back to the other side of the desk and finished what she started. As she worked, her mind wandered over what it would have been like to take Lyra out on an actual date. To kiss her on the lips instead of everywhere else. To wipe away the memories of the sparkling stripper swinging around the silver pole with the practical prosecutor positioned perfectly to propel Zoe into the next stage of her life.

Her phone rang, drawing her attention to the last person she wanted to talk to: her mother. A woman who was never proud of Zoe's success. Lyra and her mom would probably have gotten along well because they both thought Zoe needed a girlfriend.

She set the phone down, letting it ring through. Getting told she needed a girlfriend after being told off wasn't going to help her become the next District

Attorney.

6

The phone flew from Parker's hand when the leather case smacked her arm. As she tried to save it from hitting the ground, the lid of the coffee cup popped off and the walls smashed under her grip. Creamy iced coffee sloshed upward from the crunched plastic, soaking through her white cotton top. She let the rest of the drink fall to the ground. It splattered around her feet, leaving speckles of tan on her scratched, secondhand loafers.

Parker's gaze rose from her now see-through shirt to the back of the woman click-clacking away in Jimmy Choo's. Red faced, she yelled, "I wasn't just standing here, and you didn't just hit me!"

The woman didn't turn around, let alone apologize. She simply made her way through the doors labeled: Attorneys Only.

Parker closed her eyes. She counted to five, letting out a deep breath, then exhaled until her count reached ten.

The wait for the drink she couldn't really afford had already taken fifteen minutes. If she tried to order again, she would be late for her jury summons. She wasn't sure what kind of penalty it would earn her, but she wasn't going to chance sitting behind bars once again. She had to do something about her shirt though. The coffee shop would at least have a bathroom for her to fully assess the damage.

She turned back to Starbucks outside the Downtown Phoenix Court House, nearly running into someone else. Her feet left the ground when she jumped to avoid another collision.

'Am I invisible? Like, does no one see me standing here?'

Sharp green eyes of a gangly teenage girl searched Parker from her hair line to the crotch of her wet pants. The girl's oily hair hung around her face, partially concealing the blackheads covering the kid's nose and chin like freckles. She chewed on the already cracked lips, then held up Parker's phone.

"Thank you," Parker offered, checking to see if the screen had shattered.

"Parker? Is that you?"

She looked up from her phone to find Dilynn smiling at her. The woman clutched her own drink, handing a second cup to the teen still silently standing beside Parker. Dilynn moved to pull Parker in for a hug but stopped when she saw the coffee still coating the exposed cleavage Parker's shirt couldn't cover.

"Oh, dear." Dilynn's eyes quickly snapped up from where her eyes had fixed on Parker's breasts. "What... uh...." Dilynn cleared her throat before trying once more. "What happened?"

Parker glanced at the Attorney's Only door before wiping her coffee-soaked hands down her maroon pants.

"I think the person whose parking spot I snagged just sought revenge."

"That's terrible," Dilynn said. She took a step back and bit her lip. The blonde eyebrows rose to form a deep crease across her forehead. "What are you here for?"

"Jury duty." Parker pulled the shirt out from her body as an early fall breeze whipped through the courtyard. Her eyes rose to the skyline, searching for any hint of a storm.

The girl began to dig through her backpack. Several papers tried to flee the chaos within, but she pulled out a blue thermal shirt. Her finger ran over the size small sticker. She picked it off with scabbed over fingertips, then held it out to Parker in the same way she'd held out the phone.

"No. I can't," Parker said. She forced a smile on her face as she shook her hand at the shirt.

"Your bra... its showing." Each word scratched over the girl's tongue. The green eyes fell to the concrete, but she pushed the shirt towards Parker once more.

Dilynn studied the girl as a broad smile spread over the older woman's face. She took the shirt and forced it into Parker's hand.

"Thank you, Olivia," Dilynn praised the teen in a sugar-coated voice more suitable for a young child.

Parker ran her fingers over the rough material, appreciating the promise of warmth in case the grey clouds made it to Downtown.

"Oh, and Parker, it was great meeting you last weekend. I meant it when I said I would really love to talk with you about joining the Greyson family." Dilynn turned to the quiet girl. "Don't you think Parker would be a great addition to the staff, Olivia?"

Olivia's arms pulled her sweatshirt around her tightly. Her head fell once in what Parker took as a nod of agreement.

"Thanks. I would...." Parker started, but Dilynn's attention was drawn to something over her shoulder. Turning, Parker saw a large man in a suit waving to Dilynn and the girl.

"I'm sorry, honey, but we have to get inside." Dilynn squeezed Parker's sticky hand.

There were thirty dollars left in her bank account. The fridge was empty enough she'd driven the cabaret yesterday. She'd been unable to get out of the car when she saw the spot her ex had ended their relationship in once she'd gotten off stage. Going back to work there would mean walking by the spot to go in and leave every shift. A constant reminder of being treated like trash wasn't something she'd wanted so she drove away.

Fate wasn't something Parker put much belief in. Running into Dilynn again felt like it though. To not call the woman would mean truly shutting the door to a job she needed. And she couldn't blow another opportunity to prove to herself she was more than a trashy stripper.

"I'll call you tomorrow," she called after Dilynn.

The blonde threw up her hand, waving as she moved towards the giant in the expensive suit. "I look forward to it."

Parker slipped back into Starbucks, heading to the counter to find out where the bathroom was. The woman behind the bar pushed a venti drink towards her. "Iced coffee with a whole lot of specialness."

"Thank you." Parker took a sip of the drink, realizing the barista had duplicated her order perfectly. For a moment she didn't feel invisible.

"The Commander is a great lawyer, but she gets in a zone and forgets the rest of the world exists," the barista explained. "Ari told me you needed a new drink."

Parker quirked an eyebrow at the familiar name. "I'm sorry. Who?"

"The cunt that hit you and walked away," a woman said from a large leather chair in the corner of the lobby. "Anais, quit calling her by that name. Her head is already too big to fit in the door."

Parker glanced between who she could only assume was another lawyer and the barista, Anais, with a huge smile.

Anais pointed at Parker's shirt. "The one who crushed your drink is Zoe Robinson. She's a prosecutor. Sorry, all the other lawyers call her The Commander."

Parker looked across the courtyard at the door for attorneys. She'd only seen the back of the woman's head, so she couldn't be certain it was the same Zoe Robinson. But if it was, then Zoe hadn't changed. She'd probably seen Parker and felt the need to remind her ex-girlfriend that she wasn't important enough to notice. Apparently, Parker was important though, or a ghost that haunted Zoe with everyone calling her the ironic pet name Parker had given the pillow princess.

"She commands nothing," the other woman added. "Just another reason people hate lawyers."

"And that's Ari," Anais said, nodding towards the woman with possibly more of a grudge against Parker's ex. "She's a big shot too, and her head is just as big, but her manners are better unless Zoe is around."

Parker studied the lawyer's incredible bone structure. The high cheek bones and sharp jaw line reminded Parker of Zoe. She stared longer than she probably should at the rage in the pale hazel eyes that were watching the door to the courthouse. Ari's face causing Parker's left hand to itch with a need sketch the woman's profile.

"Karma is not on that asshole's side today," Ari declared, smiling into her drink as she met Parker's gaze. "She thinks she's doling out justice; however, I have a feeling today she's going to get smacked off that pedestal."

The coffee bar came to life as milk steamed. It provided Parker enough time to not need to respond to Ari. Unfortunately, the lawyer's critical gaze was still staring at Parker, and a finger tapped her nose.

"I know your face." After a moment of careful analysis, the lawyer's eyes grew. "Oh, you have no idea how much I wish I could've been there that day. You don't want to be here though. My mother, DA Williams will be here in a moment. Maybe change and take your drink because she won't have to think about who you are."

'First Evie, then Zoe. Now Nia fucking Williams. What the fuck did I do to deserve this?' Parker asked herself as she made her way through the crowd to the restroom.

'Karma is clearly pissed at me too.'

Security made Parker throw out the last fourth of her drink when they called her name. They handed her a laminated pink placard with a huge "2" printed on it and told her to get in line by her number.

Looking around, Parker took in the sixty-five other individuals with numbers. Her last name was Carter but the older lady with the last name Aguilar was just handed number sixty. Parker decided whoever got to choose these things was seriously confused. There was no chance she'd be giving up weeks of her life to come back here.

It took twenty minutes for people to order themselves numerically. Standing in line by a number wasn't complicated; however, the other potential jurors made it out like it was.

A small woman stood in the middle of the semicircle developing as people lined themselves around the hallway, and announced, "Hello, I am Judge Miller's bailiff, Guiterrez, and I am going to lead you into the courtroom. Jurors one through fourteen will be seated in the jury box and everyone else will be seated in the audience area. Numbers sixty-five and sixty-four will you hold the doors for the line, please?"

Sixty-four looked as though he would fall over under the weight of the door, so sixty-three took his place. Parker waited for the bald head in front of her to start walking, which he did only when the bailiff gestured him within.

All the suits in the courtroom stood as the jurors entered, as well as the white-haired judge in the wizard-looking robe. Parker smiled weakly when she recognized him, just in case he too recalled putting her on a bus to the detention center. Then her eyes landed on the owner of the shirt she now wore.

Olivia stood alongside the tallest suit in the room. The girl glanced back at Parker in the parade of disgruntled civilians before dipping her head down. Dilynn hadn't noticed Parker because she was preoccupied with her phone, standing directly behind the wooden railing separating her from the lawyer and girl.

Parker didn't envy Olivia. Briefly, she considered if she shouldn't pull the same stunt she'd used last time she'd been called for jury duty. Sixteen dollars a day wouldn't pay her rent though. And she now had a clear-cut opportunity to get kicked off the jury and out of the courthouse without causing as much of a scene as she had last time.

She scanned the rest of the courtroom until she reached the prosecution's side. Her eyes locked on the lawyer with dark hair tightly twisted into a bun at the base of her neck, shifting her weight uncomfortably in the same Jimmy Choo's Parker had purchased for the woman years ago. A present Zoe couldn't actually walk in when she got them. Almost a whole night's tips because Parker was trying to match the gifts Zoe would give her.

The gift hadn't mattered three days later when Zoe broke up with her for earning it on a stage in her thong after coming in with Zoe's asshole brother. The man who'd known Parker was Zoe's but still tried to get Parker on her knees the week before in the private dance room.

Zoe turned to the jurors from the pile of papers she was sorting on the table. Her eyebrows raised high enough to tell Parker that Zoe wanted to see her as much as she wanted to see Zoe. Knew even though she'd stopped dying her hair in grad school, her ex recognized the girl she used to be.

The borrowed thermal shirt felt as though it disappeared. Parker's skin itched as the hazel eyes ran down the front of her. She closed her arms over her chest, and she hoped Zoe wouldn't recognize the purse tucked under her arm.

Her gaze dropped to the ground, and she walked faster to close the distance between herself and Juror 1. They were ushered into the jury box that any television crime show would be jealous of.

'I must have been a really bad person in a previous life.'

7

Zoe's eyes landed on the wet spot running down the fitted red pants she had watched walk out of Starbucks. Her morning was already a mess with Nia's daughter, Ari calling her a cunt while she waited for her drink, and that was after the redhead in red pants stole her spot and hadn't even held the elevator in the parking garage. It was petty revenge on the woman she hadn't recognized, which was now coming back to bite her in the ass.

"Shit."

It came out before Zoe could fix her face into any form of deniability as the woman, she'd once loved, walked by her. She took a deep breath, inhaling the subtle berry scented body spray lingering from her ex. She caught sight of a stained shirt and thick novel peeking out of the familiar tattered Coach bag.

'I bought her that bag for her birthday.'

Her eyes dropped to her shoes. The scarlet red reminded Zoe of the negligée her ex was in on stage when their eyes met. She realized the woman would recognize the gift Zoe hadn't been able to part with. The heels that squished her toes, but never failed to help her get a guilty verdict.

Irene, her co-counsel, stood beside Zoe with the list of jurors. As soon as the stripper passed, Zoe yanked the list from Irene's hands. She tore through the profiles, until she found it. A star marked in the corner of the page. She wanted Juror 2, Parker Carter. Needed a younger female who would be more likely, in Zoe's opinion, to cave to the older men she'd planned to load the jury box with.

'She'd said her name was Michelle.'

Zoe scanned the rest of the juror profile page. The woman wasn't a stripper anymore. She was a therapist.

She looked back at the box. Scanned the other members only to not appear to be looking at Parker Carter. Her ex used to be blonde, and Zoe hated the way her fingers itched to tuck the loose tress of hair that had fallen in the woman's face. The woman who knew every secret and desire Zoe held. The one who'd slept pressed against Zoe's back for a year yet had never told Zoe that her name was Parker. A name that seemed to fit the now redhead much more than Michelle ever had.

"Problem?" Irene whispered as jurors continued to file by.

A long list of problems ran through Zoe's mind. The first was calling Juror 2 trash when she and Zachery saw Parker on the spotlit stage with cash hanging out of her thong. The second was that Zoe didn't have another juror she actually wanted. The third was that the woman's presence reminded Zoe of one of the worst moments of her life after Ari had nearly spit at Zoe for trying to put the past behind them. The fourth was that Parker looked more beautiful with red hair, making her seem like she aged like a fine wine. And five... she couldn't think of a fifth problem because she was staring at the back of Parker's turned head. Besides the color change, Parker's hair had the same curl at the end from the flip she would do with her straightening iron before she left the house. It cascaded past her shoulders, just as it had when Parker walked away from Zoe's broken heart that wasn't worth even trying to fight for.

Her lip was pulled back between her teeth, and she dropped her gaze to the paper when Parker turned to look directly at her. She searched for anything that would tell her why Parker had lied about her name for a year, just like she'd lied about being a stripper. If she could find the answers to those questions, maybe she could understand why Parker just walked away instead of reminding Zoe that it didn't matter what her job was. Zoe had told herself that multiple times in the following months, but she'd never believed it because Parker had left without even seeming to care Zoe had said such hateful things to her.

Irene cleared her throat, bringing Zoe back to the courtroom.

Without looking at the jury, Zoe carefully answered, "I *may* have hit Juror 2 with my purse earlier, and I may have, by the look of her pants and the fact she changed her shirt, spilled coffee all over her."

Irene inhaled obnoxiously loud. A similar sound Zoe was accustomed to hearing from her mother when she had to report she was still single. The older attorney's disapproval was not helping, and Zoe knew she had to fix this herself.

'Michelle. Parker. Doesn't fucking matter. You can't be here,' she said to the woman without moving her mouth. She searched through the other names to find a replacement.

It took almost ten minutes for every potential juror to enter. Once the door holders were seated, Judge Miller gave permission for everyone else to sit. Zoe still did not have a replacement. She had banked on Woods wanting to keep Juror 2, which would give her the chance to eliminate the single mother and the grandfather of two little girls. If she kept her ex, then she would have to look at the former stripper every day of the trial. She'd have to acknowledge the woman she'd finally convinced herself was below her would now be a deciding factor in the most important trial of her life.

"Good morning, ladies and gentlemen." Judge Miller began as he recited the well-practiced script in a drolling baritone. "I want to thank you for your haste in getting seated. Before we begin the process of determining who will stay for this jury, I will provide you with a brief description of the charges and the time frame this trial will take."

He picked up a form, beginning to read in an even more boring timbre. "The charge against the defendant is second degree murder and trespassing. The defendant is accused of breaking into a man's home and killing him without a premeditated...."

Zoe examined the potential jurors seated in the box while the judge continued to talk. All of them were listening carefully, except Juror 2, who rudely stared at the ceiling.

"This trial is scheduled to begin next Wednesday and will take place over the next three weeks. Your obligation as a juror is to listen to the information brought forth before you and determine beyond a reasonable doubt as to the guilt of the defendant. We are asking for quite the time commitment from you, and we respect some of you are unable to comply with this sort of obligation. Does anyone have any questions regarding this?"

Juror 12 stood up with a worn baseball cap clutched between his weathered fingers. He cleared his throat. "I don't speak English well. I need a translator. Juries need people like..."

Zoe willed her ears to stop listening. Twelve's public facebook page was filled with his grandchildren. He was getting eliminated so he wouldn't associate the teen with the little girls that looked a little too much like Moore. Which meant, she still needed to find a new Juror 2 rather than listen to his speech that was too much of a social commentary on institutionalize racism for her. As a mixed raced female, she didn't need a lesson from an old man on what it was like to have people doubt her because she had just enough melanin in her skin to not be white, but hair not curly enough to be Black either.

She scanned the jury again, tabulating the number of female faces. She paused at Parker leaning back in her chair like a hostile teenager, her head rolling back and forth.

"Focus, Commander," Irene growled.

Zoe's cheeks heated up at being caught watching Parker. She needed to divert her attention, so she took the opportunity to get a feel for the tiny brunette mostly covered by her opposing counsel, Landon Woods. Olivia's awkward adolescent body hunched at the table, looking solely at her own hands wrestling with each other. Zoe only realized Olivia was picking at her cuticles when the girl brought a single finger to her mouth. She let her hair fall around her face, so it was hidden.

"Thank you for your willingness to participate with a translator. At this point, is there anyone feeling they are incapable of being unbiased and acting within their civil duty?" Judge Miller asked.

The number two pink placard could not have entered the air any faster. Zoe watched the redhead bounce in her seat, begging to be dismissed from the jury. For a moment, Zoe remembered a time when Parker had begged for her attention.

"Stop smiling. Woods is watching you," Irene hissed at her.

Woods was watching Zoe. He smirked at her, then nodded in the direction of Juror 2. She was correct in assuming he would want to keep the woman.

Judge Miller called out the numbers in order as he went around the courtroom. Irene quickly notated every name attempting to be dismissed.

"Thank you all for your patience. I am going to have a momentary conference with the attorneys."

Zoe watched Parker huff and lean forward, catching her face in her hands. Fighting an urge to laugh at her, Zoe straightened her shoulders and proceeded to the bench. The bailiff hit the button that played a loop of white noise over the speakers in the courtroom.

"I would like to keep jurors 2, 8, 7, and 9," Woods requested.

Judge Miller's eyes shifted to Zoe, "Depending on their reasoning for dismissal, I would not be opposed to having juror 7 stay, but I wish to strike jurors 8 and 9. Juror 12, I would also wish to release, along with 4."

"And Juror 2?" Judge Miller asked. The whole group looked over at Parker rocking herself in her chair like a child.

Zoe bit her lower lip to keep from laughing. She recognized Parker's ploy. Had been the victim of the woman's childish behavior from time to time. It had always gotten Parker her way, so it made sense for her to try it here. She made the decision it wouldn't work this time though. She needed Parker to see what she'd become.

"While she is desperately trying to seem too immature to be here, I would like her to stay."

Woods tilted his head and looked back at Juror 2 again. "*You* are okay with rolling eyes number 2? She's a behavior therapist for troubled teens."

Zoe looked at him with her court day mask in place. "I am curious to know her reason for her bias. I would expect her to feel obligated to stay."

Judge Miller nodded, releasing the lawyers from their place before the bench. While they walked back to their seat, Parker's head rolled left and right.

The white noise was switched off, and Judge Miller called the numbers jointly agreed to be released. People shuffled out of the box, but Zoe paid them no mind. Her eyes were caught in a stare down with a set of brown ones measuring her coldly from seat two.

Parker only stopped staring at Zoe when Judge Miller called her number, "Juror 2, could you please explain to the court your reasons for claiming bias."

'Please don't say you know me,' Zoe begged. 'I'm sorry. You will never know how sorry I am. Just please don't say you know me.'

Parker opened her brown eyes wider and tilted her chin slightly inward as she stood up and spoke directly to the judge. Zoe couldn't believe the woman still deliberately made herself appear more childlike when she talked to authority figures.

"Your honor, thank you for taking the time to address my concerns and biases based on my personal ideologies."

The trailer slang Parker used in college had vanished. A wave of regret washed over Zoe. Things could have been different if she'd hung around long enough to see the woman the sparkly girl grew into. She could have forgiven her.

"My first concern is that my work with youth would pose a significant problem for me seeing this young woman, who was kind enough to loan me a shirt this morning after the petty prosecutor struck me with her briefcase and dumped coffee all over the front of me without so much as looking back to apologize. At this point in time, the only person that needs rehabilitation is the state's prosecutor or at least some finishing classes."

Parker's hand waved at Zoe dismissively, even though her cheeks flushed highlighting the freckles that speckled her face. There were one hundred and fourteen freckles last time Zoe counted.

"However, despite my interactions with both sides, I feel that my bias lies in how the judicial branch of government has become a punishment system without rehabilitation."

Parker's eyes shifted to Olivia. "Maybe I just believe too much in the good in people or am a twisted anarchist... but I do not feel that I could properly sit on this jury and claim to judge this girl's actions. I know that I have personally made many mistakes in my life, and while I strongly believe in accountability, this court does not offer her that."

Turning back to Judge Miller, Parker's chin raised. "No, it offers only the court's illusion of safety for society by claiming to determine the defendant's guilt and then lock her away in a manner that is only deemed justifiable for all non-human beings. And even then, there are a large number of people that would argue even that is inhumane. Basically, I don't believe in the system of incarceration, nor do I feel that it would cause this young woman to pay her debt to society."

Zoe held her breath, noting Parker barely took one herself, like the woman feared if she did, she would give up her opportunity to completely ruin Zoe's chance of winning this case.

"... after all the debt being paid for her incarceration would be paid by myself, Zoe the petty prosecutor..."

Zoe's eyes grew at the sound of her own name coming from the familiar mouth.

"... every juror in this room, and even yourself, Judge. For it is our funds, from our work that pay to keep her locked in a cage. This is against my moral compass; however, if you feel that reasoning is unacceptable, then I would also like to state that I work with troubled teens, and since this trial is looking to be several weeks long, I don't feel that having me here would benefit society. After all, I am a civil worker that provides *actual* rehabilitation therapies to youth, which are far more worth everyone's time than me sitting in this uncomfortable chair."

Judge Miller knocked on the bench as several of the other jurors in the room began to clap. The sound pulled a soft seductive smile to the redhead's face; a smile Zoe knew all too well. One that had fallen when the woman looked down at her from the stage while cupping her massive breasts with thumbs grazing her hard nipples. It had been the last time Zoe saw Parker smile.

"Order, please," Judge Miller requested with the same tone her grandfather had used with Zoe and her brothers when they were children.

The other jurors slowly ceased their claps of approval. When the room was quiet, Judge Miller smiled at the woman kindly.

"Ms. Carter. We meet again. I am sorry the Commander seems to have assaulted you this morning. Would you like to press charges?"

Parker softly chuckled and dropped her chin once more, before looking up at the judge. "No, sir. I'm just going to drive around until I see her car and key it."

"Ha!"

Zoe's head snapped in the direction of laughter to find Olivia Moore with her hand covering her mouth and eyes locked on the table in front of her.

Miller also let out a chuckle, which caused the blood to rush to Zoe's cheeks. He tapped his knocker lightly against his desk as others laughed at Zoe's expense.

"I see having you on this jury may cause you many conflicts and disrupt these proceedings. I hereby dismiss you, as well as call a thirty-minute recess. I feel it should give you, Ms. Robinson, an adequate amount of time to replace Juror 2's coffee so your car may maintain its paint. Court will resume in thirty minutes."

Zoe took her seat and tossed down the juror sheets she'd crumpled in her hands. Pinching the bridge of her nose, she attempted to regain control.

Footsteps stopped alongside her.

"Anais... she said she knew you... and she..."

Zoe looked up to find all the confidence Parker had when addressing the court had vanished.

"Who?" Zoe asked.

The redhead shifted her weight and avoided all eye contact with Zoe as she said, "The barista. Don't know why I thought you would know the person's name who made your coffee every day, but she said you were normally a nice person, so sorry for embarrassing you. I just really didn't want to be on this jury. I wasn't... I mean... I'm not going to key your car, and.... I wasn't about to tell anyone about, you know, so sorry."

Zoe stared at the creased info sheet on Parker in front of her. The page didn't give a single real detail about who Parker was now besides her job title.

"I'm sorry for hitting you, and even more sorry for not stopping to check on you. That was just rude and, as you said, petty." With a heavy exhale, Zoe added, "I'm also sorry for—"

"Don't." Parker held up her hand just enough to put a wall up between them. "It is what is it."

Zoe's head shook. She tried to figure out how to fix this since she finally had a chance. Nevertheless, nothing came to her. Just like nothing had come to her each time she'd seen Parker turn the other direction on the college campus. Frustration settled in her chest at her inability to create a solution, which turned into anger.

"You lied to me," she quietly growled.

"Huh?"

"Your name. I never knew your actual name. Almost a year and you never told me your real name."

"Wouldn't have made a difference," Parker stated more quietly. She sighed when she added, "I was nobody to you then, and when I leave, I'll be nobody to you again."

Parker started to walk away but stopped. Her frame had curled just enough to make her into a walking comma, but her head rose just enough to make her into a semi-colon.

"She was a really sweet kid this morning." The tress of hair Zoe wanted to touch was pushed roughly behind Parker's ear by her own hands. Her jaw worked over whatever she wanted to say carefully.

"She's a murderer," Zoe stated. Then looked at the kid chewing on her fingertips because surely there wasn't any nail left. She reminded herself, "She killed a man."

"Has she been evaluated?" Parker turned just enough to suggest she was looking back at Zoe. "Young girls.... Ones that keep themselves unkept and stare at the ground usually don't...."

Zoe narrowed her eyes at the stripper turned therapist. She felt the venom she'd swallowed after being humiliated in front of everyone rising once more, and decided Parker wouldn't just get to walk away without being bit back.

"It's none of your concern now. Had you stayed on the jury, you could have requested the information." Zoe pointed at the door. "Now, you walk away, and she is left with whoever doesn't pitch a fit about being here," she hissed.

Parker's head tilted just as she had the first day Zoe had handed her a coffee outside the library. She did not say anything else to Zoe. Her body didn't flinch, and her face didn't contort. She wasn't sorry, just like she hadn't been sorry that night. And once again, she turned away from Zoe. She:

Turned the wrong direction.

Walked directly to the money behind the scenes.

Shook Dilynn Greyson's hand that pulled her into a hug.

Smiled at the older woman like she'd won a best actress award.

Zoe's eyes narrowed as she considered if Parker Carter had intentionally planned her little speech to tamper with the other potential jurors. She knew Parker wouldn't have known she was called for this jury. But Zoe couldn't be certain what Greyson was capable of. She even scanned the room to see if Nia's ex-husband was hiding somewhere to report back to his boss, Sylvia Winters.

Zoe turned back to find Judge Miller still in his seat. This was rare, he normally retreated at any given recess. Zoe followed his eyes to where Parker and Greyson stood talking. She studied the glint of recognition and ran over his words about Parker and him meeting before. There was something resembling pride buried within the pale blue eyes.

When Parker left Greyson, Judge Miller's gaze followed the redhead out of the room. Everyone present knew Parker Carter, and Zoe needed to know how. She pulled out her phone, clicked the safari app open, and typed in 'Parker Carter'. The first hit read, "Daughter of convicted serial murderers, James and Janice Carter, arrested for assault of ADA Nia Williams."

8

Middle aged women with their messy buns and grannies sporting their grey bobs occupied all the front seats for the weekly book club event by the time Parker made it to Changing Hands Bookstore. She stood on her toes searching for anywhere she may have missed. The armchairs were filled, along with the folding chairs brought out for the event.

When she scanned the tabletop within the First Draft bar, she noticed a single unoccupied barstool facing the meeting area. Squeezing through the people in her same predicament, Parker clutched her beer to avoid wearing it like last month.

She managed to make to the seat before the older woman coming from the other direction. The legs of the metal chair protested against the wooden floor as she celebrated making it to the chair before the woman. That celebration ended with a sigh when the purse in the seat came into view.

She'd have to stand again if she wanted to stay. Looking down at her beer, she realized she at least needed to drink it before she left because it had cost a fourth of what remained in her bank account after the Starbucks fiasco. Another really dumb purchase since there was no actual guarantee she was getting the job at Greyson Academy.

'Stop wasting your food money on liquid calories,' she admonished herself.

She turned, trying to find another path through the people crowding the bar. Stuck without a clear exit lane, she hovered over the back of the chair as the dark-haired woman beside the saved seat met glanced at her.

They shared a smile before a path opened up. Holding the beer away from her chest, Parker started to leave.

"Wait," the woman said. She smiled again as her thin hand took the purse from the seat. "Siéntate"

The purse was set next to the once read book, and the woman leaned away from the chair. Parker's breasts grazed the woman's arm as she attempted to slide between the chairs. An awkward apology was offered as her face burned with embarrassment. But the woman's lips pressed into a sly smirk, when she said quietly, "Nothing to be sorry for."

Once she was settled in the confines of the chair, Parker offered a half whispered, "Thank you. I was just thinking that I would have to finish my beer quickly since standing at these things isn't fun."

"No problem."

Parker sipped her beer after setting the library copy of the novel in front of her. She scanned over the simplicity of the Kate Spade bag as the bitter beer faded to a fruity hint of pineapple. She liked the size of the purse and decided she'd search on OfferUp for something similar after landing the job at Greyson Academy.

"Whatcha drinking?" the purse's owner asked. The dark eyes didn't look Parker's way this time. Instead, the woman leaned casually against the bar still watching the crowd participate in the small talk Parker found so difficult.

Parker set the glass down. "It's called Church Music."

"I keep meaning to try that one. Creature of habit, though. I know I like the Cold Snack." The caramel toned hands tilted her own glass of porter colored liquid bubbling as it moved. "Venturing out can be dangerous."

"Dangerous is an interesting choice of words when considering if you should try a new beer." Parker smiled at how quickly she'd managed to respond.

"Maybe it's a gateway to other dangerous behaviors, like talking to a beautiful girl at a bar."

Parker tilted her head and took another look at the woman beside her. Then, her eyes searched the tops of the other people's heads as she tried to determine if the woman was implying Parker was not beautiful since she was talking to Parker.

With a raised hand and flushed cheeks, the woman choked on her drink. "Wait. I... that didn't come out right. I didn't mean to imply that you're not... Shit. Just... discard, por favor."

Parker tried to hide the blush rushing to her cheeks behind her glass. She couldn't help the tickling fluffiness run from her chest to her arms at someone noticing her while she was fully clothed.

"And you're right," the woman said, casting a glance Parker's way. "Dangerous is too harsh. Adventurous is probably better."

Parker looked at the woman's profile as her eyes crinkled in the corners when her scarlet painted lips spread into a smile.

"Well," Parker licked her lower lip and instantly wished she'd remember to pack Chapstick. "There's something to say about a person that knows what they like and sticks to it. It demonstrates true loyalty, which is hard to come by."

"I'll drink to that." The woman raised her glass. "Here's to sticking to what you like."

They clinked glasses and drank.

The woman shifted in her seat, turning toward Parker. "So, do you come to Book Club often?"

"When I actually read the book." Parker carded her fingers through her hair. She bit her lip as her finger ran over the top of the dense novel. "I don't always finish in time, so I don't want to ruin the ending by coming."

"Makes sense. I only come when my mom is too busy to come with my sister. I'm Lyra by the way."

"Parker."

"Parker." Her name rolled off Lyra's tongue slowly, every syllable enunciated. There was no denying Parker enjoyed hearing her name caressed by Lyra.

Lyra smiled, gesturing to the gathering. "So, you're here. Which means you must have read this week's book."

"Yeah, I didn't think I would make it through, but I had time while I was waiting for jury duty today."

Lyra held up the paper back in front of her, flipping through the pages. "I'm not that much of a thriller book person. I mean, it's all predictable. When you know the way the stories have to go, it kinda takes the fun out of it. I blame my mom. She writes books and she taught high school English."

She held up the book to an open page, pointing at a star in the margin. "Page 56 was when I knew the narrator killed the husband." Above the star Lyra had scratched notes, like she studied every single line. Following the star though, the notes disappeared.

Parker raised an eyebrow. "Did you stop reading there?"

Lyra shook her head. Her onyx hair fell into her eyes, then she pushed it back. "It's not about who. I mean, not for me. The why is more interesting. All the good questions start with why. Like why someone as beautiful as you is alone at Book Club?"

"You're alone," Parker stated.

Lyra held up a finger as she took a drink. "I am waiting for the sister."

"Possibly," Parker said with a slightly cynical squint. "But... you didn't save her a chair."

"Well, technically I did." Lyra's smile turned smug. "Until I didn't."

"So, I'm sitting in your sister's seat."

Lyra waved the words away. "Public space. You're in the seat, she's not. It will piss her off to not get her way. Honestly, I'm doing society a service by reminding her she can't always get her way."

"So, you didn't save your sister a seat to piss her off?"

Lyra reached over and picked up Parker's book. She flipped through the bare pages. "No notes."

"The librarian probably would have been angry at me if I returned it all marked up."

"You didn't have an inspiring English teacher or you'd have post its." Lyra set the public copy down. "When did you figure out who did it?"

Parker didn't miss Lyra's avoidance of the question. The therapist in her wanted to explore the relationship dynamic that would cause Lyra to actively want to piss her sister off. However, the single lesbian in her chose to see where the conversation would lead.

"At the end," Parker said.

"Did it shock you?" Parker watched Lyra study Parker's face like she was searching for something.

"No." Parker turned away from the intrusive gaze towards two older women having a heated debate a few rows of chairs in front of them. When she felt like Lyra's eyes were no longer on her, she added, "It... it wasn't really what I cared about."

"Why?"

Parker's head dropped as she laughed. She turned to find she was wrong to believe Lyra had turned away. Finding the woman sporting a devilish grin, Parker stated, "Your favorite question."

"The only important question." With her beer, Lyra gestured to the space between them. "When the answer is possessed, there's a moment of peace. The chaos stills." She held up a finger. "But only for that moment."

Parker considered the chaos between them. The spark of electricity that had tingled her nerve endings when the stranger called her beautiful even more than the accidental graze that had her nipples still pebbled. The way she could talk to Lyra without her body begging for a protective bubble even though they were strangers. She wasn't sure if the answer calmed the chaos, then she would want it.

Nevertheless, the possibility of her-awkward-self ruining a chance to talk to a gorgeous woman who read and spent time with her family was scarier.

"I cared about the paintings," Parker confessed. "The way the author described the colors, the strokes. I think about things sometimes as though I am in a scene someone is painting. It's one thing to look at paintings, but to read the creation of a painting is a different experience."

"So, your why wasn't the murder but the behavior that followed it," Lyra stated.

Parker shrugged. "It's what I do."

"You're an artist."

"No." Parker laughed at the thought of her mediocre work being considered art. "I do behavior therapy through art."

Lyra sat back in her chair. Her arms crossed over her chest, closing herself off. "You work with trauma kids?"

Parker felt the flickering flames between them smoldering as Lyra pulled the oxygen into her closed off form. The chaos Lyra described shifted in one direction. Parker imagined the artist painting the scene taking straight strokes with the brush starting at Lyra and ending the paint in jagged strips at Parker's chair. The painter tried to push Parker away without removing her from the picture.

"Yeah. Well, sort of. I am hoping to start a new job at a school."

The hairs on Parker's neck and arms stood like tiny warriors ready to fight the attack behind her as a raucous voice bellowed, "Bitch, you didn't save me a seat."

Parker's shoulders rose to her neck protecting her lifeline from the voice, but Lyra leaned forward. She brought the beer up to her lips to hide the growing smile before looking over Parker's shoulder, where Parker knew Evie stood.

Casting a glance back, Parker saw Evie's furrowed brow drop as her eyes darted between Parker and Lyra.

"What are you doing here?" Evie asked.

"Obvious, isn't it." Lyra held up Parker's library book, waved it once, then set it back down. "She read the same book we did."

"She's your sister, huh?" Parker pulled her book closer and looked over the crowd to see if anyone had decided to leave.

Lyra took another drink, larger than the last. With a roll of her eyes, she said, "Yes. And I just need to ask that you don't judge me by her grisly behavior since you two have clearly met before. E has the ability to make the worst impressions on people." Lyra turned and glanced between Evie and Parker, "But if you two ever—"

"No!" Parker and Evie cried out in unison.

Lyra exhaled heavily. "Thank God."

Evie shifted her feet, putting a hand on the back of Lyra's chair. "Did you call my mom yet?"

"Our mom," Lyra corrected.

Parker scanned Evie up and down, taking in the feminine chic of the woman's bohemian style that just didn't fit with the woman who was cased in a bullet proof vest last week. Even though Evie was a threat, Parker felt the need to sketch her in her various forms. Maybe even split her torso to show the woman's three sides all connected to the same legs or even just a genie like wisp. She realized she was staring too hard at Evie when the woman's brow formed a wrinkle across it, and she looked down at her body before meeting Parker's eyes again with a slight blush.

She turned back to her beer, hoping she could pull off nonchalance as she asked, "What does it matter to you?"

"Why," Lyra corrected again with eyebrows raised. "The why is way better than the what."

Parker smiled as Lyra grew more interesting with each turn of phrase. She decided to take Lyra's advice. "Why does it matter to you if I did or didn't?"

"Because." Evie's arms crossed over her chest. The purse on her shoulder fell to the crook of her arm.

"'Because' is not an answer, Everleigh Greyson," Lyra practically sang.

Evie narrowed her eyes on her sister. "Shut the fuck up."

"Why?" Lyra's head cocked to her sister as her lips spread, showing perfectly aligned teeth.

"Because if you don't, I'll make you," Evie hissed.

All Parker's muscles locked up as Evie said the same words she'd used before sending Parker chin first into the steel desk within their cell. She wanted to tell Lyra Evie could make people shut up, that she is completely capable of it. That she would do it. But Parker didn't because the last time she interfered she had to drink her meals through a straw.

"No, you won't," Lyra stated as her eyes rolled once more. "Obi would lose their shit since I'm their favorite."

Then Lyra smiled smugly and winked at Parker. "I can be your favorite too."

Parker held her glass up, trying to hide the fear spreading throughout her. "Already are."

Lyra clinked the glasses together.

Leaning closer to Lyra, Parker asked, "Who's Obi?"

"Our mom's partner. They identify as non-binary, so after much searching, our other sister, Sadie and I found out in Yoruba Obi means 'other parent'."

Evie huffed, still hovering like a helicopter in the space between the backs of Parker and Lyra's chairs. "I can't believe you didn't save me a seat just to talk to a girl. And not just a girl but her."

"Sister code, section 18: a sister will respect her fellow sister's attempt to engage in creating a meaningful relationship. You should know it since you wrote it. Then again, you have always been a hypocrite." Lyra glanced at Evie. "And I can't believe you were late, again, but since you're going to be such a baby just take my seat."

Lyra's left leg hit the ground harder than the right. Parker tried not to look, but the metal brace running from thigh to calf caught her attention.

When Parker looked up, she found Lyra studying her again. She tapped her short, manicured nails against the top of the brace. "Yeah, some sister right. She shows up late. Then I give up my chair to stand with only one good leg. And that is why I'm the better sister and the favorite."

Lyra leaned against the bar. Her shoulders flexed as she tried to support her weight against the wood. Parker considered offering her own seat, but then worried Lyra would think she pitied her. Experience had taught her that no one wanted someone that pitied them.

Parker sipped her drink as Lyra's soft arm rested against hers. She turned to face the crowd, before she asked, "Is there a code for sisters that always show up late also?"

"I think I could fall in love with you," Lyra said, smiling at the drink.

"Sit down, asshat. And for the record, I wasn't late. Book club still hasn't started yet."

With a bit of work, Lyra settled back into her chair.

Parker's fingers traced the raised lettering on the book cover. She wondered if she would ever have the courage to write a book, tell her story. The story Dilynn probably knew, and she needed to be prepared for that in her interview tomorrow.

Unable to just walk in blind, she decided to ask, "Did you tell your mom?"

Evie tossed her purse on the countertop. "Look, I didn't have to say anything. You don't know her though and... what we went through is, like, a prerequisite. Mom and Obi will only hire people who understand the trauma. You get it. You were there. Shit, you were there with me and the fucking guard. And she... she literally built the school for people like us. People like you and me and Lyra and sister Sassy. She even hired this one girl that went to school there and she doesn't even like her, but she knows that even Charliegh understands these kids. Kids that came out of juvie. Kids that got kicked out of their homes. Kids like me who didn't have anyone. And she did it so they could have better odds than we had. Because our odds were shit, and we got lucky. We got out and turned out well."

"Well, she turned out alright. You on the other hand..." Lyra didn't finish her sentence, she just widened her eyes and sucked in her lips.

"Lyra, seriously, dude," Evie's hands ran up and down her face. "Please, just shut up."

"Why do you care so much about what I do?" Parker asked.

Lyra chuckled and held her beer up to Parker. "That is a good why question. And she hates you asked because it means she has to admit she's not a sociopath."

Evie stepped back, her gravelly voice dropping as she held up three fingers. "One, fuck her. She's just trying to get in your pants by being mean to me when she actually loves me. Two, I'm capable of remorse hence the apology. And three, look, I never should have busted your face for telling me to back off your friend. I know I already said I was sorry, but you will never get how sorry I actually am. How much I hate who I was. So, when we ran into each other, it was like the universe saying we didn't meet on accident. We have this connection. And you're here now and I'm here now, so we need to just be okay with being in each other's lives."

Parker dissected each of Evie's sentences trying to figure out what she meant by them being connected since they hadn't seen each other since they were both relased. She struggled specifically with the idea that they were meant to be in each other's lives. Her fingers picked at the dry skin on her lower lip, pulling pieces off until it hurt. Then, she focused on trying to hide that her lip was bleeding from the nice sister.

Evie squeezed her way in between Lyra and Parker, cutting Parker off from the only reason to stay in the seat. Out of the corner of her eye, Parker saw Lyra's head peek around Evie. She cleared her throat, but her sister didn't move.

Suddenly, Evie jumped back, holding her breast. Her eyes were murderous as she hissed at her sister, "What the fuck?"

Lyra turned, puffing up her chest. She dramatically held up three fingers and fixed her facial expression to match Evie in perfect mockery. "One, you standing as close to her as possible talking about the universe wanting you all to be together, like some Eminem and Stan shit, is making her uncomfortable."

Lyra's serious eyes turned to Parker.

"Two, don't worry; she's not hitting on you. She's just shit at apologies, and she thinks that she can just say sorry for pounding in your face and that you will just forgive her. She still hasn't gotten over me not forgiving her for hitting me, and that was almost a decade ago." Her gaze flitted to Evie. "And I still don't forgive you, but I do love you and I would take a whole ass bullet for you so stop ruining this for me."

She turned her attention back to Parker and waved the third finger.

"And three: I would love the opportunity to hit on you in public with dinner, flowers, and a limited amount of dancing. Just give this little cyborg a chance."

"I need a drink," Evie stated before Parker could respond. She walked away muttering about Lyra being an asshat as Parker watched Lyra wiggling her third finger.

A tall woman tapped a microphone but didn't speak until the rumbling of the other participants shifted their attention to her. When it was quiet, she announced, "Welcome to Book Club!"

The moderator had a bubbly personality that brightened the faces of even the older women arguing before. With a smile, she welcomed everyone and opened the floor for reflections on the book Parker hadn't loved or hated enough to have anything to say about it. She'd only begun coming to the book club meetings because they'd reminded her of a class she took in college where her psychology teacher brought in novels for them to examine instead of textbooks. She'd learned to dissect the young adult protagonist's personality traits and link them to one of their earlier traumas. She also learned to focus on actions instead of just what people said, because people lied. And she learned that a lot of the time they lied to themselves to the point that their verbal lies were actually their truth.

Zoe had tossed her heart into the gutter at the start of that class, and Parker hated that she saw herself as the poor kid and Zoe the oblivious well-off kid in every story. The books always seemed to have one of each, however, the analysis had helped her understand how Zoe could love her one moment and despise her in the next. And in the end, the books only verified Zoe wouldn't ever get that the world wasn't her playground, but the character like Parker would save the day.

Watching the audience of book club gave Parker more unknowing participants to observe and analyze as she sketched complicated social psyches. Photo books in her head linked together themes of what people viewed as norms in the society in which she lived but didn't understand. These weren't her people like Echo and Xio, who understood the world like she did. They were Zoe's people. Lyra and Evie's people. And living in a world where Dilynn Greysons were going to judge her, meant she had to understand how they perceived injustice. Then, just maybe, she would be able to blend in.

One by one, members shared their thoughts, delving into themes, characters, and plot twists with fervor. Some offered insightful analysis, while others shared personal connections they felt with the story. Laughter and nods of agreement punctuated the conversation, creating a lively atmosphere filled with intellectual stimulation and mutual appreciation for the novel Parker wasn't sure was really that good. However, Lyra was obviously uninterested in the conversation.

"So, how about you let me take you out Friday night?" she asked.

Parker took a moment to think about the offer. She wouldn't be completely opposed to a date with Lyra, even though the woman's sister was Evie. The woman was beautiful, and her witty banter amused Parker more than anyone else she'd dated, possibly ever. Her mind wandered briefly to Zoe, but she shut that down immediately.

Her stomach did a little flip at the idea of going out for a meal. Real food cooked to be eaten rather than tolerated, but that would be against the rules Xio had taught her about dating. She had to have at least enough money to cover her own plate, and the beer she'd purchased was already too much of an early celebration for the job she didn't have yet.

"I promise my sister won't interrupt either," Lyra said. "I won't tell her where I'm going. Though that is kinda part of the sister code in case you're a serial killer or something. But I'm pretty sure my sister, Sadie is the serial killer and the odds of knowing two in your lifetime is pretty slim."

Parker glanced over, not sure if Lyra was hinting Evie had already told her who Parker's parents were. She'd met her fair share of weirdos and creeps fascinated with hooking up with a serial killer's spawn. In the world of true crime, Parker had been a childhood star of enough podcasts to cause her for a brief time to go by her middle name.

Lyra was scanning the room, instead of trying to read her like a book. She didn't seem to notice the woman directly below them had turned and glared at Lyra. She must have noticed though because Lyra shifted her body closer to Parker. She was close enough Parker could catch the subtle trace of cherries and chemicals. She knew the little black bottle of grit cleaner, which didn't help the spiral Parker's mind had taken.

She decided Lyra didn't even know she and Evie knew each other, so it was unlikely that Evie had the chance to tell Lyra anything about where she came from. That would happen on a phone call tonight, so she deflected from Lyra's question.

Whispering to not get another angry glare from the people in front of them, she asked, "You work with cars?"

Lyra's eyes narrowed momentarily. Her hands flipped up and down as though the cleaner was still there.

Parker shrugged, then explained, "You smell like GoJo."

Lyra pulled her phone from her purse, unlocked it, then handed it to Parker. A weather worn yellow truck sat in a driveway with its hood open. Lyra and Alex Trikru leaned into the hood, their arms and shirts covered in grime and grease.

"That's my baby," Lyra stated, gazing at the image once Parker handed her the phone. "Obi and I are restoring her. An old Chevy long bed. But I'm not a mechanic anymore. I am an Assistant District Attorney for family court." She smiled when Parker cast her a questionable gaze. "Yeah, I work with troubled youth too. And Egotistical Evie already shared that I was one. But yeah, the whole therapist thing threw me for a second. You never know when someone is going to start examining a piece of your puzzle that maybe you have off to the side for a reason."

"I get it," Parker stated. "I mean, you now know that I met your sister in juvenile detention. So, how about I work on my puzzle, and you can work on yours."

An audience member stood up to provide an overzealous critique of the time jumps between chapters. Parker studied the violent manner that the woman used her hands to slice through sentences as they exited her mouth like she was trying to cut them into bite size pieces, so people would understand her. Parker began to count the number of times the woman started her sentences with, 'I mean,' and thought of how Echo did the same thing because she never thought people understood what she'd said.

She'd made it to six when Lyra asked, "Do you work on cars?"

Parker forced a social smile on her face and whispered, "No. My dad used to though. He was a mechanic."

Evie squeezed between Lyra and Parker's chairs like they weren't just talking. She slid her beer in the small space provided as she stared at her phone. Parker never thought she'd be happy to see Evie, but her return ended the conversation for Parker.

In the middle of taking a long sip of her beer, the phone was held out in front of Parker. Dilynn's face was smiling on Facetime causing Parker to almost choke. The last thing she needed was for Dilynn to see her drinking the day before her interview.

"Hey, Mom. Look who I ran into at Book Club doing the flirty flirt with Lyra."

Several older women turned, giving Evie passive aggressive cues to shut up. Evie pulled an ear bud from her ear and handed it to Parker who was occupied with trying not to aspirate.

"*Parker!*" she heard as she held it up to her ear.

"Hi, Mrs. Greyson," she whispered.

"*I'm so happy you have agreed to come to interview with us.*"

Dilynn's face was pulled to the side by a pair of marker-covered hands.

"*Mama. Looks at mes,*" a child whined in the background. "*I's tattedtoos. Looks me tattedtoos.*"

Evie turned the phone back on herself. "Wait, she already called you? When I asked—"

"You raised a stalker," Lyra chimed in.

Evie glared at her sister, then turned back to the phone. "Lyra didn't save me a seat."

"She was late, Mom."

"Shhhhhhhh!" A woman from in front of them hissed. Evie took the hint and walked away from the meeting area with her phone.

Knowing Evie would come back, Parker took a chance. She got up and moved her stool, so it was directly alongside Lyra's. The other woman didn't say anything, just smiled into her beer.

They listened as the crowd took turns answering the moderator's discussion questions. Lyra had side comments regarding most of what they said, but she whispered them quietly into the bubble Parker had created with their chairs.

"So next week I will pick you up in my baby. We have dinner and watch a cover band play in Heritage Square. There's this pizza place there that is amazing, and they make personal pizzas so we can each reveal a piece of our puzzle."

Parker felt the words caress her cheek and neck, softly smoothing away the tension twisting at the thought of going out with her bosses' daughter. Her mind stopped picking at the knot of complications, focusing on Lyra's comment about the pizzas.

"How does pizza reveal someone?"

"Well, you have the pineapple only ordered by the devil's children. The meat lover's pride. The supreme settlers." Lyra tapped a finger to her lips, then added, "Not to mention the direction of the first bite."

"Everyone bites the tip first."

"Not everyone." The corners of Lyra's lips raised seductively as she leaned closer. "Some people start at the crust and work their way to the salty rich tip."

Parker's chest fluttered, and warm tingles spread over her arms and down her torso. Two fingers came to rest on her lips as she tried to shake away the blush rising in her cheeks.

"See, pizza can tell a lot about a person."

Unable to focus on Book Club anymore, Parker said, "Let's get out of here."

Lyra slid down from her chair. She moved around the back of Parker with her half-finished beer and held out her hand. Evie came up just as Lyra turned to lead Parker out of the overcrowded bar area with their hands clasped.

"Seat's all yours," Lyra said.

"You're leaving me?" Evie whined. Her eyes scanned over the strangers, and

Parker felt momentarily bad for the woman, who apparently only came when someone accompanied her.

"We're going to go look at the books," Parker said.

Before she could offer Evie to join them to ease the other woman's clear anxiety, Lyra interjected, "We, as in her and I."

"Fine," Evie said, taking Parker's seat. She tugged at her shirt, then hunched over her beer with her eyes locked on the book Lyra had left.

Parker remembered the woman was the reason she was released from juvie early. Recalled waking up in the hospital with her jaw wired shut and only one eye able to open. She didn't need to ease Evie's discomfort after being tossed back into the world without anyone to even care she'd survived.

As they wandered through the aisles together, they discovered shared interests and exchanged recommendations. Their laughter mingled with the quiet rustle of pages as they both perused the young adult realistic fiction section. Each had a distinctive taste in books, and Parker noticed Lyra tended to pick up books with a darker skinned female on the cover. The only one that stood out from Lyra's other selections was a thin book with a plain deep gold cover. A small boy was imprinted on the cover, holding on to a string of birds.

"Have you read this one?" Lyra asked, holding it up for Parker.

Parker took the copy of *The Little Prince*. She checked the back just to make sure, then said, "No."

"Okay, I'm getting it for you." Lyra kept it tucked close to her chest, and Parker took that as a sign it was something important to Lyra. "When you go out with me, you can tell me which adult you grew up to be, and which you want to be."

As they rounded the shelf and headed down the next aisle, Parker tried to avoid looking at the covers with mutilated bodies for the zombie books. She'd seen enough torture in her life to despise horror and gory renditions of too real pain.

"So, what is the most interesting thing that has happened to you this week?" Lyra asked.

Parker picked up a copy of *Unwind*. She wasn't a fan of the new cover design with the lines of doll faces on book three, but book one was still at least pretty chill.

"You read this one?" she asked.

"No," Lyra said with a shake of her head.

"Well, I'm getting it for you," Parker stated, holding it close to her like Lyra had done. "And to answer your question: I got out of jury duty by telling them I didn't believe in incarceration. I have an interview at your mother's school. Oh, and I met you."

Lyra stopped.

Her mouth was open, and she looked Parker up and down for a moment. Then, she slowly asked, "You're the redhead that tried to blow up the Commander's jury?"

"Uhm... I guess," Parker answered. She tucked a lock of hair behind her ear. "Do you know her?"

"Uh... we work in the same building, so I heard about it." Lyra turned back to the shelf and immediately picked up another book. She put it under her arm with *The Little Prince*.

"What's that one?" Parker asked.

"Your other must read." Lyra handed Parker the thick book.

The lush green forest decorating the cover didn't make Parker's stomach queasy, but the scarlet hue of the ground floor suggested there would be lots of blood within the pages. Her finger ran over the raised lettering of the author's name: Greyson Dillion.

"That's my mom's first novel. Since you have an interview with her, you should read the book. She's Priya and Obi always says they are Morgan, even though she wrote the book before meeting them. There's a whole story about a catfish smelling troll and a badass princess that she never wrote, but if you even read the first few chapters it will give you some insight into them before you meet with them."

Parker flipped open the cover and read the description. She chewed on her lip momentarily, then decided to ask, "Whose Atlas?"

"Princess Pain in the Ass," Lyra said with a roll of her eyes. Then she looked around like Evie might pop out from around the corner like she'd been summoned.

"Are you in the book?"

A smile rose up Lyra's face, and she said, "You can tell me over pizza and wine."

"You're not going to give up, are you?" Parker asked with a soft sigh.

"If you say no, then I will 100 percent give up and ask you to be my friend." There was a sad honesty in the delivery of Lyra's stance on annoying someone to go out with her. It was wrapped around another note of rejection Parker was all too familiar with. "However, if you say yes, then I won't give up. I'm a Gryffindor."

With a soft chuckle, Parker said, "Well, I'm a Slytherin, so I'm pretty sure we are enemies."

Lyra held up a finger, then left Parker in front of the shelf with all of Greyson Dillion's novels. She pulled out a book that didn't seem to be in the original series. The girl on the cover had hickory eyes and a dark set of goggles atop her onyx hair. A blow torch had been gilded into the cover in a scarlet and gold foil that drew Parker's fingers to it. She had a weird need to try and see if it was actually hot. This had to be Lyra's book, because the steampunk theme just screamed the mechanic hobbyist. She flipped to the back cover and took in Dilynn's warm smile.

She only looked up as Lyra came back, waving another book in the air.

"This right here is she-who-shall-not-be-named's proof that Gryffindors and Slytherins can in fact be friends." Lyra tucked the third book under her arm, then glanced down the aisle. "Let's get out of here before I buy the other half of the store I don't already own."

Parker hummed in agreement. She was already short two books in matching Lyra's gifts, but she couldn't afford more. Her own uneasiness grew as she handed over the credit card to pay for the one book she said she was buying for Lyra. She watched the card mystically wisp away half of what was left in her bank account.

"I'll go to dinner with you, but not Friday."

Parker licked her lip, then bit it. She needed a paycheck before she could go out with Lyra, but she needed an excuse that didn't tell Lyra she was dirt ass poor. Her eyes settled on the books that Lyra was paying for.

"It will take me at least a week to read those," she said, pointing to the bag that the cashier had left for her.

Lyra pulled out her phone and said, "Siri, send the hot woman next to me a text saying I can't wait to have dinner with you."

Parker felt her ass vibrate. She pulled the phone out of her pocket and looked at the message. "How did you do that?"

"Magic." Lyra stated. "You didn't learn that spell in year one?"

Parker shrugged and toed the ground. She looked up with just her eyes, and decided to remind Lyra what she was getting into.

"They don't deliver letters to Azkaban."

"Well played," Lyra said with a nod. "Well, you text me when you are available for dinner. I promise you won't regret it."

Patrons flooded the walkways as Lyra slid the bag of Parker's assigned reading onto her wrist. Lyra walked backwards until Evie body checked her. She turned back, calling through the other book club attendees fleeing the store, "I will be eagerly awaiting my call to adventure!"

9

Zoe poured another glass of wine and set it on the patio table. She watched the Arizona skyline steadily shift from blue to red, then purple to pitch black as she alternated between sipping the wine and inhaling the nicotine vapor. Her downtown apartment patio was anything but peaceful with the Light Rail train beeping as it pulled into the station. Nevertheless, sitting in her office when she knew Lyra wouldn't be coming was pointless.

The wine was supposed to ease the knots twisting in her neck muscles. It wasn't working though. The only accomplishment thus far was increasing her nausea and making her eyes unable to focus on the case notes on her laptop.

She picked up the pink cards she'd brought home. The newest one lay on top of the pile, and she studied Parker Carter's name.

'Things could have been different between us.'

She set that card to the side, then flipped through the others. No one was potentially more problematic than the redhead.

Her fingers wrapped around the thick file on Parker. Nia had eagerly handed it over after hearing Woods managed to get the therapist added to the witness list. Parker's file was different from the one Nia had on Everleigh Greyson. She hadn't just kept the details of Parker's juvenile conviction, but everything public she'd done over the years. Clearly hitting the DA put her on a permanent watch list.

Zoe flipped through the employment records dating back to when Parker got her first job at Christy's Cabaret. She'd worked for a year and continued to strip all through undergrad but stopped before graduate school. She recognized the date immediately. A shame rose in her as she realized Parker had quit her job after Zoe broke up with her. There wasn't another job listed, and more guilt flooded her system as she began to worry her action had caused Parker even more financial hardship, since she clearly had to poor to even consider becoming a stripper to begin with.

After a moment though, she considered if maybe she had gotten Parker on a better life path. Licking her lips, Zoe smiled at the fact Parker did all of this. Come so far from where she'd been.

In a separate section, Nia possessed a list of Parker's known associates; a short list. There was a bar owner that went by Echo, who was married to an Assistant Principal. A friend who had ODed last year. And Xiomara Horna, a last name that led the cartel industry until Nia had locked up Jose Horna before Zoe was out of high school. All of the names were linked to the juvenile detention center

Parker had spent high school. And the last name made Zoe's brows rise. Everleigh Greyson had been locked in the same cell as Parker.

Zoe was beginning to think that it was no accident Parker had ended up on jury duty. The only thing that didn't make sense was the fact that she tried to get kicked off. If Greyson was paying her, it would have been better to be there. She could have convinced the jurors to let Olivia off, or at least caused a mistrial.

'It had to be a coincidence.'

There was also a list of women Parker had dated. That list longer than the associates caused Zoe's shoulders to drop at the realization Parker had moved on, while Zoe was still standing still.

Zoe ran over the names again, letting out a *whew* as she realized her name was missing from Parker's batting line up. The moment was replaced with a slight burn of jealousy at not being important enough to make the cut. They'd dated for months. Publicly.

Not making the list caused Zoe to wonder what made those other women better than her. Zoe cataloged all the women she'd met whom she measured by her connection to Parker. She'd never been able to move out of the initial stages of dating or casual sex with any of them because they'd never made her feel as important or strong as the tiny blonde who sparkled in direct sunlight.

She picked up a newspaper clipping from the file. It was a photo taken the day Parker had attacked Nia on the steps of the courthouse. Two police officers held the sixteen-year-old's sagging frame. Even in the grainy grayscale image, Zoe could see Parker's face flooded with tears as Nia stood glaring down from the top of the steps. Zoe hated how much it reminded her of the way Ari looked as she walked off the graduation stage with her diploma that neither of her parents had bothered to show up to see her receive.

Leaning back in the rocking chair, Zoe tried to connect the information from Nia's file to the girl shimmering on the grass outside the library. She hadn't known Parker's skin sparkled because of leftover body glitter from working the night before. Parker never told her she was a stripper. Never told Zoe about spending the last years of childhood behind bars. Never felt comfortable enough to share a sliver of her past or present.

Her stomach twisted tighter as Zoe realized Parker hadn't given her a real name because she had probably been scared Zoe recognized her. And she'd been right to be scared because Zoe had googled Michelle Carter when they first met, only to find the woman didn't have a digital footprint. A puzzle piece that fit into Parker's then narrative. After getting to know Parker, Zoe just thought she didn't like social media since she avoided cameras and typically wore a baseball cap everywhere she went. Parker had claimed it was to avoid getting more freckles, but Zoe understood now. She even understood the cold gaze she'd gotten when she'd walked up to Parker at the library after finding countless blogs by people fetishizing the woman when she was barely eighteen. Sites with paparazzi style photos had captured Parker from stalkerish distances, and there were so many by too many middle-aged men.

She remembered the day Zachery had texted her. Remembered how he'd asked her to go out with him. How he'd laughed at her discomfort when he pulled into the cabaret's parking lot. He'd promised her it would be an eye-opening experience. Promised she'd learn a few things for the girl Zoe posted photos of on Myspace when Parker didn't know she was being photographed. She'd learned how Parker paid tuition and rent by sitting at the edge of the stage. Learned the real reason the tiny blonde, who fit perfectly into her big spoon, looked like a modern-day vampire.

'Someone like me doesn't bring white trash home to meet her family,' replayed in her head.

She took another long drag from the vape and stared at the starless sky. An airplane steadily made its way to Sky Harbor Airport through the darkness, sending Zoe down another rabbit hole to the top of the parking garage outside Terminal 4.

Zoe pressed against Parker's back and rested her chin against the smaller woman's shoulder. She could still smell the John Frieda Sheer Blonde shampoo Parker used. Her arms wrapped around the woman's middle pulling her in closer, never close enough. As each plane vibrated their bodies during their landing, Parker would tell a story about the passengers aboard. The adventures other people had and one day Zoe would have because they were all the places Zoe had told her about. All the pins in the map of exotic destinations hung above her bed in the one-bedroom apartment her parents provided for her.

'She never planned on forever.'

Zoe picked up the pink card again. The only thing she'd managed to write on it was Parker's name. She chewed on the inside of her bottom lip, then her top.

"I could destroy you," she told the card. "Everything you've worked to overcome. I could take it all away."

Her eyes fell to the file again, and Zoe considered what she could take. Parker wasn't Officer Everleigh Greyson. She didn't have a rich mommy to bail her out. She didn't have anyone according to Nia's file.

She was alone.

Alone as she had been when they met in the mandatory Psychology study. And when Zoe approached her with a coffee after stalking her a few days later. And on Thanksgiving when Zoe called Parker from the back porch of her parents' house. And when she turned in the parking lot without a word and walked back into work.

Zoe picked up the glass but found it empty. She tried the bottle, but it was empty too. She shook her head at the realization she'd finished an entire bottle of wine, alone.

She considered texting Lyra to apologize and inviting her over. Lyra could help take her mind off Parker. Remind her she wasn't alone when she didn't want to be.

Placing the phone on the table, she vowed not to drunk text anyone tonight. Justified she was alone on her patio because she'd had a hard day at work. She wasn't like the stripper turned therapist, whose father waited on Death Row and mother locked behind bars, never to see society again. No, Zoe had worked hard her whole life to be able to sit in her house at peace.

'Just like Michelle...' The voice in her head stopped, then self-corrected. 'Just like Parker had worked hard to sit in her house at peace.'

Zoe made the decision not to bring up Parker's juvenile record. She also decided to leave the part about Parker being a stripper out as well, primarily so Parker wouldn't feel the need to share their brief relationship. If nothing else, she owed it to Parker for calling her trash.

'Olivia Moore could grow up to be someone just like Parker did. Someone who understood hell enough to help others out of it.'

The thought bulldozed through the barricades of Zoe's mind without tapping the brakes. Then, it dumped toxic waste in her head and poisoned every idea she'd had about protecting society.

"I'm too drunk for this," she told the part of her she'd imprisoned to get through the trial.

Leaving everything on the table, Zoe made her way to bed. Even with the ceiling fan on high, the room was too hot. She peeled off her tank top letting the sheets cool the burning in her skin. She sank into the pillow top mattress and tried to ignore the part of her that missed the way the tiny redhead used to curl up behind her. She created a cocoon in the pillows to hold her just as she had when Parker laid beside her. Only when she was secured in the bed she'd made, she allowed the darkness to swallow her.

But the darkness leads her down the familiar Phoenix street as a streetlight flickers above her. Past the drugged out homeless walking across the busy road, to the silent neighborhood. Past the three-foot chain link fences and weed-filled yards to the run-down house.

Vincent Gibson's bloody body lingers in the window to the kitchen where he'd been murdered. He leers at the woman with the teenager. Parker's thin arms hold Olivia Moore's shaking frame. Parker whispers to the girl crying like the sixteen-year-old in the photo.

Zoe doesn't need to hear them. She knows what is said because the words came from the moment Zoe wishes she could take back.

'No matter what anyone says. You're not trash, and you're not disposable.'

10

The high school administration building lobby wasn't buzzing with the energy of students, parents, and faculty moving to and fro. Upon entering, Parker was greeted by a quiet hum of conversation floating from the offices down the hall and the occasional ringing of phones from the reception desk. There was no 'hello' or 'welcome to Greyson Academy' from the girl sitting behind a desk.

Parker had a moment to scan over walls plastered with colorful bulletin boards showcasing student achievements, upcoming events, and important announcements. This was the high school experience she'd gotten for two years. Never had she participated in a school function, but her eyes immediately fell to the blue sheet sprinkled with glitter announcing the start of a dance team.

The tryouts were in two weeks, and Echo had mentioned teachers made extra money for helping with clubs. If she got the job, maybe that was something she could do. She shook that thought away. No one would want a former stripper working with the dance team.

"Sign in," the girl behind the desk stated. She tossed a pen atop a three-ring binder. "You the lady that Greyson is waiting on?"

Being called lady caused Parker to look behind her as though she missed someone else in the tiny lobby. Then she realized she was the lady to this kid, even though she didn't see herself as that much older than the girl who was probably a student. She was old though. Old compared to the girl who apparently thought Parker was about to hit thirty.

"Uhm... yes, I am here to see Mrs. Greyson. I am—"

"Greyson!" the girl shouted. "The lady's here!"

Parker jumped at the complete lack of formality, and the pointed tip of her heel moved to the side. Her ankle popped, and she immediately felt the pain radiating up her leg. She'd been in worse predicaments with heels larger than these before. Had twisted her ankle countless times while trying to land her twist around the pole to the right beat, so she breathed through the pain as Dilynn walked down the narrow hallway.

While the woman's smile spread to her ocean blue eyes, Parker tried to fix her shocked face at Dilynn's loose fitting black t-shirt and skinny jeans. Echo had helped her shop at Goodwill yesterday for professional clothes, but apparently forgot to mention Dilynn dressed casually for work.

"Parker!" Dilynn's voice bounced off the empty walls of the hallway striking Parker with each echo.

The redhead bit her lip, regretting her choice of shoes. Her six-inch heels raised her significantly above the petite principal as Dilynn bypassed Parker's outstretched hand, pulling Parker down into a tight embrace.

Parker searched for an exit. Then she remembered her checking account balance. She tapped Dilynn's back, unsure of what to do with the rest of her body.

"Thank you for coming in today." Dilynn said. She wrapped an arm around Parker's back, guiding her down the hall.

Parker scanned the walls covered in signatures. Dilynn hummed, and smiled as she explained, "I read once that kids tag walls because they want there to be some indication that they existed. When they enroll, we have them sign the wall as proof that they are here to do something beyond existing."

"What will you do when you run out of space?" Parker asked.

"You know, I haven't really thought about it." With a shrug, Dilynn added, "I guess we'll just build a new wall somewhere."

Dilynn held the office door open and gestured Parker within.

"Welcome, Ms. Carter," Alex said once Parker breached the doorway. They casually leaned against the large desk in the middle of the room, adjusting their tie in a fitted vest.

They extended their hand towards Parker.

Parker could hear Echo's voice in her head saying, 'Clasp tightly but don't squeeze. No Jell-O arm either,' as Parker met Alex's hand with her own and shook it firmly.

Alex smiled at her as they said, "I heard about your speech at court. Good for you, standing up for what you believe in."

"Good? She was great!" Dilynn announced proudly. She gestured to the armchairs positioned in front of the desk.

Parker lowered herself carefully, placing her purse in her lap. She adjusted the suit jacket she'd found on the juniors' rack, double checking her entire torso was covered prudishly.

Dilynn flopped down into the adjacent chair, tucking her short legs under her. "So, I know this is quick since we just saw each other at court on Monday, but I wanted to get everything put in motion."

"Dilynn doesn't give people a chance to change their mind," Alex threw in. Parker noticed the way only the corners of their mouth rose in a subtle smirk as they watched Dilynn like they were waiting for a reaction.

With an exaggerated eye roll, Dilynn defended, "Wonder why I would ever do that? Sounds like a response to trauma."

Parker looked back and forth between the couple as the blonde lowered her chin and glared at Alex, who appeared to find the ceiling very interesting.

When neither of the school owners moved or said anything, Parker cleared her throat. But it didn't change the way Dilynn and Alex were sharing a bubble, while Parker sat on the outside wondering if they would even hear her if she said anything.

Parker wiggled her toes in her shoes trying to wait them out. Then, she shifted in her seat like she'd rung a doorbell and was waiting for someone to answer. Finally, she said, "I am sorry that I didn't call you earlier."

Dilynn waved her hand as though she was capable of swatting away the words before they ever reached her ears. She looked Parker squarely in the eyes, and the smile vanished from her lips.

"So, let's just get something out of the way." Dilynn's feet dropped to the floor. She tapped the armrests a few times, then took a deep breath. "Evie. Evie and you have a... colorful history. She asked several times if you called, and I could see when she put you on Facetime that you were just as uncomfortable as the last time she saw you. Apparently, she's heard a lot about you from your friend Xiomara Horna. Evie and Xio work together closely to help get kids who are trying to leave the gang life behind here. I need you to know, Evie didn't have a lot to say about you other than you'd be good for the school."

"Which means that whatever transpired between you both was not one of Evie's finer moments," Alex added with a loud sigh.

Dilynn shot Alex a look Parker read as 'shut up.'

Alex's hands raised in surrender, then folded in front of them.

Turning back to Parker, Dilynn's face retained the same serious expression she'd told Alex to shut it with. A bubble grew in Parker's throat while she waited for Dilynn to drop whatever grenade she was holding. The woman sucked her teeth, and Parker felt like a test question Dilynn was trying to answer.

"Look, I'm just gonna be upfront with you, I googled you," Dilynn finally spit out.

The air became trapped in Parker's chest. It fought against her diaphragm and her ribs. Attempting to escape until her blood was forced to settle in her limbs. Her legs grew so heavy, she couldn't move even though it was time to leave.

Dilynn reached over and patted Parker on the knee. "And I am only telling you so we can just move on past it."

Parker still couldn't breathe, so she sure as hell could not speak. Her mind ran over the 'move on past it' repeatedly, until her brain settled on Dilynn being ineffective at googling. After all, no one just moved past the conversation when a job applicant attacked a District Attorney or is the only child of serial murderers. Those are not things people just accept.

"So, the job—"

The air broke loose as the question escaped Parker's lips, "You really don't have any questions?"

Dilynn's whole body quaked as a witchy cackle made Parker's eyes grow wide. The redhead turned to the only sane person in the room, Alex. She looked for any clue as to what was so funny and got nothing.

The smile returned to Dilynn's eyes, watering with her laughter. "A hundred and one. Primarily how good did it feel to punch Nia in the face?" Then she waved her own words away. "No. No. You don't have to answer that."

Dilynn sighed. "When Evie found out I googled you, she made it clear you never talk about what happened and to leave it alone."

Alex huffed in annoyance, before interjecting, "And bringing it up to you right when you come in is clearly leaving it alone."

Dilynn swatted away their words. Her face settled in a perpetually playful smile.

"Okay, smooth and political are not my strengths. From me you will always get overly honest and straight to the point. I just don't want you to be worried all the time. It's out and now we can talk about the big picture." Dilynn quickly held up a finger, "However, if you, like, ever wanna talk about it, especially the punching Nia part, my door is always open."

With another huff, Parker heard Alex mutter, "This is why I do interviews."

"We both know this isn't an interview," Dilynn snapped back.

Alex's eyebrows had risen so far up their forehead Parker questioned if the dark lines were ever there to begin with. "Can we at least pretend to be professionals?"

Dilynn looked back to Parker, "Sorry, I'm not good at pretending. The reality is I decided to hire you the second Olivia spoke to you. The kid has not spoken to anyone since she got here. A year ago. And you got her to speak and laugh in one day, which means if you are willing, I—"

Alex cleared their throat.

"*We* are ready to offer you a job here."

Alex stared their wife down. "You are never interviewing people again. You threw away any bargaining chip we—"

"When do I start?" Parker cut them off before they possibly caused Dilynn to change her mind.

"You don't even know how much the job pays," Alex stated. Their eyebrows returned to normal forehead position but furrowed in the middle.

Parker shrugged and dropped her chin a little before looking up at them staring down at her. She inhaled deeply and looked at the scratch on the toe of her shoe.

"I need need this job. No one will hire me after they google me." She licked her lips, tasting the desperation of her words. She turned to Dilynn, adding, "And Echo likes you, and Echo doesn't like anyone."

Dilynn's head tilted, her eyes searching Parker's face. It took a moment for Parker to realize the source of the confusion. She held up her hand.

"Sorry, I mean Marissa."

"Echo," Dilynn said the name like she was trying it out. She looked back at Alex. "Did you know she went by Echo?"

Alex raised their shoulders, then said, "Well her bar is called Echo's Escape."

Dilynn folded her arms over her chest. "Why didn't she tell me she went by Echo?"

"Because you and Simone can't play nice, so it's not like we get to hang out," Alex stated blandly.

Dilynn narrowed her eyes at Alex, "Your best friend is impossible."

"So are you, but I am still friends with you," they said, their lips forming a matter-of-fact line across their face.

"Aren't y'all married?" Parker asked, then remembered she was supposed to be professional and admonished herself for slipping into her trashy talk.

"Yep," Dilynn stated childishly. "Which makes us not friends."

Alex's hand came to their face tapping their cheek with a single finger, then vigorously rubbed with both hands like they were attempting to scrub away their obvious frustration. Dilynn got to her feet. She didn't say anything to Alex, just placed a hand on their bicep.

Parker diverted her eyes and took in the office. The overly simplistic decor demonstrated that not a lot of thought had been put into the room beyond the standard furniture and a wall of filing cabinets. The only personal touches were pictures of Evie, Lyra, the toddler from the party, and another young woman who looked so much like Alex it made Parker wonder if Alex had a child they had brought into the relationship. She turned to analyze the ambiguous build of Alex's frame. She stopped herself as her eyes started to wander down in search of an indication as to what Alex's chromosomal make-up was.

'It's none of your business.'

She took mental snap shots of their facial structure though. Wanted to try her hand at capturing the careful image they'd constructed to ensure pegging their biological sex was difficult.

Dilynn interrupted Parker's thoughts. "So, I was hoping you would actually start today. Landon, Olivia's lawyer, got approval to add you to the witness list because if you get her to talk, then you will be the only person with any kind of information."

Parker's eyes grew, "You mean like now now?"

"Yeah. Is that okay?" Dilynn glanced at the still empty courtyard. "I mean, if it doesn't work, it's fine. But I was hoping you'd be willing to meet with her today for an initial eval."

"Don't you need me to fill out paperwork?"

Dilynn waved away the words once more.

"Alex and you can handle it later today. Olivia has an open period in twenty minutes. I can give you a tour and show you the art building. You'll only have a few minutes to get situated. I'm not expecting miracles but like I said, we are kind of on a time crunch."

"If this is all too fast for you, it's okay to tell Dilynn no," Alex offered.

Parker considered if she would be capable of running an effective evaluation with nothing to go off. The reality was no, but the other reality was if she started today, then she could start getting paid since Echo's money ran out. Rent was due on the first, so Parker realized holding off would likely mean an eviction notice.

"No, I'm good to start." Then added, "Like I said, I need need the work."

Alex nodded. "Okay, come see me after your session. I'll put together the employment contract and we'll get you on the payroll."

"We also can get you your signing bonus today, if you'd like?" Dilynn offered.

"Signing bonus?" Alex looked at their wife.

'Bet they're counting to one hundred right now,' Parker told herself. The thought brought a smile to Parker's lips.

"Yeah, the thousand dollars for all new teachers," Dilynn said, staring at Alex whose confusion fell behind a stoic mask.

"Of course. How could I have forgotten?"

Dilynn clapped her hands together. "Great. Let's get going."

Parker followed Dilynn out of the office's side door as Alex mumbled to themself, "What does she think this is, the NFL?"

Once they were within the courtyard, Dilynn held her hands up like a toddler showing off their masterpiece. "So, this is it."

Parker walked alongside Dilynn until she felt her left heel crack. She stutter-stepped without Dilynn noticing anything was wrong.

The underside of the shoe flapped with each step she took. Parker tried to listen to the details of the school but keeping herself upright became her sole priority.

"When we had it built several years ago, we didn't want the traditional buildings..."

Parker shifted all her weight to the balls of her feet. Her calves burned more than the Arizona sun they stood under. She moved from left to right, trying to relieve the stress from her feet.

"Everything looks like a house, but what would be, like, the living room or a master bedroom is a classroom instead. There's a full kitchen downstairs and the independent living is...."

'She gave you a job and a fucking bonus. You can stand on your toes for as long as you have to.'

Dilynn's tiny body barely took a breath between her long-winded paragraphs. Before Parker could process what was in one building, Dilynn was talking about another. She explained every detail of every building, and Parker tried to keep up with what was what.

"That's the science building. It actually has two classrooms on the bottom floor. Mona Ramirez is our chemistry and physics teacher, and Tylor Reichard takes care of the biology and health classes."

Parker slowed slightly to trail Dilynn. The fake leather dug into the top of her feet, and her tiny pinky toe screamed for relief.

'Just shut up,' she told her feet. 'I can sit in the room. Just have to get to the room.'

Dilynn pointed out another building at the back of the U-shaped courtyard. "That one the kids call the book building..."

'I'm never gonna remember this shit.'

"... run by Charleigh Marshall. Her and Mona actually were part of the first graduating class, and they came back to work here."

As they passed the one building out of place, Dilynn explained, "This one was Alex's idea..."

'For the love of God, I just need to sit down!'

"...We also have several lunch carts where the students can work at selling their creations."

Parker nodded along as Dilynn's words strung together, entering Parker's ear, only to twist into an impossible knot Parker was unable to untangle. She tried to go through the different buildings and remember what classes were within and who taught them, but Charleigh Ramirez teaching math didn't sound right to her. The only information she held steady was she could go to the weird looking building and get ready made meals for lunch.

Parker's stomach growled at the anticipation of a meal in the near future. Unfortunately, the sun had already passed the high point of the day, meaning lunch was over. She'd have to wait until she left to get something to eat.

"And this house is the art building." Dilynn's words pulled Parker from thinking about falling on her face and her empty stomach. They stood outside the smallest house. Across the blue door "Pollock" was painted in broad box letters.

"Pollock? As in Jackson Pollock?" Parker asked, immediately regretting her own participation in delaying them getting inside.

"All of the houses have a name because numbers and letters just felt wrong. When we were building, Evie said that classrooms and cell blocks always felt exactly the same," Dilynn explained.

"I mean, she's not wrong," Parker contributed, grateful Dilynn didn't appear to care she'd been locked up alongside her daughter for three months. "Why Pollock?"

"He challenged the norms. Plus, it makes me think of Julia Roberts in *Mona Lisa's Smile* trying to change the world for her students." Dilynn gestured to the courtyard. "I like to think we are doing that here."

Doors smacked open as teenagers suddenly filed out of houses. The humans with questionable fashion sense formed herds, roaming through the walkways, over benches and porch railings. Their voices ricocheted off every surface, chasing the peace from the courtyard.

Parker found Olivia in the mass of students walking alongside a bubbly girl talking enough for both girls. They paused only long enough for Olivia's 'friend' to wrap her arms around a giant boy whose tattoos reminded Parker of Xio. She definitely recognized the gang brand on the side of his neck as one of the first things Xio had covered when she began recreating herself. The boy would probably do the same, just as Parker had tried changing her name for a period of time and dying her hair. She scanned the sea of students realizing many of the kids looked to be from Xio's neighborhood, and she smiled at the thought of the barback working to keep kids from ending up like she had.

"Oh, and we don't have bells," Dilynn suddenly threw out.

The last of the stragglers made their way through doors, which shut behind them. Dilynn nodded to the door still unused before them. The steps creaked as they made their way up. Parker followed, curious of what lay within.

Dilynn had not been joking about the building being a house. They passed the kitchen immediately as they entered. They continued through the common room to the back of the house. Once through the double doors, Parker was finally in a more familiar space. The room was mostly empty. A few tables and shelving units, but otherwise the space was void of distractions.

"This is it." Dilynn ran her finger over the table, grimacing at the dust.

Parker nodded and grabbed hold of the table, trying to lean casually against it on the unbroken shoe.

"Since the semester has already started, you don't exactly have any classes. We have a few kids who expressed interest in art, so we already have the basic supplies. Paints, pencils, markers, paper, canvases, and such are available and on the shelves. Neither of us are art people, so just tell me or Alex what you need, and we can order it."

Parker looked at Dilynn, chewing on the inside of her lip. "I thought you needed someone to teach?"

"Well, we haven't actually had an art program. This space was originally set up like the library was, so kids could use it. However, when Simone said Marissa's friend needed a job and you were an art therapist, we figured we could create a new program." She tucked a hair behind her ear. "So, we figured if you started now, then you could get your feet wet with just doing behavioral therapy and then we could look at scheduling you a class beginning in the spring. Honestly, I think it would be better to schedule you just one actual teaching class. Then maybe we can do some small group sessions for similar traumas, and still leave you half the day to work with individual students. But that's all for later. Right now, I need your focus on Olivia, so she is the only person you will see, and after her trial we will have you sit with our school social worker and try to figure out what to do for the rest of the day. And.... Well, I will confess, Alex didn't know you were going to start today, but they'll get over it."

Parker tried to envision what she could possibly offer in the capacity as a teacher. She had not taken a single teaching course. And the brief time she spent in high school had been buried in so much trauma she didn't have insight into what a high school class should look like. Her muscles twitched and she considered the fastest way out of the building and back to her car.

"Look, I know this may not be what you wanted, and I know there's a history between you and Evie, but this place is really something special. If you give it a chance and you hate it, then it is what it is. But please take a chance."

Parker looked back at the woman. She knew 'it is what it is' on a personal level, and she appreciated Dilynn possessed a cut and run understanding.

"Thank you, Mrs. Greyson. For the job. For the made-up signing bonus."

"It's just Dilynn." Dilynn's lips pursed in amusement. "You figured it out?"

Parker gave her a slight shameful smile. "I just really appreciate the opportunity, and I won't mess it up."

A slight chuckle fell from the woman's lips, and then she said, "Well, I hope you mess it up a little. I mean, it's how you get better. So, fail some. Fail today, or tomorrow. Just don't quit, okay?"

Parker threw out what she thought about Dilynn being a cut and run comrade. "Okay," she said.

"I'll leave you to get set up and go get Olivia."

With a deep breath, Parker scanned the shelves for an idea of how to get started as Dilynn left. As soon as the door was closed, she took her shoe off and searched the shelves for glue or tape. Once her shoe was somewhat secure, Parker set up a table with several large sheets of paper and some markers. She decided to start out basic. Just ask Olivia a few questions about where she grew up and her family, then she'd see where it led.

She barely had time to internally script two questions before the door to the house opened once more. No footsteps suggested someone had entered, but she turned. She nearly jumped out of her skin when she saw a shadow of human coming into view.

Olivia hovered in the doorway like a ghost. Her oversized clothes were so dark Parker felt the artist wanted the girl to be a black hole. Not even 'hello' was reciprocated. Parker started painting a picture of Olivia in her head. She'd used 'pitch' black with a fine tipped brush to basically scribble Olivia's clothes and face.

When Olivia continued to shift her weight from side to side, Parker realized Olivia was not going to move without permission. She briefly wondered if the girl had picked the habit up from juvenile detention, as she too remembered not being allowed to move until given instructions. Parker gestured inside and asked the girl to sit down.

The therapist chose to use a shade brighter than the actual blue color for the walls surrounding the girl as she mentally painted each stroke towards Olivia. She added a new stroke of blue for every question Parker asked. They were steady and straight questions that each were absorbed into the girl's dark drab. They'd been sitting in silence for thirty minutes. Every question got lost in the void around the girl who didn't look up from the table. Parker even briefly wondered if the girl had headphones in so she couldn't hear Parker at all. There was no way to check though. Not without touching the kid who clearly wanted nothing to touch her.

Her questions had fallen flat, so Parker turned to asking for things that would give her something to start with. She requested a drawing of Olivia's favorite animal. That was also blatantly ignored.

'Guess this is why Dilynn said it was okay to fail today.'

Whoever Parker had met outside of Starbucks was gone, and the replacement had learned how to even speak silence with her body.

The door to the building opened and closed. Voices could be heard from the teens while footsteps stomping up the stairs shook the walls. The ceiling began to creak as the students reached their rooms. Parker figured the school day must be ending.

Olivia's blank page lay on the table between them. Parker felt a spark of hope when Olivia picked up a marker. With a shaking hand, she wrote in the top corner her name, and pushed the paper across the table.

Parker knew she was done, but she continued to sit there.

"Thank you for coming today," Parker said.

Olivia got up from her seat, and pushed her chair in. She didn't say goodbye, just opened the door to the classroom carefully and left. Left with the marker still tucked into her sleeve.

Parker stared out the window. She ran over every question she'd asked. She searched her memory for how the girl moved when Parker spoke but couldn't identify anything of substance. The chair had more personality with paint speckles decorating the seat than the girl who barely breathed in almost an hour.

She finished painting the scene in her head. Added her own body in the picture. She was transparent though. They were in the same room but existing in different universes. Parker painted her mouth open, then tried to waver the lines that led to Olivia, only straightening them out before they reached the girl. She wanted to remember how the girl didn't see or hear her.

Knuckles rapped against the door, pulling Parker from her analysis. She turned to find a younger, more nervous version of Dilynn Greyson, wrapped in an oversized cardigan shifting her weight in the doorway.

"Hi... uhm... I'm Charleigh. Charleigh Marshall," the woman offered. "I teach

English. You must be the new art therapist."

"Parker. Parker Carter," she said, getting to her feet. She made her way to the doorway Charleigh seemed unwilling to breach.

"It's nice to meet you." Charleigh offered her hand to shake, and Parker followed suit. "Greyson said that you were working with Olivia today, and I wanted to stop by and give these to you."

Charleigh held out a stack of mostly empty pages to her, then explained, "This is Olivia's work. She doesn't have a strong grasp of writing or reading at this point. She's working with Andrew, the reading guru. But the work she does turn into me sometimes has pictures on it. I'm not a picture person. I prefer the words. I figured if anyone could make sense of it, hopefully it would be you."

Parker flipped through the pages. All of them were either worksheets or lined paper with Olivia's first name written in the top corner. On one page, Parker was able to make out a tent. Another there was a van. Then, a swing on a worksheet about figurative language. And a lot of singular eyes. Almost every page had an eye staring out at the viewer, carefully outlined in black and shaded with pencil and a red pen.

"I thought maybe it was the Illuminati symbol at first," Charleigh provided. "I don't know why, but I have found that most kids from juvie talk about the Illuminati. But it doesn't have the triangle. So, I don't know. But I just wanted to help."

Parker licked her lips. Everyone in juvie knew about the Illuminati, and most of it was tied to the concept of success being only available to those who were chosen. A scapegoat at times for kids to cling to that their lack of success was due to the oppression by those in power. She couldn't explain that to this woman who'd clearly never been locked up.

Charleigh shifted her weight with her eyes looking everywhere but at Parker. The woman's uneasiness made Parker's arm hair stand on end.

"This is more than I got," Parker confessed. Her hand held up the blank page she hadn't remembered taking with her from the table.

"You'll get there," Charleigh offered with a small smile. "I mean, you're here, so Greyson has faith in you."

Parker laughed, a hand coming up to pull on the back of her neck. "She seems like she has faith in everybody."

Charleigh shrugged. "I mean, not everyone. But she used to say faith in someone is often what's missing in life."

The woman's eyes fell to her own oversized cardigan. Parker remembered Lyra saying that Dilynn used to be an English teacher, and if Parker hadn't seen the pictures in Dilynn's office of the fourth daughter, she would have assumed this human standing before her was Dilynn's kid. She definitely seemed to have the black sheep demeanor.

"Anyways, welcome. If you need anything just let me know."

She waved as she turned to leave.

"Thank you," Parker called after her new co-worker. She wasn't sure if Charleigh heard her.

Parker stared at the creepy eye etched into all of Olivia's work. She didn't have long to study it before the door opened. She'd thought it was another student headed upstairs.

Turning back to the images, she let the footsteps blend in with the beat from the music coming from above them. The eye appeared to be the same in every picture, and there was no denying Olivia had an artist's eye for detail. She was holding two pictures up to compare them when dark combat boots entered her view.

Parker jumped back. The papers crunched to her chest, as she tried to catch the breath she'd lost with the "Jesus fucking Christ," exiting her mouth. As though the man was pissed at her for using his name in vain, the room's quiet was snapped with a loud crack.

Her heel snapped off the bottom of the shoe, sending Parker to the ground. She bounced as her ass abruptly hit the concrete floor.

"Fucking shit," she said now laying on the floor with papers floating gracefully towards her.

"You sound like my wife," Alex said with a soft laugh and an extended hand to help Parker up.

Parker let herself be hoisted back to her feet as if she weighed nothing.

"Sorry," she whispered, realizing Alex was the epitome of professionalism.

Alex picked up the heel from the ground, twisted it in their hands, then held it up.

"Did your shoe break?"

Parker pulled the other half of her shoe off her foot. "Looks like it."

Alex studied the scotch tape that was split from where it had been wrapped chaotically around both pieces, then they sat down. They pulled their boots off and revealed a pair of Super Mario Brother's socks. They wiggled their toes.

"Here," they said, holding out the boots.

"I can't wear your shoes."

"They may be a little big, but you're barefoot and the concrete is going to be hot as hell. At least I have socks on." Alex nodded to the door. "My wife can be a bit jealous so carrying you across the courtyard would probably get me cut off for at least a month, and I can't have that happening."

With a cocked eyebrow, Parker challenged them. "What would your wife think if I left here wearing your shoes?"

Alex's eyes crinkled with their smile. "She'll probably rub my feet for their sacrifice as she tells me I am the nicest person alive."

Parker took the huge boots from Alex. They were heavier than she anticipated, and she almost dropped them.

"Dilynn hates feet," they mused as Parker slid each foot easily into the dark leather. She felt like a child playing dress-up when she stood.

Alex stretched out their legs and wiggled their toes once more, before looking at Parker.

"Ready to fill out that paperwork?" they asked.

"Yeah."

Before she could gather the papers Charleigh had given her, Parker's stomach announced itself. She tried to muffle the declaration of hunger with a hand over her stomach. It didn't work, and her stomach shouted again that it had been a full twenty-four hours since it had last been fed.

"We have shoes in the office," Alex said, pulling a folded slip of paper from their pocket. "I'm sure we have something that will fit you, and then Dilynn said she wanted to take you to lunch as we fill out the forms. And this is your signing bonus."

She unfolded the check. It was a personal check written out from Dilynn's private account. Even had the woman's address in the top left corner.

"She didn't have to do this," Parker said, looking up at the woman's partner.

With a slight bobble of their head, they gestured to the school. "She didn't have to do any of this. That woman... she does what she wants, when she wants, and how she wants. If you try to give it back, she'll pout and do something more extreme, so if you were like me, and you don't like gifts, then I would take the new signing bonus that the school offers and let her feed you. Feeding people is what she does."

The money was a debt Parker would have to pay back. A debt she'd pay by breaking through to the silent kid. She folded the check in half again and slipped it in her shirt, having at least enough sense to turn from Alex before doing so. After paperwork, she would go to the bank instead of St. Mary's food bank.

Parker folded up Olivia's work and put it into her purse. Looking back at the markers and the papers on the table, Parker left a seed of hope for a better tomorrow. She lifted each foot awkwardly stomping her way after Alex Trikru, who had taken off running across the courtyard.

11

The laptop keys were treated brutally. Each one was pounded under Nia's red painted nails like she was trying to personally kill the device. Zoe's laptop was taking Nia's abuse, so she didn't have to. Whatever had spurred Nia's sudden interest into Zoe's life had the woman equally elated and terrified.

She sat in her chair, but she felt like a little kid again with a need to spin around like she'd done whenever her father took her to work. He had tolerated Zoe in his chair, but that was only after that one time she found Ari being spun around like it was a top while their dads talked about some case for the Winters Group. Nia had never been as kind, so Zoe sat like a rod had been drilled into her spine to avoid displeasing the woman her father held to such high esteem.

"I honestly thought that one day it would be Aribella who would replace me, but she chose that snake of a man," Nia stated, now spearing the trackpad. "Never thought Sylvia Winters would own my ex-husband and my daughter. No matter what, you stay away from Winters. She'd throw money at you, but then you will owe her. And owing a Winters is a lifelong indebtment."

Zoe didn't remind Nia that she'd been the one to send Ari to her dad's. If nothing else because Ari coming out had given her a leg up in the race, they'd apparently been running against each other their whole lives.

Nia flipped the laptop around for Zoe, revealing the Maricopa County Election website. She cataloged the filing date for all of her paperwork as January 1st and that she would need more than 6,000 signatures to get on the ballot. Other than that, the information was sparse.

"The paperwork to get started is simplistic enough," Nia explained. "Then there's the fund raising, but I can set up dinners with the people you need to know."

Zoe's eyes grew at Nia's offer to help her build a network. "Wow. Thank you."

Turning her attention back to the computer, Zoe considered what she would put into her statement of purpose due in just three months. She decided the key focus would be protecting society by being hard on first time offenders, and everything following would have to go back to that point.

She was silently constructing her statement when Nia interrupted her train of thought. "The crucial component of getting elected is your public image."

With a nod of the head, Zoe turned her attention back to Nia. The older woman stared out the window at the sinking sun. A single finger tapped on the metal window frame. Then she abruptly turned back to Zoe still seated at her desk.

"You're not married. Do you have a boyfriend?" she asked.

"No."

"Why not?"

Zoe chewed on the answer. She knew Nia well enough to know the answer would change the offer to help. Zoe hated this part of being a lesbian, the constantly coming out and worrying how it would impact her future interactions with the person.

As casually as she could muster, Zoe said, "I'm gay."

Nia's head tilted and scanned over Zoe like she'd never actually looked at her in all the time they'd known each other. Fear crept up Zoe's shoulders as she wondered if Nia would realize the first girl she'd kissed was the daughter who'd been disowned. That the prom proposal Ari had held up for Zoe was because they'd been living in the closet together since middle school. If everything would change now Nia knew Ari left because Zoe had broken her heart.

The woman smiled though. With a wave of her hand, she said, "Shouldn't be a problem. What does your girlfriend do?"

Zoe sucked her lips in and scrunched up her face. Her eyes wandered over her desk.

"I don't have one."

"Why not?" Nia asked. But before Zoe could answer, Nia followed with, "You're not in the closet, are you?"

"No. No. No." Zoe's hands waved in the air, swatting away even the suggestion of a closet. "I came out in high school. My dad was supportive so long as I didn't advertise. And the last couple years, I've just been focusing on work."

"Hmmm."

Nia looked around the office. Zoe searched as well, wondering what her boss was looking for. She didn't have any photos up, and she'd always shied away from anything remotely rainbow to keep her promise to her dad.

"Get a girlfriend," Nia instructed. She pulled out her phone, tapping against the screen as Zoe stared at her wide-eyed.

"But—" Zoe tried.

"And don't use one of those dating apps. Go to one of those girls only bars."

"Get a girlfriend," Zoe choked. "Like tomorrow?"

"Yes. You people always like to jump into things anyways." Nia exhaled a loud breath. "That's what Aribella did with that he-she she married, but that's because she couldn't keep her legs closed. At least she had babies before he cut off his cock."

Parker's nineteen-year-old smile flashed in Zoe's head. Zoe quickly rubbed her face with her hands. It would be more effective if she could scrub away the actual memory of the past and present versions of the woman, since no matter how hard she tried Parker was always lingering in the back of her mind.

"Not just a girlfriend. Doctor, professor, something in the service field with a title. Someone with family money is even better. They will help finance your campaign." Nia shook her head and sat in the leather chair across the desk. "Did you think you could honestly do this without a family image?"

"Well, yes." Zoe started. Then explained, "I thought it was better to be single and gay in Arizona since the voter population is primarily red. I mean, if I'm single, then no one even needs to know I'm gay. My dad said that would be best. That's why I had to turn down Ari's proposal to prom. My dad said to keep my personal life private."

Nia nodded momentarily as though she understood. "A lot of red voters have gay kids or grandkids. Some have the flaming nurse who provided hospice for their granny. Plus, all the blue voters will show up to support the gay so with the swing, being homosexual will actually play in your favor. Just stay away from the tranny pedophiles and the ones that look like men. Most people favor two women that are obviously women than the other creepy stuff."

Her explanation made more sense than Zoe ever considered even laced with the homophobic additions. What didn't add up to Zoe was the immediate need for a girlfriend. She chewed on the question wondering if the answer was obvious and she'd look stupid for asking.

Slowly she leaned back in her chair, owning her space. Reminding herself, Nia wanted to help her because she saw Zoe just as capable as she was. With her shoulders back and her gaze steady, she raised her arms in a carefree "W" as she asked, "Why do I need a girlfriend then?"

"Family people are trustworthy. When you're single and successful, people question what's wrong with you. Especially as a woman. They'll label you as a cutthroat dyke if you can't hold down a relationship. So, why don't you have a girlfriend?"

Zoe looked out the window silently running over the argument at being an out lesbian wss not necessarily a career killer. It countered the lessons she'd been taught her whole life about her chances of political success as a member of the LGBTQ community. She thought of her mother's constant pressure to settle down against what her father and brothers had warned her about.

Nia's acrylic nails strummed against the leather, pulling Zoe back to the conversation. She realized Nia was waiting for an answer.

"Oh, I didn't realize you were asking me a question."

With eyebrows raised, Nia tilted her head.

"Sorry. Uh.... I spend my time going over case files. A lot of late nights at the office. Last girl I took home woke up to crime scene photos on the breakfast bar, and she was not happy. Figured it was safer to stay out of the dating circle for the time being."

As Zoe spoke, the answer to the problem came to her.

'Apologize to Lyra. She wants me, she said so. She knows the end goal of being DA and she's supportive. Plus, she's used to me working all the time.'

"Well, it's not. Also, get a house. Put down some roots and leave the photos in the office," Nia stated.

'Lyra said she lives with her sister and the sister's boyfriend. They have loud sex. She would probably jump at moving out.'

"Any skeletons? Someone that could stand in the way or make a scene. Crazy family members."

"You've known my family longer than me. So, you know... one of my brothers is a social studies teacher in Gilbert. The other just left the Navy, honorable discharge. You know my dad and my mom. I think mom being an NICU nurse at Banner is a very non-skeleton type of closet. Very G rated."

"Yes, your mother was always the perfect housewife." Nia's stare returned to the window where the sun was practically gone. "The Gibson case is going to have to make you interesting. Tomorrow, Officer Greyson is taking the stand. Are you ready?"

Zoe reached for the file on Everleigh Greyson and held it up. "Yes, I read the file. I have what I need."

"Good. That should be all."

Nia moved to get up.

"Can I ask you a question?" Zoe asked, realizing at once the irony.

"Yes."

"Why do you have a file on the Greysons?"

Nia sat up straighter in her chair. Her finger pushed the hair that wasn't in her face farther back. She opened and closed her mouth, and her eyes momentarily looked just over Zoe's right shoulder.

"I'm sure you know that I came from Maryvale." Nia points out the window. "I grew up just over the freeway. Gangs run by people like Gabriel Horna are the same monsters Greyson stops from going to jail terrorized my family so I do whatever I can to protect the people in the community."

Zoe looked out the window but couldn't see anything but streetlights and cars.

"Dilynn Greyson and Sylvia Winters used to be an item. While they are not together anymore, they are still a constant problem. Buying judges' seats. And Dilynn... she throws money around like it could buy her whatever she wanted is almost as bad as Winters." The older eyes refocused on Zoe. "She acts like her motives are pure with all those kids but each one of them just makes her pockets deeper, since she houses them in group homes. Then the school is funded using public funds, so she is getting double paid for each one."

Glancing out the window, Zoe considered the power someone like Dilynn had. She was clearly gay, and since she was in the habit of buying elections maybe obliterating her daughter's reputation on the stand would not be in Zoe's best interest. However, making an enemy of Nia was something her father had been adamant about not doing. He had always supported Nia, even though he was one of the more powerful lawyers for the Winter's Group before he retired. He had pushed Zoe to be a DA like Nia, instead of working for Winters like Ari had ended up doing.

Nia licked her teeth before she said, "Dilynn Greyson collects on those criminals and then they go back to the neighborhood where I grew up. You know the 3034s, well Greyson's kid was locked up with Gabriel Horna's daughter. I haven't been able to prove it yet, but I think they all are connected to the cartel, and I think that Greyson is laundering money for them and getting a piece of the action. Probably using those kids like mules."

"I understand," Zoe lied. She couldn't imagine what Nia's life had been like growing up. She understood only enough about the streets of Maryvale to know she shouldn't go without her brothers. And she also knew Parker currently lived there and was friends with Xiomara Horna. Had been in a relationship with the head of the 3034 gang before they'd met according to Nia's files.

Nia got up from the chair and gathered her Mikel Kors bag.

"When you discredit Everleigh Greyson, it will remove her influence in the police department. That's the only way to dismantle Greyson's hold, by removing her hands in the system. One finger at a time."

"I'll help you in any way I can," Zoe promised.

"Just make it clear tomorrow that Officer Greyson should never have been issued a badge. You do that and I will get you elected." Her mouth spread into a large grin.

Zoe stood and made her way around the desk to Nia. She took the woman's outstretched hand. "I won't let you down," she promised.

"I know you won't. You're the perfect person for this job."

Nia looked down at her phone and smiled. "Aribella says there's a lesbian club on McDowell and the 51 freeway. Echo's Escape. Go out and let your hair down a little... but not too much."

12

The parking lot of Echo's bar wasn't busy, which wasn't unusual for darts night. With good news to share, Parker practically pranced from her car to the bar. She didn't even care Echo was going to yell at her all night, because she had cash in her bra to buy the woman a beer. A beer that was kind of like paying Echo back for the $300 loan since the profits would go straight to Echo's wallet.

"I'm here," Parker declared, throwing the door open. With a broad smile, she asked the woman behind the bar, "Does your partner ever play darts with you anymore? Or did she get tired of you yelling at her constantly?"

Parker slapped her bag on the bar and plopped her body down on a stool as Echo carefully dried each glass before putting it in the cooler.

"I didn't call you to play tonight."

"You said you needed me." Parker's eyes narrowed. "I rushed home to change to come and help you."

"I do need your help. Two of the girls called out sick so I need you on the floor tonight."

Parker ground her teeth at the woman. Her arms folded over her chest as she looked at the almost empty dance floor. Today she'd gotten a real job that didn't involve booze or boobs, and she wasn't even going to get to celebrate.

Echo set the towel down. She leaned against the wooden surface. The bags under her eyes were more prominent than the last time they'd seen each other.

"Please, princess. This is my one night out and I need this."

Looking up at the ceiling, Parker counted backward from ten. With each number, she thought of a time Echo came to her rescue. She had more than ten.

"Please, Princess Lucifer." Echo said, taking Parker's hand and bowing down.

"Fine," Parker huffed.

She got down and moved around the bar to the inside. She stripped off her t-shirt to the tank top underneath and pulled the hair tie out to release her ponytail. She flipped her head down and scrunched her fingers against the roots to add some volume. When she stood up, Echo was staring her down.

"What was that?" Echo asked.

"That's her fuck me look," Xio said, coming up behind Parker and wrapping an arm around her waist. "Looking hot as ever."

Parker elbowed her former lover in the gut, then turned to the masc feigning hurt. She pointed to the strap in the woman's pants, and said, "You keep that pussy breaker away from me."

Xio adjusted the bulge, then shrugged lightly. "You got implants; I got a dick. Silicon is gonna keep the doors open tonight."

"Neither of you better try to sneak off to screw the customers," Echo stated. Her eyes locked on Xio, then added, "And you better not try to screw her on my desk either."

"That ship set sale a long time ago," Parker declared more to remind Xio than Echo. "Besides Xio prefers a different girl every night."

Parker reached into her shirt and pulled each breast up until the lace of her bra peeked out of the top of the tank top. She looked up to find Xio standing close enough to hit again.

"You were the one that didn't want the candles or dinner," she reminded Parker.

"You were the one still screwing your ex-boyfriend and got knocked up," Parker snapped back. "I told you I didn't want kids."

The sound of the camera shutter clicking pulled Parker's gaze from Xio's defeated face. The bartender had snapped a photo of Parker and Xio practically nose to nose, staring each other down, before there was any chance for Parker to protest.

"What are you doing?" Parker snapped. "You know I don't like my picture taken."

With a sly smile, Echo said, "Getting you more customers."

Parker grabbed a tray, and silently hoped that photo wouldn't wind up on any of the serial killer blogs. She made her way over to the dart players gathering in front of the boards before Echo could get another photo.

The team she'd played against last week whistled as she approached, greeting her like an old friend. She didn't tense up when one pulled her in for a hug, instead fell into an old routine of flirtatious touching and batted eyelashes.

The bar pulsed with laughter, music, and the clinking of glasses. Parker weaved between tables with ease, her steps purposeful yet fluid. Each interaction was met with a genuine smile and a twinkle in her brown eyes.

At one table, a group of friends chattered animatedly while their drinks dwindled. Parker approached with a tray balanced expertly in one hand, effortlessly gliding into their conversation with a witty remark. As she took their orders, her attentiveness was palpable, ensuring each drink choice was noted with precision.

Moving to another table, she encountered a couple engrossed in a deep conversation. With a gentle touch on the shoulder, Parker interrupted their dialogue with a respectful apology. They looked up, greeted by her warm smile. Without missing a beat, she smoothly took their order.

Throughout the evening, Parker's familiarity with the serving role made her feel like a success. Whether it was refilling glasses or simply sharing a moment of flirty camaraderie, she approached the customers with a blend of professionalism and genuine care that had her thinking maybe holding down two jobs for a while wouldn't be a bad idea.

Parker picked up the three dollars from the table and stuffed it in her bra before clearing away the empty bottles. From a few tables away, she watched Echo laugh with the other dart players. It was nice to see Echo relaxed. Her chest felt tight as she searched for the last time Echo had been so carefree with her.

"Get me a Coors Light, bitch," someone called from behind her.

With her fingers dug into the tray, Parker reminded herself not to throw it. Reminded herself she was too weak to establish dominance in a women's prison, even if she was sent there for decapitating the woman with her Olympic level discus throwing skills.

Parker turned to see the soggy loaf of bread looking a little burnt with the home dye job and the overly dramatic black eye makeup unblended around her bulbous eyes. Andrea set an empty beer bottle on the table.

Shaking her head, Parker said, "I know you didn't just say that."

Andrea smiled as she looked at the people at the table with her. Then she shrugged and stated, "Figured you'd be used to it. I mean you bark at strangers and come whenever your master calls. Just an obedient. Little. Bitch."

"Please, don't make me hit you," a familiar voice stated.

Parker searched until she locked on Zoe's hazel eyes staring at Andrea. Zoe got up from a stool and made her way to the table Parker had just cleared. Glancing at the stool by the bar, Parker wondered how she'd missed Zoe sitting there.

"Who the fuck are you?" Andrea growled at Zoe.

"Someone who won't tolerate someone else talking to another person like—"

"They're trash?" Parker finished. She watched Zoe's eyes fall to the ground, then her teeth bit into her plump lower lip.

The confidence Parker had in her role serving tables fell with her shoulders at Zoe's unexpected presence. She scanned the floor, mapping the shortest path without any obstacles away from Andrea and Zoe.

"Parker, I need another bucket," Echo called.

Parker looked up but found her only friend still engrossed in the people around her. She searched for Xio next, but the woman was leaning over a customer while the dark-haired femme put what was probably a phone number into the pocket closest to Xio's fake dick. No one else knew Parker, so she would have to navigate her way out alone.

Silently, Parker took her leave from the situation. But even with the growing space between her and the bullies, she could hear them talking.

Parker loaded the tin bucket with six beers and filled it with ice. She grabbed a Coors Lite for Andrea and a Heineken for Zoe, hoping it was still the lawyer's go to beer. She stared at the green bottle remembering all the times she watched Zoe raise one to her perfect pillow lips.

'Don't go there.'

She returned, dropping Andrea's beer off first. Then she handed the second bottle to Zoe. Zoe's fingers grazed hers as she passed off the drink. The momentary contact burned Parker at the thought of what could have been if Zoe hadn't turned out to be as big of a douche as her frat boy brother.

Parker glanced back at Andrea downing the beer she'd just been handed. The woman was already drunk enough to talk shit, and Parker made a note to not walk to her car alone tonight.

"I dated this girl in college," Zoe called over to Andrea. "She worked at a club and told me that when someone would call her a bitch, she would fuck with their drinks."

Andrea was mid-drink when Parker saw the pieces click into place for the dumber woman. With a glance at the bottle, Andrea set it on the table. The people around her laughed, and Parker harnessed the courage needed to lift her lips in a smug suggestive smile.

"She once said someone was running their mouth, calling her names because she refused to give out her number, so she put Visine in their beer. She said it immediately rerouted the shit from their mouth to their ass." Zoe looked at Parker and took a drink of her beer, then asked, "How's life been since college?"

The table behind her exploded with laughter. A chair made a loud scraping sound against the concrete floor, and Parker turned in time to see Andrea make her way to the bathroom.

"Thanks," Parker offered.

Zoe smiled at her like the first time she held a coffee to Parker outside of the library. Smiled like she hadn't broken up with Parker for doing what she could to pay the bills and tuition. Like they could have this friendly banter back and forth after Parker had walked away hiding her tears. They fell for hours after she'd left early, unable to finish her shift. Fell for days as she hid in the back row of the class they shared, afraid of what other humiliation Zoe had planned.

Parker walked away again, unable to pretend that being near Zoe was okay. The bucket was an excuse to head to Echo. She needed the safety net that her worried friend always provided her.

She stood alongside Echo, hiding behind the woman's size. A friend of Echo's handed Parker a business card with a phone number on it. With a gentle smile, the woman shifted her weight as Parker took the card and put it in her pocket. She'd send the woman a text tomorrow and let her know she was seeing someone, even though she'd only scheduled a first date with Lyra for the following Friday. It would be kinder than ghosting her.

After taking a few more drink orders, Parker made her way back to the bar.

She leaned against the polished wood, waiting for drinks that she'd called to the girl working the bar. Taking a glance back over her shoulder, she watched Zoe drain the last of the beer in the first bottle.

"Give me another Heineken too, please."

With the tray loaded, she moved through the tables dropping off the various drinks and collecting the empty and abandoned bottles since Xio was now busy flirting with a different woman. With only Zoe's beer left to deliver, she dragged her feet to the table Zoe still leaned against.

She put the beer on the table this time. Her teeth chewed the inside of her lip until she couldn't hold the question any longer. "What are you doing here?"

"Not really sure honestly. I was driving by and thought, 'what the hell?'" Zoe stared out at the dance floor. Then without even looking at Parker, she said, "You look good. Grown up."

Parker's head tilted as she studied the woman Zoe had grown to be. "You look exactly the same."

The corners of Zoe's lips raised as she hid her smile behind the mouth of the bottle. She took a long drink of the beer before she spoke. "I'm going to take that as a compliment."

Andrea swore loudly at the dart board, pulling Parker's attention from Zoe. As she'd expected, the woman was getting angrier as she got drunker.

"Did you fuck with her drink?" Zoe asked.

"Not hers."

Parker watched out of the corner of her eye as Zoe momentarily examined the green bottle, just as Andrea had a little while prior. She let out a simple huff and took another drink.

"I deserve that."

They both stood there as the uneasy silence of the words not said enveloped Parker. She had other drink orders to take and tips to collect, but she couldn't get her feet to move.

"So, you work here and at that school," Zoe stated. "For how much that woman gets to run that school you'd think she'd be able to pay her therapist enough to only work one job."

Parker glanced over at Echo, wondering if her protector knew that the woman responsible for breaking her best friend was standing in her bar.

"Helping out my sister tonight. I don't actually work here." Her eyes then narrowed at Zoe. "Are you even supposed to be talking to me since I'm, like, the enemy?"

Zoe sucked her teeth, pulling a vape pen from her pocket and taking a drag. Parker smiled. Zoe had finally given up smoking.

"Didn't know you'd be here, and we are not talking about anything that would put the case in jeopardy."

Parker followed Zoe's eyes to a group of femmes dancing on the floor in celebration. She'd taken their drink order when they had first arrived as they patted the taller blonde in her black lace tank on the shoulders.

"The blonde in black just got accepted into medical school. Bet she checks all your bougie boxes. Go tell her you're the hot shot you always dreamed of becoming, buy her a few drinks, and see if you still have game."

Zoe's chin dropped. She twisted the bottle in her hand. "Look, Parker."

"Look at what? You?" she snapped.

Parker turned from the brown eyed stranger on the dance floor to the hazel eyed stranger still holding the green bottle. She stared into her ex hoping that she'd ruined whatever Zoe had planned on accomplishing.

"I see you. You did what you said you were going to do and I'm happy for you. Okay. I don't wish misery on you."

'Well maybe a little.'

Parker exhaled slowly. "What is it that you want from me?"

Zoe took another drag on the vape pen. Shorter this time. The vapor came out in bursts as the words broke free from the slouched shoulders that barely held up the hopeless looking lawyer.

"Are you happy?" Zoe asked.

'She's got to be shitting me.'

Parker strummed her fingers against the tray that she used to steady herself. 'Asking me if I'm happy. What the fuck is there to be happy about? Never having a girlfriend because I'm scared of them finding out anything about me. Barely landing a job interview and only because my friend knew someone. Being alone.'

Parker licked her teeth and stared at the Coors Lite lamp hanging above the bar. "What is it you said to me at court? Oh yeah, doesn't concern you. You walked away, so the person that is not going to pitch a fit about being here gets to know shit about me."

"Michelle."

Parker froze. Her mind lost in a time when she thought changing her name would change where she'd come from. Who she'd come from.

The ground shifted from quicksand to a landslide. Parker's whole body moved but not in the right direction, which would be away from Zoe. Instead, Parker was falling, her feet unable to keep up with her momentum, only the table stopping the tray in her hands as it collapsed against her chest. Backwashed beer, watered down liquor, and a half a cup of a designated driver's soda soaked through Parker's shirt, pants, and thong. Everything on the tray tumbled and shattered on contact with the concrete around her green Converse Chucks.

Parker closed her eyes as a hammer tapped from within at the front of her skull. She was cold, wet, and pissed as she turned to where Andrea held on to the table with Zoe two inches from the woman's nose.

"It was an accident," Andrea stated.

"Like hell it was," Zoe growled, her shoulders no longer slumped. Her fists white and ready to fight.

Parker held her breath, wondering why this Zoe hadn't been there the night her brother had called her a dirty whore; when just hours before that perfect mouth had peppered her back with kisses as fingers danced a ghostly waltz over her naked flesh until she was dizzy and tingling with the possibility her future held brighter days than a spotlight on her bare skin three feet above drunk and drugged out men waving paper bills in the air.

"What's going on?" Echo bellowed over the music.

Zoe didn't move, even though Echo was practically sharing the air the other two women were breathing as she positioned herself as close as possible to the potential fight.

"She just pushed your server into the table."

"I didn't push her. I just stumbled a little and I ran into her."

"Bullshit, Andrea," Echo said. "You're just pissed that everyone laughed at you not once but twice because you were running your mouth, and someone said something about it."

"I didn't push her," Andrea growled

Echo pointed at the door. "Get the fuck out of here."

"You're kicking me out?" Andrea looked at Echo and then held her hand out, "What about her? She put shit in my drink."

"No, she didn't. I just made you think she could," Zoe said, backing up just enough to put her body between Andrea and Parker.

"Go!" Echo barked.

Andrea pushed off the table and made her way to where her friends were all glaring at her. She grabbed the cheap purse and left.

Parker looked down at the mess around her. With a shaking head, she half whispered, "Sorry, Echo. I'll clean it up."

"Xio!" Echo shouted at the woman getting a lap dance from the woman whose hand had been in her pants. "Get your ass over here."

Echo took the tray from Parker's hands.

"Xio's supposed to be working, not getting off on the dance floor," Echo grumbled. She nodded to the bathroom. "You go clean yourself up."

 Parker's hands shook as she pulled the tank top up and over her head, only to replace it with the t-shirt she'd worn to play darts. She pulled at the neckline hoping it would help her breathe. Hoping more air would stop the pounding in her skull. When it didn't work, Parker rubbed at the spot on her forehead where the internal hammer was still tapping out an SOS signal.

The door opened to the small two stall bathroom. Zoe's perfect face with her perfect hair, and perfect clothes moved into the tight space and hovered behind her.

"What do you want, Zoe?"

"Are you okay?"

"I'm fine," she lied.

Zoe pulled at the back of her neck. Then she said, "I need to ask you a question."

Parker sighed and opened her eyes. "What?"

Zoe leaned against the tampon dispenser behind her. She looked at Parker in the mirror. "Was it all a lie?"

"Does it matter?" Parker felt all the energy she had left draining out of her with each of the words.

"It does to me." Zoe's hand came up again to pull on the back of her neck. "I have thought about that night... well too many times. We had something special. And then everything happened so fast it was like you were there and then you were gone."

"That's what happens when you throw someone away."

Zoe sighed. "What I said was out of line."

"No shit."

Hazel eyes rose from the ground. "You meant the world to me, and then it was like I didn't even know you, but I always wondered if things could have been different."

Parker stared at Zoe's pitiful face. All of the anger she'd locked away came bursting through the door in her head, and she realized what the throbbing was.

"Didn't realize you've become so environmentally conscious. Look, I'm not looking to be recycled. I am 100 percent biodegradable though so don't worry, I'm not going to taint your life," she hissed.

"I'm sorry," Zoe whispered. Then her eyes rose, "I'm sorry. But I was hurt because you lied to me."

Parker turned as the walls began to close in on them. She held onto the sink, drawing strength from the stainless steel. "Tell me what I lied to you about? I'll wait."

"Your name."

Parker rolled her eyes and she shot back, "That wasn't a lie. I was trying to remake myself. Also, you didn't find out I gave you my middle name until court. So, what did I lie to you about that hurt you so badly that you called me a piece of trash in the parking lot of the place that I worked?"

"You never told me you were a stripper."

"Again, I didn't lie to you." Parker's arms folded across her chest, protecting her heart from another attack. "It was the only job I could get to feed myself, to put a roof over my fucking head. Give me one example of a time I actually lied to you."

"It was a lie of omission."

"It would only be a lie of omission if you ever asked where I worked. You didn't. In fact, your pickup line was 'I'd love to get to know you. No majors, jobs, or childhood details. Tell me who you want to be.'"

The door opened pulling both Parker and Zoe's eyes to Echo's large frame blocking most of the doorway.

"Everything okay?" she asked.

"Yeah, she was just leaving," Parker stated.

Zoe let out a heavy breath and turned to leave.

"By the way, did you get the Visine story from your brother?" Parker asked before Zoe even had a chance to turn completely away.

Zoe's head turned back to her with brows scrunched in the middle.

"He was a regular." Parker's lips turned up in disgust. "One night he came and paid for a private dance. Halfway through, he told me how pretty I looked in his sister's bed but that I would look better on his cock. Didn't realize you took pictures of me naked in your bed and showed them to people, but yeah, I was the one that betrayed you."

She held up her hand when Zoe opened her mouth.

"It's done. But I slipped the shit in his drink. A week later he brought you in."

Zoe's eyes fell to the floor and then rose back to Parker.

"You never wondered how he knew?" Parker asked.

Eyes scanned her face. Parker knew Zoe was looking for her tell, the hint of blushing that would show if she was lying. But Parker knew it wasn't there.

Zoe left the bathroom without a word. Left Parker to study the metal tampon dispenser. Parker felt the guilt twist in her gut. Felt remorse for ruining Zoe's image of her brother, her best friend. Remorse for what could have been if she'd never squirted the clear liquid into the Fireball shot.

Echo moved into the tight space, allowing the door to shut behind her. The hip hop music and women laughing filtered through the cracks as Parker picked at the skin on her lower lip until it bled.

"So that was the bitch from college," Echo stated.

"Yep."

"You okay?"

Unable to look Echo in the eyes, Parker counted the dings in the cabinet under the sink. When she got to seven, she said, "Nope."

"Can I help?"

Her finger pulled at a loose string on her shirt, ruining the hem. As she played with the damage, she answered again, "Nope."

13

After leaving the bar, Zoe drove straight to Zachery's house. She sat in the car outside the three-bedroom townhouse, running over the day he'd asked her to go to the strip club. Recreating the conversation and searching for any possibility Parker was lying.

When she couldn't find any way to explain why he'd asked her to go to that club or how he'd waited for her reaction as she sat alongside him, she tried to talk herself into confronting him. Tried and failed.

Ashamed of her cowardice, Zoe left the driveway in the same fashion as she had left the club years prior. Tears and snot smeared across the back of her hand as she choked on the lyrics to The Script's "Breakeven." Zoe screamed the whole way back to her apartment, only replacing the screaming with the slamming. Slamming of doors, buttons, and her purse on the entry table to the empty apartment.

Parker's words echoed in her head like Zoe still stood in the bathroom looking down at the woman. The woman's sentences smashed through the memories she'd altered to feel less guilty about the verbal assault she'd used to tear Parker down. Every justification she attempted to create sounded too much like Zachery.

Exhausted from crying, her mind drifted from reality to restless sleep only to wake sweat soaked before dawn. The dream lingered on replay as she got out of bed. She tried to catch her panting breath, but it was controlled by the beat of the music that pounded only in her ears.

The college aged Parker swaying her hips back and forth until she straddles Zachery's lap. Parker with long blonde hair cascading down her back as she rolls against the man under her. Small hands hold the back of the chair so she can press her naked breasts to his stupid smiling face until the pale skin of her back blocks all sight of him. Hands come off the armrest, clasping around Parker. Holding her in place as she pushes the face away from her chest and begs Zoe for help. Zoe yells at Zachery to get his hands off her girlfriend but it wasn't her brother when the head tilts back and laughs at the pain he is causing. The buzzed head of Vincent Gibson jeered at the woman fighting him.

Zoe tried to wash the image from her mind as she scrubbed the sweat from her skin in the shower. Tried to rinse away the screams from her mouth as she brushed her teeth. And tried to swallow the disappointment in herself as she chased four Motrin with a glass of water. Still Vincent Gibson's sneer wouldn't leave her.

He needed to leave though, because in a few hours she was going to destroy Everleigh Greyson so he could have justice. Because murder was never justifiable according to her father. Even though Zoe had spent the better part of the morning contemplating different methods to murder her brother and get away with it.

The courtroom was too bright for how tired Zoe was. The court reporter's fingers typed as Irene flipped through papers beside her. The jurors appeared as bored as Zoe, which she felt would play in her favor. An inattentive jury would wake up when she made the woman on the stand lash out at her. At least that was what Zoe was hoping for. Nia had walked her through how the older woman had broken the officer's calm demeanor when she was fourteen on the stand. Got the woman who now looked to be closer to six feet than Zoe was to let loose a verbal stream of cuss words that earned Nia's friend an acquittal.

Zoe kept Officer Greyson's file closed on the prosecution table. Her eyes were unable to focus on the pages due to sheer exhaustion.

"Officer Greyson, tell us about the night that you first met Olivia Moore," Landon Woods instructed.

The woman looked no different from every other time she'd sat on the stand as a witness for Zoe. This time she'd chosen the wrong side though. Forgotten she was meant to protect society, not help her mother make more money by standing in the way of justice. And it almost didn't seem to bother the officer, just like the court records from the juvenile trial transcripts Zoe read, where the woman helped more than fifty of the 3032s gang members get out of a drug charge and sent to Greyson's school.

The only sign of discomfort was how her hand rested on the neck of the Kevlar vest, periodically pulling it down. Zoe tried to ignore the familiarity of the action. Something Parker did every time she wore a shirt that touched her throat.

"It was 10:32pm. I was on patrol heading west on McDowell when I saw the defendant stagger off the sidewalk into the street and then back to the sidewalk. Her behavior was erratic, and I was concerned that she was going to hurt herself or someone else by walking into traffic," Officer Greyson explained.

"So, you stopped to check on her?" Woods stood on the opposite side of the room from where Officer Greyson sat alongside the jury. The space between them was so great that the jury would naturally pay attention to the witness over him.

"Yes." she answered, then looked at the jury. She was speaking directly to them.

"And what happened then," Woods prompted, walking casually towards Zoe's table.

"I approached her and asked if she was okay. She said her head hurt. She was squinting and just standing as she swayed slightly from side to side. I radioed dispatch for a DRE or Drug Recognition Expert," she looked to the jury, "because I suspected her to be under the influence."

"And was she under the influence?"

"Yes, later tests found she was under the influence of Rohypnol and Opiates."

"What happened next?"

"I asked her for identification. She said she didn't have any, so I asked her for her name. She told me her name was Olivia but refused to give me a last name. It was then that I noticed she was bleeding from her arm. My partner, Officer Stallard, radioed for Fire and Rescue."

"Officer Greyson, when your partner radioed for Fire and Rescue, how did Olivia respond?"

"She became agitated. She cried saying she didn't want any more pills and for anyone to touch her."

"Then what happened?"

Officer Greyson took a breath. Her eyes glassed over as she appeared to go back to the scene.

"She tried to run into traffic. I wrapped my arms around her, locking her arms to her chest, and pulled her back onto the sidewalk. She screamed at me to stop touching her and that she couldn't do it anymore. Then she threw her head back and broke my nose."

Woods moved to the defense table and leaned against it. Drawing the jury's attention. Zoe studied the way they followed him, and then she looked at the girl. Her eyes were on the floor, so it was impossible to see if she was crying, but the shake accompanying each breath didn't leave much to anyone's imagination.

"Besides the blood on her arm, what else did you notice?"

"She had bruises on her wrists, like she had struggled with someone."

"Like someone holding her down?"

"Yes."

"How dark were the bruises? Were they fresh, still red? Or were they dark, like they had been there for a while?"

"I don't remember."

He held up an enlarged photo of Olivia's wrist to the jury, and then walked it up close to Officer Greyson.

"Officer Greyson, is this an old bruise or a new bruise?"

"It's old."

"So, in your opinion, the cause of this bruise took place days before Vincent Gibson was killed."

"Yes."

"So, these marks could be evidence that Gibson was holding Moore against her will."

"Yes, it is possible."

"Could that explain the Rohypnol in her system?"

Zoe was on her feet, "Objection. Calls for the witness to speculate."

Judge Miller looked at Woods. "Sustained."

Woods smirked at Zoe with his back to the jury as he asked, "Officer, are you familiar with what Rohypnol is more commonly known as?"

"Yes."

"And can you tell the jury what it is most commonly referred to as?"

"A roofie or the Date Rape Drug."

Zoe knew where he was going. She knew the drug would be brought to the jury's attention; however, she didn't anticipate the looks of uneasiness on the jury's faces or the way Juror 3's eyes saddened as he stared at Olivia Moore.

"So, Olivia was walking down the street, day-old bruises on her wrists, and actively bleeding from a slice on her arm after being roofied?"

"Yes."

"Then what happened?"

"I waited for Fire with the defendant. When Fire arrived, they stated that she had excess blood on her," Officer Greyson explained.

Woods moved directly in front of the witness stand. Zoe was impressed with how he used his body to change the impact of his girlfriend's testimony.

"What does excess blood mean?" he asked.

"Olivia had more blood than they felt would come from the wound on her arm. She had fresh blood in her hair, spattered on her neck and forearm that would not have come from the wound on her arm."

"What did you do next?"

"I called for a crime scene tech."

Woods smiled at Officer Greyson. "I just have one last question, Officer Greyson. Since you were the first person to engage with Olivia, do you feel that she was physically strong enough to murder a grown man, a prison guard that was a foot taller than her and had one hundred pounds on her?"

"Objection. The witness cannot—" Zoe tried but was silenced when Officer Greyson chose to answer.

"No."

"Your honor," Zoe called out again, "The officer cannot possibly know what the defendant would or would not be capable of."

Judge Miller considered momentarily, and Zoe decided he was stalling. It didn't matter what he ruled. He'd given the jury enough time to chew over the idea coming from a witness in uniform testifying for the defense.

"The jury is ordered to disregard the witness's last statement."

"No more questions, your honor," Woods stated. He unbuttoned his jacket and sat down.

Judge Miller didn't look at Zoe. He looked at the witness on the stand with sad eyes. His chest fell as he said, "Ms. Robinson, your witness."

Zoe stood, pressing out the wrinkles in her black jacket and buttoning the top button. She opened the file filled with the life of Everleigh Blake Greyson.

She willed her hands to not shake and her head to commit. Justified that she had to do this to keep society safe from Olivia Moore. At any cost.

It didn't stop her heart pounding. It didn't stop a small voice in the back of her head saying, 'Don't do it.'

She took a few steps forward and turned back. Dilynn Greyson sat in the same seat she had been in since the start of the trial, only she wasn't staring at her phone like she had while Zoe's witnesses testified.

Blue eyes seemed to be pleading with Zoe. They crinkled at the edges, but she didn't break eye contact. Zoe could hear the woman begging her, even though Dilynn Greyson never said a word.

The frazzled blonde had interfered with justice too much already. Had probably sent Parker into the jury to force a mistrial. Built her wealth by pretending to care about those kids she housed at her school.

Zoe turned back to the jury. She reassured them with a smile as she pictured the carefully scripted and practiced words jotted on the legal pad. When she mentally made it through, she began.

"I met with Mr. Gibson's neighbors, friends, and co-workers. All said he was a good guy. Four of them sat in that same seat explaining how he was always trying to look out for the young girls living on the street."

She paused so the jury had time to remember that narrative of the deceased, then she gave them a specific detail to cling to. One that wasn't provided in earlier testimony because Brandon Collins, the shelter's owner, had declined the request to provide a character testimony.

"He spent one weekend a month at Open Doors Homeless Shelter serving food. He would use part of his pay to buy socks for the homeless. Like I said, a good guy. A guy who will be missed by Open Doors Shelter in need of volunteers, at his job where his dedication kept inmates safe, and by his friends."

Turning to face Officer Greyson, Zoe raised a single eyebrow. "But you sit on that stand casting doubt on his character."

"Objection, where's the question?" Woods called.

Judge Miller looked at Zoe from the corner of his eyes, his body still angled at Officer Greyson. He warned, "Ask a question, Ms. Robinson, or release the witness."

"You said the bruises on Ms. Moore's wrists were bruises at least a day old. You can't be certain that the victim, an upstanding citizen, ever put his hands on Olivia Moore before she killed him in his kitchen, can you?"

"No, but it's still likely," Officer Greyson stated.

Zoe scrunched her eyebrows theatrically. "I don't understand. You are claiming that it's likely the girl was restrained by Gibson for over twenty-four hours, roofied, then killed him an hour before she broke your nose?"

"Yes."

"And why is that, Officer Greyson?"

Officer Greyson growled, "Because young girls don't just brutally murder people for no reason. Abused kids who have no way out, they sometimes fight if they have no other choice."

Zoe willed herself to look at the jury. Convinced herself it would be easier to tell the truth if she was speaking to them, and not to the woman on the stand. One who had always been a critical witness in her prior cases. Something that wouldn't be possible once she was discredited.

"And you would know, wouldn't you?"

"I don't understand the question," Officer Greyson answered, but Zoe knew she would understand. This was her warning to get ready. The little piece of her soul left had convinced her to give it before it curled up into a ball and shut up like she told it to.

Zoe turned to find Officer Greyson staring at her mother.

"You don't know about vicious girls who attack innocent grown men and then cry rape. How could you not understand since you are one of them, aren't you?"

Zoe waited for a reaction. Waited for an objection. For the officer to cry. The scene she'd imagined coming true.

But Woods didn't object. She'd expected him to object, but he didn't. She had expected to argue. He was her fiancé. His high school sweetheart. He should be trying to stop this.

And she should be crying in her mommy bought uniform. She should be pleading for credibility. Yet she wasn't.

"No," the officer said, but it was weak. Officer Greyson's lips moved like she had more to say, but she didn't. Her eyes remained locked on her mother.

Zoe moved until she stood between the mother and daughter. Then, she waited for the stone-faced woman to look at her. To acknowledge that it was a mistake to come into her courtroom and try to blow up her chance at being the next District Attorney.

She did not look at Zoe though.

The air in the room was thicker, and Zoe had to take twice as many breaths to get the oxygen she needed. Zoe felt her face crack as her voice raised, "Officer Greyson, you claim that little girls can't get angry and lash out at people. Yet, you know firsthand that they can because as a teenager you did just that."

She paused. Pushed her frustration into the same space she'd locked away her conscience. Then she carefully continued at a steady pace of neutral cadence.

"You smashed your stepfather's car with a softball bat after getting drunk.

When he fought back, you swung at him. Then, you went to school the next day and cried rape to your teacher. You were so convincing that she paid for your lawyer. She paid to get you out of juvenile detention. And you got out because you are a great liar."

Zoe tapped the wooden bar separating herself from the jury.

"You got out of the assault charge. Then, you went right back to drinking while living in your new rich mother's home. So please explain to the jury how you know that little girls don't just snap and attack people."

Officer Greyson opened her eyes. Zoe could tell she wasn't looking at her, so she followed the line of sight directly to Olivia Moore.

Olivia Moore looked at the officer like she saw her.

When she went to turn back, Zoe scanned the jury. She understood why Woods didn't object. Two women in the front row of the jury stared at her through narrowed eyes. Juror 9's fists clenched around his notepad so tight that his knuckles were white.

'Don't worry, I hate me too.'

"Your honor, no more—" Zoe tried.

"No one believed me." Officer Greyson's gravelly voice cracked as each word came out slowly. "Even though I was covered in bruises. No one believed me because they said he was a good guy."

"Your honor," Zoe tried again. "I have no more qu—"

"You, Zoe Robinson, are the reason little girls try to and sometimes succeed in killing the person who beat them, raped them, tried to kill them. I can't even count the number of times I have sat in an interrogation room with you as you asked victims of abuse or domestic violence, who finally fought back, to explain why they didn't just ask for help. Why they fought back instead of pursuing legal action."

Zoe's gaze snapped toward the turquoise eyes that now looked her straight in the face. The woman's glare launched daggers towards Zoe, and she felt the first hit her in the chest at being blamed for girls getting raped.

"You, Zoe Robinson. You are the reason. Because they know that no one here will help them."

She felt shame rise in her, running over how she'd spent years blaming Parker for hurting her when it had been Zachery.

"It's why running into traffic is a better option than sitting on this stand pointing a finger at a good guy. It's why breaking a mirror off a car is the only way to get removed from their hands even after DCS comes. It's you and your boss and everyone else who covers up what they do because tearing apart a girl on a stand makes you feel safe."

Officer Greyson tugged at her vest once more, a little harder this time.

"The first thing that those good guys do is convince you that it's your fault that they hurt you. The second is tell you no one will believe you, even if you ask for help."

Judge Miller cleared his throat. "Officer Greyson, if you say another word, I will have to hold you in contempt of court."

Officer Everleigh Greyson wiped a single tear from her cheek. She looked Olivia Moore straight in the eye, and said, "Whatever he did to you, it wasn't your fault."

Judge Miller only lightly tapped his knocker to the heavy wooden desk. His jaw worked together slowly while the muttering in the courtroom grew to a low roar. He had to knock once more, but again there was enough time for the jury to sit with the testimony by the woman who hadn't screamed at Zoe. The woman who held her shoulder's higher as she looked at the kid in a way that said she wasn't going to let anyone hurt her.

"Bailiff, please take Officer Greyson into custody."

14

"Olivia, it's great to see you," Parker called with her mouth still full of Shrimp Maruchan when the door to the art building opened. She peeked around the corner to make sure she hadn't just made a fool of herself.

Olivia looked up for the first time since they had started their sessions. Parker attempted to not act surprised but felt it on her face that she failed.

"Uh... I thought today we would try painting. Just let me get rid of this." She waved the cup in the air, then turned abruptly. "Oh. I have another if you are hungry. I only eat the shrimp ones, and apparently that's weird. The chicken grosses me out though. It's the only kind you can get in Durango though. I had to wait a year to earn enough money to buy one, and now I can't stand it."

Sharing personal information was definitely against the rules. Nothing else had worked yet, so Parker felt sharing she got where Olivia was coming from might just get her to see there was life after juvie. Something she didn't think was possible for several years after being processed.

Pulling the spare cup of process noodles from the cabinet she'd put her lunch time stash in, she held it out to the teen. Olivia shook her head but tucked her hair behind her ears. She didn't have ear buds in, and she communicated.

"Well, here keep it for later then. I promise it doesn't even really taste like fish. Just salt and noodles."

The cup was taken from Parker's hand and turned as though Olivia had also not had time to earn enough money to buy one while locked up.

"Okay." Parker dumped the liquid into the sink, then dropped the cup in the trash as they walked to the art room.

Olivia ran her fingers over the brushes on the easel already set with the canvas.

"What... what do I do?" the girl half whispered.

Parker eyes grew, unsure what to do with a talking Olivia. She quickly gestured to the paints and handed her a pallet. "Choose whatever colors you want, and some white and black. You'll be able to create different shades then."

She picked up several shades of blue, examining each label before putting it back or setting it down.

"Are you looking for a particular color?" Parker asked.

Olivia set a lighter shade of blue down and picked up another. "My mom once said the color doesn't really matter, it's the name of the color." She checked another label and popped the lid. "Choose a name that means something."

"What's that one's name?"

"Pah... Pah-ill-A-deal..."

"Can you spell it?"

"P-H-I-L-A-D-E-L-P-H-I-A"

"Philadelphia," Parker provided.

"I been there." Olivia kept the bottle in her hand.

Olivia spelled several of the names for Parker when she couldn't just sound them out. It was hard for Parker to keep track of which ones Olivia kept, and which she put back, but blue was clearly the teen's favorite color.

Parker cataloged the information in her very thin mental file on the girl. Tried to remember to tell Olivia when they cleaned up that she just had to leave them on the edge so she could write down the names later.

When Olivia returned to the canvas, she sat staring at it. Parker knew not to rush her. This first painting would give her the greatest information about Olivia and what she'd gone through in her life, if Parker didn't rush it; however, her patience was wearing thin in the thick silence.

Rolling the brush between her fingers, Parker considered what she could do to get Olivia started before she lost her mind in the quiet.

The ceiling began to creak under the weight of the teenagers returning to their rooms on the floor above. Thumps from bags being dropped jolted Olivia, whose shoulders shrank to the ground. Tupac's voice found a pathway through the floor, fighting against the silence.

Their time was already up. Parker's session should be done. The girl had to know it too, and her chin fell as though she was just as disappointed in herself as Parker was at failing to make the big break through.

"School is over," Parker said quietly. Flipping her brush in her hand. "We can stay here if you want though. However long you want."

She could see the green eyes peeking out from under the hood. Olivia appeared to be searching Parker, before she turned back to the canvas. Quietly, she confessed, "I don't know how to paint. I... I think I know what I want to paint... but I don't know. It won't look good."

"Painting isn't about knowledge. It's about expressing yourself. There's no right or wrong," Parker said.

Olivia picked up a brush. "Am I supposed to talk while we do this? I'm supposed to talk to you, right?"

Parker chose a brush as well and flexed the bristles. "Would you like to talk?"

'Dumb ass questions. Shut the fuck up before she goes silent for another year.'

Olivia set down the flat brush, switched to the linear brush and dipped it in the palest color on her pallet. "Clouds shouldn't be hard, right?"

Parker hummed in agreement. Then added, "You can make them look however you want."

The water-based paint, thin tip, and Olivia's shaking hand left many crude sketch lines. Parker chewed on the end of her brush, watching as Olivia silently formed a rough circle a little higher than the center.

Parker pulled the brush from between her teeth when she felt the soft wood crunch. She'd ruined the kid talking with her stupid question and now she was going to sit here through another day in silence. She had six days before she was supposed to testify. And at this point, Parker had nothing to share.

"Did you come here because of me?" Olivia asked.

Parker considered the question, then realized she was ruining her opportunity again. "Uh, kind of. I actually met Mrs. Greyson a week before you loaned me that shirt. I was worried about taking the job though because I knew her daughter when we were younger, and we didn't get along. Then, the trial and everything... I didn't have anyone to talk to when I was on trial."

"She doesn't like you to call her that," Olivia stated.

With her head tilted to the side, Parker asked, "Who?"

"Greyson. Greyson and Trikru. No Miss or Missus." Olivia scraped her tongue against her teeth, then added. "They... they don't like it. Greyson or Trikru."

"Thank you," Parker said with a smile. "No one told me. I bet you learn a lot from watching people. Listening to them."

Olivia swirled her brush between blue then black, but quickly rinsed the paint off in the cup of water Parker had set up for her.

"Do... do you have friends here?" Olivia asked.

"Honestly, no," Parker confessed, hoping it would show Olivia honesty was safe here. "Ms. Ramirez seems nice and friendly, and she's pretty funny how she's always trying to make something explode. Earlier this week, I got hit by the Mentos and coke experiment."

"Marshall is her friend," Olivia stated. "They are sisters. Greyson doesn't like her."

"Ms. Ramirez?" Parker probed, learning a lot from the kid who'd spent a year watching and listening to everyone around her.

"Marshall. She doesn't like Marshall. Likes everyone else. Not Marshall though."

"Oh. How do you know?" Parker asked.

"There's a picture of Ms. Ramirez and her on Marshall's desk when they were my age, and they're always together."

"I meant that Greyson doesn't like Marshall."

Olivia glanced at the door as though she was checking to see if Dilynn was standing there.

"The air changes." Olivia licked her lips and continued to paint. "When Greyson comes in, Marshall looks like a question mark. And the air is hard to move in. Only in the book room. The air doesn't change in other rooms with

Greyson. Just with Greyson and Marshall. And Marshall wants her to like her."

"How do you know?"

Olivia glanced back again at the door. Even more quietly, she said, "She does everything Greyson says. Everything. She... she wouldn't have gotten in trouble like I did. I learned to do what I'm told, so I know Marshall is doing what she is told to not make Greyson angry."

Parker added Olivia's acute observation skills to the list of things to remember. She also made a note to pay a little closer attention at the next staff meeting to Charleigh Marshall. The woman had been kind every time Parker and her were in the same room, but she figured it was her own inability to talk to people that stopped the woman from engaging with her.

"Have you made any friends in your classes or your roommates?"

Olivia stared at the canvas as she added more paint. "Kinsley's nice but she's nice to everyone. She doesn't ask me questions. Everyone else is scared of me. They leave the kitchen if I go in there, so I just eat the Lunchables because people get scared when I use... utensils."

"Sounds like Kinsley is someone that would make a good friend."

Parker began at the center of her own canvas, mimicking the movements she'd watched Olivia make. Recreating the image, the girl was painting in an attempt to understand.

"What class do you like the best?" Parker asked.

Olivia held her brush still momentarily. "Reading with Mr. Johnson. I'm getting better. He says I'll be able to read the actual books that Ms. Marshall assigns soon."

Olivia blended a darker blue with white and covered her outlines as a cloud took its form. Parker used a random color on her pallet and continued to mimic the girl's movements.

"Have you lived in Phoenix your whole life?" Parker asked in an attempt to keep Olivia talking.

"No."

'No yes or no questions. Did you forget everything they taught you?'

"When did you come here?"

"After my mom died. My aunt and I moved from Pennsylvania."

"I'm sorry for your loss. When did she pass?"

Olivia added puffs on the top of the larger circle, like ears to a cloud face.

"I was ten, so I lived with my aunt."

The cloud had a face, then a rounded body. Arms stretched out. Then legs straight out.

"Where's your aunt now?"

Olivia started with the palest blue at the top corner, but she stopped. Choosing another shade, much darker she started to paint over the lighter color, the dark paint spreading faster and with less care. Each stroke blended the edges of the cloud until the cloud figure looked about to rain.

"Her boyfriend killed her because we left."

Olivia changed brushes. Added grey to the outline. Shaded the areas around the neck of the top of the cloud. Then shaded over the edges of the four extremity looking protrusions.

"I went to the shelter where I saw the people lined up. My aunt had a friend there, so I went there, and I found her like I was supposed to. She knew a guy that helped girls like me find a place to stay. She said it wasn't safe on the street. Said the cops would put me in a stupid foster home. My mom told me all about those places."

Olivia's cheeks reddened. She pulled closed the zip-up hoodie, even though a shine of sweat gathered on her forehead. She stared at the cloud with eyes but no smile.

"I don't want... He said that no one... I just want the voices..."

So many pieces to the puzzle were trying to come out of Olivia's mouth at once that Parker couldn't focus on one detail long enough to consider what Olivia was even trying to say, let alone follow the girl's movements on the canvas.

The girl jabbed the brush into the white then ground it against the canvas until the eyes were gone and the nose disappeared.

"No faces... Always foggy..."

She stabbed the brush into the darkest blue. The bristles smashed against the plastic pallet were pushed back to the canvas spreading them in every direction, like Olivia's words.

"So many voices."

She darkened the ears of the cloud figure, covering them until they ceased to exist. The figure, now blurry faced, sat surrounded by darkness. Alone.

Parker jumped when Olivia swiped at the cloud, disconnecting what would have been the head from the rest of it.

Then again.

And again.

Each strike was harder and faster than the last. Her hand swiped in a wild arc over the canvas. Each contact wiped away the original figure. The cloud disappeared into darkness one sliver at a time. When there was no light left to aim at, she penetrated the canvas with a vengeful thrust.

The material screamed as it split open, globs of paint dripping to the floor one smack at a time.

Olivia's paints dropped to the already speckled floor as she hit the ground. With the ruined brush still clasped in her hand, she pulled at her dirty hair trying to rip it from her head. Her cries caught in her throat but were still enough to drown out Tupac.

Parker wiped away a tear from her cheek, slid down from her chair and sat next to Olivia rocking herself on the cold floor.

The brush clanked against the concrete as it fell from the girl's quivering hand. Olivia's hands spread tears, snot, and pitch colored paint down her cheeks.

The house creaked as the occupants above them stomped out of the room. Their steps shook the paintings on the walls Parker had hung as they left the building with a slam of the door.

Parker watched the pool of paint forming on the floor from the droplets falling from the painting. Carefully, she asked, "When you look at your piece, how does it make you feel?"

Her tone flat, the girl asked, "What am I supposed to feel?"

Parker remembered sitting with Nia Williams when she thought the woman had cared about her. She'd asked the lawyer preparing to prosecute her parents the same question. Only Nia had done it wrong, telling Parker she should be angry. That she should feel betrayed and scared of what would happen to her when she became an adult, and her father came after her. She hadn't understood that all his victims looked exactly like her only later in her life. By then she was too angry with Nia. Too betrayed and scared of how the woman had used her. It was when she decided to study psychology. To learn how to talk to kids who might be angry, scared, or betrayed so they could decide for themselves and not ever feel like she was manipulating them. That she could be trusted.

"Feelings come from inside you. No one can tell you what to feel. They can only tell you what they think you feel."

Olivia's eyes fixed on the battered canvas. She moved her mouth as though she was trying to say something, but nothing came out.

"I'm going to list some words, and you stop me if the word feels right."

Olivia nodded.

"Alone."

The girl didn't move.

"Angry."

She blinked a few times but gave no indication that Parker should stop.

"Disappointed."

Olivia looked away from the canvas.

"Okay, so disappointed. What do you feel disappointed in?"

With eyes trained on the corner of the room, Olivia whispered, "I made a promise."

"What was the promise?"

"To keep my mouth shut," Olivia said through gritted teeth.

Parker began to ask another 'what' question, but her mind flashed to Lyra swirling a beer as she said: 'why is the only way to calm the chaos.'

"Olivia, why did you promise to keep your mouth shut?"

Olivia licked her cracked lips and turned to Parker. Her emerald eyes looked at her unblinking as she whispered, "I killed him."

Parker felt the shift in the air. The chaos Lyra had promised was settling, and Olivia breathed. Tears welled in her eyes, but they didn't fall.

"I killed him and I'm not even sorry he's dead because..."

Parker waited.

Waited as Olivia lifted her hands palms up. She looked over the paint that covered her fingers as they hung cupped in the air. Then she nodded, the tears evaporating without collapsing the dam.

"Everyone is safe now," the girl whispered, nodding again.

Parker chewed on the word 'everyone.' The word had seemed deliberate, but if she was wrong then it meant something else was going on with the girl. The way her face shifted with each turn of phrase was disconcerting.

"Olivia, was someone else in the house with you?"

Olivia looked back at the painting. Her eyes scanned over it like she'd never seen it before. She reached out and touched the pool of blue paint, rubbing it between two fingers.

Casually, the girl explained, "He wasn't going to touch her. I'm stronger. I can take it, but she wouldn't stop crying. He tried to take her, so I stopped him."

"Who is her?" Parker asked slowly.

"She couldn't take care of herself. It was my job to take care of her, so I did. I kept her safe and when I go to jail, she'll still be safe."

Questions flooded Parker's mouth. She tried several out silently, but none were right. She knew she was running out of time when the girl stood up.

Olivia's shoulders had risen from her normal hunched position. She moved about the room gathering paper towels, cleaning the spilled paint, rinsing out her brushes, and scrubbing the paint from the pallet. She saved the damaged painting for last.

"What does she look like?" Parker asked.

Olivia licked her lips as she carefully picked up the canvas and walked it slowly to the trash. She stared at it for several moments, then softly placed it in the bin.

"She had so much hair. Green eyes. And dimples."

The girl turned and made eye contact directly with Parker. The pitch streaks now hardened into a mask. Her green eyes set, the softness and uncertainty gone. Her lips parted in a reminiscent smile, just enough to show her two dimples.

15

The receipt for Officer Greyson's contempt of court fine was paper, not soap. Zoe couldn't use it to wash away what she'd said. It was just a thin paper that had sliced her thumb in the crease, causing her to hiss.

She hadn't waited for Officer Greyson to be released. The paper cut was clearly a warning to run away before the woman's patience broke and the violent disposition appeared as finally promised. Zoe knew she probably should have left the woman there and let Dilynn Greyson get her out. Woods could bring up Zoe's remorse in court. Use it against her.

The jury was already against her. She didn't even have to look at them to feel the way their collective breath was trying to push her to the other side of the room. Losing the jury was losing the case. That part of her soul she'd locked away behind the closet door was whispering through the keyhole.

'You saw her. You saw them both. You saw them all.'

She didn't know who her was. There were so many hers. So many females who were against her, like she wasn't on their team. Like she didn't understand bad things happened to women, which was why she wanted to be the District Attorney. That was how she would make sure the people who hurt whoever the 'her' the voice was talking about were put away.

'I did it to protect people,' she told herself.

Shaking her head, she declared that she was not going insane. Too much work had been done. Too much had been sacrificed to get her to this point.

"I am protecting everyone," she said aloud to her reflection in the elevator. "I am keeping people safe."

That part of her that said she was wrong for what she planned to do to the officer screamed through the keyhole. Then it began pounding on the closet door in her head.

She barely made it back to her office before the pounding in her head shifted to her heart. Her body shook with each hit. That part of herself she didn't need right now was going to get through the barricade if she didn't get some back up.

She called Nia.

Called Nia again when she didn't answer.

Then again when she was sent to voicemail.

And again, but it only rang once.

And again.

And again.

Zoe squeezed the phone, so she didn't dial for a seventh time. Seven was her lucky number, but she knew this wasn't her lucky day. With both hands wrapped tightly around the device, she fought the urge to throw it through the seventh-floor window.

She shook the device and growled at the ceiling, "Where the fuck is she?"

Nia hadn't answered one of Zoe's calls since Everleigh Greyson was taken into custody. With everything riding on this, Zoe had expected Nia to be there. Maybe if she had been there Zoe wouldn't be second guessing everything that had happened.

She'd done what Nia had asked. She'd made the Greyson daughter look like a liar, which according to Nia, she was.

'You knew it was wrong and you did it anyways.'

Zoe tried to swallow the guilt, but her throat refused to let her push it down. Instead, acid pushed the wickedness back to her tongue, where the sour slime stuck to the roof of her mouth and teeth.

'Nia treated Ari like shit her whole life, did you really think you were special?'

She had thought that. Believed Nia chose her because Zoe had proven herself. And Nia had said the gay thing wasn't an issue. Even told her to get a girlfriend.

'Go talk to Lyra. Lyra will know what to do,' the voice offered. The first helpful thing her brain had come up with so far.

The woman was one floor away. After a quick stop to the restroom, where she repeatedly tried to rinse the repulsive taste of remorse from her mouth, she took the elevator down to the sixth floor and walked along the corridor looking for Lyra's name.

Lyra didn't have an office on the sixth floor according to any of the doors. Zoe sighed, wondering if Lyra would even want to see her. Parker hadn't wanted to see her but that was because she'd waited too long to apologize. She decided with Lyra there was still a chance to make things right.

The mirrored finish of the elevator door gave Zoe the opportunity to fix the smeared eyeliner on the top of her eyelid. She unbuttoned the top button of her shirt. Lastly, she unwound the tight bun from the base of her neck, and let the dark locks unwrap. Her fingers carded through the denser portions until her shoulders and upper back were covered.

The fifth floor looked exactly like the sixth, so it made sense Zoe had gotten them confused. It's not like she had been down to Kiddie Courtland before. As she made her way down the hall, searching each of the names of the closed and dark offices, she realized Lyra probably went home.

'No, she was always working late. A workaholic like me.'

She had to try though. If nothing else, she'll find the office and come back tomorrow to ask her to dinner or surprise her with lunch. Zoe got to the end of the hall and still had not found Lyra's office. She stopped at the end and looked right and then left. There were offices on each end, but only one door was open.

She took a step, but the heel of her shoe slipped on the smooth wax floor. Searing pain shot up her calf as Zoe's ankle popped. Barely catching herself on the wall, Zoe choked on the pain.

With eyes pinched shut, she took a test step. The pain was there, but not as bad. She could make it back to her office and change her shoes so it would not suck as bad walking through the parking garage.

A cell phone rang within the office a few doors down. Zoe stopped when she heard Lyra, "Hey, Mom. Yeah, I'm still at the office.... Yeah, I heard... I'll get the pie on my way.... Yes, I'll pick up Sadie too... Hey, I love you and we'll get her through this... Okay, see you soon."

Zoe limped her way to the open door.

Lyra didn't look up from the yellow pad. Her hand paused momentarily but then continued jotting down notes. When she reached the bottom of the page, she flipped to the next and kept writing.

"I'm busy, Zoe," Lyra stated just as Zoe raised her hand to knock.

Zoe glanced at the door jamb wondering momentarily if she had knocked and not realized that she had knocked. Her hand dropped to her side.

"How'd you know it was me?"

"You can't walk in heels. Never could, so your steps are uneven."

Zoe nodded at the information and smiled that Lyra had taken the time to learn her walk. It gave her hope Lyra still cared about the possibility of something between them.

"Why are you here?" Lyra asked.

Zoe's brows scrunched in the middle. 'Why do women keep asking me that?'

Her gaze drifted around the office she'd never visited before. She pulled on the bottom of her jacket, unsure of what to do with her hands or any part of her body since Lyra still hadn't looked at her.

"I wanted to see you."

Lyra peeked over the top of a pair of black metal frames, then cast her eyes back to her notes. "Why?"

"I missed you."

Lyra set her pencil down, followed by her glasses.

"Me?"

"Yes, you. I missed telling you about my day, and I thought—"

The chair squeaked in protest as Lyra leaned back, her hands folding over her chest.

"You what, Zoe? Thought that since you had a bad day, I would feel sorry for you. Bend over so you could fuck me on my desk and call it the change of venue I asked for."

"Look Lyra." Zoe moved towards the seated woman. Made her way around the desk and pulled Lyra's chair out from under the table. Her eyes fell to the metal brace running up Lyra's leg.

'I literally know nothing about her.'

Zoe swallowed. She'd have to digest the new knowledge that Lyra wouldn't be able to dance at a fundraising event later. Right now, Zoe needed to make peace. Needed to commit to being a better person for Lyra.

"I messed up. I didn't realize how much I want you in my life until you weren't there. I can't promise that I will stop working late, but I can give you what you asked for. I can do real dates. I can do sleepovers. I would like to show you the best of me since you already know the worst of me."

Lyra rolled her eyes. "I do now. "

"Now?"

Lyra pushed up from her chair, sending Zoe backwards.

"You know when I first met you, I was awestruck. This intelligent, beautiful woman stood before me. I bet you don't even remember the first time we met because if you had, you probably would have more sense than to be coming to my door tonight."

"I... uh." Zoe's fingers fidgeted with the bottom of her blazer. Her mind flashed through the first time she remembered Lyra.

"Go ahead, tell me. Where did we first meet?"

'She can't think I forgot.'

But the look on Lyra's face told Zoe Lyra thought just that. Zoe swallowed the excess saliva in her mouth, trying to think if there was anything she may have missed.

Lyra leaned against the desk, and Zoe realized that Lyra always made it a point to sit or lean against something in her presence.

'She doesn't think I would accept her disability.'

With a tilt of her head, Zoe considered how to make Lyra know she still thought she was beautiful. She reached out and took Lyra's delicate fingers in her own. She rubbed her thumb over the warm skin as she started at the beginning.

"We ran into each other in the elevator. You were calling for me to hold the door. But then when you got to the door, you tripped."

She looked into Lyra's eyes and lied. "I caught you. Your hands grabbed my arms... and I know this is going to sound dumb, but I swear I had never been so warm before."

Lyra rolled her eyes again but didn't pull her hand away. She squeezed Zoe's fingers instead, which encouraged her to continue.

"You had dropped your coffee on my briefcase and offered to help me rewrite my special file of notes that had gotten ruined. That whole day, I was so worried that you were straight and that I was being stupid that a woman like you would possibly consider me as something more than a co-worker."

Zoe stepped in front of Lyra and placed her hands on the thin hips.

"I ... I wasn't sure how to talk to you when you arrived, so I kept fumbling over my words." With a head thrown back, Zoe laughed. "I must have sounded like a mumbling idiot. You were just so cool. I know that's stupid and again cliche, but it was like nothing could rattle you. And it was intoxicating."

Zoe rested her head against Lyra's and inhaled the soft coconut and lime tropics. "I became addicted to your presence so quickly. Just being in the same room made everything that was going on in the world, all the hurt and the pain and the death that I see every day just disappear. So, I took a chance, and I kissed you."

They breathed together, neither suffocating the other.

"I couldn't stop kissing you because it was more important than breathing, and it still is. I haven't been able to sleep. I've sat in my office every night thinking about where you were, what you were doing."

Zoe placed a hand on Lyra's jaw, holding it softly.

"I know I messed up, but if you need more, then I can try to give you more. You need dinner that doesn't get Doordashed to my office, then we can go get those tacos you like. I never considered that you would want anything like that from me, and when you offered it, I was afraid."

Her thumb stroked the smooth skin of Lyra's cheek.

"Please, honey. Just give me a chance to show you."

"You just did."

Zoe couldn't stop the smile from spreading across her face.

"You showed me, you have no idea who I am. Or that the first time we met was at a fundraiser thrown by my mother. Dilynn Greyson."

All of the air was forced from Zoe's lungs as Lyra's knee slammed into her sensitive core. She staggered backwards into the wall of bookcases behind Lyra's desk. Finding a grip on a shelf, Zoe held herself up as she turned back to Lyra.

"Or that the cop on the stand that you attacked today is my sister. And how about how you stood in court today and used your power to protect the good ol' boys and blame the child victim."

Zoe tried to stand but her whole body protested.

Lyra walked around the desk with only the slightest limp. She turned back to Zoe still trying to regain her composure.

"You know it's shit like that..." Lyra stopped and shook her head. "Your privileged ass couldn't know. Anyone that knows could never say what you said. Could never do what you did. Because the abuse fucks you up for fucking life."

Lyra lifted her chin and stared at Zoe. She sucked her teeth then shut her mouth. After several blinks, she said, "When I first met my mom, I was barely eighteen and I tried to get her to fuck me so that I could stay in her world for one night." Lyra held up a single finger. "Just one night."

Tears slowly trailed down her cheeks, "I convinced myself that if I was a good enough lay, then maybe she'd let me stay longer. I had to give her something and it was all I had to offer. Because I had never met a decent human being before then."

Lyra wiped away the tears with the back of her hand.

"My own biological mother tried to sell me to her drug dealer when I was ten. And I showed up on Dilynn Greyson's front doorstep after I'd just ruined her life by fucking her fiancé for two years. He was a fucking youth counselor. Another one of those good guys that little girls try to ruin with their lies." The laugh that came from Lyra splattered her pain against the office walls. "Yeah, he was a real good guy that spent his days helping young girls in foster care, and then he came back to his secret apartment, drink a few beers, smack me around, and tell me I was lucky to have someone like him."

Zoe couldn't move, couldn't look away.

Lyra's eyes narrowed, and spit flew from her mouth with each following word. "And Evie. Evie was twelve years old. Twelve years old when her stepfather raped her on Christmas Eve."

Lyra's upper lip curled, revealing her teeth. "Christmas fucking Eve a kid should be watching The Grinch and waiting up to see if maybe Santa really is real. Did your background check tell you she lived in hell for two years? Or that your idol, Nia, let that asshole get away with it because he paid for her campaign?"

"Lyra, I—" Lyra held up her hand, slicing Zoe's sentence off.

"If you're not planning on confessing that you are a complete and utter piece of fucking trash, then don't even finish that sentence."

Zoe opened and closed her mouth. Her chest was so filled with rage she could barely breathe. The more she tried to think of a way to make this right, the more her words twisted into knots before they reached her tongue.

Her head hung as she whispered, "I'm sorry."

The toxic laugh that broke through Lyra's lips, permeated the air. Bile rose in the back of Zoe's throat, as Lyra hissed, "Sorry for what? Treating me like a fucktoy? Treating my sister like garbage? Or because you let Nia play you like a fucking fiddle?"

Zoe closed her eyes.

She rewatched Parker walking away with her head hung and shoulders slumped through the dark parking lot as she laughed. Rewatched Lyra unable to make eye contact with her while she put her clothes back on. Rewatched the smile grow across Nia's face as she told her, 'You're the perfect person for the job.'

She opened her eyes to find Lyra leaning against the window frame. Her tears had returned, and Zoe wondered how many times she hadn't noticed Lyra silently crying.

"I'm a piece of trash," she whispered.

Lyra shook her head.

"Just go."

Zoe ran her fingertips over the raised letters on the door, Lyra Trikru-Greyson, as she left. The clicks of her heels on the marble floor echoed down the empty hall.

Her ankle hurt. Her crotch hurt. Her pride hurt. But more than any of that, her heart hurt at how she'd let herself be manipulated into hurting others.

The elevator opened as soon as she'd hit the button, like it had known to wait for her. She stared at her reflection, recategorizing the people in her life into two files. She labeled one fix and one break.

'Lyra, fix.'

'Everleigh Greyson, fix.'

'Nia, break.'

'Ari, fix.'

'Parker, fix.'

'Zackery, break.'

The elevator dinged as it opened to the seventh floor.

Zoe pulled off her shoes and padded silently down the hallway. When she opened her office door, her eyes landed on the green-eyed teenager's blank stare.

'Olivia Moore. Fix.'

16

Parker heard Dilynn on the phone making her way to the art room. She quickly finished laying out each of the drawings Charleigh Marshall had given her on the table, and then leaned over them to appear busy. Turning only when she heard Dilynn directly behind her, Parker put on her work smile for the woman who hadn't yet looked in her direction.

"You're making it more complicated than it needs to be," Dilynn chastised. "The teacher is not going to check your sources to make sure that every article you cited is perfect. Stop looking for the perfect quote and find one that sorta works. Explain then how it works."

Dilynn set a large bag on an empty table in the room before looking over at Parker. She pointed to the bag then to Parker.

"For you," she mouthed.

Parker made her way over to the table and opened the bag expecting to find new supplies she hadn't yet requested. Instead, she found multiple shoe boxes.

"Hold on, baby." Dilynn put the phone to her chest. "What you don't like, I can return."

Putting the phone back to her ear, she said, "Just write the paper and then I can help you fix it, Sadie. I have to go." And then, "I love you, too."

The first box Parker pulled out of the bag contained a pair of Cale Hann black classic heels. They were sleek and similar to the pair Parker had snapped in two the last time she'd seen Dilynn.

Dilynn flopped down onto a stool and watched Parker look over the shoe.

"Okay, I know it's weird, but I totally made Alex check the size of the pair you broke, so they all should fit."

"I can't—"

Dilynn raised her eyebrows at Parker and then looked down at the faded black Tom's on her feet currently held together with black Duct tape. "You're right. You can't go to court in taped together shoes."

Parker pulled out the next box, this time revealing a pair of black Steve Madden Troopa Boots. This pair was a minimum of $70, and Parker knew that because she looked at them every time she went to the outlet mall.

"Mrs. Greyson, you already gave me a job and a bonus that came from a personal checking account."

"And I cosigned for an apartment for Charleigh and Mona when they first started here. I paid for Andrew's educator certification test and fingerprint clearance card when he was completing his reading certification. So, really this is the least that I can do."

Parker ran her finger down over the smooth leather toe of the boot. Remembering Alex's warning that Dilynn would just get more extreme if she didn't give in, she said, "Thank you."

A smile spread across the older woman's face, revealing perfectly aligned teeth. "I consider this place a second home. All the kids and the staff are members of the Trikru-Greyson family, so expect to be treated like such."

"Why is the school only named after you?" The question was out before Parker thought about how rude she must sound.

"Alex and I have different passions and... well, this venture began and I had a partner that insisted the school was in my name. My partner, Ms. Winters comes by occasionally so you will meet her. But she promised me when we were together she would help me when I was ready to make my dream come true. Alex and I had barely met, and they came with me to help me get it started. But at that point it was just me."

Parker sat down and pulled off the Toms. She fixed the laces of the boots to run all the way up, before putting them on as Dilynn continued to explain.

"After we got married, we kept our own last names because a lot of the kids we bring here... well, their parents think they are sending them to a conversion camp. It's easier to play off when we are not tied by name. They are also very insecure about money. The shortest answer is that they are insecure about our distribution of wealth, but the truth is we built the school when Alex was still groveling for being a catfish. This is my dream, not theirs. And my business partner insisted this was my legacy, so I needed to put my name on it. Originally, I was going to name it something dumb like Second Chances or Refuge, but Sylvia told me, and I quote, 'Pull your head out of your ass.'"

Parker mulled over the information, before stating, "I dated someone that came from money in college. I tried to hide my lack of it but found just going to places and doing things with her was like culture shock."

Dilynn nodded again. "Yeah. Growing up with or without money really does impact someone's approach to the world. For example, Evie and Sadie spent most of their adolescence with me so when we go shopping, they never look at a price tag and just pick out everything they want. I can't even imagine how Levi is going to be since I didn't get my girls until they were teenagers. Lyra, on the other hand, price checks everything, and shares Alex's penny-pinching skills."

"That's why Lyra calls Evie a spoiled brat?"

"I used retail therapy too much with Evie because I wasn't trying to be her mom when I first got custody of her. I just wanted her to stop hating me and when I bought her things she smiled. I honestly didn't become a parent until Lyra, Sadie, and Alex came into our lives."

Parker held up the boots that she still had yet to put on her feet. "So, you are trying to be my friend?"

Dilynn tilted her head as she looked at the door. She chewed on the inside of her lip, then rubbed her face. She took her time like it wasn't two hours since she should have been home getting ready for job number 2.

The woman cleared her throat before she answered. "I didn't think of it like that because honestly when I was shopping for you, I was thinking about how I wished I would have met you before you were in that place with Evie. And..." She held up her hands, "I won't pretend to know you, but I know a little about Marissa, I mean Echo, and she said that you were her only family so I imagined that you were probably in the same boat, like my girls cling to each other, and I just thought that I wished I'd known you so you wouldn't have had to go through so much in your life. Plus, I realized why I recognize you. You were waiting by the bus stop when I came to pick up Evie from Durango. She told me I should have chosen you instead of her, and I was going to offer to take you where you needed to be, but you took off. So, I guess it was more of a mom gesture than a friend gesture because you should have someone to look out for you."

Parker counted the stitches running across the toe of the boots in her hands. She had forgotten about the blonde who'd come to get Evie. A part of her had been envious that someone as terrible as Evie had a mom who clearly cared about her when she'd had no one. She was good having no one when she watched the white car flip around and come towards her. Moved to hide behind the tree until the car drove away.

"Do you have contact with your mom?" Dilynn asked.

Brown eyes raised to meet the woman seated across from her. The woman's promise not to ask questions apparently no longer existed. No one had asked her about her mom in so long, and a part of her felt like Dilynn knowing and asking was different than the creepers who showed up when she was younger.

"I don't. She's in prison." Parker unzipped the inside of the shoe and pushed her foot in. "She... She basically helped my dad kill all of those women. They... well the FBI people that, like, study serial killers do these, like, interviews and they explained that she'd been, like, brainwashed into thinking that if she didn't help him, then he would kill her."

"I'm so sorry, Parker."

"You know the weird thing was, we were just like every other family in the neighborhood. I mean except that we were happier. Like the front they put on was so real when everything happened, I thought something entirely different was going on."

Dilynn got up from her chair and moved to hug Parker. But Parker got up and took a step back. She waved at Olivia's work. "I'm sorry. I just... Can we... um... talk about Olivia?"

"Yes, of course." Dilynn didn't move though. "But..."

Parker looked up from the floor she was studying.

"You're not alone, okay. I'm here if you want to talk. Alex is here. You need anything, we're here for you."

The tightness in Parker's chest made it difficult to breathe. She bit her lip to keep it from trembling as she begged the tears not to fall. It only made her need to cry worse.

'Get your shit together.'

She listened to Dilynn's footsteps shuffle to the other side of the room. The air around her pressed against all sides of her body. She willed herself to breathe. To take in as much air as possible and then slowly breathed out through her nose.

"You said in your email that Olivia did a painting and while she did it, you made a copy of her motions. So, this is what she worked on until she... shifted?"

Parker looked up to where Dilynn was pointing at the original. She reheard the canvas's protest against the brush being forced through the material.

"That's a nice way of putting it," she said with a shake of her head.

Her feet moved easily in the comfort of the new shoes as she made her way over to Dilynn and the paintings. Her hand covered her mouth as she considered holding back. Then she breathed and confessed. "I gotta tell you, I have been in... well, you know.... but I have never been as scared as I was when she stabbed that painting. It was like someone else was in control other than the kid that I had been working with."

Dilynn looked over Olivia's piece. "Court yesterday was tough. Actually, it was horrible. That prosecutor, Zoe Robinson, is a bitch."

Parker snorted. "Oh, I know."

"What?" Dilynn asked with raised eyebrows.

"I'm sorry. I just... never imagined you to be a swearing kind of person. You seem like all Mother Teresa."

"Only at work, hun." Dilynn rolled her eyes. "Or when Alex is around. The rest of us lowly Greysons were meant to be pirates on the open seas. Actually, that's a great idea."

Dilynn pulled out her phone from the oversized cardigan. She tapped against the screen quickly before depositing it back into her pocket. "Sorry, I have to write it down or I will forget."

With a nod, Parker said, "Lyra said you write novels. She even bought me one of them. It was your first one."

"Yeah, it's how I deal with all of the world's shit."

Parker smiled at the second swear word.

"I have actually been meaning to talk with you about Lyra."

That smile fell.

'Shit. Of course, she wouldn't want her daughter to date the kid of a serial killer.'

"When I met her, I didn't know she was your daughter, or I wouldn't have—" Parker tried to explain. "She was so persistent though."

Dilynn held up a hand. "No. No, Parker, I am not trying to... Fuck. Let me start this over again."

With a step back, Dilynn pushed her body up onto the tabletop. She huffed and shook her head. Her tiny feet kicked back and forth.

"I didn't mean to imply that you can't date my daughter. I am happy that Lyra and you met, and that you enjoy each other's company. It's just... oh my god, how do I ever write when I can't even speak?"

Parker bit her lower lip, not sure if she was supposed to respond or not.

Dilynn's hands rubbed up and down her face, smearing her eye liner under her eyes like a cheap robber's mask. She smiled when she looked up at Parker.

"So, Lyra is the strongest of all of us Greysons. She is the kindest. She is the most accepting. She is the one that when the mis-match patches of our family start to tatter, she just swoops in with a needle and thread and sews everything back together."

"She hides her pain and vulnerability the most," Parker interjected her own opinion.

Dilynn's hands shot towards Parker, causing Parker to jump back. "Exactly!" she exclaimed. "When shit gets hard, you won't even see her break a sweat. Even after the accident and her leg... she just pushed through with a constant smile on her face."

Her hands dropped from the air, and Parker found it easier to breathe without Dilynn flailing around.

"She refuses to ask for help," Dilynn said.

Parker scrunched up her lips. "She doesn't want pity."

"I am glad you recognize that. You're going to have to let her do things even when you don't think she can do them. You're going to have to support her problem solving."

"You know we haven't even been on a date yet, right?" Parker asked.

With a shrug of the shoulders, Dilynn sighed. "I know." She held her hands up as though she was trying to stop herself. "I know it's just that this is more complicated than her just meeting someone. You're a part of our family so it's not as simple."

Parker quirked an eyebrow, "So don't break her heart?"

"Actually, I was going to go with don't rush into anything. And..." Dilynn bit her lip. "Just break her heart quickly if you're going to do it. Don't drag it out. Don't try to make it work because of your job because she's looking for the long term. And if you're not feeling it, then please just don't lead her on."

Parker scanned the room, then the new boots. When she raised her eyes, she was met with pleading ocean blue eyes.

"It took me a week to call you about a job I needed so desperately that I was going to the food bank for food boxes. I'm not the rushing kind."

"Yes, but my daughter is."

Parker swallowed the information and felt it sit in her throat.

"Lyra has accomplished so much and she's looking for the next stage of her life. Her sister is already there, and any day now Landon is going to propose—"

Parker held up a hand, cutting Dilynn off as though she'd learned the secret method of slicing sentences through observation alone from the older woman.

"Landon, as in your lawyer, Landon Woods?" Parker asked.

"Yes, he and Evie have been together since high school."

Parker carded her fingers through her hair. With eyes on the ground, she tried to put all of the pieces of Dilynn's run-on sentences together with the fragments to understand what Dilynn was suggesting.

Her fingers pressed into the center of her forehead as she tried to push away the potential headache from all of the what ifs and if-thens ricocheting around her brain.

"So, when Evie gets engaged," Parker swallowed. "Lyra will be looking to do the same thing. But Lyra made it sound like Evie was the co-dependent one."

"I'm sure she did, and a part of her is convinced that she only does the things she does to make sure Evie is okay and happy. She doesn't think anyone sees her and that she has to always be strong, but I'm her mother. I know, and I have to do what I can to protect her. To keep people from hurting her, at all costs."

'I have to do what I can to protect her.'

Parker looked at the paintings. Her mouth opened. Then she closed it. She pointed to her copy of Olivia's work and traced an imaginary outline to the figure. Then she tapped her finger to her mouth as Dilynn's words played in her head again.

'I have to do what I can to protect her. I'm her mother.'

"Parker?" Dilynn called, but her voice sounded like it was at the end of a tunnel.

The shelves holding the paint called to Parker. She'd watched Olivia pick up the bottles and read the label. The ones she didn't like, she put back where she'd found them. The ones she had chosen, ended up gathered at the end of the shelf.

Parker turned back to Dilynn.

"I'm sorry, I don't mean to change the subject but what you just said. I was going about this all wrong."

She picked up the bottle and read the names of the colors aloud.

"Borrowed light. Dodger Blue. Distance. Brittany Blue. Philadelphia Sky"

"Are those the names of the paints?" Dilynn asked.

"Olivia picked the colors based on the name. She's originally from

Pennsylvania so Philadelphia makes sense. Dodger, she was on the run."

Dilynn repeated, "Borrowed light, distance, and Brittany."

"Olivia.... She said she had to protect her." Parker's hands came up and pulled at the roots of her hair for missing the obvious. "I thought she was talking about herself."

"Like a split personality?" Dilynn asked.

"Yeah, that is what I thought." Parker moved back to the canvas with her outline. "But what if..."

She took a marker from the table where Dilynn remained perched. She quickly drew an outline around the whole image.

"Sorry. I am so stupid. How did I not think of this?" Parker said to herself.

"What?" Dilynn asked.

Parker added eyes and a mouth that she remembered seeing Olivia draw but missed putting on her own canvas.

"When a teen works on their first piece," Parker explained as she added a nose. "It never fails that they look to create something for someone else."

Holding up the canvas to Dilynn, Parker asked, "What does that look like to you?"

"Like something you'd hang in a nursery."

The air settled for the first time since Dilynn had entered the room. The chaos ceased just momentarily as Parker clung to the answer to why Olivia killed a man.

She swallowed. "The key to this whole trial was never if Olivia killed Gibson. She told me flat out that she did. What never made sense was why she did it. What if Olivia wasn't trying to protect herself? What if she killed that man because she was trying to protect her child?"

"Like a baby?"

Parker nodded. "She said she had to protect her. When I asked her to describe what her looked like, she said lots of hair, green eyes and dimples. That may be the only image she has of her child, and he took the baby from her."

"Why didn't I... I should have..." Dilynn's hand raised to her lips. From behind her fingers, the woman whispered, "Olivia has a baby, which means she was fourteen when..."

A knot twisted in Parker's stomach.

"She said she couldn't let him touch her. She was strong and she could take it, but she couldn't let him touch her."

Dilynn's pale face turned and met Parker's eyes.

"Evie was the one that arrested her. She didn't have a baby with her. Evie wouldn't have missed a fucking baby. So, where's the child now?"

17

The metal chair rocked against the uneven paving stones outside of Pizzeria Bianco with every move Zoe made. The September air stagnantly sagged around her as she stared at the half empty wine glass. From the small table, she watched couples approach hand in hand and groups of friends laugh as they gathered for a get together.

She scanned the half-eaten pizza in front of her. It was good, but she found herself unable to finish. Not when her stomach was punishing her for all the pain she'd caused.

Her mind replayed the look on Evie Greyson's face when Zoe called her—the star witness on so many of her cases— a liar. When that didn't make her feel shitty enough, Lyra's silent tears dripping from her chin came to the forefront of her mind. The sisters each overcame the types of struggles that would make a tear-jerking Netflix movie, where Zoe would undoubtedly be the villain.

A part of her wondered if she had the ability to flip her story. If the movie was about her and dating, instead of the sisters' struggles, she would probably never recover in the fans eyes after Ari, Parker, and Lyra were all treated like crap in a bullshit attempt to protect her future. The women, including Ari who'd been cast aside by everyone in her life, were testaments of what Olivia Moore could do if given the chance.

Zoe knew she would never fully understand their struggle. Not when she had been praised for never having to struggle because sports and academics came easy to her. She was handed every opportunity under the condition she didn't announce her sexuality in the way her mother was pushing for now her father didn't remember he had children. The woman who accepted her and her gayness enough to constantly push her into settling down with a girl, while ignoring the fact her brothers were single.

She tried to wash away the disgust she had for herself with another sip of wine. The cabernet left a bitter taste in her mouth, but she decided it was better than the guilt continuously rising in the back of her throat.

"Excuse me, but can I steal this chair? Or are you expecting someone?" Zoe looked up from her glass to find a thin man with a hand on the back of the spare chair. She nodded soberly, wondering how she ended up so alone.

She checked her phone for the time, but the little red bubbles reminded her of all the unread texts and missed calls she had from her family. The family who taught her it was okay to hurt others as long as she came out on top.

She let out a heavy breath and searched the sky for even a single star. The yellowish haze from the antique streetlamps overpowered the downtown light pollution and blocked any hint of a space beyond the historic square.

"Can I get you anything else?" the waiter asked.

Zoe set her glass down and wiped her mouth with the napkin. "Just the check, please."

"Sure thing." He picked up her plate and disappeared.

Zoe went to take another sip of wine, but the waiter returned faster than she had anticipated with the bill. She glanced at it briefly before sliding a credit card into the black folio.

She drained the last of the wine from the glass, the liquid running around the lump in her throat. Nothing seemed to ease the destruction of reality that she'd allowed to happen. Her imagination running over the mangled bodies of the women she'd betrayed to protect her own sense of self.

'Lyra was right, I didn't understand.'

Zoe's finger traced the top of the glass as she watched a band setting up at the other end of Heritage Square. She considered staying to see who was playing since there was nothing waiting for her but an empty apartment and the bloody crime scene photos she still couldn't explain.

Chairs protested against the ground just behind her as more guests were seated. She looked back down at her phone at the latest notification that Zachery was trying to reach her.

"Can we talk?"

Zoe looked over her shoulder, then ran her eyes up the bullet proof vest to Evie Greyson's pale eyes. The officer's hand hung on to the top of the vest, as she looked down at Zoe.

"Uh... someone took the other chair," Zoe said. She turned, looking for a spare chair at one of the other tables but all were filled.

"I don't need a chair."

"Oh, okay... uh... just give me a minute and we can go someplace less crowded." Zoe held up the folio and waved it at the waiter. He nodded to her, finished setting down a tray full of drinks, and retrieved it from her hand.

Evie scanned the other patrons, then the dimly lit courtyard between the restaurants housed in the historic buildings. The lapel mic screeched to life on Evie's shoulder. Evie leaned closer to her mic listening to the woman on the other end run through a variety of numbers as her hand twisted the knob on the radio to turn down the volume.

The officer didn't answer the call. Her head straightened and stared across the courtyard. Zoe followed the officer's focus to two female silhouettes walking side by side towards the pizzeria. They gently bumped into each other, and Zoe smiled softly at the sweetness of the interaction.

When the waiter returned with the check, Zoe quickly scribbled in the tip, the total, and her signature. Gathering her things, she nodded to Evie and made their way to a less densely populated space. A large tree blocked out most of the streetlights' glow, providing them more privacy.

Evie positioned her back to the building so she could still see the rest of the courtyard. She tugged at the vest, this time with both hands.

Zoe heard the shuffling feet of the silhouetted women pass behind her as she waited on Evie to say her peace.

"You paid my fine. My mom said she went to pay it, but it had already been paid," Evie finally stated. "So, I asked around. I want to know why. And I know it happened before Lyra kneed you in the crotch."

Zoe's tongue ran over her teeth. "She told you about that?"

"We tell each other everything. Like how you have been keeping her your secret friend with benefits. Made her feel like she wasn't good enough to be seen in public with her." Evie shook her head. "You know, she stopped wearing her brace so you wouldn't be ashamed of her even though she was in so much pain? You're lucky I'm not what you say I am or I would beat the shit out of you."

"What I said..." Zoe shook her head. "I was out of line."

"You realize how many people we locked up are now going to file an appeal because you called me a liar?" Evie shook her head. "You seriously fucked us both over with your bullshit."

Evie's hand dropped to rest on her belt, next to her gun. Zoe's core tightened and arms wrapped across the front of her.

"I owe you an apology."

"I didn't come up to you for an apology. I don't even give a fuck as to why you paid my fine." Evie looked over Zoe's shoulder, pulling Zoe's attention to follow her gaze. "I just didn't want you to ruin my sister's night."

The two women they had watched walking through the shadows had passed them, waiting outside of the pizzeria. Zoe immediately recognized Lyra even though she'd never seen the woman in casual clothes before. She'd never imagined Lyra to be anything less than a lipstick femme, but the faded band shirt hung perfectly to her narrow frame. Lyra's face spread into a warm smile as she pushed her hands deeper into the loose-fitting jeans.

Zoe squinted at Lyra's date. Her mouth opened as she took in the copper hair, fake boobs, and round ass. She'd know that ass anywhere, but the warm laugh dancing off the pavement sent the still air into a frenzy around Zoe solidified her worst nightmare. She'd not only lost Lyra, a woman who checked all of the boxes for an ideal girlfriend, but she'd lost her to Parker.

"She's met someone who doesn't feel the need to keep her hidden," Evie said, pulling Zoe back into the shadows. The darkness concealed her from the two women who deserved a night to laugh more than anyone else.

Zoe's skin burned. With shut eyes, Zoe embraced the shame she'd caused each of them to suffer. Accepted her turn in the shadows.

"Thank you," Zoe whispered barely loud enough to hear herself over the pounding of her own heart. Her mind felt fuzzy, and the ground shifted under her feet. She opened her eyes to find Evie hadn't moved, her body rigid as a guard at Buckingham Palace.

"She says you weren't always like this," Evie stated.

Zoe shook her head because Lyra hadn't known she'd been wrong. "I wish I could corroborate that, but I have always been like this."

Evie's head tilted. "Are you upset about losing her or losing your case?"

"Who said I was upset?' Zoe asked, the fog in her brain blown out with the question.

"I know a little something about regret." Evie narrowed her eyes on Zoe. "The inability to eat. Downing a half glass of wine meant to be sipped. The constant looking for a sign from the stars but not finding anything but more darkness."

Zoe felt the weight lifting as Evie labeled the earthquake crumbling Zoe's reality. She held herself tighter, hoping to stop the shaking but she couldn't control the quaking in her chest.

"I regret losing her and the woman she's with."

Evie's head tilted. "You know Parker?"

"We dated in college. She was... she was the first woman I'd ever loved."

"She's the only woman you've ever loved," Evie corrected.

Parker and Lyra's laughter hit Zoe in the back. Two separate shock waves crumbling the walls of the fortress she'd built to keep out the loneliness.

Music filled the air from the other side of the courtyard. She glanced back to see Lyra's arm draped over Parker's shoulder, the way she'd done when Parker was hers.

Her feet moved before her mind had a chance to tell her to get away. She backed up until her shadow returned to her side, and the darkness no longer threatened to swallow her.

"I need to go," Zoe choked out.

Evie followed a step slower than Zoe was able to move. Zoe stopped so abruptly, Evie practically ran into her.

With hands up, Zoe promised, "Look, I'll stay the fuck away from her. Away from Parker. I'm sorry for hurting you, embarrassing you, and even more for making Lyra think she was nothing more than a secret. Neither of them deserves half of what I put them through."

"Where are you going to go?" Evie asked.

Zoe's hands ran over her face as she tried to wipe away the monster she'd become. Shaking her head, she answered, "I don't know."

"You shouldn't be alone right now."

"Why the fuck do you care?" Zoe snapped.

Evie tugged at the top of her vest. Her feet shifted as she looked towards the sky. Zoe followed her gaze, hoping she'd see something. Anything. But as Evie had said before, there was nothing but more darkness.

Evie let out a deep breath, pulling Zoe back to the courtyard.

"I don't really give a fuck about you or your guilt. I came here to see my sister and honestly because it's a little fun when I mess with her dates, but I saw you where they were going, and I just knew I had to get you away from her." Evie cast a glance over Zoe's shoulder, but Zoe didn't follow this time. She waited until Evie met her eyes. "Parker is like us. She's messy and complicated, and she and Lyra will be good for each other."

The woman's jaw shifted back and forth, like she was chewing on what she wanted to say. There was clearly a lot, but Zoe had to breathe out the breath she'd been holding before Evie began.

"You're mean," she finally said. Evie sucked her teeth, then added, "You treat people like rubbish. But my mom always says those are the people that need someone the most, and I know it's the truth because I was really cruel to a lot of people, like Parker. I still have a lot to make up for in this life. So, if you don't want to be alone right now, my shift ended thirty minutes ago. We can go to Denny's up the road and get some pie. Pie always makes things a little less shitty."

Evie's lips scrunched up, "Plus we could plan a little revenge on Nia for setting us both up."

Zoe stopped breathing. Her eyes searched Evie for answers but found nothing on the surface.

"What are you talking about?"

Evie checked around them and took a step closer. Then she whispered, "Nia called my mom after court to ask for campaign support. Said that she needed help from good people like the Greysons if she was going to beat you in the election."

Every muscle in Zoe's body solidified into stone as her mind felt Nia's lies wash over her in a flood, sending her downstream towards a waterfall.

"She what?"

With a shrug, Evie said, "My mom and Aunt Sylvia said she played you. Figured if you hurt me, she'd get my mom's money. And if she gets Mom's money, then Aunt Sylvia would contribute next."

Zoe searched every word from Nia, every document in the file on the Greyson family. She looked for where she'd missed the trap.

"Your aunt is Sylvia Winters?" Zoe asked. "I thought they were exes."

Evie's head bobbled some, before she said, "We're a found family. Sylvia isn't actually my aunt, but it's easier to explain than her and my mom were not in a relationship but in a relationship, and there were like three weeks when they were engaged when I was in high school, but now they are business partners, and it's weird but I know she has slept with both my parents, but yeah... our family is complicated."

That was a lot of information that Zoe stored for later evaluation. The narrative Nia had given Zoe of the Greysons hadn't delved into Sylvia Winters as much, but Zoe had learned from her own research that the Greysons and Winters had a long history. Not as long of a relationship as her father had with Sylvia Winters's dad, since he was the elder's personal attorney. Her dad hadn't been of the mind to tell her much about Sylvia when she'd gone to see him. So, when that failed, she'd tried to strike up a conversation with Ari that morning at the courthouse Starbucks. Nia's daughter had called her a cunt though, and 'accidently' dropped a hot latte down Zoe's pants.

"So, are we going to Dennys?" Evie asked.

"Does your mom get her money from the school she opened?" Zoe asked, needing to sort through which parts of Nia's tale were lies.

Evie laughed, and then rolled her eyes. "She could, but she puts every last dime back into it. She literally pays herself five dollars a month. It's all public record on the charter school financial records. You can pull up where every cent goes. She writes bestselling novels, and she inherited a lot of money when her dad died that Aunt Sylvia's people invested for her. Mom has her own maths people now and they manage all of our money, but no, Mom doesn't steal from poor kids."

"So, she just gives it all... back to the kids?"

Evie nodded. "Yep. Every kid has a college fund with their foster care stipend that gets paid to the school of their choice when they graduate for tuition, meal plans, dorm costs if they go out of state. She also pays for her employees' shit, like apartment down payments and I think she just bought Parker a bunch of shoes because her shoe snapped when she was on a tour and Obi, my mom's partner, had to loan Parker their boots, which I hear was hilarious because Obi is like a giant compared to Parker. Wish I had been there to see it."

Evie stopped talking, then looked at the ground. "My mom. She's a legit good person. I can only hope that one day I can be as good as she is."

Zoe looked over Evie's shoulder to the sky. A single plane flew over them. She held onto the hope it was a sign she was meant to meet Evie tonight.

"So, pie?"

Evie held up a hand. "As long as you promise not to order the booger looking one."

Zoe racked her mind for what pie would constitute booger pie. Then asked, "Pecan?"

"Ew, that one is gross too, but I was talking about the slimy lime that looks like a sinus infection oozing from a white girl's nose."

Her stomach clenched as Zoe pictured key lime pie. "That is so gross and so accurate." Then she nodded. "Okay pie."

They walked together towards the parking garage.

"I still don't like you," Evie stated, breaking the silence.

"I don't like me either."

18

'Just take it slow.'

Dilynn's words repeated in rhythm with the water from the pool just below Parker's apartment. Parker rested her head against the front door looking over the source of Dilynn's plea. She couldn't stop the words to focus on the finger tucking a lock of auburn hair behind her ear.

Lyra placed a hand on the door and leaned in for a goodnight kiss. She paused, hovering over Parker's lips. Parker swallowed as she held Lyra's gaze, contemplating what the kiss would mean to the other woman. She wanted the painting of this first date in her head to end in warm hues though, not shaky lines. Especially after the moan Lyra let out when she reached the tip of her pizza. Because Lyra ate pizza backwards like a weirdo.

Inhaling slowly, Parker closed the distance between them. Her back came off the door, so she wasn't trapped as their lips pressed together gently. Noses touched and they shifted. The kiss deepened as they melted into one another.

The crickets sang a duet with the pool water in the still apartment complex when they released each other. Chests rose and fell together. Parker's feet stayed planted so Lyra could lean against her.

"You don't have to go," Parker half whispered, half pleaded.

She traced the flickering light of a plane across the sky, wondering if Lyra was interested in traveling. With hands resting on Lyra's hips, Parker searched the dark features unsure if she was looking for an indication of this being a one-night stand or that Lyra was jumping. She couldn't be sure, which was actually scarier.

Parker closed the distance once more. Their lips danced to the beat of Parker's heartbeat. The pressure of the day and the pain of the past lifted its veil from over her. The kiss chased the woman's mother from her thoughts as she settled into the comfort and safety of Lyra's warm embrace.

Lyra rested her forehead against Parker's. She licked her kiss swollen lips, then she quietly said, "I want—"

Her words were cut off and her body went rigid. Her arms no longer held Parker but gripped her as though her life depended on Parker supporting her weight.

Parker pulled back only enough to look up at the woman just a few inches taller than her. "Are you okay?"

Lyra's teeth dug into her lower lip. The umber eyes looked to the sky as she opened her mouth and inhaled. Parker watched Lyra's mouth close, white teeth peeking out as she bit back into the bottom lip Parker had just been kissing.

"What's wrong?" Parker asked.

"My leg... cramping," Lyra answered through clenched teeth.

"I got you," Parker said. Shifting her weight, Parker wrapped Lyra's arm around her neck. She held still, taking the other woman's weight as Lyra lifted the toe of her checkered Vans and kneaded her thigh through the jeans. The brace hidden by the baggy jeans caught Parker's attention and guilt rose in her throat for having made Lyra stand for so long.

"I'm sorry," Lyra said through gritted teeth.

Parker had no clue as to what she could do to help alleviate the pain etched across Lyra's face. She couldn't for the life of her figure out if asking how she could help would hurt the other woman's pride anymore.

They stood still until Lyra put her toe back down. Little droplets of sweat had accumulated on her brow, but she exhaled a heavy breath.

Lyra shifted so Parker was free. With a hand pulling at the back of her neck, Lyra moved to the landing guardrail. It shifted under her weight, forcing Lyra to rely on her own body for support. Her knuckles were white from the force of the hold she had on the rail.

"I was in a car accident. Piece of metal from the door got lodged in my back, and it basically fucked everything up. They said I wouldn't walk again," Lyra offered with a weak smile. "I did it though."

"Do the cramps happen often?" Parker asked, her eyes watching the water in the complex's pool ripple.

"A few times a week."

"How do you manage them?" Parker tapped the railing, running over the question again in her head. She realized it wasn't the question she wanted to ask. "Wait, I don't mean, like, how do you deal with the pain. I mean, like, what do you do to work the cramp out?"

"Well, when they happen in the front like that one did, I can't really do much until it fades. The best stretch would be to pull my foot up and back. Like raise it to my ass. But it's one of those things I can't do by myself." Lyra wiped the sweat from her forehead onto her jeans. "I tried once by laying down, but I couldn't get it back down. I was stuck on the floor because I couldn't get to my phone, so I just laid there waiting for Evie or Landon to get home."

"I could... you know...." Parker fumbled with her keys. "Help stretch it out."

Lyra pushed her hands in her pockets. Shaking her head, she said, "You don't have to... you know... pretend to still be interested."

A soft breeze rustled the leaves of the palm trees surrounding the pool. Parker's stomach twisted in a knot as she felt the chaos pushing her to back up. She picked at her lip, realizing Lyra may not be giving her an out but looking for one herself.

"So... I'm just going to say it. If I'm a bad kisser, then you know, you just have to say so. I'm a big girl."

Lyra's eyes grew, her body turning to Parker. With hands out of her pockets, she waved away the chaos between them.

"No. No," she said. Her hands fell and she shook her head slowly. "You are not a bad kisser. An amazing kisser. Maybe the best kiss I've ever had. You're beautiful. Intelligent. Sweet. Sexy."

An uneasy laugh burst from Parker. She ran over the time she'd spent with Lyra trying to figure out how this brilliant and kind human could think all of that bullshit.

Lyra had it all, just like Zoe. And the more she thought about it, the more her shoulders drooped. Parker could not find anything to offer the woman beside her. She imagined the disappointment on Lyra's face when she figured it out. She could see the beautiful Latin features turn to disgust when the woman learned where she came from.

Parker sucked her teeth, and then exhaled the breath she hadn't known she was holding. She weighed the options and decided it would be better to see it now than later.

"So, there's something," she started, but then stopped. She couldn't just list her fears. She had to give Lyra an out as well as an opportunity to stay.

She started again. "So, I'm just going to tell you some things. If you still want to see me, then we go in and watch a movie. If it's too much, then just say good night. Like a safe word, you know? You say good night, and we'll just not make shit weird."

Lyra's face twisted suspiciously, then she slowly nodded.

Parker licked her lips before looking out at the dark sky. She followed another flickering light, making a quiet wish that one day she would move through the sky like a star against the night. Her lungs expanded as she inhaled as deeply as possible.

"My parents are in prison because they killed a total of twelve women. I spent my adolescence in juvie after punching Nia Williams in the face, and when I got out, I got a job as a stripper." As she finished, she huffed out the last of the air she had in her lungs.

She stood still as a statue, staring at what might be an actual star. Wishing on stars were for princesses in animated films, not those born from walking demons. There wasn't a point, but she found herself trying it anyways.

The metal railing shifted when Lyra started to move. Parker's fingers clung to the railing, and she braced herself for the two words she'd promised wouldn't make shit weird. She jumped slightly when Lyra's hand came into view.

The woman slowly took the keys Parker held over the edge. Lyra held them up, examining each carefully until she chose one to put into the deadbolt. It unlocked the door like Lyra had used the key before. She didn't wait for Parker, just walked into the poorly furnished apartment. Turning from left to right, she scanned the entirety of the space, then she disappeared around the corner.

"Is it weird that you live in the same apartment complex that Obi did when they met my mom?" Lyra called from inside. There wasn't a chance for a response before Lyra asked, "Where's the power button for this TV?"

Parker's feet moved even though her head was still spinning around the idea Lyra could actually be interested in her knowing the truth. The television was already on before Parker had a chance to close the door.

With a proud smile, Lyra pointed to the screen. "I found the secret button."

The woman walked to the middle of the couch. Parker raised her hands. "The springs on the middle—" but before her words could catch up, Lyra flopped down. The cushion gave out immediately, and Lyra's knees were practically to her nose as she made it straight through the couch. "Are broken," she finished, willing herself not to laugh.

Lyra's eyes bulged. She tried to push her way out, but the old couch just creaked. "Your couch ate my ass!"

Parker's head fell back. Chest spasming as she wheezed out air that quickly turned to laughter. She held her stomach, unable to do anything to help Lyra.

The woman encased in the couch pushed at the cushions, then her arms disappeared as she tried the floor. Suddenly one shot up, and she called out, "I saved your remote!"

It took Parker several attempts to get her laughter under control. Lyra continued pulling various lost items from under the cushions as Parker made her way over to the woman.

"Hey, a quarter," Lyra stated, waving it in the air.

Parker held out a hand to help Lyra up, but the woman quickly pulled her hand back to her chest.

"I'm keeping this," she said, cradling the found treasure.

Laughter shook Parker's chest again as she promised, "All yours. Consider it payment for your injuries, Miss Assistant District Attorney."

With narrowed eyes, Lyra tucked the quarter in her bra. Parker reached out and locked her hand to Lyra's wrist. She pulled until Lyra escaped the hole of rare return.

Parker put her arms around Lyra until she was confident the woman had her footing. She pulled back when Lyra narrowed her eyes again. The woman quickly patted her chest, then dug into her bra to retrieve the quarter.

With a roll of her eyes, Parker pointed to the corner of the couch. "That side's safe."

Lyra smiled with her hand still gripping the retrieved coin. She sat down, this time slowly. Lyra quirked an eyebrow at the hole.

"Where you gonna sit?"

Without a word, Parker pulled the three throw pillows from the other side of the couch. She lifted the center cushion and stuffed the pillows underneath. Then she too carefully sat down.

"Sorcery," Lyra said. A smile played at the corners of her mouth as she handed over the remote. She placed her arm on the back of the couch behind Parker.

The Netflix logo danced over the screen. Parker clicked a few buttons suggesting various options until Lyra stopped her at *Love Actually*. "That one. It's my favorite."

Parker leaned her head into the crook of Lyra's arm. "It's one of mine too."

While the movie introduced the various characters, Parker learned that Lyra didn't just talk through book club. She talked through everything.

"I fell in love with this movie after Obi moved in. It was like all the chaos in our lives had brought us together." Her grip around Parker tightened and lips pressed against her head. "I like to think that life works just like this. Like we're all connected, and our stories are all apart of other people's stories."

Parker hummed in agreement.

"Thank you for sharing before. I don't want to seem like I am competing against you for the most traumatic life, but I do understand what it means to have shitty parents."

Parker watched the characters fumble around each other, quietly chewing on Lyra's words. When she thought of Lyra, she'd only connected her life to Dilynn and Alex's seemingly perfect relationship. Same with Evie.

She listened to Lyra's breath hitch momentarily. "My bio mom... she was a drug addict. Prostitute. Anything really to get her next fix, and she... she tried to sell me to her dealer."

Parker's arm wrapped around Lyra's middle. She held her the only way she could without moving.

"I know what it's like to not want people to know where you come from. So, just know... you don't have to explain anything that happened in the past if you don't want to," Lyra stated. She licked her lips. "But..."

'Of course, there's a but.'

"I feel like this could be something. Like something really good, so wouldn't it just be better to, like, pull out the shit we've been carrying around and dump it in the toilet together, rather than use it to throw at each other later when we are hurt or insecure?"

Her head rose and fell with Lyra's steady breathing. The woman made it sound so simple. But Parker wasn't even sure she had keys to all the locks she'd used to hide away the past.

Parker weighed what telling Lyra would cost.

The hurricane in her past had been swirling at a level five for longer than she had memories. She struggled with whether just saying it aloud really was going to cause the storm to dissipate, or would she just temporarily find herself within the eye.

'Last time you opened your mouth, your whole world fell apart. And when you didn't, it also fell apart.'

She wondered what it would be like for even a moment of calm skies. She yearned for that moment.

"I have never talked about it," she half whispered.

Lyra gave her a gentle squeeze.

"I was the one that turned my parents in." As the forbidden words left her mouth, Parker didn't feel the calm she'd hoped. The rain from all the tears she'd held in pounded against the walls she'd built until one began to leak.

Parker listened for Lyra's heart to beat faster; for her breathing to change. However, she couldn't hear Lyra's heart over the pounding in her own ears. So, she waited to feel the other woman's body tense up.

"That must have been terrifying for you," Lyra said. Her finger ghosted over the exposed skin on Parker's arm. "Do you want to tell me what happened?"

"No," Parker said, unable to lift her eyes to look at Lyra. "But you said that by finding the why would calm the chaos. And I'd really like the chaos to chill the fuck out for a hot minute."

Lyra's fingers continued their gentle caress, never staying in one spot too long. "Does your chaos revolve around the guilt for turning them in?"

She considered if she'd ever felt guilty for calling the police. Fear making her skin itch was what she remembered as she sat in the interrogation room. A foggy confusion had hung around her weeks afterwards as she tried to reorganize her memories to understand what ADA Williams told her after she asked what felt like thousands of questions that didn't make sense when all Parker wanted to know was if her mother and father were alive. Guilt for calling the police wasn't a thought though, because when the haze lifted, she'd been angry that she'd been ditched in a foster home with five other kids.

"I didn't know I was reporting them. I was hiding in my closet because I thought..." She swallowed. "I thought it was my mother. I thought someone had broken into our house and I thought my mother was being murdered."

The singular scream echoed in Parker's head. It clearly wasn't her mother's voice now she'd heard it over and over again. The tools she used to block it weren't working this time because there wasn't enough paint on her pallet to force shut the music box she'd locked it into when dreams of being a fairy ballerina died as well.

She closed her eyes when she heard the woman cry out in pain again and started at ten. At nine, she remembered the shame she'd felt for not going to help her mother, instead choosing to cower in the closet. Eight brought the storm to the surface as the hurricane destroyed the dam. Seven and six blurred together as she tried to wipe the tears and snot away but ended up only smearing it all over her face and arm.

Lyra told her, "You're safe," at five.

She was on her feet by four so Lyra couldn't touch her. Just like she'd shrank farther into the closet when the police threw open the folding door and she was sure the murderer was coming for her next.

Three was when her body started shaking and the room tilted. She held a hand to the wall at two and pushed until the ground became level again at one. At one she felt like she couldn't breathe, but words started to fall out.

"I wasn't supposed to be home." She tried to breathe but no matter how many breaths she took her lungs still felt empty. "I was... sleepover. The party and the closet."

She closed her eyes and found herself in a different closet. This time she wasn't alone.

"Seven minutes of hell they should have called it. I couldn't stop him from touching me and when they opened the doors the others just laughed. They laughed, but I was able to run away because the doors were open."

Her eyes popped open. Tears were no longer falling when she turned from the wall she was supporting to the woman balancing her weight on her knees. Those umber eyes showed her no pity. They understood, which made the rest of the words easier.

"I walked home and knew my parents would be in bed. I tried to make it up the stairs to my room to just go to bed, but I heard the scream. I heard it and I ran to hide. I hid while my father killed that woman and my mother watched. And I just wish I'd had the courage to scream. If I hadn't hid, then maybe, maybe she'd still be alive."

Lyra shook her head. She pushed up from the couch, still shaking her head. Her hands were raised in the air. "You did stop it. You stopped it from happening to someone else."

Parker stared at Lyra as though the words were written on her face. She read them over and over again. She read them and ran over how many more women they could have killed if she hadn't come home that night. Each time she read the words, the rain fell a little softer and the wind howled slightly quieter.

"I never..." Parker started, but then stopped as the little girl hit a high vocal note on the television. The Christmas melody felt as wrong in September as she suddenly felt about everything, she'd convinced herself of all those years.

"I never felt guilty for calling the police."

Lyra nodded. "You felt guilty that you didn't help the woman."

Parker shook her head. "I don't think I ever felt guilty. I was angry. I was angry that I hid. I was angry that they destroyed my life. Our life. I was angry that I had ever been born. Ashamed of being alive when they took so much."

The room didn't shift again when she released her hold on the wall. Her arms relaxed and her chest didn't feel like it was still clamped in a vice grip.

A yawn took control over everything as her limbs became as sturdy as a Jell-o Jigglin'. Lyra's warm hands softened the gelatin until Parker melted into the strong embrace. The memory of having to support Lyra dissolved as she let herself be held.

They didn't move as Parker watched the credits roll up the screen. She wondered what came next. The snapshot into all those lives ended but she was still standing in the wreckage of a storm that had raged for more than a decade. And she had no idea where to start.

She tilted her chin to see Lyra. The woman who hadn't run away, and still stood despite all the odds that she'd had stacked against her.

'She's the strongest of all the Greysons.'

Parker couldn't find a single instance where any member of that family had lacked the tenacity to take on the world. She didn't know if she'd ever have that kind of strength, but she'd always forged her own path anyways. Found family in Echo, and even Xio. It wasn't as huggy as the Greysons but she knew good people stood when the world was crumbling, and she felt like Lyra would fit in her pictures without feeling out of place.

"Can you stay with me?" Parker asked, not as unsure of what might come next with Lyra. "For tonight?"

Lyra hummed in approval, and let Parker lead her around the corner to the bedroom. She was sure the room was nothing compared to how Lyra was used to living. She hoped seeing her naked would at least be a distraction from the fact Parker's clean clothes lived on her bed, only being exiled to the floor after she'd worn the outfit.

Parker rummaged through the pile that would no longer be deemed clean once she threw it all on the floor so Lyra would have a place to sit. She found one of the first promo shirts Echo made when she bought the bar and a pair of shorts. She held them out to the other woman, who raised an eyebrow at them.

"It's clean I swear." Parker said, looking at the shirt. She sniffed it for a good measure. "Yep, fabric softener, not boob sweat."

"What if I sleep naked?" Lyra asked, wiggling her eyebrows at the woman.

Pulling off her own shirt, Parker watched Lyra's cocky grin shift to surprise. When she was satisfied with Lyra's reaction, she reached back and unhooked her bra. The benefit of implants was nothing really shifted whether she was wearing it or not.

"Those are—"

"Expensive," Parker interrupted. She cupped each breast and looked down. "I've been considering taking them out, but I think I will wait a year or two, until I'm sure I don't have to go back to dancing."

Lyra wet her lips. Words didn't appear to be her friends because she repeatedly opened her mouth, then shut it.

Unbuckling her belt, Parker couldn't help but enjoy the way Lyra was looking at her. She'd always avoided undressing for her previous partners. Never wanted to feel like she was just taking off her clothes for them. Lyra didn't seem like the type to do it for her though. So, she peeled away her pants until her thong was the only thing left. She smiled at the sound of Lyra taking a very deep breath.

Holding up the shirt she'd retrieved for Lyra, Parker said, "I do not sleep naked. But I don't have to be wearing anything for awhile if you... if you want to be naked with me."

Lyra's eyes cinched, then she waved at Parker. "You are so beautiful, but I... I have messed things up before by doing things too fast. So, please put your shirt on because I might implode if I open my eyes and you are still so sooo sooo naked."

With a soft chuckle, Parker slipped the shirt over her head.

"It's safe," she promised.

Lyra peeked out through her fingers, then shut them again. "Nope. Not safe. Just as sexy with clothes on."

"You're ridiculous," Parker said, pushing Lyra playfully.

"I was already attracted to you, and now..." her voice cracked almost painfully. "Fucking eh, I'm.... No, I'm going to do right by you. At least three more dates. Three more dates and then... then, I'm going to—"

Parker straddled Lyra's lap. She pressed her chest just under Lyra's chin, chuckling as the woman's breathing stuttered. There was the slightest nuzzle between her breasts, before the dark gaze met hers.

"I can feel how... uh... excited you are," Lyra whispered, her lips finding Parker's throat. "And I want to. Please know, I want to so, so badly."

Parker lowered her lips to Lyra's. No one had ever said they would do good by her, well besides the guys who came in promising sugar baby style allowances. Guys like Zoe's brother, who were liars.

Lyra's hands held on to Parker's thighs. They almost migrated to her ass, but one hand moved to pull her deeper into the kiss. A kiss so hungry, yet gentle. Oxymorons were all Parker could think about. Needed want. Weak with power.

Pulling back, she rested her head against Lyra's. She played with the hem of Lyra's shirt. Then whispered, "May I help you get ready for bed?"

"If you touch my nipples, I am not going to be able to control myself," Lyra whispered. "It's, like, a trigger, and I'm, like, so into you."

The shirt came up and over Lyra's head. Her breasts were contained in a well fitted sports bra that Parker pulled off next. She was tempted to test Lyra's resolve, but decided seeing what could come after teasing the woman for three whole dates felt more worthwhile. After all, she'd slept with Zoe and Xio without even a date, and both of those ended quickly.

"Why did you say that I wouldn't want to be with you because you got a cramp?" Parker asked, pulling another shirt from the bed.

"Oh, a why question," Lyra said with a pained chuckle.

"Your favorite."

Lyra's head popped through the top of the shirt, and she quickly pushed her arms through their respective holes.

"There are things I can't do," Lyra admitted. She took a deep breath that rushed out with the next words. "Look, I will do everything I can to keep your needs satisfied, but there are things I won't be able to do."

"Someone hurt you," Parker said, scraping her fingers over Lyra's scalp.

"It's all fun and games until they see, and I tried to hide it last time. Tried not wearing my brace and to be... normal." Lyra licked her lips, and apparently didn't like the taste of her own words. "I'm in pain a lot, and I won't take the drugs. Can't take them because I was... my grandmother said that I was probably born addicted to the drugs my mom used. When I got hurt, they gave me the good stuff, and it was really, really hard to stop."

Her eyes searched over Parker's face. Whether the woman realized it or not, Parker was very skilled at masking all her emotions.

"There will be cramps and days that hurt too much to get out of bed. There are still physical therapy appointments, and my grandmother was talking about a new surgery that might help because they would take like nerve tissue, or something like that, and they graft it in, and it might... it could. But I will be in a chair again for months if I did it, and you should really think about that."

Her chin fell, and she shook her head once more.

"At some point, I will be in a chair. It's not an if, it's a when. And that changes things for people."

Parker stood up, which she realized was the wrong move. It was a choice she wished she could take back, but that wasn't an option. So, she moved on with her plan.

She pushed Lyra back on the bed. Her fingers played with the button on the woman's jeans. With one hand, she popped the button open, then slowly unzipped the woman's pants.

"The funny part about always ending up as the person others throw away is that I'm not society," Parker explained. She chose to focus on the little four leaf clovers on Lyra's boxer briefs rather than look at the woman's face. "I'm not people. I don't fit, so you can't measure me by what other people would do because I will probably do the opposite."

She tugged at the pants until Lyra lifted her hips. They were loose fitting jeans, so she didn't have to peel them away like she had had to do her own. The brace pressed a deep indent into the caramel flesh like Lyra had tightened it extra to make sure she wouldn't appear to be struggling.

Lyra reached down, but Parker's fingers closed over Lyra's on the metal contraption.

"Please let me do this," Parker requested.

With a lip between teeth, Lyra nodded. Her fingers released the control she had to Parker but found purchase in the laundry under her clover covered rear.

Carefully, Parker undid several clips. She gently pulled the brace down Lyra's smooth leg and sat it with the rest of Lyra's clothes. With a hand just above Lyra's bad knee, she asked, "May I touch you?"

Lyra swallowed and nodded again.

Parker glanced around and left Lyra momentarily to retrieve a bottle of lotion. She coated her hands, then added a decent amount to her palm. Deft fingers smoothed in the lotion over Lyra's thigh, gently kneading the flesh until they located the source of the cramp from earlier. She applied pressure until Lyra hissed out a breath. She waited for Lyra to signal she was okay before rubbing out the knot.

"Thanks," Lyra breathed out.

Parker helped Lyra into the shorts, then used both her arms to pull all the laundry from the bed. She tried not to appear embarrassed with not bothering to clean up. She knew herself well enough to know Lyra would have ended up in her bed tonight, especially since it had been so long since anyone was in her bed.

"Heat is expensive, and so are comforters," Parker confessed as she looked over the heap of clothes.

"I'm like a furnace," Lyra said, snuggling in close. "No comforter needed."

Lyra pointed to each side of the bed, so Parker patted the edge farthest from the wall. She used it to her advantage once the light was off to crawl over Lyra, taking her time to press against the woman and steal another kiss.

Lyra met each motion, showing Parker she too was struggling. Her hands found their way under Parker's shirt, and the caress of fingers against her skin that was anywhere but her breasts had Parker's head falling back and her core pulsing.

"Get off me," Lyra whispered between nips along Parker's neck.

"I don't wanna," Parker said, grinding her hips against Lyra.

Lyra's smile was huge, but her hands fell to the side of the bed instead of touching Parker anymore. Something that had Parker's obstinate side pouting and worries beginning to rise in her.

"Get off me and in the morning, when we have breakfast, we can call that date

2," Lyra stated, shoving Parker to the side just hard enough to make Parker laugh. A slender arm came around Parker's middle, securing her to the other woman's radiating heat. "Then lunch can be date three."

Her nose nuzzled into Parker's neck and her hand held just under Parker's breasts.

"And for dinner, I'll have you on the table. Then dessert on the couch of no return. Then a snack in bed. Then--"

"So, you're just planning on staying all weekend?" Parker asked.

The chaos that had calmed was back, because Parker wasn't the girl people wanted to U-Haul. Especially not successful lawyers from rich families. Because she couldn't be a secret girlfriend from her bosses. The bosses who knew too much about her already.

"I like to sleep under clothes fresh from the drier," Lyra confessed instead of answering the question.

A police siren sung its tragic melody into the dark night, finding the path through the cracked second story window. The air carrying the song was crisp, but Lyra hadn't lied. She was so warm, Parker wondered how the woman survived the summer.

"Does the stripping thing really not bother you?" Parker asked with eyes closed.

It was an easier question than asking if Lyra was trying to U-Haul. She'd watched the damage of moving in too soon when Echo hooked up with Simone.

Lyra pressed a kiss to Parker's shoulder. "Oh, definitely a turn on, not turn off. I bet you can roll your hips so well. I can't pick you up and fuck you into a wall or anything, but I can't wait to see how bendy you are. Can't wait for you to roll those hips on my face."

She had to press her thighs together. For someone wanting to wait almost twenty-four hours before she fucked her, Lyra was riling her up enough to ruin the lace of her thong.

"That will be my snack tomorrow. You on my face so I can watch."

Pressing her ass back into the woman, Parker warned, "If you don't stop talking, I'm going to give your tongue something to do."

Teeth pressed into her shoulder, pulling a shameful moan from Parker's lips.

"Don't threaten me with a good time," Lyra whispered, holding Parker closer. Her finger grazed the underside of Parker's breast. "I'm already using all my restraint after you put boobs on my face. Boobs. I love boobs so much, and you teased me so you're just getting what you give."

Parker snuggled in closer. Lyra's body formed a bubble of safety that was warmer than anything she'd experienced with Echo on the nights in juvie when the thin cotton blankets couldn't keep away the cold concrete. She clung to the pillow along the wall like a life raft as the waves of possibilities rocked her to sleep.

Lyra groaned, her arms holding Parker tighter. Parker grunted, pushing the other woman off her so she could find her phone. The phone that was ringing in the dead of night.

She leaned over Lyra as she looked on the floor for the source of the ring. She tried to reach her target but had to slither farther over the woman in her bed until only her legs were still over the woman. Lyra held Parker's leg, keeping her from tumbling off the bed when she finally found her phone. One hand gripped her bare ass cheek and the need within her was reignited.

But Echo's name burned her eyes as she hit the green accept button. "Hey," she said. She looked at the screen again. "It's three am, what's wrong?"

At first, she only heard what she thought was retching and Henrie crying, then a toilet being flushed. She tried again. "Echo? Are you there?"

"Help," Echo's hoarse voice came from across the speaker. "Simone can't stop shitting. Henrie puked all over her crib and had a blowout."

Echo's voice faded and Parker knew she just heard her best friend puke on the phone.

"I can't stop—"

Parker raised her fist to her mouth as she tried to hold down her own vomit at just the sound of someone else puking.

"Please," Echo begged.

Parker scrambled the rest of the way over Lyra's now alert body. She turned the light on, the yellow glare burning her retina. She searched the floor for her sandals.

"I'm on my way," she promised.

Lyra fumbled with the brace. Her fingers repeatedly misaligned the clips.

"I have to go," Parker explained, now looking for her keys. "Echo and all of them are sick. Like sick sick."

Parker's fingers dug into her hair as she twisted in every direction looking for the keys.

"I'll go with you," Lyra said, finally getting the last clip in place.

Finding the keys in Lyra's pants pocket, the redhead snatched them up. "I don't want you getting sick too," she said. "Stay. Sleep. Just lock the door when you leave in the morning."

Lyra was already on her feet. She protested, "I'm not going to slow you down."

Parker stopped rushing. She scanned the disappointment on Lyra's face. With two steps, she was in Lyra's bubble again. Softly she held the other woman's hurt face in her hands, and said, "I am not leaving you behind. I'm sparing you from what I just heard. If I need anything, you will be my first call."

"Promise?" Lyra asked.

"I promise."

Parker pressed a kiss to the taller woman's lips as she stood just slightly on her tiptoes. "I also promise to text you when I get home tomorrow."

"To schedule our next date?" Lyra's mouth smooshed into a cute little duck face.

"Yes, in fact to schedule the next two dates." Parker ran a finger over Lyra's breast. Watched the nipple peek through the shirt. "I need to show you how bendy I can be. And my boobs haven't been worshiped properly in a long, long time."

Lyra's air rushed from within her. She held onto Parker's hips like she was going to lose control.

"That was mean. So mean." Lyra's eyes stared at Parker's chest. "I'm going to make you pay for it. Just spend hours with my mouth on those breasts and not touching you anywhere else."

"We'll see," Parker said, pushing the woman back to the bed. "I bet you fall first."

The door wasn't closed when Parker heard Lyra say to herself, "Already fallen. Just don't fuck it up. Take your time with her so she'll fall in love with you. Don't just fuck her because they always leave afterwards."

19

The live cycling class continued as Zoe slowed her pace on the Peloton bike and muted the screen. She tried to listen through the whirring of the wheel still making its way to stillness, unsure if she'd actually heard someone knocking on her door or if it was just the pounding of her own heart.

She set her feet back on the pedals, when "Zoe Marie Robinson, you open this door right now!" came from the hallway.

Panic spread through her limbs as she fumbled off the bike, catching her body before her face was introduced to the wooden floor. She scrambled up. Her mother was angry enough to yell in a semi-public space, which meant Zoe had to move her ass faster. Her legs wobbled when she tried to stand but she pushed herself from the far side of the living room to the front door.

She'd barely made it to the couch when she heard, "Zoe! You better open—"

"I'm coming, Mom," Zoe called, hoping that would stop the lecture the grumpy grandpa next door would subject her to for waking up his stupid cat.

She unlatched the chain and the deadbolt, but the door flung open before she could grab the handle. With barely a chance to move out of the way, Cassandra Robinson with her tightly fixed bun barreled through the door in full rant.

"You don't answer calls or texts. I even emailed you and you didn't respond. Someone could have died, and you wouldn't have known because you're too busy to talk to your mother. Think you're so important that you can just leave me on read. I spent two days pushing you out of my vagina with no drugs! No drugs they said because it would make you stupid, and I believed them. Yet here we are!"

Zoe's hand pulled at the back of her neck. She examined every smudge on the floor she was certain to hear about before her mother left.

A casserole dish was pushed into Zoe's chest. "Here's chicken parm. I made you a whole plate because take out is not food, Zoe."

It smelled good even though it was breakfast time. A part of her wanted to peel back the foil and pick up a piece of chicken with just her fingers. That would only lead to her being yelled at more though.

"Zachery said you haven't answered him either. I almost called the police because I was sure you'd been kidnapped."

Cassandra's head turned left and right. Her upper lip curled in disgust as she quickly moved about the living room collecting the various articles of clothing Zoe dropped throughout the previous week.

"It's a good thing I didn't call the police because they would think you were raised by ingrates with missing teeth."

"Mom," Zoe tried. She blew out a loud breath, reminding herself that she loved her mother. No matter what, she loved her mother and would not fight with her today.

"You had me worried sick. How could you ignore me for weeks?" Cassandra gathered all of the articles of clothing into her long arms and retreated down the hallway to her bedroom. She came back empty handed, but sadly not out of breath.

"Don't you think about anyone else besides the bodies in those disgusting photographs?" Shaking her head, she gestured to the living room floor where Zoe had reconstructed the crime scene like a 2d model. "People matter, Zoe, just as much as corpses."

The stern-faced woman ran a finger over one of the floating shelves under Zoe's obscenely large television. She held the filth in the air, turning to scowl at her daughter.

"This is why you're not married yet. What woman would want to come home to a slob?"

"One that wants to watch women's soccer on an 85" screen." Zoe was disappointed when her mother didn't even pause at her retort. She'd felt it was one of her better comebacks.

Instead, Cassandra looked around the room, shaking her head. "You're getting old, you know. You need to stop pretending that you have all the time in the world because the clock is ticking, and your ovaries are drying up."

"Mom!"

A single hand raised in the air at Zoe's protest, silencing the daughter. "Don't you raise your voice to me. I did not raise you to talk to your mother in such a tone."

With fallen shoulders, Zoe shuffled her way into the kitchen. Her stomach growled as she put the dish into the refrigerator. As soon as her mother left, she was going to eat half of the family size portion. Glancing at the bike, she decided she would need to ride at least three more miles to burn it off. It would be worth it though. Her mother's cooking was always worth it.

"Zoe Marie."

After a deep breath, Zoe turned back to the woman. She leaned against the countertop, and begrudgingly said, "Sorry."

The hand dropped, still covered in dust. Cassandra raised her chin and stared into her daughter's widening eyes. Her lower jaw moved just enough that Zoe wondered if her mother was also gifted with the ability to vividly imagine murdering someone. "Unacceptable, Zoe Marie. That is not how you properly apologize to someone. You must—"

"Look them in the eyes and say the whole sentence," Zoe recited. She sighed, tried to find a way out of this, and then looked her mother square in the face. "I'm sorry for not answering your calls or texts."

"Better." Cassandra made her way over to the kitchen island to a low stool. "Not great, but better. So, tell me what is wrong."

Zoe ran her hands over her face and tried to wipe away any hint of her blushing. Then she lied, "I've just been busy with this case."

"Don't lie to me, Zoe Marie," her mother warned. "I spent fourteen hours in labor because you had to come out with your eyes out and they had to keep pushing you back in."

"Ew, Mom."

"The doctor literally shoved his entire hand in my—"

"Oh my god!" Zoe held her hands over her ears. "Stop!"

Cassandra let a wicked smile spread across her face. Only when her daughter resumed her sullen position did she start again. "Tell me the truth or I'll tell you about the hemorrhoid you caused."

"Jesus!" Zoe let her head hit the granite countertop with a hard smack. She regretted it instantly because she was pretty sure she just stamped the image of some doctor's hand coming at her face in a dark tunnel into the front of her skull forever.

She sat up rubbing her forehead. "Fine. I just... Do you want some coffee?"

The older woman relaxed against the counter, folding her hands together. She said, "You will talk while you brew."

"Yes, ma'am."

Zoe pulled the bag of coffee beans from the freezer and measured out the correct amount into the grinder. She let the noise fill the space as she considered how much she could tell her mother without becoming a further disappointment.

Once the grinder stopped, her mother asked, "Zachery said he hasn't heard from you since fishing. Did your brothers say something stupid?"

Zoe licked her lips, and then her fingers to separate the coffee filters. "Not exactly." She added water to the machine, chewing on her bottom lip. "I've just been dealing with some things and this case really is brutal."

She looked over her shoulder, hoping to find Cassandra distracted by something other than what she was saying. But hazel eyes watched her removing mugs from the cabinet.

"Remember the girl I dated in college?" Zoe asked as the mugs clanked against the counter in front of the coffee maker.

"The stripper."

Zoe's head snapped up. She'd never told her mother about Parker being a stripper. She'd only said she was dating someone, then that she wasn't.

"I heard she was a stripper from your brother." She watched her mother roll her eyes for what she thought was the first time in her life. "I don't know why your brothers made such a big deal about it. I mean, I went to my lesbian friend's bachelorette party and there were several strippers there. Very nice girls. So down to earth when they talked to me. All of them working their way through college, much like that little blonde you were dating."

Zoe's mouth opened. Her feet planted her body midway between the counter and island.

"Close your mouth, dear," Cassandra stated. "A bug from the ecosystem in your sink will fly in."

Zoe glanced at the pile of dishes and back at her mother. Her mother waved her hand in the air. "So, the girl in college. What happened? Please don't tell me that sweet little girl was hurt and you're prosecuting the bastard that killed her."

"How do you know she was sweet?" Zoe asked, finally able to move her feet.

"Your photos." Her mother smiled warmly for the first time since she'd entered the apartment. "She was never looking at the camera. Always dreaming. I wish you would have brought her around."

"Where did you see the photos?"

"Zachery showed me when you kept her hidden from the family. I don't know why you never brought her around." She pointed to the sputtering machine. "On the myplace thingy."

It was Zoe's turn to roll her eyes. "Myspace, Mom. It was called Myspace."

She poured the steaming liquid into each mug and retrieved a bottle of vanilla Almond coffee creamer from the refrigerator. She held it up to her mom, who shook her head. "I prefer it black like your soul."

Zoe's head tilted back as she stared at the ceiling, once more reminding herself that she loved her mother.

"Anyways, back to the point, counselor."

Zoe shook her shoulders in an attempt to dislodge her growing frustration. She handed her mother the cup, then looked at the liquid within her own mug changing colors as she added the creamer.

"Parker, that's the girl's name. She... she was on my jury."

"That must have been very uncomfortable for you since she dumped you."

"What?" Zoe snarled at her mother, "She didn't dump me. I broke up with her, and I was—"

"A jerk."

"What?! How did you—"

"You have a meanness to you, dear. Always have. Just as mean as your brothers." Her mother sipped the hot liquid. "I love you but your coldness towards other people is not something you learned from me."

"Can we just—"

"Yes, get back to the point."

Zoe dropped her chin. She mumbled out the truth. "I called her a piece of trash."

Cassandra set the cup down. Zoe glanced up to see the woman's lips set in a straight line. "Go on."

"Well, I ran into her after she was dismissed from the jury. She was helping her friend that owns a lesbian bar and there was this woman that was calling her names and dumped a tray of drinks on her. I was so mad because even though I hurt her I realized that I still have feelings for her. But to complicate matters worse after she was dismissed from the jury, she started working with the girl that I am prosecuting for murder. She's a therapist now. So, I have to prep for when she's on the witness stand. But anyways, I defended her to that crazy woman that dumped drinks on her, and Parker got all pissed—"

"Language."

Zoe reworked the sentence in her head, then started again. "She got very defensive, and she told me..." She swallowed the shameful tears threatening to break through. "She told me that Zachery used to go to the bar that she worked at, and he said some really messed up things. When she refused to sleep with him, he took me to the bar and humiliated me for dating a stripper."

She rolled her head until her neck popped, releasing some of the built-up tension. "I didn't know about what he'd done, and he backed me into a corner with all of his shit talking so I broke up with her in the parking lot after she got off stage. And I just feel betrayed and angry. And I feel like that was a turning point in my life. I thought I was better than her, and when I saw her in my courtroom, I tried to make her stay on that jury to prove that I was better than her. And it's not how you raised me, I know."

Zoe stood up. Her finger tapped against the mug. She sighed and looked at her mother, hoping to find some sort of understanding, but the woman just continued to stare into her.

Unable to handle the silence, Zoe continued, "Now, everything feels like it is spiraling out of control. I let my boss manipulate me into saying some horrible things to a witness. I tried to destroy her on the stand and accused her of lying about being a sexual assault victim, so the jury hates me. Plus, I literally ignored like everything a decent person would notice to convict this kid of murder when she was probably raped for like a long time by the guy she killed. And my career is blowing up, which I thought I was going to prove how I was better off without Parker in my life."

"Is that it?" Cassandra asked.

"No."

Zoe pulled at the back of her neck again, and then threw the rest into the air with all her other secrets. "I lost another great woman, Lyra, because I was a dick and the witness that I hurt on the stand turns out was her sister, but I didn't know that because I treated Lyra like I only wanted to sleep with her. Which I mean that was actually true and then when I tried to fix things with her, I made it worse because I literally was only trying to win her back so that I could put out this image that I was stable and dependable for voters so that I could become the next DA. Then I saw Lyra on a date with Parker last night, and they were actually happy. Which sucks because I remember making Parker happy."

She tapped her chest where her heart should be but felt like it was missing.

"Parker smiling and laughing at my jokes was, like, the greatest feeling ever and I won't ever get to be the one that makes her smile again because her and Lyra are a good thing. I know they are a good thing. They are two good people that deserve each other, but I still want them to not work out so that I can show Parker that I can be better. I can be better, and I can make her smile again because I think about her all the time. Like all the time."

Zoe closed her eyes, running over everything she'd said. Trying to think of anything she missed.

Cassandra's mug clinked against the counter, drawing Zoe's attention back to her. The woman tapped two fingers to her lips.

"So, you love Parker?"

Zoe nodded.

"But Parker is now with Lyra. And you hurt both of these girls while dating them. Now you want the chance to still be with Parker, even if that means hurting the other girl, Lyra, for the second time," Cassandra summarized.

"Yes. I mean, no. But yes." She looked at her mother pleading for permission to go after the girl she wanted.

Cassandra took another drink of her coffee. Then she looked her daughter square in the eyes and instructed, "Leave those women alone."

"But what if Parker is my one true love?" Zoe reached for the fairytale that she remembered being read as a child by the woman across from her, "Like Dad was for you."

"She's not," her mother answered with a slight shake of her head.

The conversation not going how she'd wanted reinforced the reality her mother didn't understand. She needed to know going after love was the right thing to do from the person who loved her.

"How can you be so sure, though?"

Cassandra reached across the island and took her daughter's hand.

"Honey, I say this with all the love in my heart for you. Parker sounds like she's probably been through hell in her life. The type of person that others pick on, like the girl at the bar that dumped the drinks on her. Girls like your stripper turned therapist are usually treated like shit because they have a sweetness to them that others can't match, so they try to bring them down. They deserve someone equally sweet, which you say Lyra, your other ex, is." She tapped Zoe's hand. "And you don't have that kind of sweetness. Your daddy and brothers are gravel and grit, and you're just like them. So, you stay away from that girl. You let her be happy."

Zoe's teeth dug into her bottom lip. She ran through her memories, trying to find one example where she too had been sweet. When she came up empty, she tried, "I can be better."

But Cassandra shook her head. "Doesn't matter how great you could become now that you realize how cruel you're capable of being. That memory of you telling her she's trash will always be there. You'll always be another person that pushed her down and left her to figure out how to get back up. There's no fixing that."

"But we could get passed it. I could give her a better life. I could spoil her. I could show her that I think she hung the moon."

Cassandra released her daughter's hand. "Let's say you did that. You did work it out. Get married and have kids. You'd want to teach your children to not stay in a relationship with someone who breaks them down. But you can't do that while you romanticize your relationship where you tried to break their mother. You have to move on."

Zoe hated how much it made sense. Hated the way her mother's logic was impeccable. The reasons why it would be toxic and couldn't work, but she didn't want to accept it.

"When are you going to talk to your brother?" Cassandra asked.

Poison filled her veins at the mention of having to speak to the man who'd ruined her chances at happiness. She confessed, "I really just want to hit him. I mean, he ruined my relationship with Parker."

"How?"

Zoe's jaw dropped. Her mother was able to repeat practically everything she'd told her, but she'd somehow missed the part where her brother had caused all of this.

"He took me there and embarrassed me because I had been dating a stripper. He knew I would break up with her."

Her mother's eyes rolled again. "It's not Zachery's fault you were cruel."

Zoe stood up straighter. Her arms coming up to make her into a "W". "But, Mom, he put his hands on her. He put his hands on my girl when he knew she was mine. He said that if I stayed with her then I was bringing trailer trash into the family."

"Zoe Marie, women are not property. I don't belong to your father, just like Parker never belonged to you. And if she did belong to you, then you should have taken better care of her."

"If someone put their hands on you, Dad would defend your honor," the lawyer reasoned.

But Cassandra shook her head "no" once more. She pointed at Zoe. "You proved you're not her knight in shining armor when you stripped that girl of her self-confidence. You did that. And don't you compare yourself to your father. Your daddy was always so proud that he raised you up to be a fighter. 'My daughter, the big shot lawyer that fights for the voiceless,' he'd say. It's a good thing he can't see what type of fighter you've become."

"Mom," Zoe tried.

"I thought we taught you to fight for what is right, what is just."

"You did."

Cassandra raised her chin challenging her daughter. "What was right about calling Parker trash?"

"Nothing."

"What was right about what you did with that other girl, Lyra?"

"Nothing."

"And what about this case?"

Zoe's fallen face shot up. "What about the case?"

"You're going to drop the charges, right?"

"Mom, I can't just—" but she was cut off with a held-up hand.

"How old is the girl on trial?"

"Fifteen." Then Zoe mumbled, "She was fourteen when it happened."

Zoe's mom narrowed her eyes. Her voice dropped an octave when she said, "Zoe." But she stopped and sighed. "You want to hit your brother in the face for touching a grown woman, but you can't drop the charges for a child defending herself that you think was brutalized by a grown man."

"It's not that simple," Zoe stated.

"You're starting to sound like that witch, Nia." Cassandra's glare rose to the ceiling. "I understand that your father and her were close from working together, but she is not a good person. You remember what she did to Aribella. You know what kind of cruelty she is capable of."

"Cause that was any better than you and dad keeping a conversion camp pamphlet on the fridge," Zoe shot back.

Cassandra licked her lips. She didn't acknowledge the fact that neither of them had been actually okay with her coming out.

"If the stripper girl, Parker, or that other girl you kept hidden away had killed this man to protect this girl, what would you call it?" her mother asked.

"A heroic act." Zoe nodded her head after, confirming her initial reaction.

"But you're calling a child that defends herself a murderer."

Zoe thought of Zion on the boat. Remembered the resemblance to Gibson. "What if she hurt Zachery or Zion?" she asked.

Her mother folded her arms across her chest. "If your brothers hurt that little girl and you were charging her for murder, I would pay for the girl's lawyer."

"So, you're saying some people deserve to be murdered?"

Cassandra let out a huff of air. Zoe could see the wrinkle deepening across the woman's forehead. Her mother looked out the window, then back at her. "I can argue this with you all day and night. That won't change your mind. But ask yourself this, if that child hadn't killed that man, then where would she be now?"

"Still with him being abused."

"Or?"

"Dead."

"So, the question is, why do you think some lives matter more than others?"

Zoe stared at the blank television screen, contemplating the question. Wondering when she determined that some people were worth more than others. Which brought her back to Parker dancing on the stage. Her body swinging on a pole under the spotlight played across the screen. She remembered the look of fear in the girl's eyes when she saw Zoe.

Cassandra got up, blocking Zoe's memory from replaying.

"You can think while you clean," she instructed. "Start washing the dishes, while I go get the rest of your science experiments from your bedroom."

20

The droplets of water glided down the steamed-over mirror in the bathroom. Parker's rear had gone numb from sitting on the floor with the toddler snuggled against her chest as the shower ran at full temperature.

Tiny fingers rubbed softly over the silver pendant hanging from Parker's neck. The necklace brought the song to mind and off her tongue.

"Momma said there'd be days like this," she half whispered to the exhausted child. The memory of a steam filled room crashed against Parker's chest. The storm Lyra had chased away the night before returned when she closed her eyes and saw the same pendant hanging from her mother's neck.

She sang the same lines over and over until she choked on the tears. The words were replaced with a hum as she couldn't recall the rest of the lyrics.

Henrie began to cough and choke on the mucus that was coming loose. Parker patted the naked back of the girl, helping her get it up and out. She too was exhausted, but it didn't matter. Her niece needed her while her moms slept away the sickness.

When the coughing subsided, Henrie rested her head back against Parker, and closed her eyes. Her little nose struggled to get air past the congestion. Parker looked at the snotsucker Echo had handed her before they went into the bathroom. She'd vowed she would not be sucking anything through a tube from the child's nose, but that vow was wavering with every strangled breath. She picked up the tube and examined it. There was a filter midway through it, so it wasn't like the boogers would get in her mouth.

Henrie's little foot came up and kicked the tube out of Parker's pincer grip. The child whined and rubbed her boogery face all over the sweaty shirt Parker adorned. "I know, monster. I know. But she said it would help you breathe."

Parker looked at the terrible device again and tried to talk herself into being able to use it without puking. There had been enough vomit. She picked it up again and accepted that it would have to be done.

Henrie whined again, twisting to get out of Parker's hold. The wrestling match began and ended with Henrie on her back and hands held to her chest as Parker did the unthinkable. She bit down on the mouthpiece, aligned the other end of the tube with the child's nostril, and sucked. She gagged as the other end began to fill, but she didn't stop.

Screaming wildly, Henrie did everything she could to escape. She thrashed against the bathroom floor mat and landed a few kicks to Parker's legs. The job was done before Henrie formed actual tears, which Parker took as a win because she knew from experience where there were tears more boogers would follow.

She scooped the wild child back into her arms, but the sweet snuggle monster had vanished. Apparently, the terror monster was reinvigorated by the fresh oxygen rushing into her system. Parker's eyes rolled as regret itched its way under her skin for having given up the opportunity to cuddle the girl.

In the year that Echo had been a mother, Parker had done minimal baby holding. She'd never held a child before Henrie. The fear of being responsible for a human incapable of helping herself was overwhelming.

The phone beside her read 5pm. They'd been in steam for almost thirty minutes, and with Henrie moving about, she decided it was time to leave the sauna. She shut off the water and dried her face from the sweat that had begun to accumulate on her forehead. Henrie held up her pudgy arms when Parker squatted down to the child's level.

"You hungry, monster?"

Henrie put her fingers of both hands together, tapping them. Parker recognized the baby sign language as a request for 'more,' which caused her to pause.

'More what?'

The tiny fingers repeated the gesture until the girl's eyes scrunched together and she whined in frustration.

"What do you want more of?" Parker asked.

The signing continued as Parker held up the towel and wiped her face again, wondering if Henrie thought it was a game, but the toddler only whined more.

"Are you hungry?" she asked this time.

The toddler smacked her fingers together more vigorously and Parker realized her mistake. What she thought meant more was actually Henrie's sign for food. "Sorry, little beast. I get it now. Let's get you some apple sauce."

The air hung around Echo and Parker as they sat on the back porch. The attack on the house had been violently fast but left just as quickly, leaving Echo and Simone with a messed-up sleep pattern. Echo took a drink from the bottle of water as Parker rocked in the chair across from her. The redhead hummed into the coffee cup when she took another sip hoping to buy herself enough energy to drive home. She'd been up for almost twenty-four hours, and she was exhausted. Her head felt like it was being split in two from the lack of sleep.

"Thanks for coming," Echo said. Her face was less pale, and her eyes weren't as glassy. "I owe you."

Parker rubbed her fingers against her temple hoping it would ease some of the tension, then said, "You would have done the same for me."

They drank and listened to the crickets. Parker felt their fast-paced chirp was played specifically to torture her. The thought of torture led her down the fear of having to take care of Henrie and possibly coming up short, which traveled to the memories of the baby's namesake, the original Henry.

"You ever wonder why O.G. Henry didn't call? Why she just gave up?" Parker asked.

"She said she was going to break up with that girl, Kayla. You know the rich bitch that she met at the place you two danced." Echo set the bottle down, then pulled her legs up to her chest. A finger ran up and down the stubble on her thick legs. "Henry was an addict. She was a twitchy little ball of sunshine sure, but underneath it all... I mean, you remember the nightmares. The way she would scream. I still wake up to her screaming, even though she's been dead for more than a year. I know it's not like a ghost, but I don't think she planned on dying. I know they said it was just a typical overdose, but that girl she was with was bad news. Is still bad news, but she has the money to buy her way out of shit."

"Why did you name your withdrawing baby after her?"

Echo's laugh wasn't real. She still smiled like it was though, then nodded to the house.

"Simone was not a fan of it either, but she came so soon after Henry had passed, and she came into the world the same week the original left it. It was like giving her a second chance at life. Like, if I could get her through the worst, then maybe I could fix it. I mean, I was the one that fucked it up. I kicked her out and sent her back to that club after I found her in my office snorting coke. So many chances, but I shouldn't have turned her away."

Parker considered the life Echo and Simone had given Henrie. The life none of them had ever really known, well except Simone. Simone was raised right with the family and care. Parker marveled at how their paths had basically been decided by a coin toss. People like Simone got stability and people like them got constant chaos. She couldn't shake away the feeling that sometimes it felt the cards were stacked too high against their people.

"Did you ever think about giving up?" Parker asked.

"No." Parker felt Echo's eyes on her. "Did you?"

"After you left, yes. Henry broke and Evie showed up." Parker watched a gecko crawl around the porch light, pouncing on the moth resting against the stucco. "Officer Marcel was always in my face, and it just got worse when you left, and I just didn't want to fight anymore."

"I'm glad you didn't quit," Echo whispered.

Parker rocked back and forth. Her empty stomach sloshed with each motion, but she couldn't stop moving, afraid she'd fall asleep. She couldn't sleep when this was the first time Echo and her had time together like this. Time when Echo wasn't working or Simone hovering over them.

"Did you ever question if you'd even be alive right now? I mean, I never thought I'd be alive now. Like when I went to juvie, then the club. When I was in college, there was never actually an end goal. I just kept going day by day because I figured at some point it would just all be over. That I would be here and then I wouldn't," Parker confessed.

Echo's neck popped several times, then she returned to the same position. Her jaw worked over her words before she found ones that must have tasted right.

"How did you end up in juvie? You never said what you did."

Parker leaned back in the chair until it threatened to dump her out on her head. She rubbed her hands over her face, before settling back into the same to and fro motion.

"I punched a county prosecutor in the face."

"You did not!" Echo stated, sitting up straight with eyes wide and alert. "You?! Princess Parker punched a prosecutor!"

Parker nodded. A smug smile spread across her face at the memory of Nia Williams sitting on the courthouse steps holding her nose.

"Oh, I did." She looked at her friend. "Possibly the best day of my life was knocking that bitch on her fucking ass."

"Why did you hit her?"

"After my parents were arrested, she said that she'd be there for me. She acted like she actually cared about me. Now thanks to all my therapizing schooling, I know I transferred my need for my mom to her because she was there, and I spent so much time interviewing with her, and she would buy me ice cream and got me school supplies. It just seemed like she actually gave a flying fuck about my life."

The gecko slinked across the wall, gobbling up another unexpecting insect. It munched carelessly as Parker remembered Nia chewing her up and spitting her out.

"So... she put my parents away and then just Houdinied her way out of my life. She dumped me in a foster home." Parker smiled weakly at Echo, knowing the bad name that foster homes have. "The parental units were nice; I mean as nice as they could be to a bunch of traumatized teenagers. But there were a lot of us. Six including me, plus they had adopted two. There were these three boys, and..."

She stopped. Stopped talking, then breathing.

She focused on the fan whirring, until her heart settled enough to just say what happened.

"I called her for help after the first time one of the older boys raped me. I called her again when they came for me as a group. She didn't answer, but I kept calling. Then one day she showed up at the house. She accused me of just trying to get her attention and said that my lies would 'ruin those boys' lives.' She called me a stalker and said if I didn't stop calling her that she would file a restraining order."

Parker curled her legs up into the chair while chewing on her thumb nail until it bled. She'd never told anyone after Nia had shown up at the house. Now looking back, she realized that was the point she'd decided no one would ever see her.

"When did you hit her?" Echo sat watching the younger woman like an overexcited child surrounding a campfire.

"I saw her on the steps of the downtown courthouse after the hearing when the judge severed my parents' rights. And I just hit her." Parker smiled again as she rubbed her knuckles. "I hit her knowing she'd put me away. Which at the time seemed better than being raped every time they got me alone." Her eyes rolled when she added, "Which wasn't because then there was that guard that was on my ass the moment that I was processed."

She knew Echo had spent years following Officer Marcel into the storage closet. Years of being molested, only for Parker to find out after Echo's release the woman beside her had done it to protect her. A protection she couldn't provide on the outside. Parker had decided a long time ago never to tell Echo she'd suffered for nothing. She couldn't keep it in anymore though.

"I tried to stop it from happening," Echo said, the excitement in her voice gone. Her eyes were closed when Parker looked over at her.

With a shrug, Parker stated, "There was nothing you could do. Nothing anyone of us could do. And because she was a girl, it's not like anyone would take me seriously."

The gecko wiggled its way under the light fixture, giving Parker no further distraction.

"You know," Parker started, then sucked her teeth. Thinking about all the shit cards she'd been dealt. Accepting that even though she'd survived most people's worst nightmares, she hadn't let it break her. She'd regained the power to just be.

"I think that's why stripping was so easy for me. It wasn't like people hadn't seen me naked before, and when I was up there, I was in control. Like for the first time in my life I was in control of my body and since so many people would do anything to see it, touch it, I figured why not make money off it? And it got me through college. Gave me the ability to support myself, rely on myself. And I finally... finally... learned that I wasn't less than others. Even when Zoe, that girl from the bar, told me I was a piece of trash, I knew it was bullshit. Because people don't pay to see trash. People throw away trash, and she thought she was throwing me away. But I walked away and decided that I would never pretend to be less than I am ever again."

Parker held up a hand, "I mean, I cried that my girlfriend broke up with me, but it wasn't because she thought I was trash. I cried because I let her think she was better than me. That she thought she had the power to break me."

"Then why do you act broken all the time?" Echo asked. "I mean, you have these moments where you are totally badass, like with Andrea. When you were serving that night, you talked to people with no issue. But most of the time you hide away. Pretend to be invisible."

"I guess...it's, like, customers ain't scary to me." Parker considered if what she'd said was true. Deciding it was, she nodded at her own assessment. "I think that I'm actually scared of people that care about me. I always wonder if today is the day that they will stop caring. So, if I just keep my mouth shut, stay out of the way, then they'll still be there."

"You think I'm going to leave you?" Echo asked.

"Not leave. Just stop caring. So, it's easier to stay quiet and not give you a reason to not want me around anymore."

"I'm not going anywhere," Echo said like a promise. That was something Parker thought was true. Echo always told the truth or she wouldn't' say anything, but a part of Parker didn't know what was true and what was fake.

"I hope one day I stop wondering if this is the day. Just like I hope one day to see a future beyond right now."

A breeze gently blew through the palm trees surrounding Echo's pool. The crickets put their fiddles away and let Parker's words drift into the night.

Parker found the freeway of planes in the sky. She watched the blinking lights rise in the sky, leaving the Devil's playground. She smiled at the realization that she'd been born in Hell to two demons, then wondered which of the seven circles she currently resided in.

She yawned, which was mirrored by Echo. Setting her bare feet on the cool concrete, Parker felt her body relax. "I need to get home before I pass out."

"You should stay, it's late," Echo protested as another yawn ripped through Parker.

"I miss my bed," Parker said, letting her body extend into a long stretch before standing. "I'll call you tomorrow."

21

The BMW's air conditioning blasted in Zoe's face as she sat outside Greyson Academy. She flipped the visor down and checked her eye liner in the mirror. She wiped the corners of her eyes, but it only caused them to water more. She slapped the visor shut, then the vents away.

Students passed by the gate, chatting animatedly. Some were covered in tattoos, others plastered in rainbows or neon. All of them carried backpacks and books. But she didn't see a single gang flag hanging from a pocket or wrapped around a head. She regretted putting faith in the lies Nia had spun.

With a heavy breath, Zoe ran through her apology. Nothing Evie said about her mother prepared her to face Dilynn Greyson in the flesh. She swallowed the pride she'd clung to as a lifeline and stepped out of the car.

The office assistant smiled warmly as she made her way through the eerily quiet lobby. The girl looked like she could be a student, but Zoe made an active decision not to assume anything.

"How can I help you?" she asked. A finger twirled a lock of hair as she chewed on the pen in her hand.

"I'm here to see Mrs. Greyson." Zoe placed her hands on the counter, then removed them.

"Oh yeah." She glanced down at the computer in front of her. "You must be... Zoe Robinson."

"Yes, that's me," Zoe said. She looked down at the black fitted suit. The bottom was wrinkled, and she tried to press them out, but was jarred when the assistant pushed her chair on wheels into the hallway without getting up.

"Hey Greyson!" the teen yelled, "That lawyer lady you hate is here. The young one. Not the nasty boomer. You busy?"

Zoe stood still, unsure of what she was waiting for.

"Send her back," came through the open door down the hall.

The assistant turned her chair back to Zoe and offered a fake smile. "All the way down. She's waiting for you."

Zoe passed a wall of signatures. Read over the vinyl sticker proclaiming that all who signed were here and mattered. It wasn't a long walk, but she took her time looking over all the kids Evie said her mother helped. So many names, and a new guilt rose in Zoe's throat when she found Olivia's name written in careful print.

She knocked on the frame when she reached the door and saw Dilynn

Greyson sitting in a chair on the wrong side of the desk with her name on it. Blue eyes rose to meet Zoe, but Dilynn didn't bother to get up. Instead, the tiny blonde folded an oversized cardigan around herself and gestured to the seat across from her.

"Thank you for taking the time to meet with me, Mrs. Greyson," Zoe said as she entered the room and sat in the chair offered.

"Just Dilynn," the woman stated. "I told Landon he had to be here. Just in case someone said something stupid."

Zoe smiled at Landon Woods standing in front of a window overlooking the vacant courtyard of the school. Landon looked at Dilynn staring at the photos on the wall, before casting Zoe a forced smile. She'd gotten to know the man through his girlfriend. Learned that the cocky man she saw in the courtroom was a persona he never held outside of it.

"Of course," Zoe said. She folded her hands in her lap, but it felt weird, so she shifted in the leather seat and clasped the armrests. She tried to relax, but Dilynn's coldness made the hairs on her arm and neck stand.

'Just say it,' she told herself.

"I should start with an apology," Zoe said, searching the other woman for any indication she was even listening. When she got nothing, she tried again. "The way that I—"

"Attacked my daughter." Dilynn's gaze had reached her face. Her eyes were as cold as the Pacific, and the dark eye make-up made her look fiercer than she'd let on when she sat in court.

Zoe nodded. "Yes, that is the most appropriate word to use. I was out of line and the things I said..." Her eyes fell to her own hands, unable to meet Dilynn's challenging gaze. "It was unforgivable."

"Yep," Dilynn said, popping the "p" at the end of the word. Her tongue probed the inside of her mouth, and she leaned back in her chair.

"I—"

"Ms. Robinson, let's just—" Dilynn started, but Landon's large hand came to rest on Dilynn's shoulder, stopping the woman mid-sentence.

"Momma G," Landon warned softly.

"Yeah, I know. I know," the older woman stated, waving her hands in the air. She folded her arms over her chest and huffed.

Zoe squirmed when Dilynn's eyes narrowed in her direction. She started to open her mouth, then closed it as Dilynn ran her tongue along the bottom of her front teeth. The tiny woman's leg bounced on the ball of her foot.

Landon's hand fell back to his side. Calmly, he started, "What do you—"

"You know what, fuck this nicety bullshit." Dilynn's shoulders rose, her posture straightening. She looked Zoe dead in the eye. "You're an asshole, and that bullshit you spewed is unforgivable. But here you are trying to be forgiven.

What did you decide to grow a conscience all of a sudden? Walk into my school in your knock off suit and expect me to be nice because you think you're some big shot." She rolled her eyes and waved her hand in the air. "Well, screw that. I met my niceness quota for the day. So, if you are here to ask me for money or anything else like that snake of a boss of yours, then I hope you trip on those stripper heels on your way out the mother fuckin' door."

"Language!" a voice called from somewhere else in the office.

Zoe wasn't sure where the voice had come from until a head of chocolate curls peeked through the door. "The walls are thin so stop yelling cuss words."

Dilynn rolled her eyes again. She pointed at the head in the doorway, "Zoe Robinson, this is Alex Trikru, my partner and keeper. Pronouns are they and them, and don't fuck it up. And this is the county prosecutor that—"

"Managed to hurt two of my daughters in less than a month," Alex finished. They closed the door softly as they entered. Landon shrugged his shoulders as Alex said, "I thought you promised to keep this civil."

They made their way around Dilynn, leaning against the desk at their wife's side. With arms crossed over their chest, Zoe noticed the toned biceps stretching the fitted button-up. As petite and soft as Dilynn appeared, Alex countered it with their stoic mask of indifference and firm frame.

Zoe raised her brows and forced a smile at Alex.

"Is she here to ask for money too?" Alex asked, pulling Dilynn's glare from Zoe.

Dilynn's attention was diverted momentarily to something outside. She got up and made her way to the window.

Landon cleared his throat. "Momma G. Obi. Let's hear Zoe out."

Zoe looked at the combat boots that weren't even laced on Dilynn's ridiculously small feet. They brought a smile to her face. This was the woman who'd raised Lyra and Evie, and she should have expected the fire balls being launched at her.

"I had pie with Evie a few nights ago. You both raised a hell of a woman," Zoe admitted, hoping the couple would break down some of the barricades. "She thinks I'm an asshole too, as does my mother. And, I have had to come to terms with my need to make some serious changes in my life."

"That's a start," Dilynn stated vacantly.

"I promise to show you that I don't want to be an asshole." Zoe held up her hand, "And I didn't come here for money or excuses. I actually came to speak with you about the trial and Olivia."

"About fucking time," Dilynn proclaimed. She turned back to Zoe only for a moment before the outside drew her attention back.

Zoe watched Landon try to swallow the chuckle. He looked at his girlfriend's mother, and Zoe couldn't miss the admiration in his eyes.

"I will be filing a motion to have Olivia's case dismissed," Zoe said. She rummaged through her bag and pulled out the paperwork, handing it to Landon's eager hand.

"Why the sudden change of heart?" Alex asked.

Zoe's skin itched as their eyes searched over her face.

"I'm going to be straight with you." Zoe leaned against her knees hoping to close the distance. "I have ignored the circumstances of what caused Olivia to murder Gibson, but thanks to your daughters I can't anymore. I can't live with myself if I continue to pursue this case."

She expected Dilynn to turn back around, but the woman's fixation on whatever was outside made it seem like she wasn't even listening.

Zoe sat back, her shoulders slumping but then she remembered Alex Trikru was watching her. She quickly straightened her posture and clasped her hands in her lap.

She checked to find Dilynn still staring out the window and figured it would be best to try again. "I would like the opportunity to work with you, Dilynn. And Olivia. To find out what actually happened to her so that we can right her name. She'll be an adult one day, and it will be important that her real story paints her as something other than a murderer."

Dilynn moved from her position and left the room without acknowledging anything Zoe had said. Everyone watched her curiously until she was out of sight.

"Did I say something to piss her off?" Zoe asked Landon.

He shook his head as the blonde returned, being tailed by Olivia.

"Alex, did Parker call in sick today?" Dilynn asked.

Alex looked at the ceiling, considering the question. Then answered, "No. She called in yesterday, but I haven't heard anything from her today."

"Well, Olivia says she's not in the art room." Dilynn grabbed her phone from the desk, hit some buttons, and held the phone to her ear.

Zoe glanced over at the teenager standing as close to the wall of the office as possible. The girl looked up only for a second but when her eyes met Zoe's, she dropped her chin back down. Hair fell in front of her face. The girl was terrified of the monster Zoe had let herself become, and it made breathing difficult for Zoe.

Dilynn gripped the phone in her hand. "It went to voicemail."

"I'll call Lyra," Alex said, their phone already in their hand. "You call Marissa."

Alex looked at Landon, and he nodded. "I'll call Evie."

Zoe watched the three each hold their own conversations with the people who did answer the phone. She became acutely aware of her feet and legs as she listened to snippets of each conversation.

"You stayed the night with her on Friday but—" Alex said.

Dilynn nodded, then clarified, "So, you said she left on Sunday at like 1 AM."

Landon's eyes wandered back and forth between the others. He asked, "Could you run a check for any accidents on Sunday morning around 1?"

Zoe's body became a statue as she waited for them to hang up. Her mind pushed away the information that Lyra and Parker had spent the night together. Her whole focus was on Dilynn's conversation with the person who may have been the last to see or hear from Parker.

Alex hung up first, followed by Landon. Alex went to a filing cabinet behind the desk, a finger running over the drawers until they found the one they wanted. They flipped through the files, then closed the drawer retrieving nothing. Without a word, they left the office.

Landon walked over to Olivia. Zoe watched out of the corner of her eye as he lowered his giant frame to a knee. He didn't touch the girl; just spoke too quietly to hear what he was saying. She looked back at Dilynn when Olivia began to raise her head.

Zoe's eyes peaked over when she heard Olivia's voice for the first time. "The room was dark when I got there. Her things weren't there, but I waited. Then, I figured I messed up, so I came up here." The childlike cadence to the girl's words pulled at Zoe's heart. Soft and curious at the same time quiet and withdrawn.

'You tried to send a little girl to prison.'

"That was the right thing to do. Thank you for letting us know." Landon held up a fist, and the girl's small sweatshirt-covered hand came up to give him a bump.

Dilynn set her phone down and let out a long breath. Her head was shaking slowly back and forth. Teeth chewing on her lips until she ran her hands over her face and through the roots of her hair. She stopped and pulled slightly until Alex came back with a manilla folder.

"What's wrong?" they asked.

"Marissa said Parker left her house a little after 1 AM. They all had been sick, and Marissa called her to come help with Henrie."

Alex nodded in agreement. "Yeah, Lyra said Marissa had called Friday at, like, two or three in the morning and Parker had rushed off to help them."

Dilynn sighed, then added, "I guess they had something that hit all of them so fast that they couldn't function. She stayed with them and took care of the baby. But Marissa said she hasn't heard from Parker since she left. Which means that girl is probably as sick as they were and was too stubborn to call anyone."

Landon picked up his phone again as it buzzed in his hand. "Hey, E." He held a hand over the bottom and said, "There were no accidents reported Sunday morning that match Parker's name or description." He returned to the phone call, explaining the situation.

Zoe felt momentarily relieved at Landon's intel, but it quickly vanished as she realized no one still knew where Parker was. The woman, who could have been hers and a part of her family if she'd been the person her parents had raised her to be, was somewhere sick and alone. She felt the weight of Parker's safety falling on her shoulders.

Dilynn looked at Alex, who nodded silently. "I'll pick up Lyra on my way. She said that Parker lives in my old apartment building."

Alex held the file up to him and pointed at a page within it. "Yeah, I'll text you the address so that you can GPS it."

Zoe watched the others move about the room. All anxious and concerned about a person they barely knew. They couldn't know Parker like she knew her. But they were moving while she was standing still.

The realization train hit her as she tried to convince her feet to move. Parker wasn't alone, well figuratively. All of these good people cared about her and were springing into action to run to her rescue. Just like her friend at the bar. Just like Parker had run to help them when they were ill. Parker had a family, and people who cared enough to hunt her down. Just like Zoe's mother did when she didn't return any texts.

Parker didn't need her.

Parker needed the Greysons.

The weight on Zoe's shoulders faded, and she plotted her escape. She needed to get away from this school, this office, and the Greyson family. She needed to for once follow her mother's instructions.

'Leave Parker alone. She's better off with them than with you.'

Zoe stood up as Alex kissed their wife and left. Landon finished texting what could only be Parker's address to Evie, before putting his phone in his pocket.

"I should get going." Zoe forced another smile on her face as she extended her hand toward Dilynn.

Blue eyes crinkled at the corners, then tilted to one side. "You said you wanted to talk to Olivia." Ignoring Zoe's outstretched hand, Dilynn's short arm extended towards the girl who'd become one with the wall. "We're all here, so you should tell her that you have decided to drop the charges."

Landon chortled, then said, "Well, you kind of just did, Momma G."

Dilynn shoved the Hulk-like frame that didn't budge. "Shut it," she said to him.

Zoe turned to Olivia. Bright green eyes peeked up from behind the dark hair hanging in her face. Zoe offered her a weak smile and nodded. "Olivia," she started, but stopped. The girl's eyes had disappeared again. Zoe glanced at Landon, who only offered her a subtle shrug of the shoulders.

She took a play from his book and moved towards the girl. The small feet inched closer to the wall until they hit the baseboard. and she had nowhere left to go.

Zoe reached out and took the girl's hand hanging loosely at her side. She squeezed it slightly and softened her tone. "I owe you an apology. My mother always said that you have to apologize right though, so can you please look at me?"

Slowly, the vibrant green eyes rose again. They were wide and searching for something on Zoe's face. Zoe offered her another soft smile.

"I'm sorry, Olivia. I'm sorry for assuming things about you and that no one was there to protect you when you needed them, and that people like me treated you so coldly. I'm sorry that I made it seem like you were lying and said those awful things to Officer Greyson that you heard. Because what I said..."

A silent tear fell down Olivia's face that she quickly wiped away on the sleeve of the oversized hoodie.

Zoe squeezed the girl's hand again as the green eyes faded to brown and the dark hair to blonde. She pulled the girl she knew wasn't Parker into a hug. The tiny body stiffened in Zoe's arms, but Zoe couldn't let her go.

"I'm sorry I made you think that you were less deserving of justice. That your life didn't matter as much as another person's."

Olivia's hands rose from her sides and wrapped around Zoe's arms. She clung to the lawyer that had tried to lock her away, and Zoe felt a new weight fall on her shoulders. A weight she'd never considered was in the cards for her.

The girl's face buried against Zoe's chest, which became damp with the teenager's tears. Her arms squeezed tighter as the girl's body shook in her grasp, and smothered sobs broke through the quiet office. She turned her head to press her cheek to the brown hair. Oily stink and sweat filled her nostrils but it didn't matter. She'd seen enough pain in this world to know why a teenage girl would refuse to clean herself.

Zoe opened her eyes to find Dilynn hanging on to Landon's arm. Dilynn's perfectly manicured fingers were held over her mouth. The coldness in her eyes was replaced with lulling seas. Her hand dropped to join the other around Landon's arm, and Dilynn softly mouthed the words, "Thank you."

The sobs slowly dissipated. When the girl's face came up for air, Zoe still held her. She waited for the girl to let her know Olivia was done with the hug she hadn't asked for or wanted.

"He said no one would believe me," Olivia whispered.

Zoe squeezed her again and then released her. She cupped the girl's blackhead covered cheeks.

"I know at first I made it seem like what he said was true. But it's not. Officer Greyson believed you, even when you didn't say a word. Ms. Carter and Mrs. Greyson believed you. And I believe you."

Olivia bit her lower lip and lowered her eyes. "I didn't know what to tell them when they asked their questions. I couldn't tell them what happened because most of it I don't know. It was all so fuzzy."

Zoe released one of Olivia's hands. She led the girl towards the chairs in front of Dilynn's desk. She sat across from Olivia, not releasing the connection of their still clasped hands.

"Olivia, did Vincent Gibson force you to have sex with him?"

The girl nodded. Her chin quivered.

"Did it happen right before you stabbed him."

This time the brown hair swayed side to side.

"Did you kill him because he made you have sex with him?" Zoe probed softly.

Olivia looked into Zoe's eyes, but then over to Dilynn. She licked her lips before opening her mouth. It closed as her eyes fell to Zoe's hand holding hers.

"No," she whispered.

Zoe inhaled. Question after question ran through her mind, but nothing seemed right. Nothing made Zoe feel like it would help her understand what happened better.

"Did you have a baby, Olivia?" Dilynn asked, kneeling down beside Zoe.

Zoe started to turn to Dilynn, but the girl's green eyes grew momentarily before she dropped her chin and pulled her hand away.

Olivia pulled at the baggy sweatshirt and wrapped her arms around her middle. Zoe stared at Dilynn trying to figure out what type of Jedi mind powers this crazy woman possessed.

Dilynn mouthed, "Parker."

Zoe's lips pulled up in a smile.

'Parker had gotten through before anyone else. Of course, she had.'

22

The bathroom's tile floor helped ease the fire burning Parker's naked flesh. Every breath hurt, and her diaphragm quaked through another aftershock.

'Listen up, stomach, there is nothing left. It's bile. That's it and there's nothing left of it either. You're just heaving to heave, and I can't anymore.'

Parker choked as her stomach twisted tighter. She pushed up and clutched the porcelain bowl. She prayed that it would stop, but it didn't. Nothing came out but her stomach kept contracting.

Her head lay against the toilet seat when the front door closed. She knew it was just her imagination though. She was alone. She was sure she would drown in the toilet bowl when she passed out from all of this.

"Parker?"

She hadn't imagined it. Someone was in her apartment. Someone was checking on her.

"Her car is here," the voice stated. "She has to be here."

Parker listened to the floor creak under the weight of whoever was coming.

"What the fuck did I just step in? Oh my god did I just step in puke?" a second voice cried out. Parker would know Evie's voice anywhere.

Evie was in her apartment and had stepped in her puke. Parker started to smile but the smallest movement twisted her insides tighter.

"Don't come...in," she choked again.

She couldn't stop the footsteps closing in on her vulnerable position. Her body didn't cease its heaving when Lyra cried out, "Oh shit. Evie, get a towel."

'No. No. No.'

Lyra's hands pulled Parker's puke spattered hair out of her face as she thrust her head back in the toilet.

"I got you. Just get it out," Lyra cooed.

When her heaving ceased, Parker tried to explain. "There's nothing... nothing left."

Her abs tightened, and her back was freezing as the sweat soaked skin was met with the cold air.

"Won't stop," she choked.

Parker couldn't stop the tears or the heaving until the tiniest amount of bile coated her tongue. She scraped it against her filthy teeth and spat.

"I'm sorry," she cried.

Lyra eased her way down the wall next to Parker, pulling the exhausted woman to her chest. "It's okay. You're okay. We're here to help."

There was no energy left to push Lyra away. Parker feebly tried with her words, "No, you'll get sick too."

Lyra's hand stroked the oily vomit speckled hair, "Shhhhhhhh. It's going to be okay."

"Here," said another familiar voice, but Parker couldn't place it. Her eye lids were too heavy, and her head was too tired to focus on figuring it out.

Parker felt a new form of torture as the sandpaper fabric of a towel was draped over the front of her. She breathed through her gritted teeth. It's too much, but she can't get her mouth to move to tell Lyra to get it off.

"How long have you been puking?" the familiar voice asked Parker.

She doesn't have an answer. She's not sure how long she was on the bathroom floor. She knows she went to Echo's on Saturday morning. It was still dark, but it was Saturday because she left Lyra in bed after their date. She'd gotten home Sunday.

"Sunday." Parker's throat ached as the word scraped slowly against what was left of her esophagus.

"Parker, we're going to get you to someone who can help you."

Parker squinted at the face above her that was talking. Alex Trikru looked her directly in the eyes, never casting a glance anywhere else. They smiled reassuringly. "I have to touch you to pick you up. I don't want you to be scared, but I won't drop you."

'My boss is seeing me naked.'

"Parker," they said again. "I need you to give me a sign that you are okay if I pick you up."

She lifted her head, just enough to let it fall back down, resigned to this new reality. It's not like people haven't seen her naked before. For all she knew, Alex could have been one of the many people who'd sat in the audience as she stripped. She gripped the abrasive fabric to her chest as her body was pulled from the safety of Lyra's embrace.

Alex laid Parker on the bed that she couldn't remember seeing in the last day. Or was it two? The mattress springs dug into her sensitive flesh and the bones in her body prodded for a weak spot to escape her skin. She groaned in protest, hoping her bones would understand that today was not the day to run away.

"Should we take her to the hospital?" Lyra asked.

"Her insurance hasn't kicked in yet because she just started two weeks ago. We're going to take her back to the house and your grandmother is already on her way. I called Simone and she said it was a twenty-four-hour stomach flu—"

"She's been sick since Sunday and it's Tuesday. That's more than twenty-four hours," Lyra protested. "I'll pay the bill. Take her to the hospital."

"Lyra, there is nothing they will do that your grandmother can't."

Every drawer that opened and closed sounded like bombs being dropped in Parker's skull. She didn't understand what was happening until she felt the terry cloth sweatpants being pulled up her legs. Her head was lifted, and a large shirt was pulled over. She opened her eyes, instantly grateful it was Lyra putting clothes on her instead of Alex.

Her head swirled like she was running down a drain. She gripped the shirt and tried to pull it closer. Everything was suddenly cold instead of burning.

Parker felt her body lifted once more. She looked up at Alex's smooth jaw. She leaned her head against Alex, humming the tune of Happy Days to chase away her nausea.

"She's dehydrated and that fever hasn't broken yet. No one forced fluids into her like she did for Simone and her family. Now shut up and hold the door," Alex commanded.

Parker's fingers searched over the softest sheets she'd ever felt before. She wiggled her toes trying to figure out what the weird bandage was wrapped around her foot. Her body still ached but her eyes didn't feel as heavy.

She opened them hesitantly, the smell of GoJo and oil made the space unfamiliar. She squinted and let her eyes adjust. The room was mostly dark, light barely peeked around the edges of the dark curtains. She made out a bookcase filled with oddly shaped gears and wires sticking out of them. Frames on the walls were filled with vintage cars and above the bed was a full-size classic bumper.

"Don't you start your fucking germaphobe shit, Alex Trikru!" She smiled at the sound of Dilynn's voice coming through the crack of the door.

"Cupcake, please don't make me," Alex begged.

Something out there slammed, and Dilynn was still yelling, but Parker couldn't make out the words because a loud alarm began to screech.

Her gaze settled on the slumped body sleeping in the armchair alongside the bed. The woman grumbled in an unintelligible dialect. Even in the dark, she knew it was Lyra.

The door squeaked in protest as it opened, letting the light from somewhere else in the house flood the floor. Dilynn walked into the room carrying a bottle of Gatorade.

"You had us all pretty worried," Dilynn whispered.

Dilynn held up her hand, and Parker leaned in so Dilynn could check her temperature. "Lean forward," she instructed.

Parker did as she was told but jumped when Dilynn pulled up the back of Parker's shirt and placed her cold hand on the middle of her spine.

"Feels the same, I think." She dropped the shirt and pushed Parker a little, signaling she could lay back down. "Let's be honest, I forgot the thermometer and I figured I would try to, like, supermom it."

"Kinda feels like you succeeded from here," Parker said, then panicked over having referred to Dilynn, her boss, as acting like a mom toward her.

Somewhere in the house an alarm blared loudly. Dilynn ignored it like she was unfazed by the announcement of the apocalypse coming.

The mother looked at the sleeping form next to the bed. "She refused to leave. But I guess she's gone ahead and jumped right in. Heard the first date went well." Dilynn's eyebrow raised, and the corners of her mouth turned up.

"We didn't sleep together. I mean we slept, but not like... you know." Parker looked at the IV in her arm to avoid Dilynn's gaze. She followed the tube to the bag hanging from the side of the old-fashioned bumper above the bed. "Where am I?"

"Our house," Dilynn explained. "Alex and Lyra brought you here and my mother paid us a home visit. She's a general surgeon."

Parker looked down at her stomach. Pulling up the shirt, she searched for any indication she'd had surgery.

Dilynn laughed. "She just hooked you up to a banana drip and gave you a Zofran, which basically makes it, so you stop feeling nauseated. It's basically all the stuff you need to get rehydrated and help your body flush the shit in your system. She said you're going to be fine, and she'll be back later this afternoon to remove the IV."

'Of course, they have a doctor in the family that makes house calls.'

"How'd you know I was awake," Parker asked.

Dilynn pointed toward Parker's feet hidden between the covers, drawing Parker's attention back to the bandage. "When Levi was a baby, my mom got us this thing called an Owlette. Basically, it wraps around the baby's foot and monitors heart rate, oxygen levels, and movement. It also sends an alert to my phone when there's a change. Sorry, I know you're not a baby, but I figured you'd be pretty freaked out when you woke up in Lyra's old room."

Parker wiggled her toes around. The alarm to take shelter sounded again. She looked up at Dilynn. "Sorry."

"May I sit?" Dilynn pointed to the edge of the bed as she chuckled at Parker's apology. When Parker nodded, the woman carefully sat on the edge and handed over the Gatorade. "Drink, please."

Taking the bottle from the woman, Parker tried to open it, but her arms were too weak. Dilynn took it back and quickly uncapped it, before handing it over.

"Well, my dear. My best guess is you got whatever nasty virus Simone and Marissa had. Since you didn't call for anyone to help you, you basically almost died from dehydration."

Parker took each sip hesitantly, making a note that Dilynn liked the word 'basically' a lot. The strawberry flavor coated her tongue, and she hated having to swallow it with the idea of what it would taste like coming back up, since she didn't like strawberries to begin with. She capped the bottle and set it out of the way.

Dilynn took her hand and squeezed it softly. "I bet you have never asked anyone for help and when they try to help, you push it away."

Fingers on her free hand fiddled with the sheet. She wasn't sure what she was supposed to do with Dilynn's non-boss-like behavior. Thus far she'd managed to keep the woman and her motherliness at an arm's distance. But in this bed, taped to a baby monitor made her wonder if this was how her father's victims had felt. Helpless and trapped.

"It's called hyper independence, and many of the people in this house feel like they have to carry the burden of everyone else also," Dilynn explained, clearly oblivious to Parker's discomfort. The woman's hands smoothed out the wrinkles of the sheet covering Parker like she was tucking in a child for the night.

Parker bit her lip and searched for a way out of the room. There wasn't any easy path since she was still connected to the IV. She looked at the concern etched into the wrinkles around the woman's eyes.

"Um... why do you care so much?" Parker asked.

"She's incapable of not caring about everyone," Lyra contributed groggily from her seat. "Mommy Dearest left out the part that you'll run to everyone else's aide and ignore your own safety. She's the literal queen of hyper independence, or as Obi once said a Mary Sue."

Dilynn's eyes narrowed at Lyra. "Pot calling the kettle black there?"

Lyra waved her hand in the air shooing away Dilynn's words. She wondered if Lyra had learned the gesture from the mother who seemed compelled to collect damaged young adults like a spinster collects cats.

"They called my character a Mary Sue, not me."

"The character you wrote yourself into, which the crazy English teacher taught me—"

"Shut it. You're going with your Obi so change your clothes. I can smell you from here."

Lyra picked up the shirt she was wearing and sniffed it. "I don't smell," then she cast an awkward glance at Parker.

Parker felt her face grow hot. She tried to discreetly sniff herself but regretted the action immediately. There was no doubt the rank onions aggravating Dilynn's nose was her own stench.

"Uh, can I use the bathroom?" Parker asked, finding her way out.

Dilynn stopped glaring at her daughter and smiled. She picked up the bag and the tube so Parker could slide out from under the sheet. Her legs were weak when she started to get up, but Dilynn quickly moved to allow Parker to use her as a support.

Shame coated Parker's skin, adding to the embarrassing stink now rubbing off on Dilynn's arm. She came to terms with the reality that even if she needed to escape the house, she couldn't in her current state.

"Hold up," Lyra said. She rocked in the chair to her feet, limping to a chest of drawers. From within, she pulled a fresh change of clothes and handed them over to Dilynn.

"You ready?" the blonde asked.

Parker nodded, allowing Dilynn to lead her across the hallway to the bathroom. Dilynn pointed to the cabinet above the toilet.

"There's washcloths, baby wipes, deodorant, and some new toothbrushes in there. I ask that you don't shower until my mom gets here to take out the IV. Holler if you need anything." She smiled softly and closed the door behind her as she left Parker alone.

Once fully relieved, Parker made quick work of scrubbing her pits, under her breasts, and her crotch with an excessive amount of baby wipes. Then she applied an overly generous amount of deodorant to the same areas. When she felt at least semi-clean, she looked through the various packages of toothbrushes. She settled on a standard blue one, even though she really wanted to use the one with Trolls on it.

The tingly sensation of brushing her teeth perked up her still fatigued body. The minty freshness made her feel more human and less zombie. It gave her hope that maybe she'd be able to convince the Greysons she was in the clear.

When Parker was finished, she picked up the yellow bag and opened the door to find Lyra following Alex down the hallway. Alex grumbled under their breath as Lyra pulled a holely shirt over her head.

"Here," Lyra offered a hand. She took the bag from Parker and led her down the hallway to a room bigger than Parker's entire apartment.

Parker stood with her mouth open as she tried to take in the Great Room. She knew Dilynn had money, but she wasn't expecting this kind of wealth by the way the older woman usually dressed like a middle-class soccer mom.

A little face peeked around the giant granite island in the kitchen with a bright smile. Her tiny hand lifted, opening and closing several times in a wave. Parker smiled at the little human who looked so much like Alex. Questions filled Parker's mind about how the kid could look exactly like Alex with Dilynn's deep blue eyes.

Dilynn stood with her back to them, stirring something on a six-burner stove in a kitchen that belonged in Better Homes and Garden. She turned when Lyra tried to catch Parker from stumbling on her still weak legs and dropped the IV bag. With a smile, Dilynn instructed, "Oh, good. Parker, sit. I made you some soup."

Lyra scrunched up her face and leaned in closely. "Her soup is gross. I'll bring you back something when we're done."

"Where are you going?" Parker asked, realizing they were leaving her here alone with Dilynn acting like a Stepford wife. Her eyes followed Alex with a bucket filled with cleaning supplies and the answer clicked into place without Lyra having to respond.

"Please, don't." she begged. "It's not your—"

"You sit and stop arguing," Dilynn commanded, the niceties dropped at the suggestion of someone disobeying her. Her spoon was pointing to the chair at the end of the long farmhouse table. Unsure of what else to do when Dilynn's smiling face had turned hard as stone, Parker sat.

"You two, go."

Alex's upper lip raised like they were going to growl at their wife.

"Now." Dilynn stated.

Parker stared at the table with brows raised.

"Stop ordering me around, wife," Alex said indignantly. "You're scaring Parker with all your barking. She's ill and frail, and she's already going to choke on your—"

"Say one word about my cooking, Alex Trikru, and you will be eating nothing but what your own hands can forge from the fucking yard that you'll be sleeping in," Dilynn warned, the spoon wavering in the air.

The toddler teetered around the kitchen island, giggling. Little ocean blue eyes sparkled in the light at Parker as she made her way to the table and climbed up into her own little booster chair at the end of a long bench where a coloring book and crayons awaited her.

"You owe me," Alex grumbled.

But Lyra quickly groaned. She pleaded, "Please save it until Parker can go home. Evie and I already need therapy from hearing your version of debt repayment."

There was no containing the laughter falling from Parker. She covered her lips in an attempt to stifle it, but her sore body still shook at Lyra's defeated plea. It seemed so normal even though everything about this situation was weird.

The spoon sailed through the air. It missed Lyra, which Parker assumed was its target, and smacked Alex in the back. They turned so slowly while the wooden utensil bounced twice before settling against the floor. Parker wondered if someone had flipped on the slo-mo film option for this very moment.

She looked at Dilynn standing perfectly still behind the island with her mouth open wide and eyebrows practically connected to her hairline. The blonde's hands slowly raised in the air, as she explained, "It was an accident... Meant to hit..." Her words fell to a quiet yelp as Alex charged her.

With silent grace and terrifying speed, Alex moved around the table and the kitchen island. The little girl at the table clapped and laughed wildly as Alex caught their wife trying to flee. They pulled her flush against their body and held her two hands against her chest. Dilynn screeched, when Alex flipped on the tap in the sink and fumbled with the detachable nozzle. They sprayed water all over the top of Dilynn's head, who thrashed in their grip.

Parker, who still hadn't gotten over the spoon being thrown, was now unable to stifle the laughter of Alex for once seeming to win against their incorrigible wife. The couple laughed together and reminded her of a time she swore she just imagined when her parents would laugh and jest with each other.

Before Parker could compare and contrast the only happy couples she'd ever experienced, Evie came bashing into the room. The dense frame slid on the floor, her body colliding with a hutch as she tried to stop herself. She panted as she yelled, "I thought someone was murdering you!" She held the hip she'd smacked, moaning in subtle pain. Then bent over trying to catch her breath.

Lyra laughed, pointing at her sister from the same spot that had saved her from the spoon debacle. Between her chuckles, she said, "Why you would ever run into this house with those two sickos and think someone was being murdered is still a mystery. It's like you want to catch them having sex."

Parker's eyes fell to the table reminding herself to stay in the present not the past. That normal people did run to help those they love when in potential danger. She'd written the past off as figments of imagination she'd created in parallel with the models she'd seen in stories and films. To her, relationships like her parents had pretended to have with playful banter and loving looks were an act. But Dilynn and Alex were real people who looked at each other lovingly and had kids and jobs and lived in a nice house. All of the things Parker avoided because they couldn't be real. Even when they had been.

"Shut up, asshat," Evie growled. She moved to the table and started to sit next to Parker. Then with a quick glance at the yellow IV bag, she slid her ass to the opposite end of the table, across from the toddler. "Hey, Munch."

"Ev-e!" the toddler called, her hands opening and closing at her sister. "Mama wet."

Evie rolled her eyes, affirming, "Yeah, I bet she is."

Parker followed Evie's gaze to the couple. Dilynn's arms were wrapped around Alex's neck and her eyes stared adoringly up at their face. Their hands smoothed the wet blonde hair from their wife's face before kissing her, pulling a gagging noise from Evie.

"We have company!" Evie yelled, but Dilynn swatted away her words and continued to kiss Alex. The type of kiss that said the couple had no fear of being seen by anyone.

"So gross," Evie said, turning back to Parker. Her turquoise eyes stared at Parker, and she looked to be carefully considering her words. Her mouth closed, and she shifted her attention back to her sister pushing a crayon across the table to her.

Parker squirmed in her seat and turned back to Lyra. Lyra had retrieved the bucket and was making her way out of the room. She called to Alex as she moved, "I'm headed to the car. Can you stop making out in front of my girlfriend so we can get this done?"

The air in Parker's lungs stilled. Every muscle in her body was now alert and confused as to what to do. She looked up to find Evie studying her every move. The only sound in the room was the nuclear blast warning coming from the cell phone on the counter.

"Why the fuck is the baby monitor going off?" Evie yelled. Her sentence ended after the monitor ceased its beeping, making her words echo off the walls.

Parker let out the breath she'd been holding, and her toes dug at the bandage on her foot, trying to kick away the stupid monitor. It wouldn't budge though.

'Did she fucking superglue this shit to me?'

Lyra was suddenly at Parker's side. Her eyes everywhere but looking directly at the woman she'd just announced was her girlfriend. She pulled at the back of her neck.

"I... look, we haven't talked about it, and I know we barely know each other." Lyra took a deep breath. "I didn't mean to imply that you didn't have a say in if you... you know, maybe if you were actually... if you wanted to be my—"

"You sound like an idiot," Evie interrupted. "Just let her absorb that you think of her as girlfriend material and walk away. Play it cool. Jesus, I thought you had skills."

A bowl of practically clear liquid was set in front of Parker. There were things floating in the liquid, but Parker couldn't figure out what it was supposed to be. This was definitely worse than anything she was ever served in juvie.

Dilynn pushed Lyra slightly, and told her, "Go now before you say something else to give her heart palpitations and a reason for your sister to make fun of you."

Chin to her chest, Lyra trailed Alex out of the quiet room, while Parker examined what she assumed was albino chicken and star shaped noodles floating in the opaque liquid.

Evie moved to sneak a peek within the bowl. Her nose scrunched and she moved back down the table before she said, "That looks disgusting."

Dilynn huffed out an annoyed breath, then mumbled, "So much for supermom." Dilynn's shoulders fell, and eyes cast down to the floor.

Parker picked up the spoon, scooped up the naked chicken and noodles, and shoved it in her mouth. She said, "Mmm," and swallowed everything in a single gulp. She prayed she wouldn't regret the action.

Evie gagged again, but Dilynn smiled gratefully.

"It's terrible, isn't it?" Evie asked, scanning over Parker's face.

Unsure if Dilynn was vengeful when insulted, Parker took another spoonful and swallowed again. She went for a third scoop of the miserable soup, then told Dilynn, "It's great. Thank you."

"Lyra apparently is already planning your wedding, so you don't have to kiss our mother's ass," Evie stated.

"Everleigh Greyson, you leave Parker and your sister alone. Not everyone finds their happily ever after in high school, and its awkward enough without someone making stupid ass comments all the fucking time."

"Fucking!" The little girl yelled with her green crayon raised in the air. Her tiny hand smashed the crayon against the Paw Patrol coloring book and scribbled vigorously.

Dilynn's eyes grew. She carefully tried to correct the situation. "Levi, honey, fuck is a big person word."

Levi looked her mother square in the eyes and with a well-practiced scowl stated, "I big girl!" Her little head tilted to the side, daring any of them to challenge her.

Parker choked down another bite, then said, "I read somewhere that children who swear in the correct context are actually more intelligent and have a stronger command of language."

"Kiss ass," Evie quipped as her eyes practically dislodged from the retina. She got up from the table and disappeared into a large pantry near the refrigerator.

Dilynn took a seat beside Parker, this time holding a thermometer. She ran it along Parker's forehead down to her temple.

"99.8. Looks like your fever has finally broken."

Parker forced a smile. She leaned over her soup; her IV arm resting in front of her bowl. She lifted another spoon of nasty into her mouth. She figured if she kept up the pace, she'd be done in four more bites. She tried to make faster work of it, but Dilynn stopped her.

"Slow down. I know you must be hungry, so I made plenty."

The spoonful stopped halfway to her mouth, and she stared at it. If she slowed her pace, then she would actually have to taste it, and she wasn't sure if it would be worse to shovel in two bowls or fake savoring four bites.

"You still eat like you're in juvie," Evie stated as she poured part of a bag of Cheeto puffs on the table between the toddler and herself.

Parker looked at her arm guarding her bowl. She sat up, placing her arm off to the side. Through the corner of her eye, she checked to see if Dilynn had heard what Evie said. Which she clearly had, because she was staring at her daughter as though she were plotting a murder.

Evie didn't seem to care about Dilynn's dirty looks though, because she went about munching on Cheetos with her mouth wide open. Smacking each bite grotesquely. She licked each finger loudly before shoving another bite in her mouth.

"So," Evie said with a mouth full of tangerine mush. "Does Lyra know about you and Zoe Robinson?"

Parker choked on an unchewed piece of chicken. She hacked it back into the bowl, as Evie muttered, "Guess not."

Wiping her mouth on the back of her hand, Parker sat up straight. "How do you... I mean, yes, we were together and no, I haven't exactly told Lyra yet about my past dating history. But who told you?"

Evie stared at her. "Zoe told me. Apparently, she's still in love with you. So, did you, like, break her heart?"

Dilynn quietly took a seat at the table with a cup of coffee cradled in her hands. Parker watched as Dilynn fixated at a very unremarkable section on the center of the table.

Shifting in her seat, Parker's face grew hot from the embarrassment coursing through her body at having to have this conversation with Dilynn present, let alone with Evie.

"I didn't break Zoe's heart. She broke mine," she snapped. "It was years ago when we were in college, and the claim that she is in love with me is ludicrous. She thinks I'm white trash and before you tell me that I'm full of crap, she actually said those very words to me."

Evie tilted her head and studied Parker before returning to her Cheetos. She shoved a few more in her mouth, torturing Parker further with the noise.

"Well, I saw her Friday night at the pizza place you and Lyra went to. I went to give you guys shit and saw her there. Figured it was best to get her out before Lyra saw her. Since you haven't talked about the dating history, you don't know that Lyra and Zoe broke up like two days before you all met, and I figured I would scoot Zoe's bitchy ass out of the way so you two could have a good time until she basically had an existential crisis at seeing you with Lyra." Evie turned her attention to Dilynn, "Which by the way proves that the bitch really did use Lyra so I should get to punch her, and..." Evie flipped back to Parker, "Means that you best understand that if you hurt my sister and go running back to your douchey ex, then I'm going to punch you again too."

"Zoe and I are ancient history," Parker practically spat. She ground her teeth, unwilling to back down to Evie. "And if you ever even try to hit me again, you'll be the one going to the hospital for stitches because I let you get in a cheap shot last time. I let you make me think you were stronger than me. But I'm not a little girl anymore, and I'm not scared of Bully Blake. And I am more than ready to fuck your face up if I have to prove it."

Dilynn's mug clanked against the table as she set it down. She lifted a finger and pointed to the wall. "What does the sign say, ladies?"

Parker followed the direction of the outstretched finger and landed on a chalkboard with the words, "House Rules" written at the top. In all capital letters, next to number one read: No hitting, kicking, or spitting.

"Spitting?" Parker asked.

Dilynn sighed and turned a matter of fact face to Evie.

Particles of Cheetos flew from Evie's mouth as she held up her own finger and cried out, "That was one time! And your ex fucking deserved it. AND it also says no sex on communal furniture yet there is not a single spot in this house that you and Obi haven't ruined with your fucking."

"Fucking!" the toddler called out again. Cheeto drool ran down her chin.

Dilynn's head fell back. "Alex is going to kill me."

The room settled. Only Cheetos being crunched and Parker's spoon clinking against the bowl as she stirred broke up the silence. Dilynn sipped her coffee, seeming to be processing Evie's tale.

Parker stared at the regurgitated chicken in the bowl, debating if Dilynn would still need her to eat it to feel like a competent caretaker. She couldn't do it. She'd done a lot of things she'd thought was impossible over the last few days, but this was where she had to draw the line. She set the spoon down and pushed the bowl from in front of her.

"So, since we were talking about her; Zoe actually came to see me yesterday," Dilynn mused, her fingers tapping the outside of the mug. "She said she's dropping the charges against Olivia."

"That's great news," Evie proclaimed.

"Yeah, really great news," Parker added.

Dilynn hummed. "She also got Olivia to verify the abuse."

"I knew it," Evie said.

"And I asked her about the baby," Dilynn continued. Her eyes rose to meet Parker's.

"Wait!" Evie cried out, "What baby? Olivia didn't have a baby with her."

"And?" Parker asked.

"She didn't confirm in words, but her body language said yes."

"What baby?!" Evie yelled from the other side of the table like the two women were on the opposite side of the house.

"So, what now?" Parker asked.

"What baby?" Evie banged her hand on the table.

"Zoe is working with DCS to identify any surrenders at Banner University, which is right around the corner from where Evie stopped Olivia."

"I know you hear me," Evie griped.

Dilynn winked at Parker, and Parker silently signed on to continue the torment. "Will they be able to locate the child? I mean, if she dropped it off at Safe Haven, the baby would have been placed for adoption and in Arizona all records are sealed."

"You can't ignore me," Evie said, now on her feet and waving her hand between Dilynn and Parker.

Parker didn't blink as she stared through the visual disruption at her boss.

Dilynn shook her head, then explained, "Safe Haven only places healthy kids in adoptive homes. With the number of drugs in Olivia's system, there is no way that child was placed for adoption. I guarantee she is in foster care."

"What will they do when they find the baby?"

"Honestly, I don't know. But hopefully, Olivia will have the chance to get some closure," Dilynn said. "I mean, I honestly don't want Olivia to try and be a mother to the child since she's so young and has so much to still deal with, but maybe the parents will agree to an open adoption, and she'll get updates and stuff. I think it would help her recovery process."

"Is this because I let Parker's relationship with Zoe out of the bag?" Evie whined.

Dilynn turned to her daughter, putting her mean face back in place. "How about you stop sharing other people's business and mind your own, Everleigh Greyson?"

"I was looking out for Lyra." Evie's hands shot in front of her. "She's the greatest human alive and she keeps picking losers."

"Hey!" Parker cried out.

"You were trying to prove you're the baddest bitch in the room, and you succeeded in only proving part of it. You have to stop alienating everyone your sisters date. I thought you learned that lesson already," Dilynn lectured.

Evie sat back down. Her lower jaw moved back and forth as she stared at the ceiling. Half-heartedly, she mumbled, "Sorry, Parker."

Looking over her teenage tormentor, she considered how much Evie had grown up. Dilynn had been good for her. She could understand why Evie was so protective of her family.

"When Echo met Simone, I looked for every reason Simone wasn't good enough for her," Parker confessed. She decided not to add she still hated the woman. "I get what it's like to worry about your sister."

"Why do you call her, Echo?" Evie asked.

Parker twisted her lips up into a smile. "When I was first processed, Echo was mine and Henry's block mate. I was trying to figure out how to say her last name, Echomolziski, and she yelled at me to stop looking at her tits. I tried to explain that I was trying to read her badge, and she told me to just call her Echo, because the girls were always making her name echo when she was..." Parker cast a sideways glance at Dilynn's smiling face. "Well, you get the picture."

Evie's lips curled up, and Parker saved the information that Evie became uncomfortable about other people having sex. She'd use it later as needed. Parker jumped when Evie's head snapped towards her.

"Wait. Did you screw Marissa too?"

Parker sighed and shook her head. "No. We were never like that. She treated me like a sister. Even tried to keep a guard off my ass."

"The blonde with spikey hair," Evie stated, not asked. Parker's arms itched at Evie's confession like they had when hands searched her body for the weapons both the guard and her knew weren't there.

Parker looked at the bowl still sitting on the table. She swirled the liquid with the spoon, trying to stop the phantom sensations.

"Yeah, she had a thing for redheads she always said." She smiled slightly, as she added, "When I got out, I dyed my hair blonde for a really long time."

No one said anything. They just sat listening to the hour being announced by a clock hidden within the massive house. Each tone marked another second of Parker's life she'd been free of those hands and the places she was forced to stand.

"That's why I hit you."

Parker's head shot up to Evie with her hands folded on the table in front of her. She searched through her painting of the incident because she knew that wasn't what had happened. Evie was harassing Henry for smiling. She had stood in her way and told her to pick on someone else. Evie had hit her. She narrowed her eyes on Evie, pissed she would try to pretend she wasn't a monster in there.

Evie didn't look at her though. She just bit into her own lip, chewing on the chapped skin until it bled. But it wasn't enough blood to equal the amount Parker was owed.

"I know, you think you know what happened," Evie finally said. "But it really wasn't what happened."

"Then what did I miss, because I was there?" Parker hissed. "I was there when Henry finally figured out how to braid her own hair, and she was happy. She was happy for the first time since Echo left. A real smile, and you couldn't handle someone being happy around you. So, you got in her face until she shrank against the wall and that smile she worked so hard to find fell to the floor and shattered into a million pieces and I couldn't even be there to help put it back together because I was laying in the hospital wing with my face stitched and swollen, eating through a straw."

Evie barely blinked, but when she moved it wasn't to face Parker. It was to look at Dilynn. Which just pissed Parker off more, so she added another splash of gasoline to the fire.

"What's wrong? Do you not appreciate it when someone lets everyone in the room in on something you didn't want them to know?"

Parker's teeth ground together as she thought about all the damage Evie didn't even know she'd caused. That Xio had gotten put in solitary for crossing over the line between the white and Chicana territories because crossing the line meant fighting her way through the crowd. That without Parker there, Henry had started using again, and never been able to stop. That all this time Parker knew the reason Henry was six feet under a tiny little plaque was because of Evie.

The alarm went off again, jarring Parker back into her shell.

Evie turned slowly to Parker. "I saw the way spiky dyke was always hovering over you." She sighed. "I saw her push you into that storage closet and I saw the tear tracks on your face when you were finally allowed to leave twenty minutes later. I saw it happen again when she stopped you in the showers and you clung to your towel. I saw it and there wasn't anything I could do to stop her. But I had to stop it. I had to stop her from touching you and hurting you and you're the therapist now so you probably know that while I wanted to protect you, I couldn't. Because really, while her attention was on you, then it wasn't on me. So, I could have just let it keep happening because it meant that I was safe from her. But I couldn't do it."

Evie bit her lip. Her eyes staring at her mother, who reached across the table and took her hand. Dilynn squeezed Evie's hand, and said, "Go on, tell her the whole thing."

With a heavier sigh, Evie continued, "You always protected your friend. You were a good person, and everyone knew it, which is why no one stood up for you. They couldn't handle that you were nice and kind, so they let someone else break you down. But I knew. I knew what it was like, so I figured I had to get you out of her reach. I had to get you out of there. I was already annoyed and when I saw the way your friend was so excited it just all clicked into place. I started yelling at her. I didn't just hit her. I got in her face until you stood up for her, because you were stronger than all of us. You always were. You stood up and I knew that it was my chance to get you out. I hit you, and I hit you hard. You'd be out of her reach in hospital wing. So sorry, I didn't have a better plan. Sorry you ended up with a scar, but with all the blood, I didn't have to hit you more than once at least. I originally thought I was going to have to fully beat the shit out of you. Break a few ribs, but I knew that ribs heal, having someone's hands on you when you don't want them there, that shit doesn't heal."

Parker tucked an oily lock of hair behind her ear. Biting into her lower lip, she tried to merge the two versions of the story. The fight she'd had before vanished, replaced with the shame of not fighting the guard. She considered what elements of Evie's story she could consider truth, but then she collided with a wall of lies, and she couldn't figure out which time Evie had lied to her.

"At Changing Hands, you said that you hit me because you were pissed off at the world, and that you used to punish everyone around you because you hated seeing other people happy."

Evie shrugged. Then explained, "You were clearly hitting it off with Lyra. I didn't think it would be fair to announce that you were assaulted in juvie by a guard, and I knew about it but didn't do anything to stop it."

"So, you let her think you just beat the shit out of me for no reason?" Parker asked, her eyebrows scrunched in utter confusion at Evie's fantastic decision-making skills.

Evie let go of her mother's hand and turned her body towards Parker. She licked her lips, followed by a deep breath. Parker prepared for another long-winded speech.

"Lyra is used to hearing stories about me acting like a dick. She's used to seeing me act like a bitch. Niceness is not something I'm really good at. Especially with people that matter to me. So yeah, even though I was a dick to you, you did matter to me then and you matter to me now. Which is why I told you Zoe is in love with you. If you still have feelings for Zoe, like, work that shit out, and let Lyra find someone who loves her. She's already falling for you. So, if you ain't feeling it, then you gotta let her know. Don't do the shit with her that you did with Xio, because Xio is still fucked from loving you."

Parker wiped her hands over her face, trying to process everything that was hitting her. It was too much, and she didn't have time to sort through everything and consider all of the implications, or even why Evie was so convinced that there may be some unresolved feelings over Zoe. There weren't because Zoe didn't give a damn about her. She hadn't changed since college, and neither had Parker's opinion of herself.

"This is all really overwhelming," Parker confessed more to herself than anyone else at the table. "I mean, you all have your whole family. You take care of each other. But I don't have people. I mean, I have Echo and Xio. But really that's it. But they didn't show up to help. Echo didn't come even when she hadn't heard from me because it's what I do all the time. I'm just invisible. But then you give me a job and throw money at me that I needed. Then you buy me shoes," she said to Dilynn. "And Alex and Lyra show up and, like, save me from dying when no one else—"

"I was there!" Evie protested. "I stepped in your puke!"

Parker stopped herself from waving Evie's words away, realizing she was beginning to pick up Dilynn's mannerism just as her daughters had. And she wasn't ready to consider Dilynn Greyson as anything beyond a boss because mothers were supposed to love and care about their children, but hers hadn't. There was nothing in Parker's mind that would allow herself to consider anyone could want her beyond the touch of her flesh.

"I don't think you two get it. It's just me. It was just me in my apartment accepting that I was going to die alone. Then I wake up here. A baby monitor is literally glued to my foot, a mother is cooking me chicken noodle soup because I'm ill, which side note, I'm sorry but I can't eat any more of that. Like ever again. And then you're one minute telling me not to hurt your sister but then telling me that you actually tried to protect me in juvie because you care about me and you talk about the universe has decided we need to be in each other's lives, and it's just so much because I feel like I have to be dreaming because Echo, who didn't even come apparently when I was approaching death's door, is the only person that has ever known me besides Zoe. And she bailed when she found out I was a stripper."

"You were a stripper!?" Evie squealed in excitement. "That's crazy. I took a pole dancing class once and the muscles you have to have to swing around that pole are intense. I fell on my head and ended up with a concussion. Can you still do it, and more importantly can you teach me?"

Parker's shoulders fell, and she felt her unheard words running out of the open windows of Dilynn's massive house.

"Yeah. No problem," she mumbled to the table.

Dilynn reached over for Parker's hand but stopped. She instead moved the bowl further away from Parker. Parker's eyes stayed fixed on the table, afraid to look up and see the older blonde's angry face again at her blow up. She knew better, and now she showed Dilynn she wasn't as collected as she'd let on.

"Parker, please look at me," Dilynn requested.

Parker licked her lips and closed her eyes. She knew she had to look at Dilynn, but she had to get a grip. After three deep breaths, she looked up.

"I heard you say that you have always been alone. I also heard that you are overwhelmed with members of this family making decisions for you and doing things for you that you normally wouldn't ask for. Additionally, you have been hurt before by people that you thought cared about you. Did I hear you right?"

"Yeah, that's pretty much it," Parker affirmed. Her chest felt lighter, and her breathing came easier after hearing Dilynn recap what she'd said.

"What did I miss?" Dilynn asked.

Parker reached up and scratched the back of her head, trying to figure out what Dilynn hadn't heard. But she realized it wasn't what Dilynn hadn't heard, rather what she'd failed to say.

"I don't think I said it, but the overwhelmingness doesn't really just come from me not appreciating your family. I mean, I don't really appreciate that Evie busted open my face and traumatized me to the point when I heard her voice at Henrie's birthday party that I wanted to hide in a cabinet, but that's beyond the point. I feel very overwhelmed. God, I need to find a better word, but still.... Sorry. Back to the point. I barely have had a chance to get to know Lyra, and you warned me she was looking to settle down but hearing her call me her girlfriend is a lot to process. Especially since Evie then has to bring up the only other girl that I ever dated let alone was in a relationship with. But Lyra wants me to be her girlfriend, and I'm, like, what if it all falls apart? What if she looks at me one morning and feels, like, she's not good enough for me? Not what I thought I wanted, and then I lose her. Like I lost Zoe. And this whole world where people caring about me and I'm not alone just collapses like a giant earthquake, and I find myself in a new circle of hell that's deeper and more terrifying than the one I currently reside."

"You make perfect sense. And you're right," Dilynn confirmed. "We all did pretty much jump the gun and paint a pretty nice picture of what it means to be a part of this family. We hid away the crazy for the most part, well except Evie. She wears hers on her sleeve and forehead, and apparently her fist."

Evie rolled her eyes, then held up a single finger. "I have actually not punched anyone when not in uniform in three years."

"You want a medal?" Dilynn asked dryly. When Evie scowled, Dilynn raised a finger to her, "Interrupt me one more time and you're going to eat the rest of my soup."

A single finger ran over Evie's lips like a zipper, drawing a nod from Dilynn. Then the woman turned back to Parker.

"I'm sorry for smothering you with all the mothering. I don't think I really realize I'm doing it a lot of the time. I am also sorry for lying to you about knowing about what happened with Evie when you were both in detention. I pried that information out of her the minute we stepped out of the door at Henrie's birthday party, which is why I couldn't let you run away. I knew you needed us, and I didn't even consider Lyra in all of this. I mean the chance of that happening surprised the shit out of me, which is why I then had to warn you about Lyra's codependency because I never wanted you to feel like you were backed into a corner. I wanted you to know that you didn't have to be in a relationship with Lyra to be cared about by me or Alex or Evie for that matter, though I never thought Evie would actually tell you she gave a damn about you. If being Lyra's girlfriend is that scary then tell her. Be honest. She'll appreciate it, and I can promise you that she'll give you the time you need. And if I was your mother, then I would say give Lyra a chance to prove that she isn't like Zoe. That she's capable of being as strong for you as you are for her. But I'm not your mother so you don't have to listen to me. Shit, my own kids don't listen to me. Just think about it."

The front door opened with an unexpected bang, causing Evie and Parker to jump. They looked at each other, and silently agreed not to acknowledge what the other had seen.

"We're back!" Alex called before emerging around the corner. On their face, they sported a perfectly aligned, proud smile.

Dilynn narrowed her eyes at them. "You were not gone long enough to clean that apartment."

Alex held up a plastic Starbucks cup to Dilynn and waved it in the air. Their wife jumped from her seat like she'd been trained to salivate at the sight of the plastic cup. As she reached for it, Alex's long arm shot in the air out of Dilynn's reach.

"Before I give you this, I want you to know that I did not go to Parker's apartment. I have deemed it a quarantine zone and for the safety of everyone in this house, I elected to think like my wife."

Dilynn waved her hands down to herself. "Okay, I don't care. Just give me the cup."

Evie leaned closer to Parker, "Starbucks to Mom is like crack to a junkie."

Alex shook their head and pouted. "You don't even care what I did?"

"Nope. Give me the drink." Dilynn demanded, placing her hands on her hips.

"Well, I'm going to tell you anyways," Alex stated, still holding the beverage out of reach. "I thought as I was driving: what would my wife do if she was instructed to do something she didn't want to do? My rich wife would never go clean up someone else's puke. She would demand someone else do it for her."

"Great, you made Lyra do it. I. Don't. Care. Give me my drink."

Lyra entered as though the sound of her name was the spell to make her appear. She limped in with more drinks on a tray and cast Parker a cautious look. Parker smiled at her as she approached and set a palish green iced tea in front of the redhead. She whispered, "This should be better than the chicken water."

Alex's laughter pulled their attention back to the couple at it again. They stood firm in the same spot against their wife who had resorted to trying to climb her way up their body.

"Nope, I have returned with the daughter. I actually did one better. In true Queen Cupcake style, I hired a professional to go in. Cost me $400 to get them there today, but it is by far the best purchase I have ever made."

Dilynn dropped the three inches she'd made it off the ground. "Awesome. Can I have my drink now?"

Alex narrowed their eyes at Dilynn. "That's it. I spend a fuck ton of money and you only care about a drink."

"Fuck!" the toddler called from the other end of the table. Her eyes peeked out from the inside of the Cheeto bag she'd placed on her head. Her face and curly hair were covered in orange dust.

Dilynn slugged Alex in the arm not holding her drink. "Look at what you did! You taught our daughter to say swear words."

Evie and Parker cast each other a knowing look as Alex handed Dilynn the milky drink. Dilynn winked at Parker, then amused herself with the drink in her hand, while Alex made their way towards the miniature version of themself.

"Levi, fuck is a big person word," they said, unknowing that Dilynn had tried the same tactic.

Parker watched the miniature version of Alex straighten her shoulders and tap her chest. "I fucking big girl," the girl announced, then put her whole hand in her mouth and sucked the Cheeto residue from it.

Lyra lowered herself onto the bench next to Parker. She leaned over, whispering, "About what I said before—"

Parker stopped the words coming from the worried lips with a finger against them. "We have a lot to talk about and I don't want you to think that I am not interested in you. I just need you to know me better before we put a label on what this is. For now, let's just be together. Go out and get to know each other, like really get to know each other. Because I swear to God if you eat like your sister, it's a deal breaker."

The umber eyes looked at her like Parker had given her the best birthday present she'd ever asked for. She nodded and kissed the hand that had silenced her.

"I would really like that."

Lyra pulled another drink and slid it down the table to Evie. Evie picked it up, looked at the label, and slid it back.

"Thanks, I'm good."

With narrow eyes, Lyra stared at her sister. "Since when do you pass up Starbucks? It's your favorite drink."

Evie leaned against the table. "I'm just trying to be healthier. Not drink so much caffeine."

"Since when?" Lyra probed.

Dilynn walked to her daughter and turned Evie's face up to her. They studied each other as everyone else watched, uninvited to their telepathic conversation.

"Everleigh Greyson, you can't be learning how to swing on a pole if I'm going to be a grandmother."

"Who's swinging on a pole?" Alex choked. But their question went unanswered.

With Evie's slight nod of affirmation, the room burst into loud conversation and hugs. Talks of due dates and showers chased away the tension Parker had brought into the home. She watched the celebration for a new addition to the Greyson family quietly from the outside of their circle. When Lyra cast her umber eyes back to her, Parker contemplated what a future with Lyra could look like beyond tomorrow.

23

The blinds blocked out most of the daylight within Judge Miller's chambers. Zoe's eyes adjusted as she followed Evie and Landon into the office. She took a seat alongside Landon in one of the two leather chairs set before the ostentatious desk.

Judge Miller pulled the reading glasses from his face, setting them atop a stack of manilla folders. He leaned back in his chair. His fingertips meeting in the middle as he stared Zoe in the eyes.

"Ms. Robinson, you requested this meeting. Please enlighten me on what has brought us all here," he requested.

Zoe swallowed the excess saliva that flooded her mouth. "Yes, thank you for agreeing to meet with us."

From her briefcase, she pulled out one of the many file folders she carried on Olivia's trial. She stared down at a photo from the security footage of Banner University Emergency Room. The teenager, covered in the dark blue hoodie, sat in a chair. Dark hair hung in front of the girl's face, but in her arms was a wrapped bundle.

Zoe handed the photo to the white-haired judge. "We have learned that Olivia Moore gave birth shortly before her arrest. The photo is from Banner University, and the child was abandoned in the ER by Olivia Moore."

He looked it over before setting it on the desk. "How can you be sure this girl is Ms. Moore?" he asked.

"Your honor, we identified Ms. Moore by the clothes she was wearing when arrested."

Judge Miller sighed. "So, in addition to charging the girl with murder, you want to tack on abandonment charges as well? Isn't life in prison at fifteen enough for you, Ms. Robinson?"

Zoe sat up straighter, realizing her mistake. She'd led with the wrong foot and now the old man was angrier at her. She quickly fumbled through the file pulling out the motion and double checking the papers were in order. The last thing she needed was for something to be missing and seem more incompetent than she had already.

She handed her motion to dismiss to Judge Miller. "My apologies, your honor. I should have led with that I would actually like to file for the charges against Ms. Moore to be dropped in light of her confession that she killed Vincent Gibson because he had forcibly kept her captive for several years."

He scanned the papers, then peered over the top of them at Zoe. Critical blue eyes studied her before asking, "It took you this long to realize that child was being abused?"

"Your honor, I..." Zoe took her own deep breath. "I adamantly tried to convince myself the reason for Olivia's actions was unimportant, but we both know that is not true. I lost sight of what was important."

"I'm confused, Ms. Robinson. Did you request this meeting to dismiss this case or to discuss the baby in the photo?"

"Both, your honor."

The older man looked to Landon. With the motion to dismiss forms held up, he asked, "You are aware of this?"

"Yes, sir," Landon answered. "We are very happy Ms. Robinson has decided to drop the charges against Olivia. We also are concerned about the implications of Olivia having a child."

Zoe cleared her throat, drawing the unamused eyes back to her. Her shoulder's straightened as she said, "We need a warrant, your honor." She handed over the warrant request. "We have faced some push back from DCS in locating the baby in that photo. If I just drop the charges, Olivia still walks away without justice. DNA from this child will verify that the child is in fact Vincent Gibson's child, painting Olivia in a different light. She won't be the girl that killed some guy on drugs, she'll be a child victim that heroically protected her daughter."

Judge Miller's chair squeaked as he leaned back. "Let me get this straight, Ms. Robinson. You not only brought to trial a young girl who was viciously assaulted for multiple years, but a child forced to give birth in deplorable conditions."

"Judge Miller, there are not enough apologies in this world to make up for the pain I have caused. I wasted the court's time. And I hurt people." Zoe glanced back at Evie in her uniform, standing behind Landon. "I've begun the process of making amends, but, Judge, I can't do that until I help Olivia clear her name."

"You traumatized that girl. Now, you want me to help you find a baby somewhere in the foster care system and possibly uproot the child's stability. Am I understanding you correctly?"

"Yes," Zoe nodded. Then, she processed the judge's whole statement. "Wait. No. No one wishes to uproot the child in her new home. We solely need a DNA test to determine that Gibson was the child's father and Olivia was in fact acting in defense of the newborn. The child's DNA is critical evidence."

"Intrusive evidence." Judge Miller's fingers tapped together.

"Olivia deserves justice, and I almost didn't give her that. She deserves the truth to be known," Zoe stated.

Judge Miller's head tilted as his eyes studied her. Her back straightened, ready to do whatever necessary to get the old man to sign the warrant. Afterall, Parker didn't name her Commander for nothing. So what it was because she like to bark out orders while Parker fucked her. Judge Miller had chosen to keep that name alive, so she would own it rather than hate it.

The leather bound books and dark walls blended together in the dim space as Zoe focused her stoic gaze at the judge. Zoe planned each counterattack to the blockades he could try to put up. She was ready to cite a dozen different cases to demonstrate the legal justification for approving the warrant.

"Judge," Evie interjected. Zoe turned to see Evie's hand pulling at the top of her vest. "Sorry this thing is not very comfortable. Anyways, I get it if you don't want to do it because she's asking. I mean, no one really has more of a reason to dislike her than me." Evie looked at Zoe, then turned back to the judge. "So just ignore her. She isn't what this is about. When the DNA matches, she doesn't get to take Gibson to court. She doesn't win anything. So, let's just take her out of the picture."

Evie adjusted her stance, her chin rising. "Olivia acted like a hero in an impossible situation. Her story deserves to be told, instead of the one *she* fed to everyone. And if you really want to get back at her, this is our chance. Show everyone what she said to me on the stand isn't true. That justice for girls is possible, and we do give a damn about them."

Zoe stared at the woman she'd thought was trying to be friends with her. She realized Evie wasn't trying to be her friend. She was just being a nice person to someone struggling. A part of her felt used. Another part was angry Evie was right. None of this had anything to do with her anymore. There was no glory, no prestige left in this battle. She was fighting to fight, no longer a defender of justice. Just another contract soldier putting people away because it's what she does.

She turned back to see Judge Miller's mouth rise as wrinkles crinkled at the corners of his eyes. He chuckled softly, before he spoke.

"Everleigh, I have always admired your spirit. I wish to see no more harm come to Ms. Moore. How does your mother feel about this?"

"She is willing to help in any way she can, and she said that if you wanted to speak with her, you could call her on her cell. She said you have the number."

Judge Miller placed the reading glasses back on his face. Zoe watched the judge's eyes scan through the document. She hoped there was nothing she missed.

He set the papers down once more. Zoe swallowed as his heavy stare once again fell on her. She held her breath, waiting as the man measured her.

"I will not be seeing you in my courtroom filing abandonment charges on this young girl, correct?"

"That is correct, your honor," Zoe affirmed.

"And you will never bring a case or act in the manner that you did in my courtroom again?"

Zoe nodded. "I promise, your honor."

"I will hold you to that promise."

His weathered hand turned a ball point pen open. He signed the warrant, handing it back to Zoe.

She held it tightly, looking at the scratched signature, hopeful to put this whole case to rest so she could leave this chapter of her life behind her. Since she wasn't a cop, she wouldn't have a role anymore in the case. That was unless Evie allowed her to participate.

"Thanks Judge." Evie offered while Zoe packed away the folders within her briefcase.

Zoe stood and forced a smile on her face. "Thank you, sir."

After leaving the stuffy office, Zoe walked as quickly as possible towards the exit doors. She pulled the suit jacket from her as soon as she felt the brutal sun launching its attack.

Evie stopped alongside her. Zoe's skin itched at the other woman's presence lingering next to her. Her feet were ready to flee, even if it wasn't the proper thing to do.

"Thanks," Zoe said, picking up the briefcase she'd set down to strip. "I will get the copies sent over to you. Then we're done."

"He's known my family for a long time. I'm sure that Nia told you that, but still," Evie stated. Her eyes were scanning the courtyard. "Oh, there she is."

Evie waved an outstretched hand. Zoe turned to search the people walking around the courtyard to the Starbucks where she'd hit Parker with the same briefcase in her hand. Her eyes stopped on a tall brunette with tamed curls walking towards them. The woman possessed identical features to Alex but dressed like Dilynn, which fascinated Zoe. She walked with purpose, pushed a pair of wire framed glasses up her nose, and smiled at Zoe in a way that had Zoe wanting to stand a little taller.

The woman slugged Evie in the shoulder as soon as she was close enough. Evie barely moved from the hit, and just laughed at the woman. Immediately the other girl's frustration rose to her cheeks as she clutched the hand that hit the bullet proof vest.

"What the fuck was that for?" Evie asked. She readjusted the vest and continued to chuckle.

"For telling everyone you're having a baby without me there."

"So, your immediate reaction was to punch your pregnant sister?" Evie laughed again. "This is why everyone thinks you're a serial killer."

Zoe felt her eyebrows rise. She told herself not to look, but she couldn't help it. Her gaze wandered to Evie's abdomen, but the bulky vest blocked any bulge that would have suggested she was expecting.

"I didn't mean to tell them. Lyra was all up my ass, because I wouldn't drink the coffee she bought me."

Landon chimed in, "If it makes you feel any better, I didn't get to be there either, and by the time I had found out your mom had called my mom. Do you know what it is like to have an Army Captain yell at you for finding out second hand that she's having a grandchild?" He shook his head. "It's terrible."

Zoe focused on the pavers, still unsure why she was still there. She made a mental note to learn to improve her exit game. Saying goodbye and leaving shouldn't be difficult, but for Zoe it felt impossible.

"You get it?" Evie's very violent, yet attractive sister asked.

The question drew Zoe back to the conversation as she wanted to know what it was, even though she was an outsider.

"Show her the warrant," Evie instructed Zoe. "Then we can get to work. I know you lawyers always have secret fantasies about doing actual police work."

Zoe looked between Evie and the sister who Zoe didn't know. She had no intention of providing the stranger access to the warrant without so much as an introduction. Evie must have thought she was stupid or something.

Landon chuckled when Zoe refused to budge. He said, "Zoe, this is Sadie, Evie's sister. She works for DCS. Sadie, this is Zoe. She was the prosecutor on Olivia's case."

Sadie's pale green gaze wandered over Zoe. She was definitely younger than the other Greysons, but she had a different energy to her. Not the anger of Evie or cool of Lyra. This sister was informally buzzing in a way Zoe would have found attractive if she wasn't a Greyson.

She extended her hand to Sadie. "Nice to meet you." It dropped when Sadie looked at her hand and back at her face like the gesture was a foreign concept.

Sadie turned back to Evie, "She the one?"

"Yeah." Evie nodded, her body bouncing on her toes.

Sadie glanced back at Zoe, then angry eyes narrowed at Evie. "Why isn't she sporting a blackeye?"

Evie's head fell back, annoyed. "I don't just hit people."

"I'm going to tell Lyra you love me more than her," Sadie stated.

Evie laughed. "She won't believe you."

Something in the younger sister's eyes told Zoe Sadie knew the statement to be true. Zoe tried to think of a single time Lyra had brought up another sister, but she'd only ever mentioned the one she lived with and the teddy bear boyfriend. Her eyes shot to Landon and his oversized muscles, realizing he was the teddy bear. Her lips pressed together comically as she nodded, imagining the bald brown head with two fluffy ears.

Zoe opened the top of her case and retrieved the warrant. When she stood back up, the green eyes were no longer angry at Evie but were now on her. She straightened to her full height, bringing her eye to eye with the Alex Trikru look alike.

"You hurt my sister," Sadie said.

"Old news. I already cussed her out. Mom cussed her out. Obi treated her like a grifter. And no one is scared of you, Sassy."

Evie ripped the warrant from Zoe's hand and waved it in her sister's face. "Here, you see it. Now give us a name and an address."

Sadie huffed out a heavy breath. "She's my sister too. You can't be the only one that takes on exes."

"Okay, when Lyra's new girlfriend fucks up, you can be the one to get in her face. I mean, I already broke her jaw in high school, but she's all yours." Evie's arm wrapped around Zoe's shoulders. "But this one is mine. I claimed her as mine to torment and remind her what it means to have people care about you. So, give us the file."

Sadie dug through her bag while grumbling, "Lyra is my favorite."

Evie rolled her eyes. "She's everyone's favorite."

The younger sister found what she was looking for. She pulled out the manilla folder and pressed it against her chest. Holding it protectively, she started to explain. "So, the baby is still in the system because the case managers kept turning over and stuff that should have been done didn't get done. Parent rights have already been severed but adoption hasn't been finalized because—"

"Blah, blah, blah," Evie gestured to herself. "Just give us the file, or I'll have to arrest you for impeding an investigation."

"It's not that simple. The kid is—" Evie reached for the file, but Sadie's fingers closed around it.

With a shoulder, Evie nudged Zoe. "Is it against the law to lay my little sister out in public because she's being a pain in the ass?"

"E., listen to me," Sadie stated.

"Okay, what's your deal?"

"It's Henrie. The baby is Henrie."

Evie's eyes grew. "What?" She ripped the folder from her sister's hand.

Sadie cried out, putting a finger instantly into her own mouth and sucking on it. "You cut me!" the younger Greyson whined.

"It's a paper cut. Go cry to Mom for a Band-Aid, you big baby."

Evie held the file open to the first page for both herself and Zoe. At the top corner of the page was a wallet sized image of a tiny baby with a head full of dark curls. Her face was sunken and all bone, not the typical newborn photos Zoe was accustomed to seeing with the big puffy cheeks and little old man scowls.

Zoe didn't have a chance to read any of the information between Evie's saying, "No. No. No," and flipping pages faster than Zoe can focus on a single word.

"Do you know Olivia's baby?" Zoe asked when Evie finally stared at a single page. The Notice to Provider sat in the middle of the file with the names of the foster parents: Simone Wyatt and Marissa Echomolziski.

Evie exhaled heavily. Her hand pulled at the top of her vest again. "Yeah," she said. "And fun times for you, Parker is Henrie's godmother."

Zoe's head tilted, ready to call bullshit. But Evie was serious. With her own deep exhale, Zoe said, "Great."

"Coach is going to flip out," Sadie stated.

Evie waved away Sadie's words. "Damn it, Sadie."

"Don't yell at me. It's not my fault!"

"It's not my fault," Evie mocked.

Zoe looked between the two sisters. "What's the big deal? It's not like Olivia is going to try to take the baby. Parental rights have already been severed."

"It's less to do with Henrie and more to do with Coach," Evie explained.

Sadie nodded along with her sister's statement, then added, "Coach hates our mom."

"But is best friends with Obi," Evie added.

Zoe couldn't keep up with the story or why any of this mattered. Exasperated, she asked, "Who is Obi? And why don't people in your life have names?"

Evie rolled her eyes again before bothering to answer her question. "Alex, my mom's partner is Obi. It means other parent because they are non-binary, so Obi isn't their name it's their title like Mom is my mom's title. Coach is our old high school softball coach and has always been Coach. It would be weird to call her anything else. Don't you have people in your life you have known since you were a kid and will always be someone so important that you call them by their title instead of their first name, because you will always have that respect for them?"

Zoe thought about it momentarily. Nia Williams was the closest person to her family. Her father's best friend almost. But she was the only adult and she was a terrible human.

"I guess not," she answered.

With a shake of her head, Evie said, "Well, you need to get people in your life then. And you can start with me. I'm going to be your friend, and whether you like it or not you're going to be mine."

"Only because she doesn't have any friends either," Sadie mumbled.

As Evie wrapped her long arm around Sadie's skinny neck, Zoe tried to wrap her head around the complexity of the Sour Patch Kid, Evie Greyson. She weighed every interaction she'd had with the gritty police officer to the small fragments of kindness Evie used to light the way for others. And she decided that a friend like that was probably worth more than a thousand Swedish Fish. Someone her mother would approve of.

24

The residents above the art room made their presence known with each step sending a groan from the ceiling above where Parker and Olivia sat. Olivia picked up a lighter shade of green to highlight the defined leaves of the tree she'd sketched. It was the first piece the teenager had asked for instruction, wanting to make it for Charleigh Marshall.

"A gift for understanding," Olivia had called it after talking about the book *Speak* being assigned for the class to read.

In the week since Parker had been sick, Olivia had broken her wall of silence to discuss the mundane details of the day to day. The girl's request to work on something for English class gave Parker an opportunity to get insight into the other artwork she'd produced over the last year. Parker planned to use Olivia's willingness to discuss her day to dig a little deeper into the girl's world, but so far was unsuccessful.

With Olivia fully engrossed in her work, Parker figured it was now or never. She asked, "When you draw during Ms. Marshall's class, what do you think about?"

"Different stuff."

Olivia moved on to another leaf, carefully outlining only one side of it.

"Can you describe what you mean by stuff?" Parker pushed a different shade of light green across the table as Olivia's hand moved to a different section of the tree.

Taking the hint, Olivia traded out the pencils and set about the same task. She nodded in approval as she finished another leaf. Then she said, "Sometimes it's something in the story she's talking about. She says make notes as we read. I just listen to the books or stories and follow the words. I draw what I think because I can't spell the words."

Parker pulled out the notebook page with the swing set sketch and slid it to the side of Olivia's tree. "Can you tell me about this swing set?"

"Just a swing."

Parker picked up the paper. One of the swings was positioned midair with little lines of movement above the seat.

"It's so detailed. Your skill is improving the more you draw, but I just can't get past how the swing seems to be in motion," Parker praised.

"Marshall had me listening to a story called 'The Man in the Well'."

Parker set the sketch down. "I've never heard of it. Will you tell me about it?"

"It's a weird story. There're all these kids that find a man in a well. They know he is stuck but they leave him there to die."

The plastic chair groaned as Parker leaned away from the table. Evie's confession came to the forefront of her mind about everyone knowing what was happening to her, but no one willing to help. She'd thought she was invisible, but it turned out she was far from it. Her eyes wandered from naming the constellations of paint speckles on the table to the girl that worked so hard to be invisible.

Parker scanned over Olivia's face, noticing the red splotches across her cheeks and chin where blackheads and pimples were popped. As though Olivia knew she was being watched, she wiped her face. Black lead left a streak across her cheek, but the movement caused a lock of clean hair to fall in front of her eyes. Parker couldn't force the smile down as she realized Olivia was finally starting to feel safe.

"Have you ever done something because you feel like other people wanted you to?" Olivia asked, bringing Parker back to the conversation she'd started.

"Yep."

Olivia gnawed on her lip as she leaned closer to the tree and studied the area she was working on. When she leaned back, she glanced at the swing set and pointed to it with a pencil. "I jumped off a swing like that because my friends were doing it."

She set the pencil down. While she blended the pencil marks with her index finger, Olivia explained, "When we read the story, I thought about how worried I was they would think I was scared. So, I jumped. It hurt when I fell, and I didn't want to do it again, but I kept doing it because they kept doing it. It's what I thought of when Marshall told me to make a connection between my life and the story."

A crease formed across Parker's forehead as she reconciled she'd read way more into the picture than apparently it had meant. Readjusting in her seat, she wondered if she was way off track. Chewing on the inside of her cheek, she spit out the first thing that came to mind.

"What about the eye? You draw that a lot. Is that a connection too?"

"Point of view."

"What do you mean?" Parker asked.

Olivia looked up at Parker like she was dumb for not understanding. Her head tilted with raised eyebrows as she said, "When the story is not from the character but the watcher. I draw the eye because he's watching everything."

Parker justified deserving the look Olivia gave her. She was considering why she needed it explained to her when she heard Olivia mumbled, "Like he used to do. He watched and replayed it again and again."

The door to the art room burst open. Parker jumped from her chair to her feet, blocking the girl on the other side of the table. She cast a glance back to see

Olivia had also jumped to the floor, backing herself into the shelves at the other side of the room.

"Did you know?!" Echo stomped into the room in her bulky Doc Martins.

Parker froze, her feet sinking into the quicksand the concrete floor had dissolved into. Her mind ran through anything she could have done to wrong Echo that she would know about. Every thought came back with no hint of anything that could cause Echo to be this mad at her.

Dilynn held the door, trying to steady herself as she panted heavily. "Marissa, you can't—"

Echo took three giant steps, putting her into Parker's personal bubble. Standing a full head over Parker, she glared down at the redhead. Parker's lungs begged for the oxygen Echo was consuming in the space between them. Spittle flew from her mouth as she asked Parker again, "Did you fucking know?"

Parker shook her head. Clueless as to what there was to know.

"Your new family came to see me with that lawyer bitch from the bar. They want a DNA sample from Henrie," Echo growled.

Parker stared into Echo's angry eyes and begged her to believe her. "I swear, Echo. I didn't know."

Dilynn held a hand between Echo and Parker, like it would stop whatever Echo could do to Parker.

"Marissa, I think we need to—"

Echo's neck snapped to Dilynn. "No. This isn't about you or your fucking kids sticking their nose into shit that is none of their goddamn business." She turned back to Parker. "It's about if she knew."

Parker desperately asked again, "Knew what?!"

Echo's eyes shot up above Parker's head as paint bottles fell from the shelf behind Parker. The anger radiating from Echo hit Parker in the face and chest until her shoulders stooped and she was sixteen again. Waiting for the older woman to beat the crap out of her for looking at her wrong. She flinched as Echo's hand shot up.

"Jesus. Is this her?"

Glancing up, Parker realized Echo was talking to Dilynn but pointing at Olivia. The waves of rage dissipated as Echo backed out of Parker's face into the chair Parker had been sitting in. Large hands covered Echo's face, then pulled at the short hair atop her head.

Dilynn made her way around the table to Olivia. She offered a hand to help Olivia up, but the girl rose on her own. The teen adjusted the hood of her sweatshirt to cover her head, then ducked it down.

"Honey, I'm sorry. I thought your session was done for the day. I'm so sorry we interrupted."

Olivia nodded, then whispered, "I'll go."

The hood moved up just enough for Parker to see Olivia glance at Echo, who was holding her face in her hands. Before Parker could stop Olivia and tell her that she could stay because this was her time, the girl was out the door.

The ceiling rumbled in protest as feet stomped out of a room. Dilynn looked up at the ceiling, then to Parker. "Is it always like this?"

Parker picked up Olivia's work from the ground, a small footprint stamped over the tree the girl had worked so hard on. She felt like something important had been said but for the life of her, Parker couldn't remember what it was.

The entrance to the house slammed closed, whisking out the sound of growly boys. Parker turned to Echo, now leaning on her elbows.

Dilynn pushed herself up onto the table still covered in colored pencils. She picked up a blue one, twisting it in her fingers. She sucked her teeth, before explaining, "They identified Henrie as Olivia's baby."

"She's not her mother," Echo hissed.

Parker held up her hand, "Wait, when did this happen?"

"This afternoon," Dilynn stated.

"Did you know?" Echo asked again.

The fear that had gripped her before was replaced with anger. They'd been through so much together. Too much for Echo to come at her like that.

"Why would I know?" Parker held her hands to Echo. "What the fuck do you think I have a fucking crystal ball in here? Jesus. You lost your goddamn mind, you know that?"

Echo wiped her face and shoved her battered ball cap on her head before she sat up straight. The chair creaked when she leaned back. Shaking her head, Echo said, "Henrie looks like her. Like when I saw that kid I just knew. They have the same eyes."

"She does," Dilynn stated. "But that doesn't change that you're her mother,"

Echo's fist hit the table next to her. "She fucking—" Echo cut herself off. Her fist went white as it pressed onto the table. "I've been so angry for so long at her."

Brown eyes raised to Dilynn. "Like how could she do that to my baby? How could she do all those drugs? How could she see that little girl in so much pain and just walk away? Like how did she not care?"

Dilynn dropped from the table, making her way to Echo. She placed a hand on Echo's knee, patting it softly.

"This is going to be hard to hear but that girl cared so much for your daughter she killed someone to protect her."

Echo shook her head. "But she just left. She just walked away and left her there in a chair. Didn't even put her in the Safe Haven box. Just left her in a chair and walked away. She didn't check her in. Didn't get her help."

"There were a million better paths, Marissa. But she was fourteen and heavily drugged," Dilynn said.

"She's the girl that killed the prison guard. She's going to jail for murder," Echo stated.

It was Dilynn's turn to shake her head. "The charges have been dropped. She's not going to prison."

"What about Henrie?" Echo said, the red rage returning to her face. "What about what she went through? Where's her justice? All the pain. The withdrawals. The shit we don't even know is coming. How everything is so hard for her. Eating. Moving. Talking."

Echo turned to Parker. "And you're helping her. You're helping her, so what, she can get Henrie back? How could you do this to me?"

Dilynn stood up, blocking Echo's angry eyes from staring Parker down until Parker told her everything. Holding up a hand, the blonde stated, "Parker as your boss, I am telling you right now to shut the fuck up."

Only when Parker nodded, did Dilynn turn back to Echo. "Parker can't talk to you about Olivia. As her guardian, I can."

Echo ground her teeth. The care Parker had seen Echo have for Dilynn was lost to the anger. She'd seen it before when the original Henry had been caught snorting lines off Echo's desk. When her sister had washed her hands of their broken friend.

Dilynn pulled up a chair and sat in front of Echo. "Olivia was a child, held in captivity and drugged to keep her compliant."

Echo's fists gripped the dense fabric of her jeans.

Shaking her head, Dilynn softened her tone, "I know you're angry, and I know the pain of watching your children go through life with the scars of their parents' choices. When I think of Lyra's biological mother, I want to hit her with my car, back up, and hit her again."

"I didn't want to hurt her," came from outside of the room.

All of the women turned to the doorway where Olivia stood. Thin hands pushed the hood off her head as the girl lifted her chin just enough for Parker to see her wide eyes.

Olivia kicked an imaginary rock across the floor with her hands enclosed in the overly long sleeves. Parker saw Henrie now it had been pointed out to her. The same eyes. Same dimples.

"Olivia," Dilynn started.

"I'd never held a baby before," Olivia said, silencing Dilynn. She took a step into the room. The light glinted off her own set of dark waves, as crooked teeth dug into her bottom lip. She raised her eyes to Echo.

"I didn't know what to do when the pain came. I thought I was just fat and then it hurt, and it hurt and then she was just there. So small." Olivia raised her hands up, the sleeves making a tiny cradle, Parker could see Henrie being able to fit into.

"I remembered... when I was a kid, I watched this show with my mom and they always put a thing on the tube, so I did that. I used my shoelace, and I made sure it was tight." Her eyes begged Echo to understand her.

Parker recognized the look from all the times she'd done the same thing. Prayed Echo or anyone would understand she did what she could.

The sleeves dropped to her sides as Olivia continued, "But everything was fuzzy and then more stuff came out and I didn't know what it was. But then he came." She wrapped her arms around her body. "I was making too much noise. I was supposed to be quiet."

Green eyes raised again, this time to Dilynn. "It hurt so much. And he came and he cut the tube, and I screamed at him because he was hurting her. Screaming was against the rules. I knew the rules but I screamed so he kicked me. And he took her and the other stuff that came out. And he took her. And it hurt to walk but I had to get her back. I had to get her back because she was so little. They couldn't do to her what they did to me. She was too little.

"He threw the stuff that came out to the dog. The dog that was always barking at me. Mean dog. So mean." Her body rocked back and forth while her head kept shaking. "He was bad. He was bad and I knew I had to get her away from him, so I followed him because I didn't want him to throw her to the mean dog, and I told him to give her back. I promised I would be good if he just gave her back, but he hit me. He hit me into the table and the knife was there. It was there and I stabbed him. I stabbed him over and over again."

Olivia raised her hand and stabbed the air.

"I made sure to only stab him on the side she wasn't on. I stabbed him and when I took her from him, he tried to grab me. He knocked me over, but I kept her safe. I cut my arm when the knife fell, but I got it again and I stabbed him again in his down there." Her eyes shot up to Parker. "I had kneed him once, in the beginning and he'd let me go so I knew when I stabbed him, I would be able to run. I didn't think I would have long because he always found me. He'd hold me down and put the pill in my mouth and hold my nose and mouth closed until I swallowed it. So, I left. I left and I walked. I wanted to run but it hurt. Everything hurt."

Parker held her breath, afraid if she breathed Olivia would lose her courage to tell them the why. Dilynn started to move towards her, but Parker stopped her.

"I saw the ambulance with the lights turn into the building, so I followed it. I followed it because she was little, and she was shaking, and I knew she needed help because he cut the tube."

With shaking shoulders, Olivia dropped her head. She gasped for air as tears hit the floor. Olivia cried as she said, "There were cops there though. He said he was a cop. Said he would find me like he always did and his cop friends would bring me back. And there were cops and cops are scary. So, I left her on the chair.

I told her I wouldn't say anything. I promised not to tell anyone because then he couldn't get her. He couldn't take her."

Echo got up from the chair. She took giant steps, pulling the child to her chest. Her arms cradled the sobbing girl who continued to explain, "I swear, I didn't mean to hurt her. I just wanted her to have a chance away from him. He always found me. I wasn't going to get away, but I got her away."

"She's safe." Echo said between shushes. "She's safe and you're safe. He's gone."

"I'm sorry I hurt her. I didn't—"

Echo pushed the girl back and took the wet face in her hands. She held Olivia until her eyes opened, tears running down her cheeks in streams, which Echo matched with her own. "I'm sorry you were hurt."

"Please don't hate me," Olivia pleaded.

"I don't anymore."

25

Even though the food had just been ordered, Zoe didn't feel as hungry. She leaned back in the chair doing her best to not freak out. The scene before her was worse than anything she'd witnessed in her life. Not even the three-week-old corpse of the old man ducted taped to the floor under layers of trash bags had her question life as much as Evie was at the moment.

The dressed down officer didn't look up. She simply dripped hot sauce on a spoonful of peanut butter. She wasn't even watching what she was doing as she read through a file.

Zoe closed her eyes before the spoon went into Evie's mouth. But she could still hear Evie moan in satisfaction.

"I do not understand how Henrie is not his," Evie declared. She dug the spoon into the peanut butter container again.

Returning to the case at hand, Zoe played detective with Evie. "Maybe we are looking at it all wrong."

"How else is there to look at it?" Evie asked. The spoon was pointing at Zoe like a knife as Evie added, "And don't you even suggest Olivia was a prostitute. She was fourteen."

Rubbing the frustration from her face, Zoe sighed. "That's not what I'm saying... but I have seen it before."

"Then what the fuck are you saying?"

Zoe closed the file in her hand, tossing it to her desk. It slapped against the wood. Carefully, Zoe said, "What if Gibson wasn't holding Olivia for himself?"

Evie's face paled as she stared at Zoe. The cop's mouth opened, then closed. She placed a hand protectively over her stomach as though just the suggestion would put the miniature Greyson in harm's way. Evie's shoulders rose with each deep breath. Finally, she asked, "You mean like he was selling her? But she said he raped her."

Looking at the ceiling, Zoe held her breath so nothing would accidentally fall out as she exhaled. She considered the other alternatives. If Gibson wasn't selling the girl, then she was impregnated by someone else before coming to Gibson's.

'Gibson still tried to take the baby from Olivia, so even if it wasn't his kid, he was trying to get rid of it. Not it. Her. Gibson had torn a newborn from her mother's arms,' she told herself.

"Earth to Robinson!"

Zoe looked up from Evie's stomach. She hadn't realized she'd been staring at the tanned hand cradling the unborn child.

There was another pedophile out there. Maybe Olivia was a stolen child. They knew from Parker's notes Olivia said she was from Philadelphia. Maybe her father or an uncle was the child's father. That would explain why they couldn't find a missing person's report for Olivia.

"Maybe Parker could ask Olivia about male family members," Zoe suggested.

"I can ask my mom, but the charges were dropped."

Zoe's eyebrows scrunched together. "What does that matter?"

"Parker can't tell us anything without breaching confidentiality anymore," Evie explained. "And since she hates me and you, its unlikely she will tell us anything."

Standing up, Zoe moved to the side of the desk. She flipped open a different file. Several pages of bank statements were gripped in her hand, as she explained, "I've gone through every piece of Gibson's financials and there is nothing. No large deposits, no cash deposits at all. The money trail just isn't there, so it makes me wonder if we are looking too narrowly at Gibson. What if he is part of something bigger?"

"You mean like a pedophile ring?"

"Just hear me out, okay?" Zoe asked, needing Evie to follow her through the different paths she'd been winding down. "We know that Gibson raped Olivia. She said so. She also said she was there for a long time. Your mom said that Parker said that Olivia once said that there were so many blurry faces. We know she was drugged, and if Gibson was on his own, why drug her? Why not just tie her up and do what he wanted? Think about the Olivia you arrested a year ago. She needed a bath, yes?"

Zoe made her way across the room to Olivia's mugshot. "But look at her. She has no signs of abuse other than the bruises on her wrists. And the bruises are not handprints. She wasn't held down, she was tied. She was tied down repeatedly. But in the apartment, there was no indication she was tied there. So, if you were Gibson, why would you leave her in that apartment all day by herself and then drug her and tie her down?

"I wouldn't," Evie said.

"Olivia is terrified of cops. She doesn't run from Gibson's so there is no reason to drug her or to tie her down to rape her, unless..." Zoe took a deep breath. "Unless he needed a compliant child victim for someone else. Someone else who didn't want the possibility of being recognized."

"So, you are thinking Gibson had a partner."

Zoe looked into Evie's eyes. "I think he had multiple partners. I think he had a group of people who hurt Olivia. But without any money changing hands—"

"There are other girls out there," Evie finished what Zoe couldn't stomach to say aloud. "Girls going through the same thing Olivia went through?"

"If he's part of a pedophile ring, then more than likely. I mean, that's the only reason I can think Gibson wouldn't have any money flowing in his accounts." Zoe stared into Olivia's lifeless eyes. She didn't have to close her eyes for the horrific things the girl must have seen to pop into her head. The blurry faces of sick men.

Shaking her head, Zoe added, "If he was actually selling her, then she'd be worth a decent amount. She's young. The young ones are worth more usually. So, no money means...."

When Zoe turned away from Olivia's photo, she found Evie staring through the wall across from her desk. The woman seemed lost in her own world barely breathing.

Zoe reached out and placed her hand on Evie's shoulder. "Are you okay?"

Evie moved, breaking the physical contact. Zoe felt the loss immediately, realizing she hadn't been touched in the slightest form since Lyra kneed her in the crotch.

"I had it bad," Evie confessed. She closed her eyes, but couldn't stop the break in her words as she said, "I thought... I thought I understood her, but I can't even... I mean, one person... the trauma that Olivia went through. I just can't."

Zoe sat down in the chair next to Evie.

"Look, I am sure the secondary trauma you must be experiencing by being on this case is really overwhelming. But if you—"

"Don't pretend to care, Robinson," Evie snapped.

Zoe leaned back, hoping to give Evie the space she needed. "Look, I'm just saying, if this is too much we can—"

"Fuck off." Evie wiped away the tears welling in her eyes. "I'm going to find these bastards."

A knock on the door turned both women to a large, suited man standing in the doorway. He smiled warmly as he interjected, "Sounds like you could use some help."

"Hey!" Evie said. She snorted back the mucus from the tears and got up from her seat.

The man walked into the office holding a plastic bag of Styrofoam containers. "I grabbed this from the DoorDash guy."

Evie wrapped her arms around his middle, and he held the woman to his chest protectively. "You okay, kiddo?"

Nodding into his suit jacket, Evie snorted back another round of boogers. She took the bag from his hand. He smiled as he looked at her growing belly. "May I," he asked, with his hand hovering over her stomach.

"If you have to," she huffed.

He smiled and placed his hand on the bulge that seemed to develop overnight. Shaking his head, he said, "I can't believe you're having a baby. How did my sibling and Dilynn take the news?"

With a roll of the eyes, Evie said, "Mom is excited of course, but Obi... well,

Obi still pretends that I don't have sex, so they are awkwardly avoiding any baby talk, but Auntie Jas and Mom keep going on and on about all the gross things like prepping for breast feeding and what's going to happen when the little alien rips its way out of me."

Zoe wasn't hungry anymore, and very content with the reality she would not be having any aliens tear through her. There would be no accidental pregnancies in her future.

Evie turned back to Zoe as she made her way to the desk. Quickly, she pointed to the man. "Robinson, this is my uncle, Ryder. He's Obi's brother, and he's a detective in sex crimes. This is technically his case now, but I hijacked it from him. But being all adult and shit, he said he has to come help since he is the one in charge."

"Hello." Zoe rose to her feet and extended her hand. "It's nice to meet you."

"I've heard stories about you, Ms. Robinson," Ryder said with a firm shake.

Zoe's hand made its way up to the back of her neck. She looked at the ground, "Yeah, I'm sure they are not good."

"Not in the slightest." He chuckled. "But Evie called and said not to cut you out of this case, so I'm going to let you and her play movie style cops. This is my case though, so fill me in on what you two have come up with."

Ryder took the seat Evie had been occupying, while Evie made herself comfortable with her plate of food behind Zoe's desk. She dipped her head down below the desk. "What the fuck is down here, Robinson? Your entire shoe collection?"

Zoe looked down at her bare feet. The slightest blush rose in her cheeks. She shrugged, and said, "I hate all things heels, but in court... let's just say the men pay more attention when I wear them."

"We are the weaker sex," Ryder admitted.

It would be rude to agree, so Zoe stood still. She wasn't sure what to do with the newest addition to their team. He reminded her of Alex though. There was a calmness to him that balanced out Evie's ever-present energy.

Thankfully, Ryder broke the silence. "So, where are we?"

"We were just considering the possibility of a pedophile ring," Evie answered. Red rice shot out of her mouth onto the desk as she spoke.

Zoe pinched the bridge of her nose. Silently she reminded herself it would be wrong to beat the crap out of a pregnant woman. Even if that pregnant woman just spit food all over her germ-free desk. The desk she had to sit at every day.

"What does the evidence say?" Ryder asked, reaching for the churro peeking out of the bag.

"Mine." Evie quickly pulled the bag towards her and held her fork at the man. "Order your own damn food with your fancy detective salary."

"I ordered the food," Zoe said. Then she turned to Ryder, "Not a lot."

A smirk spread across Ryder's face. "Then you are not looking at it from the right angle."

He picked up one of the files from the box lying in front of Zoe's desk. "This all the evidence?"

"Yes."

"Okay, financial?" he asked, filing through a stack of papers.

Zoe handed him the bank statements. Then she said, "No visible money exchange."

Evie's food slapped around in her open mouth before she swallowed dramatically. Smacking her lips, she grabbed Zoe's open bottle of water and chugged it. Only when the food was gone, did she say, "She suggested maybe there are other girls, and they are trading that way."

"IT turn up anything?" Ryder asked while nodding at Evie.

"Nothing on his computer other than porn," Zoe said. Then she added, "And not child porn."

Ryder hummed, switching between bank statements and the file he'd opened on Olivia.

"The girl was probably a victim of opportunity then. Any known associates?"

Zoe squatted down, thumbing through the files on the floor. "He had a small group of friends. All had alibis." Zoe's stomach twisted as she checked the file before handing it to Ryder. She'd interviewed everyone on that list.

Slowly she raised her gaze to Evie. "The detectives checked the alibis to rule them out as murderers. No one asked... I didn't ask.... They were the only people he associated with."

She let a pedophile walk out of her office and back to another girl living in hell. Put several of them on stand to talk about the man who'd raped Olivia. Forced her to sit as one of those men, or all of them, tell a room full of people that she deserved to go back to the life they'd forced her to live.

What she'd done to Evie on the stand was what she thought was her worst. When she apologized to Olivia, it hadn't been enough. There would never be enough apologies.

Ryder flipped quickly through the pages. "What do we know about these guys?"

"Two worked with Gibson, the other two attended weekly poker nights."

"Poker nights." Ryder repeated. He blinked a few times, before he asked, "In the inventory were there any poker chips, tables, space to accommodate five people?"

Zoe closed her eyes and walked through the house she'd memorized.

Kitchen table sat max four and it would be a tight fit. No seating in the living room. She'd have to double check for a folding table. She pictured the backyard. No patio furniture.

"He couldn't host," she said, opening her eyes again. "Do you think he took her someplace?"

"Neighbors ever see her?"

Shaking her head, Zoe thought about the neighbors' statements. "Homicide said no one had ever seen her."

Ryder asked, eyebrows raising. "Did Gibson withdraw cash for these poker nights?"

Zoe took the bank statements back from Ryder. She flipped through about three months' worth of information, before shaking her head.

"No cash withdrawals." She chewed on her lip for a second as she looked at all the Circle K charges. "But we wouldn't if he got cash back at Circle K. He went there a lot."

"Look at the totals. Any high amounts?"

Zoe ran her finger down the pages. "Daily transactions are a few dollars and every other week a thirty-to-forty-dollar charge."

Ryder looked up from the file. "What kind of car did he drive?"

"Honda... Accord. Yeah, an Accord," Zoe answered.

"How far from residence to work?"

Zoe hated math. She became a criminal lawyer instead of financial like her dad to not to have to do math. She rubbed her hand over her face.

"Uh... Downtown Phoenix to Perryville, so like fourteen miles both ways, give or take. He worked mid-shift so he wouldn't have hit traffic."

"Those are gas fill ups," Ryder said. He shut the file and looked back and forth between the women. "Poker night is probably code, and a crude code at that."

"What do you mean?" Evie asked with her mouth once again filled with mashed up food.

"Poker," he said. "As in poke... her."

"Fucking bastards," Zoe hissed.

Ryder held up his hand. "Hold on. This is just a working theory. We are working on the presumption Gibson held this girl for a long period of time. Where did he keep her?"

"In an apartment above the garage. And according to her, it was a long time."

"DNA in the apartment?"

"No, none," Zoe answered. "Windows were boarded up except one that was presumed to be where she climbed in to get out of the storm that hit a few days before Gibson died. Inside there were just a couple of torn up cushions. She used a bucket to go to the bathroom. Some boxes had some clothes and one of the friends said Gibson would get clothing donations for the homeless shelter he volunteered for from people he worked with. The shelter was for teens, and we just assumed Olivia took some clothes from there... but if there are others, he may have..."

"It's not your fault," Evie offered with her eyes locked on the burrito. "The detectives were supposed to figure this out. They just accepted what others said."

"But I..." Zoe sucked in a deep breath. "I talked to these guys. And I just believed them."

"Why wouldn't you?" Evie asked, raising her gaze to Zoe. "You don't know. Have never had to... know."

Ryder cleared his throat. "What do you know about the poker night players? Any with families?"

Zoe looked through the file of known associates Ryder handed back to her on the character witnesses, then she looked up, "Why?"

"To hold a woman or a girl, you'd have to have space. The likelihood of a person with a family being able to arrange a group of men to rape a girl being held for long term is slim."

Zoe flipped the pages again. She huffed out a breath. "I don't have that information. No one even thought to look."

"Okay, so that's a place to start," Ryder said. He looked at his niece who was busy shoving a carne asada burrito into her giant trap. "Evie, my darling little stalker."

Evie's eyes narrowed as the burrito stalled between her teeth.

"Search the social media accounts," he instructed.

Evie chewed slowly. She swallowed and finished off Zoe's water. Sucking her teeth, she sat back in the leather chair. "Why do you think I can do that?"

Ryder leaned back as well. His arms came up to support the back of his head. He smiled at the woman across from him.

Evie's face scrunched in annoyance. She pointed a finger at him. "Fine, but don't tell Obi. I promised I wouldn't do it again after I broke Casey's nose."

"Who's Casey?" Zoe asked.

"Cheating whore bag fuck face who cheated on my sister. You met her. Sadie."

"Casey and Evie used to be best friends," Ryder said.

"Yeah, until she took advantage of my little sister who was dealing with her own trauma to get back at me for breaking her heart."

Ryder turned to Zoe. "Casey and Mommy-to-be here had a thing in high school."

Zoe tilted her head and examined Evie. Her gaydar had never gone off on Evie. "You're bi?"

"Pan. Mom taught me sex and gender don't matter." Evie narrowed her eyes. "But back then, I was traumatized and terrified of men. She loved me and I was her first. I just wanted someone to give a damn about me." She folded her arms over her chest. "Just to be clear, you're lucky I didn't bust your face for taking advantage of Lyra."

"You're that lawyer?" Ryder said, his chin dipping down.

Zoe wet her lips. "I thought that's what you meant when you'd heard about me."

"Court stories. Heard of The Commander." Ryder let out a long whistle. "You're lucky my sibling didn't gut you. I mean, yeah Evie packs a punch but Alex has broken my nose at least four times and they are so fast and quiet."

Evie smiled. "Yeah, and to make things even better, she's all jelly Lyra not only has a new girlfriend but it's Robinson's ex."

Ryder shook his head. "I'm glad I'm not a lesbian."

Zoe's back straightened. She looked down at the bulky hetero and prepared to give him a lesson on etiquette. "What's that supposed to mean?"

Irritatingly unfazed, Ryder explained, "All the stories I listen to the girls tell is how one of you dates someone, then you break up; and someone dates the ex or the sister of the first partner. It's just so complicated and in straight relationships it's more of a bro code. You don't date your friend's ex. But then, I guess your dating pool is small as it is, so it's just not an envious place to be in."

Zoe swallowed her defensiveness.

"Back to the case," Ryder instructed. "We're going to have to flush out the possibilities with the social media stalking because if they are part of a ring and we start asking questions, then the first thing they will do is get rid of any other girls. Then we won't be searching for victims. We'll be looking for bodies."

The weight of his words collapsed on Zoe's shoulders.

"How did Olivia react when the men were on the stand?" Ryder asked.

Zoe swallowed her shame as she ran through the testimonies. With a sigh, she said, "I honestly didn't pay attention to it."

"Evie, do you think you could get your mom to go through some photos with the girl?" Ryder asked.

"Yep," Evie answered, reaching for the soda on the desk she'd bypassed earlier.

"If the girl can point out any of the men or all of them, then we could get a warrant to search the house," Ryder explained.

Zoe leaned against the wall of her office. She scratched the back of her head, making a mental note she needed to actually go home and shower tonight. Then she asked, "Could we also run the baby's DNA through CODIS? Like if the guy had an arrest, then his DNA would be on file, wouldn't it?"

Ryder shook his head. "That's not how CODIS works."

"I don't understand," Zoe said.

Leaning his weight forward on his knees, Ryder explained, "CODIS has two pools. We can put the DNA through into the unknown pool, but the only thing it would pull up is any report that the sample was connected to. All that would do would link the file to another unsolved case."

"What's the other pool?" Zoe asked.

"That is the felony pool, however, it requires a warrant, and getting one to just run a general search is too broad. CODIS laws are insanely strict because it's considered intrusive evidence."

Zoe hated those words. Those words had almost stopped them from learning Gibson wasn't actually the baby's father. That there was another bastard out there who hurt Olivia.

"We can DNA swab with a warrant, but we have to have a probable cause warrant. With that swab we could run the DNA. If it doesn't match though, then both samples get destroyed."

"So, DNA is basically a dead end," Evie said exasperated.

"Not necessarily, but I've only heard about judges ordering paternity tests in family court and that's when a mother names the father of the child. The girl cannot name four people that could possibly be the father and we expect to get the judge to require a DNA test from all of them."

"Unless the DNA was on something disposable," Zoe stated.

"I like how you think," Ryder said.

"What do you suggest?"

"First, do not expect to run out there tonight and find these girls you think are out there." Ryder looked at Evie.

The woman's face was red, and her teeth ground together.

"You have to pull yourself together," he said.

"I'm trying," Evie snarled.

"I know, kiddo, I know. "

"What's second?" Zoe asked.

"We set up stakeouts around the residences. Look for any evidence a female is being kept in the space. Additionally, keep tabs on who comes and goes in the houses. We try to identify the major players and their routine. If we are lucky, one of them could have a past sexual assault charge against them."

"They meet once a week. These girls will be getting abused while they are literally sitting outside," Evie protested.

Ryder exhaled heavily. He covered his mouth with his hand, then lowered it. "I know."

Zoe looked at Evie. Her eyes were staring into her uncle with such an intensity Zoe could swear she was plotting his murder.

Ryder leaned back in the chair again, then he shifted in the seat as Evie continued to glare at him.

"You're going to learn this when you take on a role as a detective," he said. "It's the worst part of the job. If you want to take them all down, and make it stick, we have to get their routine. And once we have it, then we can catch them in the act. That is the safest route for all of the girls. If they are all present at one place, then the other residences are left unguarded. We can safely retrieve those girls.

Then we just have the one in the house. It's the best possible option when trying to bust multiple people at the same time without tipping any of them off."

"I hate that we have to wait," Zoe said.

Ryder nodded. "Hopefully, the girl—"

"Her name is Olivia. She's a person. With a name. Olivia," Evie snapped.

"Hopefully... Olivia," Ryder corrected, "will be able to identify some of the men. It will make the stakeouts more focused. E, start stalking."

Evie held out her hand to Zoe. "Give me the list of names." She pushed the plate from in front of her, placing the paper on top of the splattered food. She pulled at the neckline of her T-shirt and Zoe cataloged the action as a nervous tic as opposed to just discomfort from being in the bullet proof vest.

Suddenly, Evie's eyes shot up. She whispered, "Brandon Collins."

Ryder moved from the chair to the desk. He grabbed the list from her and looked at it again. "How did I..." He stopped himself.

"He was a youth counselor. Said Gibson would go with him on homeless outreaches," Zoe said. She looked at them staring at each other once he'd made it to the name she'd known was there.

The burrito in Evie's hand smooshed under her grip. Meat and salsa split from both ends atop Zoe's desk. A vein in her neck pulsed violently but her chest didn't seem to move.

"You know him, I take it," Zoe stated for no one but herself.

Ryder's shoulders stooped as he ran his hands over his buzzed head. "I arrested Brandon Collins for statutory rape. Nia Williams picked up the case."

Zoe flipped through the rest of the file to where Brandon Collin's background check was. She corrected the mistaken detective, "No, he had no criminal background. No felonies."

"Because my mom didn't make Lyra press charges."

Zoe stopped flipping through pages. She looked at the woman staring out her seventh-floor window towards the setting sun. A single tear silently escaped her stoic face.

"Lyra already didn't want to and after what Nia did to me, Mom said she couldn't force Lyra to go through what she made me go through."

Zoe looked down at the picture of Collins. "He was—"

"He kept Lyra in an apartment." Evie brushed the tear away before it made it to her chin. "She was his secret girlfriend. He...." Evie choked on the words. "He was engaged to my mom. Picked Lyra up off the street when the homeless shelter ran out of beds because of a monsoon. She didn't have anywhere to go. Didn't have anyone to care and he... he convinced her he was looking out for her."

Lyra's words smacked around Zoe's skull. 'I understand more than you'll ever know.' She'd tried to get Zoe to see, to help her understand.

"When?" Zoe asked.

"She was sixteen." Evie looked at Ryder. "She never.... Do you think that she was too scared to tell us? That she was...."

Ryder's gaze gradually made its way around the room. He didn't answer the question, which told Zoe he didn't know. Didn't know but thought it was probable.

Shame burst from Zoe's gut. The bile made its way into her bloodstream. She tried to steel her features as the toxins spread. Shutting down her organs until she couldn't breathe, couldn't speak, couldn't move.

She watched tears slowly fall down Evie's red face.

The poison in Zoe's blood saturated her thoughts. Every memory of Nia shapeshifted until Zoe saw her as the demon she truly was, then Zoe grasped a single truth.

Nia could have changed the course of Olivia's fate, but the victims who needed her the most could never trust her to get them justice. She had to do better, and it would start by taking the woman's seat. Winning the election so Nia would never be allowed to let a rapist go free again.

26

Parker pushed the shopping cart towards the clunking Civic. The bags were over filling the cart for the first time ever. The first time in her adult life, she'd been able to get enough food to fill her entire pantry and freezer with mostly name brand items.

The trunk groaned when she pulled it open. Using an old crutch that lived within for this very reason, she wedged it between the floor and the hood. The bagger had messed up the perfect arrangement of Tetris she'd played throughout the store, so she had to tie bags to keep the mismatched containers from falling out.

After the crutch was tossed to the back, she looked through the dirty rear window to the cracked windshield. The car was a trooper, but it wasn't something she could ever subject Lyra to. Especially since the woman hadn't picked Parker up for their date in the beat up truck she'd called her baby.

No, Lyra was Dilynn and Alex's daughter. Her sports car was just as flashy as her parents' home. Something Parker had actually asked the woman if she was supposed to remove her shoes before getting within. Thankfully the answer had been no.

Groceries couldn't be her measurement of success. She would never have the kinda of money Lyra was used to; however, she could have nicer things. Like a vehicle that didn't require the crutch she'd used for a week because of a sprained ankle from slipping in some pole oil on stage.

She pulled the phone out of her back pocket and called Echo. The phone only rang twice before her sister answered.

"*What's up?*"

"I was thinking...." Parker played with some loose paint at the rear of the car until it chipped off, sorting through exactly what she wanted and how to for ask it without feeling like she was putting Echo in a tough spot. "You know how you're always short staffed?"

"*Yeah.*"

"Well, you should hire me," Parker stated.

"*Bitch, I have asked you to come work for me at least a dozen times in the last three months,*" Echo said. "*Why the change of heart?*"

Parker sighed. "I want to buy a new car, so let me work for you a couple nights a week."

Moving out of the sun, Parker climbed into the car. The cracked leather seat scratched her bare legs. She tested the steering wheel to ensure she wouldn't suffer any second degree burns before grabbing onto it.

"*Can you start tonight?*" Echo asked.

"Yes!" Parker said. Then she swallowed her excitement. "I mean, yeah. No problem."

"*Awesome. Be there by five for set up. Sorry. I have to go. Dilynn is coming over to talk to Simone and me, which means I have to play peacekeeper.*"

"Bye."

As she drove home, Parker blasted the music from the scratchy speakers. She checked out every car she passed, trying to decide on which one she'd like to own in a few weeks. She thought about Lyra's interest in old cars and wondered if it would be possible to get something the woman would think was cool and impressive. She didn't see any cars like that, so she wasn't even sure where to start. There wasn't space to work on a car at her apartment though. Something that went fast would probably be more impressive than looking stupid trying to constantly fix something.

Parker pulled into her assigned parking spot and hopped from the driver's seat. She was ready to start adulting. But when she opened the trunk, she instantly regretted buying so much stuff. It would be a minimum of two trips. Shaking her head, she started sliding the bags up her arms to her elbow, then doing the same thing on the other side.

The walk up the stairs to her apartment with bags weighing down her arms was no easy task. But at the top of the stairs her caramel skinned dream girl waited quietly outside of her apartment. Lyra sat in the small chair on the front patio. Her smile fell when Lyra's eyes looked up at Parker like she'd done something wrong.

"Hey," Parker offered with a shaky smile.

The concrete seemed to crunch under every step she took, and she checked to see if she'd accidentally dropped the eggs, only to realize it was all in her head.

Lyra stood up, took the keys from Parker's pocket, and unlocked the door. Before Parker could decline assistance, Lyra unloaded some of the bags pressing deep red indentations around Parker's wrists. She went inside silently, leaving Parker to trail behind her.

Parker set the bags on the counter and floor, before pointing at the door. "I have to make one more trip. Just give me a minute, okay?"

Lyra nodded, moving about the space in slow motion. It was the final clue Lyra was upset about something. Parker figured it was because she still hadn't scheduled their second date after Lyra declared they were in a relationship to her whole family.

Even though Parker knew whatever the conversation Lyra wanted to have with her was going to be shitty, she sped to the car to not leave the woman waiting.

Scooping up the rest of the items, she moved at a jog-walk up the stairs and dropped the bags on the floor.

Within the kitchen, Lyra had already begun unpacking the cold items and putting them in the refrigerator and freezer. They worked quietly until all the bags were empty. Lyra shoved the flimsy plastic bags into one and tossed the collection under the kitchen sink. Then, she took a seat at the small table in the dining room.

She rested her upper body weight on her knees and twiddled her thumbs. Without looking up, Lyra said, "So, my sister Sadie called me today."

"Sadie is the one I haven't met yet. She works for DCS, right?" Parker asked. She pulled a bottle of water from the refrigerator. She was parched but she could only bring herself to take casual sips.

"Yeah." Lyra ran her fingers through her long hair, before looking up at Parker. "She called to get Zoe Robinson's phone number. Apparently, she met Zoe with Evie while they were working on Henrie's case."

Parker took a seat across from Lyra. "Okay."

"She said she heard since you and I were dating Zoe was single and wanted to ask her out."

"That's interesting. What does you and I dating have to do with Zoe being single?" Parker asked.

"Don't play dumb."

She slowly lowered the bottle to the counter. This was a version of Lyra Parker had yet to see. She knew it was there, but even when the woman was mad at Evie, she still joked. Studying Lyra's angry face, she decided later tonight she'd sketch the two versions of the woman side by side. See if she remembered how the creases in her eyes were different when she was glaring verse smiling.

Licking her lips, she decided to participate in Lyra's need to fight. "I'm not."

Lyra sucked her teeth, then shook her hanging head. "Why didn't you tell me you and Zoe dated? Or Zoe is still in love with you?"

Parker's head fell to the side. She looked Lyra up and down. Never had she pegged the umber eyed woman as the jealous type, but here they were. Her tongue probed her mouth, as she tasted the burn of what she was about to say. She decided to say it anyways since Lyra clearly came to fight, so she could end things.

"Probably for the same reason you didn't tell me you and Zoe had regular fuck sessions in her office," Parker answered. "Or I'm the rebound from that relationship. If it even was a relationship."

Lyra's eyes narrowed at Parker.

With a shrug, Parker nonchalantly explained, "Evie has a big mouth."

Lyra's fingers ran through the hair at her scalp. She exhaled heavily, then looked to the ceiling. "We both used to date Zoe, and neither of us said anything. Don't you think that's a problem?"

Parker shrugged again. "It's not that big of a deal. I figured we just weren't at the stage of our relationship to compare batting line-ups. I mean, it was one date. Was I supposed to list out who I fucked on that date while I was trying to get you into bed?"

Lyra shook her head again and leaned back in her chair. Her hands clenched around the folds in her pants.

With a huff of annoyance, Parker said, "If anyone should be angry, it is probably me." Lyra's eyes snapped towards her. "I mean it turns out you literally broke up with Zoe two days before meeting me. So, I guess that makes me the rebound."

"You are not—"

"Don't pretend you were over her when we met," Parker said, matching Lyra's mirth. "You know I spend my days analyzing people, so just don't pretend. I remember how you freaked in Changing Hands when you found out I was the one who fucked up Zoe's jury. If this was so fucking important, then you had the chance to say right then and there she was your ex. We could have even laughed about it. I could have shared that Zoe and I dated years ago. You didn't. You kept it a secret. So, it is what it is."

"Why didn't you tell me you knew?" Lyra asked. All the frustration had dropped from her voice, but it didn't change Parker being pissed at the woman coming to her door to pick a fight with her.

"Because it didn't matter." Parker's head fell to the side. With her hands, she gestured between the two of them. "We are just getting to know each other. The first time I saw Zoe since college was when I walked into the courtroom for jury duty. The other stuff is all Evie. I haven't spoken to Zoe except one time she showed up at Echo's bar. Even that was awkward and stupid."

"Is that why you don't want to be my girlfriend? Because Evie told you Zoe still loves you?"

Parker's brow furrowed. She looked Lyra up and down, trying to figure out how her asking the woman to just get to know each other meant she had said no to being her girlfriend. Especially when the woman had demanded they take things at least somewhat slow.

Unable to come up with something else, she asked, "What?"

Lyra stood up. She reached for the high counter separating the kitchen from the tiny dining area. Then she turned back to Parker. Her hand gestured to her body. "Then what's wrong with me you don't want to be my girlfriend? That you didn't call to go out on another date?"

"I have been home for two days," Parker reminded the woman.

"But you left my mom's house, and it was just radio silence again. Just like last weekend when you said you would call but you didn't."

Parker studied insecure Lyra. Traced her eyes with an imaginary pencil, detailing the way the tiny crinkles formed around the corners and under the bags.

Carefully, Parker said, "I don't think this is about me."

"What is that supposed to mean?" Lyra snapped.

Tilting her head to the side, Parker asked, "What happened with you and Zoe?"

"We had an office romance, and it fizzled."

Parker leaned forward, scratching the top of her head. She looked up without raising her chin. "So, you're afraid of what, exactly? That I am just playing with your heart like Zoe did?"

"No," Lyra said. But it didn't convince Parker, and she was pretty sure Lyra wasn't even sure of the answer.

"Then why are you so pissed?" Parker asked.

Lyra's shoulders rose. Her back straightened as she used the counter for support. She looked out the window as she hissed, "I don't want to be your secret fucking lover. I don't want to be your plaything."

"You're not!" Parker cried out.

"Then why didn't you tell me about Zoe being in love with you still?" Lyra growled.

"Who the fuck told you Zoe was still in love with me?"

"Evie."

"SOOO," Parker said dramatically, "You talked to Sadie or Evie?"

"Both." Lyra looked at her hands, then back out the window. "Sadie called me, so I called Evie."

"Wow. Your sister really does have a big mouth." Parker leaned back in her chair again, shaking her head. "Wonder if she'd enjoy me blasting her business around. I mean, I lived with the bitch for four months. I got shit to say."

"Don't talk about my sister like that," Lyra said. Her whole body turned to Parker like she was ready to fight her. With a single finger pointed at the redhead, Lyra growled, "She may be crude and bitchy, but she also is insanely nice for everything she's gone through."

Parker laughed and continued to shake her head. "You know your family keeps saying that about each other. Oh, they are so nice, but they've been through a lot. Is that how you all operate? In your pity tales that help you justify when you treat people like shit?"

"Who in my family has ever treated you like shit?" Lyra folded her arms over her chest.

"Evie has, that's for sure." Parker raised her chin and licked her teeth. She set her face straight. "And right now, you're acting pretty crazy yourself."

Lyra mirrored her perfectly. Hurt. Pissed. Ready to walk away.

Parker sighed in resignation. "Look, if you are looking for a fight so you can end what we have, then at least pick a better one than my ex may or may not still be in love with me. I mean, seriously, Lyra. If you want a way out, there's a hundred better reasons not to date me. You're smarter than this."

"Maybe I'm not." Lyra bit back. "I mean, I keep picking losers after all."

Parker's eyes fell to the tile floor at the entryway. She raised her thumb nail to her mouth and chewed on it. She'd known it would come. Stupidly, she'd trusted Dilynn and Evie. She knew better, but she'd trusted them for some fucked up reason.

After a deep breath, Parker slowly pointed at the door. "You can show yourself out, Lyra."

"I didn't mean... I'm not saying you're..." Lyra's words tried to take back what was impossible to retrieve. She gripped the roots of her hair and screamed, "ARHHHH!"

"You can practice your pirate call for your mom's new book elsewhere."

"What?" Lyra asked.

Parker waved the question away. "Doesn't matter. I'm not going to do this with you. You clearly got some shit to work out for yourself, and I don't want the drama. I never wanted drama. I don't do jealous bullshit."

Lyra's brace creaked as she moved towards the door. She stopped before she made it to the tile.

"I don't think you're a loser," she whispered.

"Yeah, well that woman you're so worried about did." Parker stood up straight, unwilling to be seen as small and weak. "In Zoe and my entire relationship, I was the loser. Her poor loser girlfriend who was lucky to have her. And the crazy thing was this whole time, everyone has made it a point to tell me how lucky I am to have you interested in me."

"Who said that?"

Parker waved outwardly. "Your mother. Your sister. Everyone's so worried I am going to hurt you because I am such a loser I would just walk around breaking people's hearts."

A subtle smile spread over Lyra's lips. She dropped her chin and looked at Parker. "Well, have you looked in the mirror lately?"

"What the fuck is that supposed to mean?" Parker growled. Her lips curled up at the implication she was out to hurt people.

"You're beautiful." Lyra said, taking a step forward.

"You're smart." Another step.

"You take care of people."

Lyra took Parker's hands gently. "You break hearts everywhere you go because everyone wants you."

Parker's head fell backward. The anger fell off her like water droplets as she tried not to laugh.

"That was the worst line I've ever heard."

"But you smiled," Lyra said. Her body pressing against Parker's compliant form.

"I don't want to smile at you." Parker pushed against Lyra's chest. "You're acting ridiculous, and I know, you're not telling me the truth."

Lyra bit her lip and wrapped her arms around Parker. She held her so Parker could only stare at the pantry. Cautiously, Lyra said, "Remember when I told you I have been through some shit. Not the same shit as you, but some shit."

"Yeah."

"I met my mom, your boss, when I was barely eighteen. We met because I was sleeping with her fiancé. His name is Brandon."

Lyra let Parker go and sat down in the chair. She rested her weight on her knees as she stared at the floor.

"Me and Brandon were at the mall... and E and Mom were there, and we ran into each other. Evie punched him in the face and Mom called off their engagement. When we got back to our apartment, he told me to get out. He said if he had to choose, he picked her."

Lyra swallowed. "Well, I didn't have any place to go and... well, I guess you should know... I knew about him and my mom the whole two years Brandon and I were together. I was so desperate to be with him so I wouldn't have to think about the fact I slept with him to get off the streets. I wouldn't have to admit I was just a live-in prostitute that he paid for with food and a roof. But then I didn't have any place to go."

Parker watched Lyra squeeze her fists together, and then release them.

"I spent a few nights on the street. Sleeping in the parks I was used to, but it was right after Christmas. I'd left all my stuff when he'd pushed me out the door. So, I went to my Mom's house because he said she always kept the door open. Always let people stay with her."

Lyra's eyes rose to Parker. "And it was true."

"Your mom is a good person."

Lyra held up her hand. "Yeah, she is... but I didn't know that. I was ready to do anything, and I mean anything to stay with her." Shaking her head, she explained, "I tried to seduce her so I wouldn't have to spend another night on the street. And I mean, I got lucky. I got lucky my mom was my mom and not like everyone else I'd ever met in my life.

"I got luckier Obi wanted me, which I'm sure was easier than Evie since Mom and E were like a package deal, but I was theirs. I was always theirs because it was us versus them for a long time with Sadie in the middle. We're not perfect. You need to know everyone was pretending to be on their best behavior when you were sick. No one showed their real crazy, and you just didn't call."

Lyra's fingers pulled at her own hair again. "I thought I had gotten past it all. I mean, I have dated, yeah. But when I finally settled into something it was with Zoe. Zoe, who only cared about her career. And I thought if Zoe cared about me, then it meant I was valuable. I played her game. I came when she called. I kept our relationship quiet so she could move ahead. And I let her use me the same way Brandon did, and when I wanted something more, something public, she dropped me like a piece of trash."

Parker stepped between Lyra's legs and pulled the other woman's head to her stomach. Quietly, she said, "I know that feeling."

Lyra's arms wrapped around Parker, bringing her as close as possible. Then she said, "When Evie said Zoe was still in love with you, I was like Jesus fucking Christ it's happening again. Like, the person I think cares about me just uses me to go back to their ex. And I got mad because Evie said she told you to go for it if you still had feelings. And then you didn't say anything, and you didn't call. And I just thought, you know, if you didn't say anything you were thinking about it. That you had called her instead. And I don't want to go through this again. I just can't. I can't be the one who gets left for an ex again."

Parker swallowed the large amount of information laid out for her. She lifted Lyra's chin and waited for the dark eyes to meet hers. When they did, she pleaded, "In the future, please don't run to your sister for half-truths. Please don't skip over the holder of the information to the person who knows only part of the story, and the irrelevant part at that."

"She's my sister."

Parker nodded. "She's also a drama queen." She hesitated, waiting for Lyra to go defensive again. When she didn't, Parker added, "A part of her is terrified of losing you because you are her rock. Landon may be her partner, but you are her best friend, and she probably isn't even willing to admit to herself the information she gave you wasn't for you but to secure her own position in your life, as your number one."

"What couldn't Evie tell me?" Lyra asked.

Her hand cupped Lyra's face. She lowered herself to Lyra's good leg and looked her square in the eyes.

"That it doesn't matter if Zoe still has feelings for me. At the end of the day, I also lived through being Zoe Robinson's secret girlfriend. I mean I was a little less secret than you, but still. I wasn't just dropped like garbage, she told me I was garbage. Which is why I didn't want to tell you I used to strip, and why I didn't want you to know about my parents."

Parker looked over at the picture frames filled with photos of her makeshift family.

Whispering, Parker confessed, "You have this life with this family, a real family. And I have this. I sometimes have Echo, when it's convenient for her now she has a real family. I have Xio, but she also has a real family. So... I'm it. And a lot of people have said a lot of shit to me and for a while I believed them. I mean, I didn't believe Zoe when she said I was disposable, I believed she saw herself as better than me, and I guess by the stick she was using to measure I am a loser."

"You're not a loser. She's a loser," Lyra stated. Her mouth scrunched up in a mini mean duckbill.

Parker smiled and pressed a soft kiss to Lyra's cheek. Then said, "Well she lost you and that was pretty stupid."

"I mean, losing you today could have been the worst decision I ever made." Lyra's arms wrapped around Parker's middle and pulled her further onto her lap.

Swallowing her pride, Parker confessed, "I'm not afraid to be your girlfriend because I think you're not enough for me, Lyra." She took a deep breath, exhaling the words, "I'm afraid to be your girlfriend because... what happens when you realize the only thing I bring into this relationship is my ability to grind against you and my ass eating couch?"

Lyra chuckled and pushed her hand in her pocket. She withdrew a single quarter and held it up. "I keep this on me because it reminds me how much you trusted me."

Parker leaned down and hovered over Lyra's lips. She waited for Lyra to decide if she wanted the kiss. Long fingers curled themselves against the back of Parker's neck before their lips touched.

They carefully explored each other; this kiss was different from others they'd shared. This kiss was softer, not lustful. Each soothing away the pain Zoe caused the other.

When they stopped for air, with their hearts beating as one, Lyra asked, "Can I take you out tonight?"

"About that..." Parker looked at the stove clock now reading 3:30pm. "Actually, I have to work at the bar tonight. I sort of asked Echo for a few shifts a week, so I can get enough for a down payment on a new car."

Lyra's gaze fell to her brace. Something that would clearly always physically and emotionally weigh her down.

"I was actually planning on texting you when I got home to find out if maybe tomorrow, you'd be willing to do some car shopping with me. I would of course feed you lunch and dinner. Which... I believe we said would be date two and three if we did it last weekend. I mean, I don't know much about cars, and I know you—"

A cheeky smile spread across Lyra's proud face. Leaning back in the chair, she said, "Say no more. I'm your guy."

Parker's hand dipped between Lyra's legs and squeezed her crotch. She earned a quick inhale from the other woman. With a quirked eyebrow at Lyra, she said, "You're no guy."

"True," Lyra conceded as she exhaled. Then, she held up a single finger, "But metaphorically speaking, I am the guy that will get you the best deal on a reliable car. I can spot a lemon from a mile away. And I can best a guy because you can choose your ride, if you know what I mean."

Parker laughed and leaned back into Lyra's body. She felt the hairs on her arms rise as Lyra's fingers trailed ghostly paths up and down her arm. She curled against the woman until Lyra had access to her back. Then she whined and wiggled every time Lyra stopped her tantalizing graze.

Quietly, Parker asked, "So, we're okay?"

"Yeah." Lyra squeezed Parker. "But... uh... is there anyone else? Like, if we ran into them, I should know there is history."

Parker licked her lips, then sat back. "Only one other person. Xio. She's a barback at Echo's. We were... intimate for a while. Our lives are not compatible, but Echo and I still do birthdays at her house and family stuff. I should probably invite Evie because she knows Xio too, and that was the deal. We would meet up on birthdays, major events, and stuff normally family would be there for. That's it though. No one else ever mattered."

"Xiomara Horna?" Lyra asked. "Girl with the giant dick in her pants all the time."

"You sleep with her too?" Parker asked, chuckling to avoid being embarrassed.

"No. But I know who she is. She practically threw Evie through a wall six months ago."

"Her eldest son was killed in a drive-by," Parker confirmed.

Lyra scanned Parker over before she said, "She's a member of the cartel."

"You don't know Xio," Parker warned the woman.

"I work for the state. I work in juvenile court. I have aided many kids in getting out of Horna's reach and placed at my Mom's school."

"I know now that I work there," Parker confirmed. "Evie is usually the arresting officer, in fact. And I can't say anything other than Xio and Evie know each other well. Very well. So well, some of those kids probably weren't just arrested because they were selling drugs. That's all I can say, other than Evie has never been invited to shit because Xio was there when Evie hit me."

"But do you really think being associated with that woman is safe?"

Parker twisted Lyra's ponytail around her hand. This was a line for her, and she needed to establish it now with Lyra.

"I'm going to tell you a story. It's going to paint some people in your life in not a great light, but you need to understand this part of my life to get when I tell you at no point in time will I let you dictate who I may or may not have contact with that I am very, very serious."

"Are you going to call my sister a bitch again?" Lyra asked quietly.

"No."

Lyra took a deep breath. Then she nodded.

"When I got out, the first place I went to was Echo's. She was already with

Simone, and they let me stay with them for a few weeks. Me being there caused Echo a lot of problems and she is my sister, but she wanted her relationship to work out with Simone. I had to leave because Simone hates me. Hates me with a vile venom she seems to also hold for your mother, and honestly, I don't give a shit why. She might be threatened by me, even though Echo and I never have and never will be anything more than family. But Simone cut me out. I wasn't allowed at the house, the wedding, holidays. Nothing."

"I would like to state I am not a Simone fan. I know she's friends with Obi and Evie, but the rest of us Greysons can't stand her after she spread rumors my mom was a prostitute."

Parker ran her finger down Lyra's jaw. It was good Simone wasn't someone the woman liked. She would understand better then.

"Xio was all I had after Echo had to cut me out. She was the only person to text me. Only person to check on me. Brought me tamales for Christmas. And yes, we slept together. She wanted more, but she's tied to the person who took over her dad's spot. Has three kids. And that is a life I didn't want, but she still didn't cut me out."

"She loves you."

"Yes, and I love her as a friend. And I will be there for her when she needs me. I will talk shit to her like I do with Echo. None of that will change because she is my family. Her and Echo are my family. We didn't find each other. We were forced together, and we figured out how to be there for each other because you can't understand what we went through inside." Parker searched Lyra's gaze. "I bet there are things you don't understand about Evie. Like why she is always pulling at her shirt."

"That's a thing?" Lyra asked.

"It's a thing. Just like how I guard my plate when I eat, and I will not share my food. Not ever."

Lyra wet her lips, but she didn't say anything.

"You can't be jealous of Xio."

A crevice grew between Lyra's eyebrows.

"What?" Parker asked as she pushed on the wrinkle.

"I mean, I'm a little jealous of the fact she and you… made it past making out," Lyra held up a finger. "But that's only because I haven't gotten that far yet."

Parker's eyes rolled dramatically. "Hey, I tried, but you were all noble and shit."

"You didn't try that hard," Lyra stated. "I even told you what it would take for you to tell me you really wanted me that first night."

"Nipple play," Parker stated. "I mean, I can give you a purple nurple right now if it means you don't have to be jealous anymore."

Lyra seemed to be considering it. Thoroughly considering the offer, but

Parker hoped the woman still wanted to stick by her own rules. Especially since there wasn't a lot of time.

"My nipples say yes," Lyra declared. Then her arm covered her chest. "But my heart says wait. Do it right. And my heart is pretty loud. Like its pounding out some Morse Code in my ears, so I'm going to give myself some figurative blue balls once more and ask you to wait for me."

Parker agreed with a kiss. A soft kiss she hoped also would say she was done being pissed at Lyra for bringing drama to her door.

"Sorry for being crazy," Lyra whispered.

"It's fine. I get it."

Parker checked the clock again. She had forty-five minutes to get ready, which included showering, shaving, and doing her hair and makeup. She looked up at Lyra's perfect jawline.

"Want to pick out the outfit that will help me make the most tips?" Parker asked. "I want a car that goes vroom vroom, and that is going to be expensive."

Lyra's lips spread into a smile once more, but then closed to a smug grin. "Only if I can watch you put the whole thing on?"

27

Zoe flipped between each of the pre-programed stations of the BMW. She'd parked behind Zackery's new truck outside her mother's house, trying to gather the strength needed to get through her mother's birthday dinner. Under the rear of the truck, Zoe noticed the ball sack dangling from the tow hitch.

"I should kick you in your weak ass balls," she growled at the truck.

She looked up the quiet street, then checked her rearview mirror. The area was eerily vacant for being one of the first days that felt like fall was finally arriving.

The glove box popped open easily, and she grabbed the utility tool from within. Opening the blade, she looked at the sack and nodded. Grabbing the poorly wrapped bracelet from the passenger's seat, she got out of the car.

Kneeling at the back of the truck, Zoe pretended to tie her Pride checkered Vans she'd just bought to quit hiding her queerness. She glanced up at the house, then checked the street again.

"Just get it over with," she commanded.

The plastic didn't give as easily as she'd expected. She sawed the thinnest part until the truck was properly castrated. She left the useless appendage on the ground, not caring if he knew it was gone or not.

When she walked into the house, she tasted her childhood in the air. Sauteed garlic and onions simmering in tomato puree greeted her like an old dog. Her mouth watered immediately for a meal that didn't come from a bag or a Styrofoam container.

From the door, she could see the back of her brothers' heads. They sat hunched over, staring at the television. Suddenly, the Cardinals fans booed through surround sound. The boy-men jumped to their feet and screamed at the referee. Normally, Zoe would roll over the top of the couch if they were up to secure the whole area for herself, but seeing Zachery for the first time in almost a month twisted the muscles in her neck and arms until her hands clenched into fists.

Silently, Zoe made her way around the back of them toward the kitchen. She diverted to the laundry room, retrieving a Heineken from the beer fridge. As she popped the top of the beer on the bottle opener, she investigated the kitchen.

Her mother stood at the large island, pressing candy flowers into her own birthday cake. Zoe leaned against the door. She watched Cassandra quietly hum "Happy Birthday" to herself. Behind her mother, Zoe spied the freshly pressed pasta hanging from the drying rack alongside a rumbling pot.

A timer beeped from the microwave. Cassandra stopped decorating to check the marinara sauce simmering on the stove and add the pasta to the angry water. She spun the pasta carefully to keep it from fusing together.

Moving around the island, she set her beer and the disappointing gift down. Zoe pressed against the back of her mother. Wrapping her arms around the woman and leaning her chin on the slumped shoulder, she watched the noodles turn a deep gold as they danced in the water.

"Happy Birthday, Mom," she said.

Cassandra patted Zoe's arm when Zoe squeezed her tighter. "Thanks for coming."

When Zoe released her, Cassandra handed her the spoon. "In a minute, strain the pasta, please."

Straining pasta was the only task Zoe could be trusted to complete in the kitchen. A task she was happy to do for her mother because it was something she was good at. She watched the clock count down a full minute, then poured the pasta into the metal colander as her brothers screamed in victory. She shook the colander over the sink, remembering not to rinse the pasta.

"I dropped the charges on the case I was working on," Zoe said.

"Oh really?" Cassandra responded absently. "That's good, honey."

"Yeah," Zoe set the colander in the sink "Actually, we think we have identified some major players in a pedophile ring, so we are hoping we can get not only justice for the girl but locate others who may be going through what she did."

Cassandra turned the heat off the bubbling marinara. She swirled a tablespoon in the sauce, scooped up a spoonful, and offered Zoe a taste. Zoe blew on the spoon before she let it burn her tongue.

As Zoe panted at the heat, Cassandra said, "I knew you'd come to your senses."

Zoe picked up a kitchen towel and pressed it to her tongue. It did nothing to ease the burn, and her mother quickly ripped the towel from her hands.

"Don't use my good towels," her mother chastised.

With a roll of her eyes, Zoe grabbed her beer to cooled the blistered buds on her tongue.

"How did you figure out there were more people involved?" her mother asked.

Zoe took another sip of her beer. Into the mouth of the bottle, she said, "Parker actually really helped with all her work. She found out the girl killed that man because she was protecting her own child."

"Parker is your girlfriend from college, right?"

Zoe smiled at the use of Parker and girlfriend in the same sentence. She smiled bigger at the fact her mother hadn't referred to her ex as 'the stripper.'

"Is Parker still seeing the lawyer lady you had relations with?"

The smile faded.

"Yeah" Zoe played with the vape in her pocket, wishing her mother would abandon the no vaping in the house rule.

"Good for them."

Leaning against the counter, Zoe turned to the cake. She examined the incredible detail her mother had put into constructing the two-tier cake for just the four of them. She thought for a second, then asked, "Where's Dad?"

Cassandra handed Zoe an insulated metal bowl filled with the strained pasta. Then she grabbed the marinara sauce and moved towards the dining room. Zoe followed her as her mother explained, "He had a tough morning. When I went to see him, he was waiting for his brother to go fishing."

Zoe set the bowl of pasta on the table already set for four. She tilted her head and stared at the family photo hanging above the serving table. "Uncle Tommy? Didn't he die when Dad was in high school?"

"Yes."

Zoe shook her head to dislodge the flicker of panic that one day she may not remember she's old and living in a nursing home.

She watched her mother adjust the silverware on the table she'd set for her own birthday.

"I'm sorry, Mom." Rubbing the back of her head, she added, "I know you must miss Dad."

"Boys, dinner!"

Zachery whined from the living room, "But it's fourth quarter."

Shaking her head, Cassandra looked at the table of steaming food. She sighed heavily before making her way back into the kitchen.

Zoe followed her mother, while her brothers screamed at the television. They cheered for someone to keep going, then wildly celebrated what Zoe could only guess to be a touchdown.

Cassandra picked up the five and zero candles. She placed them above "Happy Birthday" scrawled in her own handwriting.

"You seeing anyone?" Cassandra asked as she moved to the trash can and discarded the plastic packaging from her self-selected candles.

"No," Zoe said, still looking at the cake. She chewed at the dried skin on her lower lip, adding 'still single' as another disappointment to the woman's birthday.

Cassandra took off her apron and hung it on a hook off the side of the refrigerator.

"You're not still pining over those girls are you?"

Zoe sighed and looked at her mom. She wished she could say she wasn't, but she had ceased trying to deny she would wait as long as it took for the chance to show the redheaded therapist Zoe was the one for her.

"I told you to leave them alone."

Cassandra shoved a towel into Zoe's hand, then began washing the dishes from the cake. She pulled the cake pan from the soapy water and scrubbed away the leftover grease and cake remnants.

"Zoe, there are hundreds of women out there. I see them all the time on the ticky-tock thing, doing their dances and being so inspirational."

Zoe took the pan that was handed to her and wiped it dry. As she placed it in the cabinet, she glanced over at the cake again. When she stood up, she asked, "Mom, why are you on Lesbian TikTok? Are you questioning your identity?"

Cassandra turned only her head and raised a single eyebrow. With a sly smile, she answered, "I started watching it to learn about how to find you a girlfriend, but some of those women.... I could be tempted."

Zoe chuckled lightly, then remembered the start of her mother's answer. Her eyes shot up as she said, "Seriously, Mom? So, you could find me a girlfriend?"

The older woman shrugged, cleaning the dishes from the homemade dinner quickly getting cold in the next room. Cassandra continued setting the clean dishes next to the sink for Zoe to dry.

Wringing the towel between her hands, Zoe shoved it between her teeth to muffle her scream. Her mother didn't bother to turn around, which made the entire situation more upsetting for Zoe.

"Why can't you just back off me? I mean, I tell you I actually give a damn about someone and you tell me I'm not good enough for her. Then you tell me you're searching Lesbian TikTok to figure out how to help me get a girlfriend."

When Cassandra looked at her, Zoe moved her hands up and down her body. "Do I have to find a wife so you can have the daughter you always wanted? Because I'm not enough for you?"

Her mom set down the sponge and the dish back into the soapy water. Her hands gripped the edge as she leaned over the sink. She pushed back up.

"Look around, Zoe Marie. What do you see?"

Zoe scanned the kitchen, eyes settling on the self-made birthday cake.

Cassandra shook her head. "I want more for you than this. I want to die knowing someone will be there to celebrate with you. To make sure you're okay. To take care of you when you're sick." Her hands came up, rubbing her face. "I keep praying you will find someone to remind you family is important. Family matters."

"I know family matters, Mom."

Her mother stared at the cake. "You don't understand how unbelievably important family is until you have no one." Shaking her head, Cassandra continued, "Until you're alone going through the days hoping someone remembers to check on you. Hope your kids will notice if you're dead. So, you do everything in your power to stay connected to them, but all they do is push you away."

Zoe noticed the cracks in her mother's makeup when their eyes met. Recognized the red rims hidden under the brown eyeliner.

"You reach out more. Hold on tighter. Try to find a way to show them how much you care about them. Pray they don't end up like you. Pray their life is better than yours."

"Mom, I'm successful. I'm independent. I like my life," Zoe tried.

"Success and independence doesn't help you when you slip and fall in the shower, but no one knows." Cassandra pressed her palms to the kitchen island. Her head hung, and the words cracked in her throat. "I watched a forty-year-old woman die last week because no one was there."

"Mom," Zoe started, but couldn't find a single thing to say.

Shaking her head, Cassandra explained, "The boys told me you don't call me back because I'm too pushy. I'm sorry. I'm sorry I care so much I don't want you to end up baking your own fucking birthday cake."

As Zoe's eyes grew wide at the f-word coming from her mother's proper mouth, Cassandra reached over and pushed the cake off the island. The glass plate shattered against the tile floor when the cake exploded on impact.

Zoe's brothers barreled into the kitchen. Zachery tried to stop himself, but Zion crashed into the back of his brother. The momentum of the collision sent Zachery face first into the cake and glass. His head popped up, covered in blue frosting and blood running down his cheek from a piece of glass embedded in the skin.

Zachery touched his cheek, then looked at the bloody frosting covering his fingers. He tried to push himself up, but more glass embedded into his hands. While Zoe stood still watching her brother transform into another crime scene photo, Cassandra moved into full nurse mode.

Unsure of what to do and unwilling to actually help him, Zoe stepped out of the way. She moved into the dining room where the steam had ceased rising from the ingredients blended together by hand. She didn't need to test the pasta, to know it had rested too long, fusing together in a lump of egg and flour. Every piece of the self-planned birthday had been destroyed by her mother's ungrateful children.

Pulling out her phone, Zoe dialed the only friend she had. After two rings and a gravelly 'hello' from the other end of the line, Zoe said, "Hey Evie. I need your help. I ruined my mother's birthday and she's turning fifty."

28

As soon as Parker walked into the bar, she felt all the employees' eyes on her. Apparently letting Lyra pick out her clothes wasn't the worst idea. However, she wasn't completely thrilled her corset wouldn't tighten all the way closed so her boobs were more exposed than usual. Lyra had been more than thrilled, but Parker worried Echo would be upset at the amount of skin she was showing.

Echo stepped out from the backroom with the registers. She quickly set them down and ripped her phone out of her pocket. Pointing at Xio and another masc lesbian, she commanded, "Go pick her up, like the dudes do in that movie *Burlesque.*"

"What are you doing?" Parker asked.

"Shut up," Echo said, moving around the bar. "They know what to do."

Xio took her bag from her and set it on the high-top table. Then they both raised her arms in a T before placing a hand on her thighs just below her ass. She laughed as they easily raised her in the air.

"Now, give me your 'fuck me' smile."

"My what?" Parker said, her face contorted in confusion.

Echo's head fell back. She held out her arms as the bartenders' hold started to shake. "You know the look you pillow princesses give when you want to be mounted like a wild animal."

The woman Parker didn't know by name couldn't hold her any longer. She felt half of her body start to fall. Xio quickly recovered, pulling Parker down to the woman's shoulders like a captured cave woman.

When she was on her feet, she slugged Xio hard in the shoulder. "Tell her I'm not a fucking princess."

Xio's chin rose, and the tattoos covering her arms flexed as she turned to Echo. "She does have a great fuck me smile. Too bad you ain't ever seen it."

Parker hit Xio again, then growled at Echo, "First off, I am far from a pillow princess, and secondly, who reads too much fanfiction now?"

"Come on. Just let me get a picture."

Parker tilted her head to the side and willed her eyes to open just a little wider. She put her pole swinging smile on as the women picked her up once more and raised her above their heads.

Echo snapped several shots before letting the two women set her back on the ground. Parker moved around Echo and peeked at what she was doing. She watched Echo change the filters until she found one she liked.

"Don't use my name," Parker reminded her. "I don't need it showing up on one of those blogs for creepy serial killer fanatics to jack off to."

Echo nodded, then posted the image to Instagram. Setting the phone down, Echo looked Parker up and down again. She shook her head.

"You do look hot, Princess Lucifer."

"Thank you." Parker looked down at her boobs, and then back up. "I let Lyra pick out my outfit."

Echo winked at her. "She clearly knows what the customers want. Oh! Speaking of the Greysons, Dilynn came to see me today."

"Yeah, you said she was coming over. Did she make it out alive?" Parker asked as she put her stuff under the bar.

Echo snorted. "Yeah. She actually came to talk to me and Simone about fostering Olivia."

Parker stood up abruptly. She looked at Echo who was trying to force the drawer into the register. "Wow."

Echo sighed, then slapped the drawer. It quickly clicked into place. Parker sucked in her bottom lip and tried not to think about how many times Echo had used that slap trick on Simone's ass to get the job done.

Wiping her hands, Echo turned to Parker. "Yeah. I mean, it's not what we expected, and there's so many questions that I can't answer. I mean, what if we say yes and she starts to think of Henrie as hers? And what does that mean for Henrie later? Is she going to grow up and one day going to be like: 'oh shit, you're my mom?'"

Parker gave Echo a half smile. "I think that's going to happen whether Olivia is there or not."

"Yeah," Echo said with a shake of her head. "I just don't know how I feel about it."

"What does Simone think?"

Echo leaned against the bar, tapping her fingers of both hands before turning just her head. "Surprisingly, she is all on board. I mean, I figured she'd say no just because it was Dilynn that asked, but the more I think about it, the more I think it has more to do with Evie."

Parker's chin tucked in as she tilted her head. "Evie?"

"When everything came out about what was happening to her, Simone signed up for the foster classes, did all the steps, but Dilynn got her out first."

Parker ran her fingers over the serving trays, searching for the one with the best grip. She knew why Evie got out being that she was a big part of the reason they were both released early. She didn't think Echo knew the details though.

"How?" she asked, wondering if there was even more to the story.

"Have you seen that house? And, I mean, look at the school. All of it was funded from Dilynn's own pocket. Well, Sylvia, the basketball player, she invested in the school as well, and probably helped Dilynn get Evie too. But, back to the point. While Simone was going through the process, Dilynn had hired herself and Evie a lawyer, started making political connections, and basically bought Evie's way out of juvie."

That settled it for Parker. Echo really didn't know anything.

"Simone has always been hella jealous of Dilynn."

Parker's tongue probed the inside of her mouth. Carefully, she asked, "Do you ever worry Simone had, like, feelings for Dilynn?"

Echo laughed. "No. I think it was more Simone felt blindsided. She did all this shit and then Dilynn just swooped in and became mommy. Then add to the fact Alex fell head over heels in love with Dilynn. If I was worried about anyone, it would be Alex. After how jealous she got over them marrying another blonde."

"So why the change of heart now?"

"Honestly, I think she sees it as a redo. She didn't get to save Evie. She thinks she can save Olivia."

Echo picked up one glass at a time and wiped any water spots from it. When Parker just stood there, Echo tossed her a towel as well.

"But you're not sure," Parker said, coming up from the other side of the bar.

Echo slid a glass across to her.

"I guess it's just complicated, because I look at Olivia and I see us. I don't know if I'm ready to be a mom to one of us. I'm barely surviving being a mom to a toddler that I have raised since she was two weeks old."

"You raised me." Parker shrugged. "And I turned out alright."

"Yeah, you really did." A soft smile played at the corners of Echo's lips while she double checked the glass she'd just wiped.

Parker set down the glass and rag. She leaned against the bar, watching Echo make her way through three glasses before picking up the half-ass one Parker had wiped.

"I am not saying do it. But I think you should honestly think about it. I mean, you could change that girl's life. You changed mine. Dilynn changed Evie's. Alex changed Lyra's."

"Thanks for the pep talk, Princess." Echo smirked at Parker as she continued her work and Parker just leaned against the bar. "Now, let's talk business. You don't have a bartender's license, so you are working the floor. You tip the girls 3% of all drink orders at the end of the night. The rest are yours. Your area is the tables in front of the dart boards and the patio. You do not walk out at the end of the night alone, no matter what. If someone puts their hands on you, you use that tray and you break their fucking face open. We clear?"

Parker stood up straight and saluted Echo. "Yes, ma'am."

"Don't call me that."

"Yes, sir?" Parker tried.

"No."

Parker's salute arm became floppy. She looked at Echo, and said, "Yes, Daddy?"

"You're sick," Echo cried out, throwing the towel at Parker's face.

Parker karate chopped it to the floor. Then with a shrug, she said, "Some chicks like it."

Parker leaned over the bar again, her arms spread wide and boobs resting on the glossed wood. Echo smiled and pulled the phone back out. Parker didn't move, accepting this as part of the penance for asking for the job.

Echo snapped another photo. Then said, "Pillow princess eyes."

Parker glared at the camera.

With a shrug, Echo corrected, "Or call me Daddy demon eyes."

The shutter noise sounded on the camera. Echo looked through the shots, then showed Parker one.

"Damn that one is hotter than the last," Echo mused. "Hopefully, this brings in more customers. There's a NWBA game tonight so we usually get a few at the end of the night, but you stay away from them."

29

The outside of the bar was quiet as a steady trickle of customers made their way through the gravel parking lot to the end of the line. Zoe glanced at her mother pulling at the black silk top in the passenger seat of the BMW. They'd stopped by Zoe's house long enough for her to change into something a little fancier than her t-shirt and Pride vans, before heading out for the birthday celebration Zoe should have planned from the beginning. Well, maybe she would not have planned an evening at a lesbian bar like Echo's Escape. But after learning of her mother's venture into Lesbian TikTok, she felt it wasn't a completely bad option.

They were able to snag a parking spot upfront, which was lucky since the line to get in wasn't short. Evie had called in a favor though, and they were apparently on a list that Evie and her parents were also on to celebrate a 50th birthday.

Zoe tried to convince herself it wasn't going to be weird with Dilynn and Alex there. Dilynn was a social butterfly according to her daughter, and Zoe had watched her mother shine at every work meeting her father dragged them too.

Cassandra followed her daughter past the line of customers outside the front to the bouncer. The greying butch held out her hand for their IDs. Zoe's brows scrunched in the middle until she watched the smile spread across her mother's face. Cassandra eagerly dugout her driver's license from within her clutch and handed it over.

"You're good, beautiful," the bouncer said, tapping it against a clipboard before handing it back.

Zoe noticed the paper only had two names scratched on it: Greyson and Robinson. Wasn't exactly a VIP list, but they still jumped the line when the bouncer didn't bother to look at Zoe's ID, even though she already had it out, moving instead to open the door for them.

While the bar was not at capacity it was extremely busy. Cassandra's wide gaze moved in chaotic waves trying to take it all in. On the dance floor, lines of queers and probably a few token allies were moving to the instructions of "The Wobble."

"There are so many women here," Cassandra said. "We should have no problem finding you a girlfriend tonight."

Zoe's eyes rolled so hard, she had to blink a few times. Taking her mother's arm, she led the woman to a high-top table providing Cassandra a bird's eye view of the room.

"Look over there," Cassandra said with a nod of her head.

Zoe turned to see Alex Trikru leaning against the bar dressed in slacks, tie, and suspenders while Dilynn talked to Parker's bartender friend.

"That's how those thirst trap lesbians are dressing now. I am telling you, you need to start wearing ties."

"Can I get you something to drink?"

Zoe turned abruptly to the sound of Parker's voice. She lost all ability to speak as her eyes ran down the mini corset tank covering only the bust of Parker's chest to the sparkling belt resting atop the skintight jeans.

"Oh, yes," Cassandra said. "I'll take.... Well, actually, I don't know what to order. It's my birthday, and I have never been to a lesbian bar before. Honey, what should I get?"

Parker smiled sweetly, and gently touched Cassandra on the arm. "I got you. You like it sweet, sour, or something that will burn?"

Cassandra considered, while Zoe was still trying to figure out how to swallow. Tapping her hand over Parker's, Cassandra said, "Sweet, like you."

A slight giggle broke from Parker's wide smile. "I can handle that." Then she turned to Zoe with the same fake smile. "And for you?"

"She would like a Heineken and your number," Cassandra interjected.

The blood rushed from Zoe's face straight to her feet, making them too heavy to run away.

"Mom!" Zoe cried out. "You can't just—"

"Shush, Zoe Marie. I told you already. I've been watching the videos, and they say femme lesbians never get hit on because people don't know they're gay." Cassandra turned back to Parker. "This is my daughter. She's a le-dollar-bean, has a good job, a very welcoming family, and she is very confident in herself."

"Oh my god, Mom. Please, stop."

Parker's face had turned a rosy pink, and she held her hand over her lips. She luckily didn't have to respond because Dilynn and Alex had made their way over to the table.

"Zoe," Dilynn said warmly. "And this must be the birthday girl!"

"That's me," her mother said.

Cassandra slipped down from the stool as Alex extended a hand to the woman. "Happy Birthday. I'm Alex and this is my wife, Dilynn. Zoe is friends with our daughter, Evie, who should be here shortly."

Dilynn reached out an arm, blocking Parker's path as the redhead was making a run for it.

"Don't run away, Parker," Dilynn said, locking eyes with Zoe. "We have a very special birthday tonight, so we are going to need some special attention."

Parker's gaze fell apologetically on Zoe before she smiled at her day job boss. "Of course, Dilynn. I just thought you already got your drinks at the bar."

Shaking the glass in her hand, Dilynn showed her party had already begun.

"I'll be done by the time you come back."

Zoe cast a glance at her mother who was looking over Parker carefully. Her hazel eyes seemed to be tracing over Parker's face, until the painted lips parted. Cassandra shifted just enough to be slightly behind Parker as she mouthed at Zoe, '*The* Parker?'

Zoe sighed and dropped her chin to her chest. She cataloged this adventure as the worst idea ever, then vowed to make Evie pay for embarrassing her. There was no way the other woman hadn't known her sister's girlfriend was working tonight.

"I'll take another Cherry Vodka and Coke." Dilynn handed Parker a credit card. "And everything for the table goes on my tab."

"Cherry Vodka and Coke," Parker repeated. She pushed the card back at her boss though. "I'm not taking that card because Echo will fire my ass if I charge her wife's bestie for anything."

Dilynn laughed, and forced the card into Parker's hand, "Simone would skin Marissa if she found out I got free drinks. And your real boss pays you more than she does. And tips better. Plus, remind her she is the one who begs you to come here to boost her business. Nice pictures by the way. We should put you on the cover of the pamphlet for the school."

"She's messing with you," Alex said, rubbing the back of their neck.

"I think the whole corset look would be great," Dilynn said, winking at Parker. "I bet our enrollment just shoots up."

Parker licked the bottom of her teeth, and Zoe's eyes grew wide. She had seen the woman test her fangs when she was about to bite back. She must not have liked the flavor of her venom though, because she smiled sweetly instead of taking Dilynn's snarky bait.

"I think, we should stick to your ball of sunshine self," Parker provided, covering her chest with her tray. "There's something very comforting about a white woman in a cardigan saving all the juvenile delinquents."

Or, she apparently did like the flavor of her venom.

"There's the spitfire Marissa promised me," Dilynn said, then finished her drink. "I was wondering when the honeymoon period would end."

Parker shrugged lightly before saying, "Yeah, I think I was poisoned by some chicken water, and I thought, well life's too short to pretend to be someone I'm not."

"Alex, what do you want?" Dilynn asked, after she licked the front of her teeth like she too had a set of fangs about to come out.

Alex's eyes squinted at their wife, then requested, "I'm going to stick with my bottle of water since I will be carrying my wife home tonight."

Dilynn's glare shot up to Alex smiling down at her. She tried to shove them away from her, but Alex barely moved. They folded their arms over their chest, then they tapped their bicep with their index finger.

Cassandra leaned across the table toward Alex. "Wait. Is that one of those domme warning signals?"

Zoe's attention snapped up to see the bouncy blonde turn a bright shade of tomato paste red. When she looked at Alex, they were calm and stoic. Only the corners of their lips raised in a subtle smirk.

"Oh my," Cassandra said, smacking Zoe's arm with the back of her hand. "I have learned so much from the tickytok."

Zoe covered her face. She peeked out just enough to mouth, 'I'm sorry' to Dilynn, who was now grinning evilly at the floor.

Evie wrapped an arm over Zoe's shoulder. She shouted over the music, "Happy Birthday, Mrs. Robinson! I'm Evie."

When Zoe stood back up, she noticed Landon casually behind Evie. He scanned the room, raising a hand to Parker's bar owner friend.

"So, what did we miss?" Evie asked. She grabbed the bottle of water Alex had set on the table meant for themself and took a drink.

Alex's head turned slowly to Evie's grinning face. They let out a slight laugh before telling their daughter, "Zoe's mother just caught your mother getting a warning. You know the BDS—"

Evie held up her hand, shaking her head dramatically. "You stop right there. I moved out of your house of unsanitary horrors to never have to know about it again."

She pinched the bridge of her nose, then exhaled slowly. As if on cue, Landon stepped closer to his girlfriend. His hand wrapped around Evie's middle.

"Let's go dance, E."

Alex encased Dilynn in their own embrace and stooped down whispering something to Dilynn. They smiled at one another, and the couple seemed to raise their eyes to Cassandra a little too predatory for Zoe's tastes.

Cassandra leaned over to Zoe. "That was a signal too. It means get me out of here."

Zoe watched Evie dragging Landon to the dance floor.

"I'll send you the video later," her mother promised.

Zoe searched for Parker, hoping her beer was on its way. Her search ended at the bar where the redhead's hips sinfully swayed. Parker had her phone out and was dancing to a different beat than the one playing in the bar.

Cassandra asked, "So, that's *the* Parker."

Zoe closed her eyes, only to open them as Dilynn's tongue ran over her teeth once more. The look was nothing short of a warning. One Zoe didn't need, but clearly her mother did before she ruined what minimal working relationship she'd salvaged with the wealthy couple.

Shaking her head, Zoe said, "Yes, Mom. That's Parker."

"She's—"

Zoe cut her mother off. "And before you say anything else, Dilynn and Alex are Lyra's parents. Lyra is the other woman I dated. I told you about Lyra. You remember Parker and Lyra are now seeing each other."

Cassandra studied the ceiling momentarily, then turn back to the couple. The older woman smiled. "So, how does the whole dominant-submission relationship work? I mean, my husband, he was always very reserved. Thirty-four years of marriage and it was the same sex every day. Missionary or me on top. Nothing risky, or anything. Just same in and out. In and out."

"Every day?" Dilynn asked as though Zoe needed to hear it again.

"Every day," Cassandra confirmed while Zoe tried to hold back her need to vomit. "You know, keep their stomach full and their--"

"Ew, no!" Parker returned in time to witness Zoe's second— or was it the third— melt down. "Mom, you can't just ask people about their sex life or tell people about yours. Especially in front of me. I don't want to know anything about yours and Dad's," she gagged, "Just, no."

After steadying the tray against the table to keep it from tipping because Parker's whole body was shaking as she held in her laughter, Parker placed a very pink and very fluffy drink with pineapple and cherries garnishing the sugar rim in front of Cassandra.

"Here's to you, Mrs. Robinson. Hey. Hey. Hey," Parker sang, ending with a wink. "Happy birthday, and may your night be filled with something or someone who excites you."

"Oh, that does sound dirty coming from someone as cute as you, dear." Cassandra sipped the drink before she added, "You know, in all my years, no one ever sang that song to me. It is nice it's from you though. So pretty indeed. I can see why you have so many eyes on you."

Cassandra reached into her purse and pulled out a crisp twenty-dollar bill. She held it up to Parker, who took it and stuffed it into her shirt just enough to show off the money like she was on stage instead of serving tables.

With a seductive wink, Parker said, "You let me know when you're ready for something a little less sweet and a little more spicy."

 Parker placed the Cherry Vodka and Coke in front of Dilynn, then handed Alex a bottle of water. She nodded to the dance floor, and said, "I saw you got jacked."

"Don't you dare wink at them," Dilynn warned, earning a laugh from Parker.

"Naw. Flirting with parents of the woman I'm dating is a little too Jerry Springer for even white trash like me," Parker stated, holding the green beer bottle out for Zoe. "Polite and pretty parents of others though, well I have been known to be petty."

"Zoe, go dance with Evie while Alex and I teach your mom all about dommes and subs, and we figure out which one she is," Dilynn instructed. When Zoe's face properly paled, Dilynn added, "Oh, and Lyra will be here soon, so stop staring at her girlfriend's ass."

Parker's head shot up, and her hand froze with the Heineken bottle in midair. She shoved the bottle at Zoe before leaving as quickly as she came.

Dilynn smiled and turned her focus to Cassandra. "So, yes there are a variety of signals that can be used publicly. For instance, the one Alex just used was a warning I was being a brat. That's one of the various submissive personas. These things are all discussed..."

Alex nudged Zoe, then nodded to the dance floor. "Run," they whispered to Zoe. "Now, while you still have a chance, because she still doesn't like you, and Parker has her full brat out now."

"So, domme-sub relationships are very carefully discussed both before and during. I know the depiction of the 50 shades of abuse that has hit mainstream media paints it all to be... well abusive, but really..."

Zoe didn't run and didn't go to the dance floor where Evie was practically riding Landon's leg. Instead, she made her way to the patio where she downed half of her beer.

Once outside, she pulled the vape from her pocket and took a deep inhale. She watched her mother for a while, then proceeded to look around at the women in the bar. Maybe she could make another one of her mother's birthday wishes come true by finding someone to ask out.

"Your mom is sweet," Parker said as she came alongside Zoe with another green bottle. "I figured you'd never tell her about me."

Zoe followed Parker's eyes through the French doors to where Cassandra was engrossed in the conversation with Dilynn and Alex.

"She seems like she is genuinely having a good time," Parker added.

"I hope so." Zoe finished the beer in her hand, handing the empty bottle back to Parker. "I pretty much ruined her birthday."

"Well.... it doesn't look ruined to me, but what do I know?"

Parker tucked the serving tray under her arm, and left Zoe to watch her mother wave her hands in the air as she told a story to the couple who listened like they were old friends.

When Lyra walked into the bar, Zoe ducked deeper into the patio. It took Lyra less than a minute to find and embrace Parker. She leaned in and said something to make Parker blush and push the other woman's shoulder. Zoe hated how she hated they were happy.

The door opened before Zoe had time to wallow in her self-pity. Evie pulled her from the smoke-filled patio. They moved to the edge of the dance floor, both watching Landon get sandwiched between two flamboyant men. Evie's hand rested on the slight bulge of her abdomen.

Tapping on her stomach, the gravel-voiced woman said, "Well, it could be more awkward."

Shaking her head, Zoe asked, "How could this be any more awkward?"

"Sadie could be here drooling over you," Evie said, with her lips pressed together in a miniature duckbill. She turned to Zoe, "Please, don't date my other sister. This little Alice Piozeki list you all have going is too much for me to keep track of as it is."

Zoe looked at Evie, trying to piece together the bit about her sister. Then she clarified, "You're talking about the sister who wanted to punch me."

Evie waved her hand in the air. "That lasted until you left. Then it was all about how fine you looked in your work clothes, and if you were still single."

"You tell her to stay away from me?"

With a roll of her eyes, Evie said, "What would be the point? It'd only make her pursue you more."

"She's a child." Zoe's eyes catalogued all the other women in the bar she designated as baby gays in their early twenties.

"I know that, and you know that. But she thinks age is irrelevant."

"Proving she's too young for me." Zoe took a sip of her beer. "Know any other queers more my age?"

"So, you're done pining over Parker?"

They both turned to where Lyra led a resistant Parker to the dance floor. The hands on Parker's hips moved her left to right as Lyra stayed planted. Parker's fingers trailed over Lyra's shoulder as she got into the new song. She moved deliberately around Lyra in a complete circle. Once facing Lyra, Parker gripped the back of Lyra's neck and slowly dropped down the front of the other woman. Her head came up to look at Lyra lustfully, then popped back up. Lyra's fingers clung to Parker's hips as the redhead put her ass against Lyra, swayed her hips, and leaned forward until her hands rested on the floor.

"Nope," Zoe said.

She chugged the remainder of her beer, hitting the bottle on the wooden railing. No matter how much she told herself to stop being a creep, she couldn't stop watching Parker use Lyra as a very willing pole.

"Well then, I have no one for you to date. But I do know someone who likes to screw with no feelings attached. Her name is Mona. She works at my mom's school. Looks a lot like Xio, over there." Evie pointed to a large masc with a girthy strap in her pants, covered in tattoos hovering over a woman. "Latina. Sharp wit and tongue that will fuck you until you don't remember your own name."

Zoe raised an eyebrow at her, "And you would know this because?"

Evie shrugged. "Landon and I have enjoyed her company. She is into women, with him being her one exception and that took time."

"Yeah, that's a negative," Zoe stated.

Turning away from her exes, Zoe tried to find someone she could lose herself in. She smiled at a woman nursing a beer across the dance floor from her. The woman glanced away, but then shyly back at Zoe.

'She'll do.'

"Wow, Zoe," Evie said. "I think I know where your gay gene came from."

Zoe followed Evie's finger to where Cassandra was dancing with a well-dressed masc woman. Cassandra's smile was brighter than any Zoe could recollect. She watched her mother's partner spin Cassandra like a little princess, and then pull her back. Maybe the night was embarrassing, but her mother was happy and celebrated.

Picking up her beer, Zoe regretted not slowing down since Parker was busy grinding on Lyra. She rolled the empty bottle between her fingers. Then asked, "How are the stakeouts going?"

Evie sighed, then leaned against the railing. "Doesn't seem like they have a set day they meet. So, one of them is setting it up."

"Any sign of the girls?" Zoe asked.

Evie hummed, taking a sip of her water. "Only at one place. Late teen is my best guess. I saw her on my watch briefly. We are trying to catch sight of the others before we go in."

Zoe waved at another server. She held up the bottle, then a single finger. When the girl nodded, Zoe turned back to Evie.

"Which of them doesn't have a set work schedule?" Zoe asked.

Evie's eyes squinted as she studied the ceiling. Then questioningly, she said, "Caliscpo?"

On the dance floor, Cassandra took Dilynn's hand. They danced to "Hey Mrs. Robinson." Zoe swore she saw her mother blushing as Alex moved between Cassandra and Dilynn. They spun both women outward and drew them back in.

Zoe turned to Evie, unsure if the question she was about to ask was one she wanted answered. But she asked anyway. "Your parents aren't swingers, right?"

Evie spit out the water she'd just sipped. The spray hit her sister and Parker as they made their way around the dance floor. Lyra cast Evie a death glare, but then smiled cockily at Zoe as her grip on Parker tightened.

"They are freaks," Evie said still trying to catch her breath. "But yes, they have had a few guests. I just hope it doesn't become a thing. I have enough sisters."

The server dropped off Zoe's beer. Before she could leave though, Zoe said, "I'm going to need another."

Evie and Zoe watched the drunken parents in confusion and concern, until they finally made their way back to the table with Alex's guidance.

Zoe sighed, then remembered the more important conversation. "Check Caliscpo's schedule. I bet they are meeting on days he is off."

30

The art room drummed with the familiar playlist from the boys upstairs. Parker hummed along with Eminem apologizing to his mother as Olivia shook the whole table from bouncing her leg nervously. Rain pounded outside as the last of the Arizona summer was blown away in the early fall storm.

Parker leaned against her hand, watching the trees sway in the wind. The song faded out, bringing the therapist back to the girl across from her. She looked over at the charcoal sketch coming to life, and Parker immediately recognized it as the same swing set, which had thrown her through a loop the month prior.

"So, today is the big day. I can't believe it's already been a month since you and I started working together."

"When do you work?" Olivia glanced up at Parker.

"I work. I do lots of work things. Like I ask you questions."

Olivia looked up from her picture again. This time she said nothing.

"Okay. Well, I... I tell you what pencils you need to use. I'm supposed to officially get an art class next semester though. And I am going to start working with more kids. Until then, it's you and me, kid. And subbing. I think Ms. Rameriz had me sub her class just so she could blame the minor explosion on me."

"That was funny. I heard you swear through the wall."

Olivia continued to detail the grass around the edges of the poles grounding the swing set. Parker appreciated Olivia's vision and attention to detail.

"Are you nervous?" Parker asked.

Olivia outlined the start of a small face. A child watched the swing set swaying softly in wait. She finished the ear, before shrugging.

"I guess."

"I remember moving to a foster home."

Parker's fingers pushed her hair back, they tangled in a knot that she brought to the front. Deftly she spread the knot out, working little sections free until she got it untangled.

"You were in foster care?" Olivia asked, looking up once more.

Parker bit her lip, and she tapped nervously against the table. She wasn't supposed to say that, but it was too late now.

"I was," she affirmed.

Olivia went back to work on the face of the child in her picture. The eyes came to life as she added fine details to the iris. Quietly, she asked, "Were they nice?"

Parker leaned back in her chair. She sucked her teeth. After a deep exhale, she said, "I'm not going to lie to you, okay?"

Olivia nodded, not bothering to look up.

"My placement sucked." Parker started to raise her thumb nail to her mouth but caught herself. Setting her hand on the table, she said, "It was so bad I intentionally got myself thrown into juvie, but it was because I was alone. You're not alone. If you hate it there, then you call me, and I'll make sure you can come back to the school."

"The one that always wears the purple hat is your friend," Olivia stated, looking up with just her eyes. "She yelled at you."

"She is my best friend. Like Marshall and Ms. Rameriz. We are basically sisters," Parker said, nodding her head. "But I will help you move if you don't want to be there. Echo would want me to do that for you. She wouldn't want you to stay with her if you didn't want to be there."

"Do I call her Echo or Marissa? The grumpy one calls her Marissa."

Parker licked her lips. She knew Echo hated her first name and Simone didn't care.

"Ask her." Parker smiled. "She loves nicknames. She'll probably give you one."

Olivia set down the charcoal. Her eyes shifted from side to side before the girl wiped her face. Dark streaks spread over the pale skin that had finally become blackhead free. She had forgotten to wear deodorant today though, and Parker wondered if Olivia was preparing to protect herself by not showering again.

Carefully, she reached over to Olivia. She'd yet to touch the girl who shied away from even the hint of physical contact. Stopping an inch from Olivia's hand, she waited for the girl to make the move. Carefully, the blackened fingers rested against hers. It wasn't exactly what Parker was offering, but Olivia was willingly touching her skin to skin, so Parker was going to count it as progress.

"Echo was also in foster care. Hers wasn't good either," Parker shared.

"Ever heard of a good one?" Olivia asked.

Parker smiled. "Well Echo and Simone have been great for Henrie. And from what I understand Greyson and Trikru's home was a good one. The officer who helped you. You remember her?"

Olivia nodded.

"Well, the officer is Greyson's daughter. And she has two other daughters as well she adopted."

"Do you know them well?"

"Mrs. Greyson's daughters?" Olivia shook her head. "Oh, Echo and Simone?"

"Yeah."

The metal braces across the girl's teeth peeked out, causing Parker to smile. Echo had always wanted braces, but the foster care dental insurance didn't cover them. Silently, Parker thanked Dilynn for doing the extras.

"Like I said, Echo is my best friend," Parker answered. "I don't know Simone as well."

"What's she like?" Olivia asked, withdrawing her hand. She didn't lean back, which Parker notated in her head.

"Well, you've been on visits with them, haven't you?"

"Yeah," the girl answered. Her tongue probed the corner of her lips, then she added, "But it's just different when you first meet people then when you live with them. I don't know the rules. How do I know when they're angry? What if I don't like the food they make?"

"Wow." Parker hadn't considered these things, but flashes of the same anxiety came flooding back. "Okay. Hold on for just a second."

Parker sent a text to Alex asking them to join her and Olivia to help ease some concerns about going to Simone and Echo's house that evening. Alex answered immediately they were on their way.

Setting the phone down, Parker explained, "I asked Trikru to come help me out because I know Echo really well, but they know Simone because she's their best friend. They will be able to answer questions about Simone better than I can."

Olivia played with the charcoal pencil.

"So, Echo... hmmm."

Memories of Echo's seventeen-year-old strut came to the forefront of Parker's mind. She smiled as she pictured Echo's smirk.

"Echo is sarcastic. She's always honest, so you will never have to question if she's lying to you. Oh, and she's loud. She's loud all the time. Think of your friend Kinsley; you know, the one who is always bouncing off the walls."

Olivia nodded once.

"Echo is loud like her. She's a big woman and her voice just booms. She loves to sing, and you will probably catch her singing when you sneak up on her. Try not to do that though. She's been through a lot like you, and she scares easy. But... you will know she's mad at you when she has nothing to say. She gets really quiet then, and that's when I know I pissed her off."

"Simone is loud too," Alex contributed.

Parker screeched and held her hand to her mouth. She turned to find Alex smiling at her. Her eyes dropped into an unamused glare. "You have to stop doing that to me."

Alex held up their hands in surrender. Their eyebrows raised as they said, "You knew I was coming."

Walking into the room, Alex pulled up a vacant chair from a nearby table. They leaned back and let their long legs spread out. Alex looked to Olivia, who had also been shocked by Alex's sudden appearance.

"I hope you don't mind I am joining you."

"It's okay," Olivia softly said. "Marshall says you are good people."

Alex tilted their head and smiled broader as they looked at the shelves behind Olivia. Their jaw worked slowly, and Parker could tell they were choosing their words carefully. Raising their eyebrows once more, they seemed to have decided on something to say.

"Simone and Marissa are hilarious. The two of them together are usually fun because they bounce off one another. They are not complete opposites, but they don't really agree on anything."

There were so many things Parker could add to the conversation. Things Alex probably didn't know, like that Echo and Simone didn't agree about anything, so Echo always gave Simone what she wanted. Or Simone had a superpower to make Parker feel like ants were living under her skin.

Had anyone asked Parker about moving Olivia in with Echo and Simone, she would have said don't even suggest it. But Echo was already backed into a corner when she brought it up to Parker, so there was no telling Echo no. She could just hope Echo was right about Simone wanting Olivia.

"Some things Olivia has asked are how will she know when Simone is angry and what should she do if she doesn't like the food they make?"

Alex looked directly at Olivia this time. They licked their lips before admitting, "Simone will yell when she's angry. It will happen immediately when she's mad. And a lot of the time when she yells, she's not yelling at you, but it can feel like it. It can be scary."

Olivia tucked a lock of hair behind her ear. She looked down at the table. Parker immediately recognized Olivia's shut down. Quietly, the girl asked, "What type of things make her angry?"

Alex studied the ceiling, then dropped their gaze back to Olivia. "She hates cleaning up after people. Simone is one of those people who has a place for everything."

"Echo is not," Parker threw in. She reached out with her foot and nudged the giant boot under the table. Alex immediately sat up and looked at her. She nodded to the girl with her head hung down. Silently, she mouthed, "Fix it."

Alex nodded and scanned the table. Then they leaned against it. They folded their hands a top and said, "Basically, if she tells you to hang your backpack up on the hook, she wants it on the hook. Not by the hook, under the hook, or even in your room."

Parker rolled her eyes. She reached out and touched Olivia's hand again. She waited for the kid to look at her.

"You don't have to be perfect. Everyone is going to make mistakes. Something to know about Echo is she only gets angry when you lie to her. No matter what you did, she'll get disappointed but not angry as long as you tell her the truth."

Alex leaned back again. They looked at Olivia softly this time as they said, "Simone hates the silent treatment. This will probably be the biggest challenge for you."

Olivia's blackened fingers came up to her teeth. She bit at the already jagged nails.

Parker tapped the table, pulling the girl's attention away from Alex. "The food thing. Echo is a terrible cook. Don't eat it if she made it honestly."

"Don't tell her that!" Alex cried out. They wiped their face, then grimaced. "She really is bad though. But it can't be worse than my wife's chicken and star soup."

Parker closed her eyes and held up her hand. "Please. Don't remind me. I'm still trying to get over the trauma."

Olivia chuckled, making Parker relax some.

Alex sighed, then added, "Simone will expect you to eat at least half of what she makes. She will ask you what you like and don't like to begin with. Are there things you know you don't like?"

Olivia shrugged. Then she said, "Peas. Hot sauce. Pudding or things that are sloppy like that."

Alex laughed. "Okay so tell her. If she makes something and you end up not liking it, it's okay to tell her you'd rather not eat it again. Simone loves to cook. I bet she'd teach you if you wanted to learn."

Parker leaned back from the table as Olivia did. "What else do you want to know?"

"What do they like to do?" Olivia asked.

Alex tapped a finger against the table. Their eyes stared at the ceiling before looking back at the girl. "Simone likes to read and watch documentaries. She's a history nerd like me. She likes to go to museums and historical places. She also really likes to work out. She goes to the gym almost every day."

"Echo also goes to the gym," Parker added. "They usually don't go together though. Echo works a lot, but she loves movies."

"What if I don't like to do what they do?"

"You all will have some things you like to do together and some things you like to do separately, and that's okay." Alex paused momentarily, then added, "Greyson and two of our daughters love to go shopping and get pedicures. One of our daughters doesn't like to do either of those things. I go to a boxing gym with one of my daughters, and Greyson has nothing to do with that. You met Evie. She loves to watch Disney movies over and over again. She does that with her sister, but Greyson and I have no interest."

"What types of things do you like to do, Olivia?" Parker asked.

The girl looked at the table. "I've never really done anything."

"How about with your aunt? You said you moved here with her when you were ten. What did the two of you do together?"

"We weren't allowed to go anywhere," Olivia confessed. She stared at the table as she explained, "She left at night and would come back in the morning. I had to stay in the room while her boyfriend had his friends over."

Alex looked at Parker but stayed quiet.

"They were loud, so I hid in the closet after one time one of his friends came into the room when I was pretending to be asleep. He tried to lay in bed with me, but I screamed and I hid under the bed. After that I stayed in the closet, and I drew pictures if we had any paper."

Parker maintained eye contact with Alex as she sat up and then leaned back. Then she nodded to them. She had to do it once more for them to understand but they leaned off the table, moving out of the center of the conversation.

"I like to draw, and I like to be outside when its light out, but not in the dark. I don't like the dark. The closet was dark and the place I was at… before I came here was dark. I wasn't allowed to have a light. And it's always loud and men yelling at each other, and dogs are scary in the dark."

Once Alex was a fly on the wall, Parker leaned over the table, closing the distance between Olivia and herself.

"Was it always like that?" Parker asked. "With your aunt?"

"Yeah, she came and picked me up from the park. We stayed in a hotel with her boyfriend, then we came here. They fought a lot. He was mad she made me stay in the room. He wanted me to go out with her."

"Okay, well then, you're right. You didn't get to do a lot of things with your aunt. Olivia, what do you remember about your mom, before you left Philadelphia?"

"She worked at night too. She slept a lot during the day, so I got up and got ready for school and then I would go to the park after school. She needed to sleep. When I got home, if she was there, we would make dinner. She liked mac and cheese. We played games and she played her guitar. She said one day she was going to be a singer." Olivia bit into her lip once more. "But she died."

"Olivia?" Parker waited for the girl's eyes to rise to her. "Did you ever go to your mom's funeral?"

Brown hair shook as the girl added new black streaks to her face. She sucked in snot, before explaining, "My aunt came when I was at the park. I was playing on the swings. She said my mom had been in an accident and she had died. She said we had to go because the people were going to come and get me and put me in a foster home. My mom told me all about how bad foster homes are, so I went with her."

Alex started to move, but Parker kicked them again. They carefully leaned back into the chair. Satisfied they got the picture this time, Parker picked up the charcoal and handed it to Olivia. She pointed to the child in the picture, and said,

"She needs hair."

Olivia took the pencil and leaned over the drawing. When she was clearly focused on the piece, Parker turned to Alex. She mouthed, "Stay put."

Alex's chin jutted out, so Parker had to repeat it before they nodded in acknowledgement.

Olivia lightly sketched the outline of the child's long hair. Then she paused. She looked up at Parker. "I don't know how to draw curls."

Parker took the scratch paper she had used earlier to answer one of Olivia's questions and demonstrated how to create three different curl patterns upside down so Olivia could watch and mimic the movements. Olivia tapped the second option and Parker demonstrated that one twice before pushing the paper to Olivia, so the girl could practice a few times without messing up her drawing.

"Had you met your aunt before she picked you up at the park?"

Olivia traced over Parker's examples before she tried two out herself. She nodded and returned to her picture.

"Mom went to work with her. Sometimes she'd come over early and hang out with me while Mom was getting ready. They would get all dressed up and do their make-up. They wore the pretty shoes Ms. Robinson wears. The really tall ones. Aunt Brittany let me try hers on once and my mom got so mad. She said she didn't want me wearing shoes like them. But my aunt, she was cool. She'd let me play on her phone. She was always really nice and told me I was pretty like my mom. Mom didn't like it. She said I was smart, but I know that was a lie because I'm the dumbest person here. I can't even read right."

Parker picked out a pencil with a finer tip from the box, then pushed it towards Olivia.

"Do you remember your mom's name?" she asked.

"Crystal. Crystal Jacobson. My name used to be Jacobson too but when my aunt came to get me, she said my name was Olivia Moore now. She said since my mom died, she was giving me her last name."

"When you lived with your mom, was your name Olivia Jacobson?"

"No."

Olivia finished the hair on the girl and moved to the girl's body. She retrieved the denser pencil and drew a soft dress flowing with the same breeze the swing swung to. Olivia's hand stopped, and her head shot up.

"What's my name going to be now?"

Parker looked at Alex. She tried to swallow the lump in her throat. She had to find a way to answer the girl without completely terrifying the kid.

Shifting in her seat, Parker angled her body away from Alex, drawing Olivia's gaze back to her. Carefully, she said, "Simone and Echo are not going to make you change your name, honey. But I need you to tell me, what was your first name when you were still a Jacobson?"

Her grip on the pencil tightened. She was no longer looking at the picture but at the table in Alex's direction.

"Aunt Brittany said I couldn't use that name anymore. She said when parents died, kids had to change their names and she changed my name to Olivia Moore."

Parker searched for a way to not say what she was thinking. She couldn't find one, so she chose to remind the girl, "I promised you I would be honest with you."

Olivia nodded.

"I know for a fact children do not have to give up their names when a parent dies. They have a choice if their name is changed when they are adopted."

Parker looked at Alex when Olivia turned to fact check her. They nodded. Then said, "When my daughters were adopted, they had a choice if they changed their name and how. They maintained their birth names, only their middle or last names changed.

Parker tapped the table, pulling the girl's attention back to her. Slowly, she said, "You didn't go through a formal adoption process. You were never in foster care before you moved here. I don't think your Aunt Brittany told you the truth. I think she lied to you to get you to leave the park with her."

"Like she took me?" Olivia asked. Then she shook her head. "No," she said, then she looked at the picture. "She wouldn't take me."

But she looked up at Parker. In the furrowed brow, Parker could see all the questions forming but getting erased and then rewritten.

"Could my mom still be alive?" Olivia asked.

"I don't know. I can just promise if you tell me what your mom used to call you, I will find out."

Parker reached across the table, then waited for Olivia to make contact. She waited as she watched the girl try to sort through her memories, understanding the constant questions about what was true and what had been nothing but lies. Wondering if life could have been different.

Olivia didn't reach out to Parker. Instead, she leaned back in her chair. Her eyes were glued to the half-drawn child staring at the swing. Her arms wrapped around herself.

"Rachel. My name was Rachel Jacobson."

31

When Zoe arrived at the station, Evie and her uncle were in a heated debate outside the interrogation room. Evie's hand ran up and down her face. She turned her head to Zoe. Whatever the two had been talking about ended when Zoe joined them.

"Everyone was there last night?" Zoe asked.

"Yeah," Evie said. She pulled at the vest more vigorously than usual. "Why the fuck can't they make these for tits?"

Zoe shrugged, grateful she got to choose her attire each day. She shifted her weight. The six-inch heel tilted a little, and she regretted the instant Karma for thinking she was better off than Evie.

Trying to hide the misstep, Zoe asked, "Collins too?"

Evie rolled her eyes. "Isn't he part of everyone?"

Zoe watched as another yawn broke free from Evie. The dark circles under her eyes concerned Zoe.

"You okay? I heard you have been here all night."

"Nope."

Shaking her head, Zoe told her, "You should go home." Evie narrowed her already squinted eyes at Zoe as Zoe held up her hand. "But I know you won't, so just stay out here. Okay?"

"Yep."

Ryder smiled at Zoe as he explained, "I had some guys get the things you requested from your office." He pointed to the stack of white file boxes next to the door. She moved the top box to the floor, granting her access to the second. From within, she withdrew a dense file.

"What's that?" Evie asked.

"Secret weapon," Zoe said. She clutched it in her hand before turning back to Ryder. "Thank you for letting me talk to him first."

"No problem. You've met with him before, so you tell me how you want to play this."

"Caliscpo is the dumbest out of all of them. Last time I spoke with him, he was really shaky and nervous. Definitely not an alpha male persona. He saw Gibson as a hero type figure. Admired his tough guy attitude. He was probably beaten as a kid, and the others never brought him up, so he is the lowest on the totem pole."

"So, be a jerk," Ryder offered.

"Yes. He'll be scared. Probably a mama's boy, so you be mean, and I'll pretend to be nice." She waved the file at him. "We can't lie to him. Speak in half sentences, and when I give you a paper, read it all the way through."

"Okay, I'll follow your lead."

Turning to the door, Zoe placed her hand on the handle. She closed her eyes and put herself back in the apartment above Gibson's garage.

Looking around the fading memory, she walks across the room to the tattered couch cushions pushed into the corner of the space. She sees the stain from when Olivia had given birth, found when she demanded the Crime Scene Unit go back to the house. Squatting down, she stares at the words carved into the exposed beam. Her finger traces over the jagged lettering. "Olivia was here." The girl's message to the world she existed when no one was looking for her.

Zoe opened her eyes, straightened her shoulders, and inhaled all the fresh oxygen she could. Caliscpo stunk last time, and she assumed after holding him in the small poorly ventilated space for most of the night meant he would reek worse. Turning the handle, she walked into the room.

Justin Caliscpo leaned against his cuffed hands. His sweat-dampened flimsy hair lay over his acne scarred face. Blue eyes stared across the table at her approaching him.

Ryder closed the door behind them as Zoe pulled out her chair. She took in the pit-stained wife beater hanging loosely off the man's scrawny frame. He sat up straighter as she lowered herself into the chair and placed the file on the table. Her fingers traced over the cover, as she met the perspiring man's gaze.

"Justin, sorry it took me so long to get here. I know you're probably freaked out, but I asked them to let me talk to you. I didn't realize they had you in here this whole time. You remember me, right? I'm Zoe Robinson, the county prosecutor." She smiled nicer this time. "I know it's been over a year since we spoke last."

Caliscpo's eyes shifted from Zoe to Ryder, then back to Zoe. He licked his cracked lips before he said, "Yeah, I remember you."

Zoe watched the protruding Adam's apple bob under the patchy covered chin. She smiled at him, and asked warmly, "You want something to drink?"

He nodded and swallowed as though the water was already in front of him.

"Get this man some water," she instructed Ryder. "I can't believe you kept him here chained up like an animal. He's a person."

When Ryder sighed heavily, she hoped he wasn't taking offense to the role she was playing. Ryder knocked on the door until it was opened.

Zoe didn't bother to turn to see if Evie was the one there. She flipped open the file, silently looking over the various handwritten documents within. Each she'd memorized from the number of uses she'd gotten out of them. She paused as she remembered the last time she'd opened this file.

The girl didn't respond to anything Zoe asked. She didn't move, and the offer for water was ignored. She'd just sat there as Zoe read through them.

Reading the pages was as much a part of the facade as the pages of words. Only one page out of all of them had actual instructions for whatever cop she was working with needed.

From over her shoulder, Ryder pointed to the sheet in her hands. He leaned in close to Zoe, then he whispered, "I am making a really good point right now."

"Yes. I noticed it too," She answered loud enough for Caliscpo's eyes to dart up to her. Maintaining focus, she pointed farther down the page, and held it up for Ryder. "And here too."

She handed the first draft college essay on why the word 'nothing' meant something to Ryder. He flipped through the document until the door opened. Handing the pages back to Zoe, he retrieved the water.

"Hmph," Zoe let out. She handed the page of her notes with detailed information on how to play the waiting game to Ryder. She watched his eyes read through the notes.

He nodded when he got to step five. At step ten, he pointed to the x on the page. Then he said aloud, "This right here. It's all in here. I told you he was the one."

Zoe sucked in her bottom lip and nodded. She scanned through another page of notes in a different handwriting. She sighed as she remembered Lyra rewriting this one for her. She set it down quicker than she normally would, then pulled out another that was a letter she'd had an officer copy when she first started. The manly chicken scratch added some realism to the ruse.

She set it down, just out of Caliscpo's reading range. She waited for Ryder to finish the instructions. When he got to the last step, he picked up the other forged letter and scanned over it.

Tapping her finger to her lips, she read over a short story she'd written one drunken night. She squinted occasionally at the questionable words on the page, not sure if she had written copulate or communicate. She smiled at how the words changed the meaning of the text and handed the page to Ryder as well.

"Can I get that water?" Caliscpo asked.

Ryder looked at the hand still holding the water, then glared at the gangly man across from them. He uncapped the lid without breaking his stare down. Setting it in front of Caliscpo's cuffed hands, he waited as the instructions had told him to. It was the last instruction; a signal for Zoe he understood.

Caliscpo picked up the bottle but set it down. They all knew he wouldn't be able to drink from it with both hands secured to the bar on the table. Ryder let a smug smile spread across his face, but Zoe rolled her eyes. She dug into her briefcase and pulled out a disposable straw. She unwrapped it and fed it into the bottle.

Zoe offered Caliscpo a forced smile, then continued to go through every piece of paper in the file again. She waited for him to take a drink as she slowly scanned each document.

When Caliscpo smacked his lips after finishing a fourth of the bottle, Zoe shook her head. She got up and left the room.

The door smashed into the wall as she pushed through it with one of the white boxes. Vincent Gibson's name was printed in big block letters on the outside of the box she dropped on top of the table towards Caliscpo. She left again, this time huffing as she slapped another box on top of Gibson's. This one had 'Brandon Collins' written on the label. She repeated the action until she had five boxes with the five names they'd connected to Olivia. This would only be the first time she'd go through this practiced act.

She opened the last box with 'Justin Caliscpo' written on it. She thumbed through the files filled with blank copy paper, random magazine clippings, and photos she'd printed from stock images. She pulled out the file she was looking for and set it on the table.

Opening it, she revealed a photo from the outside of Caliscpo's apartment. Then a close up of the fourteen-year-old peeking out of the window.

"How do you know Brandon Collins?" she finally asked, still flipping through the pages of the file.

"We... we play poker together," he answered.

Zoe hummed, then asked. "Were you playing poker last night?"

"Uh... no."

Zoe stopped flipping through the pages. She met Caliscpo's eyes and smiled. Smiled like she had when he played her for a fool.

"Good, we're starting out with honesty." She turned the photo of the fourteen-year-old in the window to him. "Who's this?"

"Uhhh... My cousin."

Zoe narrowed her eyes at him, and then turned to Ryder. "I know you said he was a liar, but I thought he'd be smarter than that."

Ryder didn't look at her. He stared straight through Caliscpo as he towered over her shoulder like an angry father. "Well, he is the organizer. Did you really think he was going to tell you the truth?"

Setting the page in her hand down of Caliscpo's work schedule, she said, "I just don't buy it. I just don't think he has it in him to plan something as detailed as this. I mean look at him. He's just a kid compared to the others."

"You still think it's Collins even after reading this?" Ryder waved the short story at Zoe with an eyebrow slightly cocked at her.

Zoe shrugged. "I figured Collins was the liar."

"But he states right here that this asshole was—" Ryder's finger pointed to the bottom paragraph of the page.

"I didn't plan anything," the cuffed man cried out.

"Bullshit," Ryder stated. He slapped the short story on the table while it crumbled some in his hand. Zoe glared at him. Destroying her documents was not part of the instructions.

"Hold on," Zoe said, taking the pages from Ryder. "Let's give him a chance to tell his side. I mean, everyone else has already made their statement."

Zoe pointed to the photo of the terrified child. "You were already caught with all of these men at your house with the girl. Every single one of them will be going away for rape of a minor, supplying drugs to a minor, and then there's the murder of Vincent Gibson."

Caliscpo held his hands out. "I didn't murder anyone." His voice cracked when he announced, "That girl, Olivia, she killed him."

He tried to stand up, but his body bounced back in the chair when his wrists stopped him from going anywhere.

"Did she?" Zoe asked.

"Yeah," he said. He tried to flip his hair flopping against his dripping forehead. "She killed him."

"When we spoke last, you'd never heard of Olivia. Never seen her before."

Caliscpo looked at his hands, then back at Zoe. "She was on the news. I saw her there."

"She was cleared," Zoe stated.

"You... you think... me? That I killed Vincent?" he asked, the panic painting his voice in pained red terror. "I... I didn't. Why would you think I killed him?"

Ryder folded his arms across his chest. "He wasn't stupid. He knew one of you would screw up. Every time you climbed on top of that child, he—"

"Okay. Okay. I..." Caliscpo's head hung. "You know."

"We don't know." Ryder slammed his palm to the table. "We are good people. We don't know what sickos like you would do to a little girl."

"I mean, I wouldn't know," Zoe said. When Caliscpo looked at her, she pointed to her tits. "I don't know what a man would do to a woman."

Caliscpo's eyes fell back to his hands. His nail dug at the skin around his thumb already bleeding. "I had sex with her. I had sex with her at Vincent's house."

"You have sex with this girl too?" Zoe tapped the photo of the girl in his home.

He shook his head. "No. No, I didn't. It was against the rules."

Ryder choked out a laugh. "You hear that? They had rules."

"What were the rules?" Zoe asked.

"Rules to play. If you broke the rules, you couldn't play anymore," Caliscpo explained. Then he added, "But once you were in, you played by the rules or you'd get taught a lesson for cheating."

Zoe hated how the words were clearly scripted for the man. To anyone else it would sound like he was talking about an actual poker game, but the knowledge it was not a card game caused bile to rise in Zoe's throat.

She swallowed her disgust and asked, "Who made the rules?"

"I don't know," he claimed, but blood rushed up Caliscpo's face.

"He's a liar." Ryder's finger thrust over the table at the suspect. "We know you made the rules."

Zoe leaned back in her chair. She tapped a pencil against a legal pad. "Let me explain what is going to happen now, Justin. Everyone else is going to State for rape, drugs, and kidnapping, while you will be going to federal prison for organizing a sex trafficking ring of minors."

Caliscpo stared at the cuffs.

Zoe continued, "You see that is thirteen years in Arizona."

"Except it's aggravated," Ryder threw in.

Zoe stopped tapping. Holding up the pen, she said, "Oh that's right. Olivia was a homeless minor. Which means life."

"Don't forget the murder charge." Ryder chortled. "Basically, you'll never see a girl again."

"It was all Brandon and Christian," Caliscpo whispered.

"See liar," Ryder said.

"No. No." Caliscpo waved his hands in the minimal space they would go. "Brandon would find the girls on the street. They were all hookers. He promised to give them a place to stay if they would have sex with us."

"You're saying Brandon Collins brought this girl to your house, and you just let her stay there so the other guys could have sex with her? Even though you knew she was a child?" Zoe asked. She pushed the photo of the girl towards him. "But you didn't have sex with her."

He shook his head. "No. No. I didn't. You didn't have sex with the girl you fed. It was against the rules."

"But you had sex with Olivia."

"I... I don't—"

"You're stuttering now. You fucking loser," Ryder growled. "Just be a man. You screwed that girl when you had the chance."

Caliscpo didn't say anything.

"How many girls are there?" Zoe asked.

"Three."

"Not four?" Zoe looked at him. The math didn't add up.

He shook his head. "No, Jim didn't have a girl. He'd gotten himself a girlfriend. And the whole thing that happened to Vincent scared the shit out of him."

"What happened to the girl he'd had?"

"He dropped her off at Jefferson. All the hookers are there outside the tents."

"Was that the plan? Was it a rule?" Ryder pushed.

"Yeah, man." Caliscpo looked at Zoe. "If someone started sniffing around, you took the girl to the tents and left her there."

"So, Brandon Collins organized everything." When Caliscpo didn't respond, Zoe's choice to start with him was validated. "Collins didn't organize, he just found the girls."

Zoe flipped through the file. She settled on Caliscpo's employment records.

"You worked with Collins. That's how you got in. What happened?" She glanced up. "Did you catch him taking a girl home?"

Caliscpo's eyes searched the room. He stared at his own reflection looking back at him.

"You caught him, and he offered to help you get your own."

"I didn't know until it was too late," he whispered. "I saw him with this girl that would always come to the shelter. They were together, but he had a fiancée and I told him I was going to tell his girl. I was joking but he said he'd hook me up. I could get my own girl. Said it was the best because she would cook and clean and all I had to do was let her sleep there and give her food."

Zoe set down her pen. She leaned against the table, so her body matched his, minus the cuffs.

"He let me pick out a girl. She wasn't a child. I didn't... I didn't like it when they were young."

Ryder growled, "You're such a pussy. I know you hurt this girl." His finger drilled the photo into the table.

"It was against the rules."

"Then what happened?" Zoe asked.

Caliscpo tried to shake the hair from his face again. Zoe reached across the table and pushed it back for him. She steeled her face to not let on her instant desire to saw her own fingers off.

"He brought her to my house. I showed her around and she did the things he said she would do. She was there for a few weeks and things were going well. Then one night he brought the others because we were going to start a poker night. I thought cool, his friends would see my girl and think I was awesome."

"And you all raped her that night," Ryder stated unamused.

"I didn't know what was going to happen." Caliscpo looked between Ryder's annoyance to Zoe. His gaze settled on Zoe. "We were drunk, and Christian gave her a beer. I told him not to because I wanted her to clean up, but he told me to shut up. Vincent told me to stop being a little bitch."

"Then what happened?"

"She got real out of it. Christian took her into my room. When he was done, the others went in. That's when Christian told me the rules." Caliscpo's shoulders rose and fell as he panted. "I said I didn't want to be a part of it. I didn't want to do any of this. But he said I was already in. That if I snitched, they would all say it was my idea."

"When was this?"

"Like ten years ago. I was... I had... Collins' hired me when I turned eighteen. It was my first apartment that I got because I had a job. He... he got me off the street."

Ryder moved across the table and pulled Caliscpo up by his shirt. The material screamed as it tore. The cuffs dug into Caliscpo's wrists, threatening to sever his hands as Ryder held him up.

Spittle flew from Ryder's mouth with each word, "You've been raping girls with your pervert friends for ten years?"

"I didn't want to do it," Caliscpo cried out. His face turned in submission to Ryder. "Christian videoed it all. He said if anyone snitched, everyone was going down, and he videoed it all."

Ryder dropped the man half his size back into the metal chair. The legs scratched against the floor.

"What happened after the first night?" Zoe asked.

"Brandon picked me up. He took me to Christian's place. He had two and he said if I didn't... he would kill me."

Ryder leaned against the table. His face stopped a few inches from the stuttering pervert. "Did that get you excited?"

Tears broke through the clenched eyes. "No. No. I didn't want to, but I couldn't go to the cops. I couldn't get out after because Christian filmed me with the girls."

Zoe nodded to Ryder to back up against the wall. Then she asked, "When did you first see Olivia?"

Through clenched teeth, Caliscpo said, "Vincent got her from Collins. Collins had taken her off a hooker's hands. She was the first young one."

"When?"

"I don't know." Ryder took a step forward. "Okay. Okay. Three or four years ago. Vincent treated her like a pet."

Zoe's nose wrinkled; the room suddenly reeked of piss. She looked at Ryder, then back to the man moving in his seat.

"Who knew Vincent was breaking the rules?" Zoe asked, trying not to gag on the smell.

"I don't know. I didn't know." Ryder moved forward. His hands rested alongside Caliscpo. "They said the rules kept us out of jail."

"Did you know she was pregnant?" Zoe asked.

The blood drained from Caliscpo's face as he rose his head. "No. No. I didn't know. They never got pregnant. I didn't know. They just got new girls when they were tired of one or they said she got too loose because they.... They liked to do it at the same time sometimes."

Ryder's hand turned into a fist against the table. He leaned closer. "Vincent's pet suddenly grows a giant stomach, and you didn't know she was pregnant." He pushed up when the man braced himself to get hit. "I told you. He's a liar."

"I didn't like them young." Caliscpo shook his head again. "I only did her once because Christian wanted to watch. He said he had to make sure I was still all in."

Tapping her pen to the apartment photo, she asked, "What happened to the girl? The first one Brandon brought to you?"

"She ran away after they.... She was crying and crying and Vincent had done the back and she was bleeding and crying, and I just left the door open and went to get a beer."

"So, you let her go," Zoe said.

"I just didn't lock the door." He closed his eyes and hit his hands against the table. "I thought... I thought they would kick me out because she got away."

"Did that happen often?"

Caliscpo shook his head quickly. "No. Christian and Vincent... they came to check and she was gone and Christian beat the shit out of me. Said he'd make sure I wouldn't bitch out."

"How did he do that?"

Caliscpo shook his head. "I don't want to—"

Ryder leaned down right next to Caliscpo's ear. "They raped you too, huh? Raped you, and you spent the next nine years making sure all those girls went through that terror too. You fucking piece of shit."

Zoe watched tears start to fall from the man's clenched eyes. She wondered if it was wrong she didn't have any sympathy for him.

"What happened after that?"

He wiped his face on his arm, then rested his forehead against the table.

"After that they only brought the ones that were too young. Sometimes when they were tired of one Brandon would take her, then he would bring a new one. They liked them young because they didn't fight back after the first time, and they didn't run away like the older ones did."

Zoe tilted her head. She'd gotten the confession, but she was trying to do the math in her head. She knew she didn't want to know the answer, but at the same point she had to know. She had to know for Lyra's family who were watching.

She asked, "Did you have a poker night at Brandon's apartment? You know with the girl you saw him with?"

Ryder looked at Zoe.

She swallowed the knowledge she'd been right about the timeline. Her gut twisted until the bile in her digestive tract burst into her blood. She hummed silently trying to keep her afternoon coffee down.

Slowly, Caliscpo shook his head.

"No, in the beginning it was just Christian, Vincent, and me. Brandon said his girl wouldn't work because he was already fucking her. Which was a good thing because he got arrested for her because she was a teenager. Christian canceled poker nights for a while until everything with Brandon got sorted out."

"Did that happen when Vincent was killed also?" Zoe asked.

"Yeah, for a couple months. Christian came and got all the girls and took them to Jefferson."

Zoe took the straw from the water bottle and handed it to Ryder who had pulled an evidence bag from his pocket. She dropped it in. She then slid a paper and pencil across the table to Caliscpo.

"Write it down. All of it. Names, dates, and any name of the girls you remember. Leave out anything, anything at all, and you'll regret it."

32

Settling in Olivia at Echo and Simone's had taken longer than Parker anticipated. She was grateful Alex had joined them and was able to talk Simone into allowing Olivia to put a lock on her bedroom door. The disagreement took longer than the installation. Simone gave when Alex said if their friend wasn't willing to help Olivia feel safe, they would take her back to the school.

A simple push button bathroom knob was removed from the actual bathroom as Simone and Alex stared each other down. There was a power Alex seemed to hold over Simone. A type of mental tap Parker wished they would share with Echo to even the scales. After unpacking and some forced conversation, Parker put her cellphone number into Olivia's new device and told her to call anytime.

She held in all of her emotions, but the car door closing was connected to the lever that would open the gates to her internal dam. As she drove behind Alex's shiny Audi, Parker's fists clenched the steering wheel. Her shrill scream broke free and threatened to shatter the windows in her car. She prepared her resignation speech for Dilynn.

She slammed the palm of her hand against the steering wheel with each word she screamed. "Every fucking thing she said was a hint at the truth and you were too fucking distracted to figure it out. You fucking failed her."

Alex blazed through a yellow light, separating their vehicles when Parker stopped as it turned red. She choked on the humid air in her car while the rain pelted the windshield. When the light turned green, she slammed her foot on the gas. The engine roared for her as she gasped for air.

Every time she started to count her way down, a part of her would hit something again and she'd forget what number she was on because Olivia was a missing kid. Just like those women her parents had killed went missing. She failed Olivia just like she'd failed before.

By the time she reached the house, the clouds ran out of rain drops and Parker ran out of energy to scream or hit anything else. Alex leaned against the porch railing running across the front. Parker followed their gaze to across the street where Levi and another toddler rolled around in the wet grass. She had to do a double take at the children who looked like twins, while a lanky teenager blew bubbles over their laughing bodies.

She counted backwards from twenty, appreciating the simplicity of childhood joy. At ten, she was able to pull down the mask of calm to hide the chaos bubbling within her. And at five, she checked her make-up in the mirror.

Alex didn't say anything while Parker climbed the stairs. They simply called across the street, "Allie, take them inside, please?"

"No problem," the girl called out.

They waited on the porch as the toddlers followed the girl into the smaller house across the way.

"Allie's my niece. My brother and his wife live there," Alex explained, gesturing to the smaller house across from them. "It's Evie's house though. Dilynn bought each of the girls a house when they turned eighteen. That was the first Greyson house though, so Evie requested that one be hers for when she and Landon started a family."

When the light within turned on, towers of boxes in the living room could be seen through the window. Cautiously, Parker asked, "Are they moving back now?"

"My brother and sister-in-law are moving into a place of their own." Alex pointed to the house with a different build, but similar size. "Dilynn owns more than half of the houses on the block already. That is the first one that has come up for sale she didn't out bid, and it was only because it's for family."

Parker forced a smile on her face, wondering what Lyra was planning to do. She would have to live alone, which she'd said she couldn't do with the pain. This must have been why Dilynn warned her about Lyra wanting to settle down. Something Parker had never even considered.

"Must be nice to have your family so close," she offered not sure what else there was to say.

"Took a long time to get here, but yes, it is."

There were eight houses on the private street. A street Parker just noticed was literally named Greyson Drive. She was about to roll her eyes when she processed what Alex had said about the Greyson kids all having their own houses.

"Which one is Lyra's?"

Alex pointed to a house with a garage built for an RV in the back. It was situated on the corner, and farthest away from Dilynn and Alex's place.

"Who lives there now?" Parker asked, cautiously.

"No one." Alex glanced down at Parker. "You and Lyra have only been together for a month."

"It could be a year, and it's still not gonna happen," Parker assured them. "This has way too much potential for people to be all up in my business. I'm an apartment or a condo type girl."

Alex held open the door for Parker, then led her past the office with floor to ceiling bookcases and a children's indoor gym to the Great Room. She sat in the same seat Dilynn had forced her into the last time she'd been there. Alex sat on the bench alongside Parker.

Neither said anything. The clock Parker had yet to find chimed out the hour as the rest of the house quietly went about its usual business.

After checking their watch for the umpteenth time, Alex confessed, "I don't do most of the talking."

Parker's finger traced a small scratch in the farmhouse table. "Me either."

"Work is different," they offered. "With the kids, I mean."

Parker nodded, glancing up only to find Alex also studying the table like all the answers in the world were written in invisible ink across the surface. Quietly she affirmed, "Yeah. Kids. And customers."

"I think it's the power of the space," Alex added. They tapped their fingers together and looked up towards the door.

"Makes sense," Parker said.

Getting up, Alex made their way into the kitchen towards a refrigerator that looked twice the size of a normal side-by-side. Parker envied the power of this space as theirs and their ability to leave the confines of the assigned seat.

"Are you hungry?" they asked.

They picked up tubs and containers within the refrigerator. Each was examined, and Parker swore she saw a container of Dilynn's soup from a month ago.

"That's not left-over chicken soup is it?" she asked.

Alex snorted, shook their head, and popped the lid. They held it up.

"No. But it looks equally bad." Their nose crinkled, and the whole container was gingerly placed within the trash bin. "I bought my wife a subscription to Hello Fresh, Dinnerly, and Blue Apron. She still insists on trying to concoct these terrible experiments. The only thing she really can cook is pizza. She makes the best homemade pizza every Wednesday night."

"Lyra mentioned that. I tend to work Wednesdays though, so I haven't been able to come."

"How about Pizza Rolls?" they asked, closing the refrigerator.

"I like Pizza Rolls."

Alex opened the freezer. They pulled out three giant bags. "We have basically every kind. Would you like combination, cheese, or pepperoni?"

Parker shrugged, then said, "They all taste the same to me."

"True." Alex looked at the bags, selected the one least full, and tossed the others back into the freezer.

They dumped the contents of the bag into an air fryer. After several beeps, it whirred to life, calling other appliances awake. A Roomba left its resting place, making its way from the Great Room towards the front of the house as ice clanked into a tray in the freezer.

"So, you and Lyra?" Alex asked, leaning against the counter of the island.

Parker waited for the rest of the question that didn't come. "Yes?" she finally asked.

"She's a good kid," they said.

Parker smiled at the awkward simplicity in their conversation skills. Trying to help the situation, Parker said, "She says she's your favorite."

Alex's head dropped but raised with a guilty smile. "As a parent I don't have favorites. However, she was my first kid."

Their emerald eyes studied Parker, then asked, "Do you want kids?"

Licking her lips, she touched the scratch again. "I used to think absolutely not."

"Me too," they said.

The whirring ended with a loud beep. Alex pulled the drawer out and dumped the contents onto two paper plates. Bringing the food back to the table, they picked one of the rolls up and bit the daintiest corner off.

"What changed your mind?" Parker asked. Then she blew over the plate, hoping to cool the hell pockets faster as her stomach gurgled.

"Lyra."

They bit another tiny portion off but hissed when the inside of the demon roll spit out its angry insides.

Parker tried to hide her chuckle.

Alex set the roll back on their plate and stared at it. Carefully, they repeated the process of biting just the corner with a new one. As they chewed the piece that really wasn't anything to chew, they said, "My parents sent me to a conversion camp when I was outted. When I came back, I ran away."

Parker tore a roll in half and blew on the inside. Before she popped the blistering torture device into her mouth, she asked, "Is it hard constantly explaining your identity to people?"

Alex huffed around the roll they'd put into their mouth. They chewed quickly and swallowed the thing practically whole. Without answering, they got up, retrieving two bottles of water. They handed one to Parker as they swallowed half of the contents of the other.

"Not talking helped because people thought what they thought."

"You seem more comfortable now," Parker said, then took a drink of the water.

Alex shrugged. "Dilynn does a lot of the battle fighting for me. She usually introduces me and my pronouns before I even get to the conversation."

"She seems to like to fight everyone's battles for them," Parker mused. "Does she fight her own?"

With raised eyebrows, they nodded as they said, "Yes, she does." They started to put another bite into their mouth but stopped. "Sometimes it will take her a while. She'll write out scenes of herself looking back on a topic, then it tends to manifest itself into our everyday lives. It was how we ended up with the school."

Parker felt a real smile spread across her face. "I feel like there is a story there."

Alex squeezed the roll, then set it back down. "Well, there is the story in the book she published about getting passed over for a promotion and Simone got the job, so her character overthrew the business and put Simone out of business. Then there's the time she decided to build a school with her ex, and she wrote a book about a private school for magic with owners who hated each other. Her partner Sylvia and her don't hate each other. They just have very different ideas of what Greyson Academy should look like."

"Interesting problem-solving skills." Parker popped another bite into her mouth. Once she swallowed, she added, "She says you have other projects than the school, which is why it's just named after her."

They sat up and smiled. "Yeah."

"Care to share?"

Alex pushed the plate away from them. Gesturing to themself, they said, "I run a program that goes to events for LGBTQA youth. Parent events, graduations, weddings, the things kids lose when they come out sometimes."

Parker's eyes widened. "Wow. How do you do it?"

Alex's smile broadened revealing their perfect teeth. "When I'm not working, I go to high schools to network with social workers. They feed me kids who are struggling, and we set them up with mentors. When an event is coming up, the mentors let me know if they need a support family, how many are allowed to attend an event, and any preferences the kid may have. Then I set the kid up with a family. We do a lot of graduations." They reached over and tapped the pizza rolls on their plate. "Sometimes Dilynn and I go. Sometimes it's Landon and Evie. My brother and his wife have gone. We have other volunteers also. We also fundraise for the kids to get the stuff they need to be comfortable in their own skin, like prom dresses and suits, graduation gowns, haircuts, binders, really anything. And we run a 24-hour support line."

"Can I volunteer?" Parker asked.

Their head tilted, and the proud smile turned to a smirk. "With all your extra time?"

Parker shrugged. "I only work at the bar a few nights a week."

Alex popped a roll into their mouth and chewed like a normal human. They finished two more before they asked, "Why are you working at the bar? Do we not pay you enough to just work one job?"

Parker choked on the pizza roll she was about to swallow and had to take a drink of water. It took her several moments to regain her composure.

"My salary is amazing," she said. She looked at her mostly empty plate wishing this was Neverland and it would magically refill itself if she just believed hard enough. "I want to buy a new car. I mean, Lyra comes from this," she gestured to the room, "and the first night she was at my house my couch ate her butt."

Parker dropped her chin to her chest. She looked up to find them watching her carefully. She shrugged again, before she said, "You've seen my apartment. I just want to show her I can have nice things, like a car to ride in she doesn't have to be ashamed to be seen in. We went shopping a few weeks ago. I found a sports car I like, but I wanted to wait until I had more for the down payment. Plus, I needed check stubs and I had only gotten paid once at that time. I decided to give it another couple weeks, then I'll go back."

"You know me and Lyra both come from the streets. You don't have to impress her by having nice things."

"I get that," Parker said with a nod. "But Lyra and you also now live like this. And when you live like this but date someone like me it puts an imbalance in the relationship. I don't want Lyra to think she has to slum it or treat me like a sugar baby to be around me. I'm not Julia Roberts, and I'm not looking to be pretty womaned."

"I like to think I taught Lyra better than that," they said. Then they shook their head. "Now my other two girls. Those two would, as you say, 'pretty woman' someone because they enjoy the power play."

Parker finished the last of the rolls on her plate. Her stomach then audibly growled, sending a flood of warmth to her cheeks.

Without a word, Alex popped the first roll they had bitten into their mouth and shoved the plate across to her. Parker was about to argue but changed her mind when her stomach protested the idea.

She swallowed another bite, then looked at them. They were checking the watch on their wrist again.

"Can I ask you a question that is just between us?" Parker asked.

Alex set their hands down. They scanned Parker's face before they said, "As long as you are not going to tell me you are going to hurt yourself or someone else, or someone is hurting you."

Parker waved her hands in the air, then quickly stopped. She admonished herself for letting Dilynn influence her so much. "None of that," she said, trying to fix herself.

Alex drew an imaginary square on the table. "Then this table is a vault of secrets. You may cast your question and it will fuse to the grains of the wood forever, locked in place."

With a quirked eyebrow, Parker asked, "You sure you're not the writer?"

They tilted their head. "Is that your question?"

"No, sorry." Parker wiped her mouth on the back of her hand. With a deep breath, she asked, "Okay, so I'm sorry that this is out of line but is Lyra always like a super jealous person?"

"Jealous, no." They held up a finger. "Insecure, yes."

Parker finished off the rest of the pizza rolls. She placed the plate on top of her empty one.

"Would you like to tell me what happened?"

A part of her wanted to drop it. If she didn't, she may end up explaining to Alex jealous and insecure are the same thing. She also didn't want to say something Alex would get defensive about. Getting relationship advice from Lyra's parent didn't seem like the best idea also. Alex had asked her though, and to not finish the conversation now felt weird.

"She found out I was in a relationship with Zoe in college and got really upset. We had our first fight a few weeks ago. I told her I was never going to let her dictate who I was allowed to talk to." She took a deep breath. "We were okay, but then she came into the bar last weekend when I was working and got pissed that another woman I dated was flirting with me. I tried to explain Xio is just a Hey Mama's lesbian, and she doesn't know how to speak without flirting, but Lyra was all growly, and now she comes to the bar every night I'm working. And I... and I just need like a heads up if she's going to turn into a green gelatinous cube every time, she finds out I dated someone before I met her."

Alex strummed the table with their fingers. "Have you ever heard the song, 'Too Good at Goodbyes'?"

"Yes."

With a sigh, Alex said, "So that song basically sums up our family's reactions to things. Well except Dilynn, but she didn't come from the world the girls and I have."

"So, Lyra is always going to try to push me away."

Alex scrunched up their lips. "I'm sorry to say, probably yes."

Parker stared at them. "And I'm just supposed to stay?"

"I can't answer that for you."

"That seems pretty shitty," Parker said to the ceiling. Her hand came up to cover her mouth. "Sorry."

With a shake of the head, they admitted, "I shouldn't tell you this, but I am going to."

Alex smiled, but the smile faded. They put the cap back on their mostly empty water bottle before trying to flip it in the air. They failed multiple times before they set it down. Their eyes met Parker's complete confusion.

"The night I was supposed to marry Dilynn, I got in my car and tried to drive away. The girls were crying, and Dilynn was standing there holding them as they watched me back out of the driveway. It wasn't the first time I'd walked out. I had walked away from Dilynn at least a half a dozen times. I think the only reason she was able to deal with me was because Evie had taught her those who push away others needed someone the most."

"So, she chased after you?'

Alex shook their head again. Their chestnut curls bounced around their shoulders. "Actually, that was something Dilynn never did. Well... she did once, but it was only to tell me I was quote unquote a fucking coward."

Parker leaned back in her chair. She could see Dilynn's red face stomping up to Alex and yelling at them.

"Dilynn didn't come after me. She just never shut the door in my face. That was the trauma you see. My trauma. I had to push and push to see if the door would still be open. The only way to test it was to walk out of it. But when I came back, Dilynn was always there."

"I remember you saying something about Dilynn not giving people a chance to change their mind," Parker added.

"My fault," they admitted. They flipped the bottle again as they worried their bottom lip. "I pushed until I knew if I pushed again she wouldn't open the door. She'd reached a point we both realized what I was doing was hurting the girls. I had to make a decision to be there with them or leave once and for all. Sadly, it wasn't even the last time I ran away. Since Levi was born, I haven't.... It's still hard though. Like an instinct in me says run and I don't fight it."

"So, Lyra's going to keep pushing me to see if I will leave her for someone else." Parker folded her arms over her chest, giving herself a hug.

"I don't think it's someone else, but Zoe Robinson in particular," Alex said. "Well, or the girl at the bar you dated. Is it the masc with the strap?"

"Xio. Yeah. So, you're saying basically anyone I dated." Parker bit her lip. "Like Lyra dated Dilynn's ex."

"That would be one of Lyra's traumas. The other part of it would be Lyra sees them and she thinks about what they can do she can't." They rubbed their hands over their face. "I hate thinking about things like this, but Lyra did speak to me about her fears about not being able to do things other soft masc and mascs can do. She is worried about being able to... satisfy you. And she's worried with her next surgery you'll have needs she won't be able to meet."

Lights in other rooms of the house flipped on automatically, drawing Parker's eyes to the hallway leading to the front of the house. She bit back her desire to tell Alex to communicate with Lyra she didn't need to be worried about Xio's dick. That she was the one who would be wearing it, and not the other way around.

"We all have them, "Alex explained. "Those termites in our head. Those fears that no matter how safe we are still burrow through the walls of our castles. Evie has them. I have them. We just found ways to deal with them."

"Like?"

"Like I told Olivia earlier, Evie and I spar at a boxing gym. She used to throw punches and words at people who threatened her position in her bio mom and Dilynn's life. Essentially, we box it out in a safe space. She gets to deal with her trauma, and I get to knock her on her ass."

"So, I just have to prove to Lyra I won't go back to Zoe," Parker stated.

"I guess." Their shoulders fell into a more comfortable hunch over the table.

They pressed their fingers together, cracking several of their knuckles at once. "I'm not the expert. I try to stay out of my daughters' relationships. That's a Dilynn area. She is a meddling mother."

The steady quiet fell around them again. Parker thought about the way Lyra had spun them away from Zoe's watching eyes when they danced at the bar. Made sure to keep her body between them at all points in time. How she'd posted in her station shooting daggers at Xio every time the woman even came close to Parker's section.

"May I ask you a question now?" Alex asked.

"Sure."

"What's your trauma?" They watched her carefully, so Parker made a conscious effort not to react. "What's the thing that will make you try to end things?"

"Honestly?" Parker asked.

Alex nodded.

"You and Dilynn."

Their head tilted as they looked at her. They covered their mouth with their fingers, gripping their lips shut. Slowly, they released their lips. "Care to explain."

Parker looked around the room, before she settled her gaze back on Alex. She took a deep breath, and confessed, "Okay, this is going to sound terrible, so please hear me out."

"Go ahead. I am not judging you at all." The look in Alex's eyes told Parker they were telling the truth, but she knew better than to trust in anything or anyone.

Parker's index fingers redrew the box against the wood. Then she spoke to the table.

"When I was with Zoe, the relationship didn't scare me because Zoe's family was out there somewhere else. At the bar, that night for Mrs. Robinson's birthday, it was the first time I'd ever met her. So, it was just me and Zoe. I was scared of Zoe realizing I was beneath her, but that was it."

She looked up. "With Lyra, you guys—" Parker stopped. "I'm sorry. Is guys an offensive term?"

Their eyes softened with the smile sincerely rising up their face as they said, "No, I know what you mean, and I don't view the context of your usage as derogatory at all. Thank you for checking, though. I don't think you realize how much it means to someone like me."

"Okay. Whew." Parker wiped the back of her hand across her forehead.

"So, with Lyra..." they prompted.

Parker fiddled with the necklace hanging between her breasts. She looked at the mother and child holding each other, wondering what it would feel like to have a mother hug her.

"I was a foster kid, and you guys are the typical foster parents. I mean the good ones. You scooped me up and brought me home. You fed me, clothed me, and gave me a job. But families scared the shit out of me so I'm not like pushing Lyra away, but I am definitely holding her at an arm's distance. It's why I work every Wednesday. It gets me out of having to come do the family stuff with you all. Like having parents that give a damn about me literally scares the shit out of me."

Alex licked their lips. Parker could see them examining the flavor of every question or statement making it to their tongue.

"Were your parents cold and distant?" they asked.

Parker looked at the pendant again. She'd never gone beyond telling anyone her parents were serial killers. That they listened and they hugged her. Never told someone they were great parents. Not even when the FBI came asking questions about their life before she'd called the cops. Didn't want to dwell in a time when things had been good, because the blood in their bathroom had ruined all of that.

"They were nice. Came to all the events. Took me to dance class. Helped me with my homework. The type of family you'd see on TV. Not Roseanne, think more Family Matters." She gazed across the table. "We were happy, I think." Parker's shoulders fell. "But... then... I mean, how happy could they be? I don't even know if my dad was capable of actual happiness. I don't know if my mom was just a DV victim putting on a strong face for me so I wouldn't know we should have been scared of him. So, it all just feels like a lie, when it was already, like, too good to be true."

Alex's eyebrows scrunched in the middle. It took Parker a minute to realize Alex didn't know.

"My dad is a serial killer. My mom participated but they said she was scared of him. That she thought he would kill her, but now I know... she wasn't his type. He only killed redheads." She tugged at a lock of her hair. "I always wondered if I would have been on his list if I made it to my twenties when he was still out."

They worked really hard to school their surprise. Didn't even break eye contact, but Parker could see them trying to process it all. Alex's chin slowly rose, then they nodded.

"I figured when we were talking about Dilynn googling me in the interview, she'd told you."

Alex slowly shook their head. A hand came up to rub their undercut once more. "She was just really excited about you punching Nia. Like over the moon about it."

She couldn't force back the smile. "Done a lot of dumb things in my life. That was my favorite though."

"Have you ever gone to see your parents?" Alex asked.

"Like in prison?" Parker asked. When Alex nodded, she answered, "No."

"Would you like to? I could go with you. You wouldn't have to do it alone."

"Some days, yes. At least to see my mom. I think about asking her all the questions that have popped in my head over the years," she confessed, clutching the pendant until it hurt almost as bad as learning the truth. "Most days, no."

Alex looked out the back window to the now dark sky. The rain had returned with the wind sending the palm trees surrounding the pool into a frenzy.

"I still can't believe I live here, and Dilynn is my wife. I wake up some days to Levi trying to crawl into bed with us, and I am in awe I am the parent to this little human who looks just like me." They paused momentarily. "Never in my life before Dilynn did I think any of it was possible."

Turning back to Parker, Alex asked, "I understand what it's like to be scared. And you have more reason than anyone else to fear parents. Is it possible to make Dilynn and me less scary?"

Parker looked up with only her eyes. Shaking her head, she sighed. "This is going to sound so stupid, but you're not a serial killer, right?"

They tapped against the table until she looked up at them once more. "No."

Parker tried to smile but it got stuck halfway. She asked, "Dilynn neither?"

They laughed as they said, "Dilynn can't kill spiders."

Parker didn't say killing a spider was different from a need to kill a person. She'd learned that much from watching the many documentaries on serial murders and reading books on Bundy, Dahmer, and Gunness. There was no way to have the profession she had without studying sociopaths and psychopaths. She trusted only one truth in her life: even good people could be monsters in masks.

"What else could I personally do to make you feel more comfortable? After all, you take great care in making sure to make me comfortable in your presence."

Parker swallowed. "Can you avoid, like, parenting me?"

Alex's eyes widened as the smile spread back across their face. "That I can do," they said with a nod. Their hands gestured between the two of them. "I am practically certain I am maximum ten years older than you. Plus, parenting does not come natural to me."

Their hands dropped with their face. "My wife, though... she cannot help it. She is a parent to everyone." They raised a finger in the air, "However, I also feel like she isn't really parenting people as much as just being there for them. She thrives off being there for people, but she latched on to being a mom to Evie and Lyra in a way that does not acknowledge the age difference.

"You see the difference though is we met our girls and even Landon when they were still children. You are not a child, but you are dating one of our children, sooo... even though you are an adult, you are put into that category as a child."

They sighed, waving their hands in the air. "I'm not good at this. Let me give you an example though. When we went out and met Mrs. Robinson, we had more life experiences in common with her than with Zoe because we have raised children into adulthood. We are in the comfortable stage of our life that middle age career life holds. While, you and Lyra, and Evie and Landon are making your way into the career world, trying to establish yourselves as adults, and reaching for the comfort level that seems to settle in your thirties."

Parker studied them. "I feel like this started out as me being a therapist and ended with me getting therapy."

Alex shrugged. "Maybe consider it more of an older queer sharing some insight to a baby gay."

Parker leaned back in her chair, folding her arms across herself in defiance this time. She scowled at her boss. "I am not a baby gay. I have been gay for many, many years."

They chuckled, dismissing Parker's protest. "Talk to me about not being a baby gay when you're married and your wife is blah blah blah don't put your workout clothes on the floor, we have a laundry room for a reason."

As Alex laughed, Parker considered the advice and the life experiences Alex shared. She walked through the possibility of Lyra having a temper tantrum every time their paths crossed Zoe or Xio, which Parker knew in the lesbian world would happen more often than anyone would like.

Leaning forward, she redrew the box once more. Alex stopped laughing and ran their hand over their face, replacing the goofy smile with a stoic mask.

"I have another question. You don't have to answer me if you don't want to, but I just wonder if you have an answer."

"Okay," they said.

"You said you left Dilynn multiple times. So, why did she keep taking you back?"

Alex's lips parted, but they didn't answer. They just stared at her. Parker knew she'd crossed a line, so her brain began catapulting ideas to her mouth. Parker choked as she tried to sort through the nonsense to create a coherent save.

"I'm sorry," she said. But she didn't give anything a chance to settle. "I was thinking about the whole Lyra and me thing, and I don't know how much jealousy I can take. I'm not someone that thrives off someone else wanting them so much I find the jealousy cute or endearing. It will be something I literally have to put up with until I can't anymore."

The explanation fell out of her mouth like she was falling from a tree, hitting every branch on the way.

"When I think about you and Dilynn. I just thought... what was going on with Dilynn? Like she was stable, her career and life were going great. And you just walked in and out of her life. Why would someone that has their shit together keep taking you back? Because if it was me, I couldn't do it. When people walk out, I'm like peace, mother fucker."

Alex looked down at the box, then back up at Parker. They reached back and ran their hand over the shaved portion of their undercut.

"I..." they started, then stopped. "You know, I was always so relieved she let me come back I honestly never thought about it. But come to think of it, it wasn't just me. There was this one night Lyra was trying to leave, and Dilynn packed her a bunch of stuff and let her take it with her."

Parker studied Alex for their reaction as she asked, "Would you say maybe her letting people leave her and come back could be her own trauma response, which then manifested into not letting people change their minds? Like, what if you didn't stop running away, but Dilynn stopped giving you the opportunity to run away? She, like, learned to read the signs you were about to run and diverted your attention."

Alex's teeth pressed against their bottom lip. They looked over Parker's shoulder. "I like to think my wife trusts people more than we trust ourselves."

Parker sucked her teeth, then took a drink of water. She checked the clock on the microwave and realized she'd been there for over an hour waiting for Dilynn to come home, so they all could talk about what to do with Olivia's real name.

She turned back to Alex. They were studying her now.

Parker replayed their last comment, then decided since they were both being honest, she'd just say it and let it be out there. "I find the concept of trust interesting. Especially the fact as a society we try to instill in people to put a blind faith in others through the concept of trust, but really it is just a weaponized version of hope that violates us when someone doesn't live up to the expectations we have for them."

Alex raised an eyebrow at her. "Are you saying trust doesn't really exist?"

Parker leaned forward and pointed to the center of the imaginary box. "Well, I think about this conversation, and I think about how the only thing that really has been established is we can only trust the negative attributes of a person." She paused, then tapped the box again, pinning her words to the table. "I can only trust Lyra will continue to try to push me away until she succeeds. Dilynn will continue to believe people will walk away given the chance, so she stops giving them a chance because she can only trust people will abandon her."

"I want Levi to grow up in a world where she trusts me to always be there for her," Alex countered.

Parker tilted her head to the side. She licked her lips, wondering if she should just shut up. She couldn't though. She had to make sure she was understood.

"You don't have control of that. You don't know what will happen, and you yourself have said you run away because you want to know if you can come back. Have you ever really dealt with the trauma that caused you to think that?"

Alex pulled on the back of their neck as they leaned back on the bench. "Uncomfortable."

"Okay," Parker said. "Has Dilynn ever dealt with the trauma that caused her abandonment issues?"

"I don't know," Alex answered.

"Well clearly Lyra hasn't dealt with her own abandonment issues. And Evie hasn't dealt with her insecurities of her place in her mother's life or you two wouldn't still need to box it out. It feels like all anyone ever does is put a plastic Band-Aid over a wound that clearly needs stitches."

Parker shook her head.

"I'm sorry this isn't an attack on your family. It's like this is what is happening all around. I mean, Zoe was ready to put Olivia in prison because she killed someone. Prison was the Band-Aid for society, but the wound was a pedophile hiding in plain sight. And that man was someone trusted to ensure the safety of others. But even then, the wound is deeper because Olivia was able to be preyed on by that man because she was kidnapped from a park by someone, she thought she could trust."

Parker ran out of air. She realized she'd pushed too far by the way Alex just stared at her with their mouth closed in a thin line.

Tucking a lock of hair behind her ear, Parker slumped against the table, barely whispering, "I'm sorry. That was way out of line."

"No," Alex said. They tapped the box on the table. "You have made some very eye-opening observations. Things I don't think anyone in this house ever considered."

Parker shrugged and looked up. She tried to put on a half-smile, realizing her calm mask had partially shattered on the table. Without it, the chaos inside of her had reached the brim of what she could contain and bubbled over the table. The imaginary box filled with her crazy until her words floated to the top, refusing to fuse to the wood as Alex had promised.

Quietly, she said, "I'm an outsider that lacks trust in anything and anyone."

"Your trauma response," they pointed out.

Parker repeated the mantra she'd only told herself as the crickets played their sad song on chilly nights when the blanket couldn't stop the loneliness biting into her flesh. "The only thing to count on is not to count on anyone, including yourself."

Alex studied her from a sideways tilt of their head. "Why can't you count on yourself?"

Parker exhaled her truth. "Because you mess up. You make mistakes that hurt you. You do it knowing it is a mistake, and you do it anyways."

"Like I runaway."

"Well, at that moment could you trust yourself to do the right thing?" Parker asked.

"That's another slippery slope," they said. "Who decides what is right?"

Parker waved their words away. "Another conversation for another time. But I would like to know, when you ran away did you believe it was the right thing?"

"Never. Not once did I walk away from Dilynn and know it was what needed to happen." They held their hands out. "I would hit myself in the head. One time I broke my hand because I punched a wall. But that was after I left. I didn't think about anything when I ran other than it was easier for everyone else. But right? No."

Parker leaned over the table again and stared at the box.

"If Lyra pushes me away, is it the right thing to stay? Or is it better to seek a relationship with someone that doesn't try to push me until I break? I walked away from Zoe when she tried to break me. Best thing I could do for me. For her, probably not because she moved forward thinking she was better than people because of her privilege. If I stay for Lyra, is it good for me? Is it good for her? Is she doing it hoping to find someone who's traumas compliment hers like yours and Dilynn's?"

She looked up when Alex didn't answer.

They were staring at her. Shaking their head slowly from side to side, they pressed their fingers against their temples. "I think you just broke my brain. I cease giving you any advice on how to deal with my daughter."

"I'm sorry."

They stopped trying to ease the headache. They reached over and took Parker's hand. Calluses scratched at her skin, but it felt nice to have someone touch her.

"You've given me a lot to think about. And honestly, I would like to talk to you again after I have had time to process the various points you made. Thank you for trusting me to have this candid conversation."

Both Alex and Parker jumped when a door in the house smashed against a wall and then slammed shut. They didn't get a chance to see who had come home when the door slammed again. Alex dropped Parker's hand, and they raised to their feet as Lyra walked around the corner with her head hung.

Dilynn rushed in after her, pulling Lyra back by the bicep. The mother's face was red and tracked with black streaks. One of her fake eyelashes had come loose, flopping against her eye until she pulled it off and tossed it to the floor.

Lyra's face was equally puffy. Her eyes red around the rims. Parker wanted to go to her, comfort her, but Dilynn was in Lyra's face.

"Let's just talk about this," Dilynn pleaded.

"What the fuck is there to talk about?" Lyra snarled. Her hands shot into the air, but Dilynn didn't flinch.

Dilynn's mouth set into a steady line. She pointed at Lyra's chest. "You don't get to monopolize the blame for what happened."

"You don't fucking get it," Lyra said, shaking her head and starting to turn away again.

Dilynn pulled Lyra back to her. "I don't fucking get it?" She gripped the taller daughter with both hands, holding her in place. "What the fuck is wrong with you? Of course, I get it."

She let Lyra go. Her finger pointed to the front of the house, as she cried out, "I brought him home. He lived there with Evie and me."

Lyra stepped into her mother's bubble. She moved until her face was inches from Dilynn's. Then she hissed, "No you don't get it. You don't get it because everything that happened... it happened because of me."

"What's going on?" Alex asked, moving towards the women close enough to start pulling hair. It was obvious they weren't sure whose side they should be taking.

"You know, I have been up for over 24 hours," Evie yelled from the front door. "The least you all could have done was wait for me."

Dragging her heavy boots against the floor, Evie made it into the room with the sister Parker had only ever seen in photos trailing behind her. She dropped the bullet proof vest to the ground.

Leaning against the wall, Evie sighed when Alex asked, "What is going on?"

"Brandon was part of the pedophile ring. He was the one who brought Olivia to Gibson's house," Evie explained.

"Brandon? As in Brandon Collins?" Alex asked. They searched Evie's face. "And you didn't tell me. Didn't warn me before you all...?"

"Uncle Ryder said you'd kill him. And we needed to bust them all together," Evie explained.

Lyra raised her arm, a single finger pointing at Evie's exhausted form. Growling at Dilynn, she said, "You and her were never at any risk, and you fucking know it." Her hand hit her chest. "And I could have stopped it. I could have put him in fucking prison and that kid would have never been hurt. None of them would have been hurt, but because I kept my goddamn mouth shut, I let him go back to what he was doing the whole time."

Dilynn's shoulders raised with her chin. She was still shorter than her daughter, but her voice was deeper and her status in the house stronger. "I paid for that shelter. I gave him access to how many fucking women. And I told you not to testify."

"Yeah, but I was supposed to be smarter than you," Lyra hissed.

"What the fuck is that supposed to mean?" Dilynn growled.

"It means you don't know a mother fucking thing about the world. You walk around throwing money at every problem that comes in the way of what you want just like Sylvia. You never slept in a gutter. You don't know what hungry feels like. You will never fucking get it, no matter how many books you write about it. You've never seen real shit because you never were on the street. You were a billionaire's sugar baby, while I was a teenage prostitute."

Evie pushed off the wall. She grabbed the back of Lyra's shirt and ripped her from the space she occupied. Lyra barely caught herself on a table behind the couch when Evie let go of her. Pressing the disarray from her clothes, Lyra slowly raised her boiling rage to Evie.

"Don't touch her again," Sadie, the silent sister, said.

"Back off," Evie warned, not even acknowledging the younger sister.

"Of course, you're standing up for her," Lyra said with a scoff. She thrust her finger into Evie's chest like a dagger. "What? Are you still scared she's going to throw you on the street? You wouldn't survive a day there you fucking fake princess."

"Shut the fuck up." Evie's growl sent Parker's eyes to the table. She didn't want to watch as the two of them started throwing punches at the other.

"Make me."

"Enough!" Alex's voice boomed off the walls. The overly large patio doors shook from the force, and Parker sank into the high-backed chair. She moved to get up and slip out through the hallway to the back bedrooms, but the chair screeched in the quiet settling in the room.

Parker looked up to find too many eyes staring at her. Too many questions she didn't want to answer. Too much anger she didn't want to become a target for.

Dilynn smeared the eye liner over her cheeks. "Oh, Parker. I'm sorry you had—"

"Had to what, Mom?" Lyra snapped, "See we aren't as fucking perfect as you pretend us to be."

"Yell at her one more time." Evie's chest puffed up. Her fists paled.

Parker held her breath, hoping one less movement would help settle the hurricane swirling within the house. She held the chair firmly to the ground, giving all her strength to keep the ground level.

"And your pregnant ass is going to what?" Lyra pressed two fingers against Evie's forehead and pushed Evie's face away. "You going to punch the cripple? It'll be just like when you beat my ass in school."

"You hit her, and I'll be the one ending it," Sadie threw in. She looked like she could be snapped in two, but there was a level of crazy in the younger girl's eyes even Parker was concerned about.

"No one is hitting anyone." Dilynn cried out. "Lyra. Baby, please. I understand you're upset."

Lyra and Evie continued to stare at each other, while Sadie was standing behind Lyra as backup.

Dilynn kept trying though. "I heard you when you said I don't understand the world you came from. I don't get what it's like to be you or Olivia. You're right. It wasn't me he kept hidden. It wasn't Evie he raped. It was you. He raped you, and you have spent years trying to convince yourself it wasn't what happened. And I did nothing to get you justice. I let him leave this house and walk back into the world when I should have hunted him down and cut off his fucking dick. I should have done what Olivia did. I should have fought for my daughter and I fucking failed."

Tears streamed from Dilynn's red eyes down her splotchy face. She held herself together with her arms but her whole body shook.

Lyra's hand came off the table and legs gave out from under her. Evie barely caught her as the strength of Lyra's being shattered. She clung weakly to her sister who moved to the floor with her. Her face collapsed against Evie's chest. Snot and tears smeared on the police uniform.

Her voice cracked as she cried, "I showed him how to do it."

Her fingers clenched Evie's shirt.

"It should have been me instead of that kid."

"You were a kid," Parker stated.

Lyra sucked back her snot as her squinted eyes fell on Parker.

"I know I'm not supposed to be here." She took a step towards Lyra who had released her sister. "But you were there when I broke. You reminded me of some key details I didn't want to remember. So, I'm going to remind you that you were a child when you met him. You told me so. You were in no better position than Olivia was, and the truth is, you got lucky. You were lucky to be the trial run for something this monster was already piecing together. If it wasn't you, it would have been someone else. Someone not as smart as you. Someone who lacked the courage to walk to Dilynn's door."

"You are stronger than most people," Alex added.

"Why do I feel so helpless?" Lyra sobbed.

"The most important question," Parker said, sitting next to Lyra but not touching her. She folded her legs under her. "I think you need to answer the more basic questions before you can get to the why though."

"You going to therapy me now?"

Parker chose not to acknowledge Lyra trying to pick a fight with her now. Instead, she asked, "What do you feel you could have helped?"

Lyra wiped the tears and snot from her face to her work pants. She looked at Parker. "I could have stopped it. I could have told him to fuck off and never went to that apartment."

Parker nodded. Then she asked, "And what would that have helped?"

"It would have shown him it wouldn't work," Lyra answered.

Parker didn't move. She only blinked to not appear as a statue. She waited for Lyra to know the truth. The truth everyone else in the room already stated and were holding on to like a lifeline in the storm rocking the Greyson-Trikru house.

"Until he tried again," Lyra finally said.

Parker reached over and took Lyra's hand, freeing Evie from the ground. She ran her thumb over the top. "Exactly. You may have been the first, but he had already decided before he met you that he was going to go after someone who was not Dilynn. He probably thought Evie would be an easy target." Parker shrugged. "That is until she turned out to be Evie."

"Hey!" Evie cried out from the place she'd found on the ottoman not far away. Then she shrugged. "Eh, I guess you're right."

Parker guided Lyra's chin up from the ground. "Is there anything else you could have helped?"

"I could have pressed charges."

Parker shook her head. Carefully, she reminded Lyra, "Nia Williams was the DA. She already had it out for Dilynn, and I know from personal experience she doesn't give a shit about rape victims."

Parker could feel Dilynn staring into her. From the corner of her eyes, she watched Alex's giant boots move alongside Dilynn's tiny ballet flats. Their feet turned towards each other, and Parker felt better knowing Alex had Dilynn contained for this moment.

"So, why do you feel helpless?" Parker asked.

Lyra wiped a new tear breaking free from her eyes. She swallowed and then tried to clear her nose by sucking in her snot. Looking away from Parker, Lyra whispered, "I thought I was special. He chose me even though he had her. The only time anyone picked me. Wanted me. Jesus, that sounds so fucking stupid. He's a rapist, and I am talking about how he made me feel special."

Parker held the trembling hand until Lyra pulled it away. Lyra wrapped her arms around her unbraced leg. She squeezed it tightly, then said, "I need you to go."

Unable to process the request, Parker stared at the floor. She ran through the words over and over again. Lyra had calmed down. She'd talked her down from wanting to hit her mother and her pregnant sister. Nothing made sense.

"I've spent the last month stressed out and waiting for you to do what he did. I wait by the phone, and you don't call when you say you're going to. You would rather die alone than call me. You flirt with everyone you see at work, and it's your job. It shouldn't bother me. But it does. And why...?" Lyra took a deep breath. "It makes sense. I need to stop chasing other people and get my own head right. I keep chasing you just like I chased Zoe. I can't keep being this person, so... I need you to leave."

Parker looked at the floor, tracing the path to the door. She pushed up from the ground, swallowed the tears, and said, "I understand."

Evie stood in Parker's way. Shaking her head, Evie said, "She needs you now. She's pushing you away because she needs you and it scares her. You can't just walk away when someone needs you."

Parker shook her head. "She needs to be able to say what she wants and have it respected. So, it is what it is. I knew from the beginning I didn't belong here."

The door closed quietly behind her. She heard Evie screaming through the wood, then something shattered inside. Lyra had promised a moment of calm when the answer to why was found. They'd shared in the moment, but the chaos was back.

Wind whipped around her as the rain began to pound against the ground once more. Parker stood at her driver's side door. Her hair stuck to her face as she scanned the wrap-around porch of the giant house.

She'd known better than to think she'd ever belong in a place like this. Known the time would come when she'd have to take the walk of shame from the almost family. The idea of happiness and people caring was for others who clung to each other. Ideas of better times would shed light on the skeletons within the minds of even the strong. Of course, she'd known she'd have to leave.

She too was far too good at saying goodbye.

"It is what it is."

33

Zoe stood outside the administration building of Greyson Academy. She took a sip of the hot beverage as she surveyed the dust covering the outside of her BMW. She managed to avoid every pothole on the dirt road to the school, but her car still looked like it belonged behind a chain link fence at a used car dealership. Glancing up at the sky, she contemplated the grey clouds hanging too low for her comfort.

"Don't you dare rain," she told the cloud.

Zoe's fingers gripped a manilla folder tighter as a gust of wind crashed against the side of her. She moved toward the door, reaching out to grab the handle when it flung open.

The metal frame smacked against the outside of Zoe's hand still clutching her coffee. Her body took the rest of the impact as her white shirt absorbed most of the hot liquid. The rest dripped down her hand holding the scrunched paper cup.

She stared at the cup, then her bra through her shirt. Every piece of lace was clearly outlined. She raised her eyes slowly taking in the shiny black boots of her attacker, then up the fitted maroon pants to the black top framing familiar breasts. Zoe's boiling blood fizzled to a gentle simmer as she stared at the mother and child pendant hanging at the base of Parker's neck alongside the freckle Zoe kissed goodnight the last time the woman had been tucked in her bed.

"I'm so sorry," Parker sputtered. She quickly pulled the shirt off her body, revealing a lace tank top. She wiped the coffee on Zoe's neck and chest, absorbing the quickly cooling liquid into the black cotton.

Zoe's lungs forgot how to function when her heart started to work double time, pushing the unoxygenated blood throughout her body. She couldn't move with Parker's hands touching her, but her brain screamed when suddenly Parker wasn't touching her anymore. Zoe's eyes snapped open to see the redhead biting her lip.

"I didn't even see you there. I was...." She bit her lip once more. "I'm sorry for, you know, touching you without asking first."

Forcing a smile on her face, Zoe felt her nipples harden as another gust of wind hit her. "I guess Karma really exists."

Parker shrugged. "But there's no nice barista here to replace your coffee."

"Maybe there will be a nice kid to loan me a shirt."

Zoe felt her face relax into the smile as laughter sprung from Parker. The high frequency sound waves bounced around the lawyer, tickling her into laughing as well.

"Well, if you play your cards right, Alex will probably give you the shirt off their back and Dilynn will show up at your next meeting with a few new ones because that's the weird shit that happens around here."

Zoe's brows scrunched in the middle, but she could not force the smile off her face. Evie had talked about Parker walking around in Alex's boots, but Parker didn't know that.

"I feel like there's a story I would love to hear." Zoe dipped her chin slightly and used Parker's own innocent gaze against her. "Maybe we could get coffee. I still owe you one from the day I ran into you."

"Smooth," Parker said with a shake of her head. "But covering you in coffee means we're even now."

The redhead glanced back at the closed door. With another sigh, the lightness of the moment vanished. "Anyways, its a story for another time. Sorry, I have to go before Dilynn sees me."

"Everything okay?" Zoe searched over Parker's head for the boisterous woman. She was ready to stand in the way of Dilynn for Parker to escape if it meant earning points with the woman looking for an exit.

"Yeah. Yeah. Everything is fine," Parker assured, but it was two yeahs too many to be true. Even if Parker's chest hadn't flushed to almost the same color of her hair, Zoe knew two yeses or two nos was a lie.

Zoe was about to call the woman on it. Take the time to check in and find out what was wrong. Parker moved so Zoe was a shield though, and her hand was back on Zoe, pressing the black shirt into the lawyer's chest. "You look good still. Take my shirt in case Dilynn doesn't like you enough to make Alex strip for you. Just remember they are kinky as fuck so make sure you change in the bathroom."

She was halfway through the parking lot when she called back, "Good to see you."

"You too," Zoe said to the back of the other woman who sped towards the dilapidated car a few spots down. She waved as Parker pulled away, savoring Parker's assessment of it being good to see her. It was much better than the usual bite of 'why are you here?'

Once the car was gone, Zoe looked down at her drenched shirt once more. Then she remembered the file. She checked it over, grateful her clothes had absorbed the coffee since the contents of the file were the whole purpose of her trip.

The door swung open again, crashing into Zoe for the second time. The cup already crushed came loose from her hand, while the rest of Zoe's body absorbed the blow.

"Damn it!" she cried out. She didn't have a chance to fix her face before she locked eyes with Dilynn Greyson

"Oh, fucking fuck nuts." Dilynn huffed. "Are you okay?"

With a pained sigh, Zoe said, "I'm fine."

"Did I ruin your coffee?"

"No." The subtle smile returned to her lips. "Actually, that was a little payback from your therapist."

"Oh. You saw Parker." Dilynn bounced on her toes. Zoe watched the blue eyes search over her shoulder. "I was trying to catch her."

"She was in a hurry."

Dilynn sighed and met Zoe's gaze once more. "Sweet to try and cover for her, but I know she's avoiding me."

Zoe pulled at the back of her neck, instantly regretting it as she felt the coffee spread to her hair. Dropping her hand, she forced an awkward smile on her face.

Tapping a finger to her lips, Dilynn pointed at Zoe. Before Zoe could react, the woman stated, "You know Parker. Maybe you can help me."

She wanted to do no helping what-so-ever. Her goal was to just be ready for if Lyra and Parker broke up, and avoiding Dilynn may be because of just that if Evie's rants about Lyra being an idiot were in line with Parker trying to avoid the woman's mother. She lied though, "I can try."

A single drop smacked against Zoe's forehead, pulling her gaze to the sky. A second drop attacked her eye before the light grey concrete turned slick with rain. Hoping for the women to be heartbroken was probably her latest round of bad Karma, and her car was going to be given a mud bath as punishment.

"Oh shit," Dilynn's hand locked around Zoe's arm and guided her within the office.

She barely had time to grip Parker's shirt close to her chest. So close she could smell the vanilla blackberry body spray Zoe had always loved on the woman.

"Sorry about all this." Dilynn stopped in the lobby, looking Zoe over. "Oh, you are not just a little wet, you are soaked straight through. Come with me, I am sure Alex has a shirt you can borrow. I doubt you want one of mine and you probably have to go back to your office so a school shirt wouldn't be appropriate."

Zoe had no choice but to follow Dilynn, who dragged Zoe by the arm down the hallway towards Dilynn's office. "Alex!" Dilynn yelled as she crossed the threshold. "I need a shirt! One of your nice ones."

She turned back to Zoe. "Alex always keeps extras in their office because I am a klutz."

"Oh, you don't—" Zoe tried, but was cut off by Alex walking into the office, tugging at the knot of their tie. Their eyes ran up and down Zoe's exposed torso, before pulling the tie over their head and handing it to their wife.

"What happened?" Alex asked.

Dilynn plopped down in a chair. It squeaked in protest. With a groan, she explained for Zoe, "Parker accidentally hit Zoe and spilled her coffee. Do you not have anything else? I'm getting really tired of young women walking around in your clothes."

Alex cocked an eyebrow at their wife. "Was she running away from you?"

"Yes," Dilynn sighed. "Apparently, she's been spending too much time with you."

With a roll of their eyes, they began to unbutton their shirt. "Just give her some space and some time. They broke up less than a week ago. She isn't like you or Evie. She needs time and the more you try to mother her the more you'll push her away."

Zoe glanced between the couple, while she fought the urge to smile. This was her shot. Just one shot to be an Alexander Hamilton. She was about to return her gaze back to Alex when Dilynn locked eyes with her.

"Is that true?" she demanded.

Pulling the wet shirt out from her exposed chest, she said, "Uhhh... well... I don't know about the mothering part, but I do know when Parker runs away, she runs away. No catching her."

Dilynn folded her arms over her chest. "Great another fucking Trikru. I'm not even sure if that means go after her or wait for her to come to me."

Alex's black button up waved in the air between Dilynn's hard-set eyes and Zoe's body. Zoe glanced over at the tight sleeves of the black undershirt pulled taught over Alex's prominent biceps. "Now you can see if the suit life is for you," they said with a smile.

Zoe's shoulders fell. "My mother."

"She is a very entertaining lady." Alex chuckled. "She's coming over for pizza. You're welcome to join—"

"Hello! Bigger issues!" Dilynn blurted out. "What do I do about Parker avoiding me? It's not like I broke up with her."

"You can't force her to talk to you."

"I'm her boss," Dilynn countered.

Zoe cleared her throat. She studied the floor as she said, "I didn't chase her when I should have. I read once the scariest people in the world are those who say 'it is what it is' and mean it. And that's Parker's go to line. Like, her life's motto. I don't honestly know if I'd gone after her, it woulda worked because she was done with me."

"Stay out of it," Alex said again, resting a hand on Dilynn's shoulder.

"But she needs people," Dilynn argued. "She just—"

"She has you and me and Marissa. When she needs us, she knows where we are."

"She won't ask for help even when she needs it," Dilynn protested. "She was willing to die of the flu, rather than call anyone."

"Yeah, but then we showed up. We changed the narrative for her, so now you have to let her decide to walk back in the door."

Dilynn pulled them closer. "I hate it when you're right."

"You're my witness she just said I'm right," Alex stated with a cocked eyebrow at Zoe.

"Is there a bathroom where I can change?" Zoe asked.

"Oh yeah. Sorry," Dilynn said. "Out the door turn left, second door on the left is the bathroom.

"Thanks."

Zoe followed the instructions and closed herself within. She gripped the sink as she swallowed the lump of guilt in her throat at the excitement tingling in her limbs. Her mind knew it was wrong for being happy Parker and Lyra broke up, but the spark had crackled through all her nerves at the renewed possibility of a second chance with Parker. After all, the woman just said it was good to see her.

Pushing it from her mind, she pulled the wet clothes from her body. She picked up the button up, then looked at the loaned shirt. It was wrong, but she pulled the black cotton tee on first. It looked almost like the undershirt Alex was wearing, but it was a piece of Parker. One she buried her nose in for longer than was necessary.

'Finish this meeting and then go to the bar,' Zoe told herself. 'She always works Wednesdays.'

With each button she fixed, she studied her reflection. Relieved her mother wasn't present to add any commentary, she turned side to side admiring the fit of the shirt.

Parker had gone out with Lyra, who dressed more like a soft masc in casual clothes and had begun to do so in the office as well. And with the redhead being attracted to soft mascs just made it more appealing. Zoe always wanted the freedom to dress like this. She fixed the buttons all the way to the top, wondering what it would look like with the tie.

When she returned to the room, Dilynn was still strewn across the leather chair. The older woman's leg bounced a mile a minute as though she was imagining running after Parker.

Alex smiled. "Looks good, but if you're going to button up you need this."

The tie they were wearing dangled from a finger. When Zoe nodded, Alex loosened the tie more and placed it over Zoe's head. It felt oddly parental, something her father never would have offered. Something she could only do now he wouldn't remember or try to send her away for being visibly gay. Alex adjusted the knot, then the collar of the shirt. Once it was fixed in place, they stood back studying Zoe.

"Your frame is well situated for ties and such."

Zoe looked down at the extra material. Quietly, she said, "Don't tell my mother."

"I won't."

Zoe took a seat across from Dilynn. "So, I actually came here to talk about Olivia."

Dilynn nodded, but Zoe felt as though the woman was somewhere else within her own mind.

She cleared her throat and hoped her news would bring Dilynn back to the moment. "First, I wanted to be the one to tell you today I got Judge Miller to revoke Brandon Collin's bail."

The glass over Dilynn's eyes seemed to clear as her nostrils flared slightly. "So, he won't be out for me to murder?"

"Going to pretend like you didn't say that," Zoe whispered.

"She's only going to murder him in a book," Alex promised, patting Zoe's shoulder. "He's been murdered in every book."

With a smile, Zoe continued. "Additionally, the arrest came at the perfect time. The legislator just passed a key bill two weeks ago changing the mandatory sentencing laws making Collins' offense of juvenile sex trafficking an automatic life sentence with no chance of parole."

"You're serious?" Alex asked.

"I am 100% serious, and I promise you, I will not lose this case. He will be going away. They all will."

"Thank you." Alex said as Dilynn's hand squeezed theirs. Tears slid down the red cheeks of Dilynn's face. Alex picked up their wife, who melted against them. Snot streaked over their undershirt as Dilynn cried.

"It's finally done."

Alex cradled Dilynn's head, pressing kisses to the frizzy blonde waves. They looked at Zoe. "This family has waited a very long time for justice we thought would never come."

Zoe nodded, then said, "I should be thanking you for not giving up on Olivia. I have learned a lot from your family."

Dilynn turned just slightly. "He wasn't.... he's not Henrie's father is he?"

Zoe wet her lips. Her eyes fell to the ground as she said, "I'm sorry, Dilynn."

"Does he know?" Alex asked.

Shaking her head, Zoe said, "Right now, he does not know. He will find out through his lawyer because it is the strongest evidence we have he in fact raped Olivia. But we also retrieved a lot of video evidence from the ring leader. He recorded everything."

"Will you take a plea?" Alex asked. "It doesn't seem this even needs to go to trial."

"I'm taking it to trial," Zoe stated. "I won't call Olivia as a witness unless she wants to have her day in court, but I need this. I need to win this publicly."

"For the election, right?" Dilynn asked, wiping her nose onto the sleeve of her cardigan. "So, what now?"

"Well, the trial will start in a few months. But I brought you a much more pressing matter." Zoe held up the file. "This is everything we acquired from Philadelphia PD on Olivia's life before she came to Phoenix. She is still going by Olivia, right?"

"Yeah. She doesn't want to go back to Rachel and she doesn't want to have to learn a new name right now. So, her mother?" Dilynn asked, taking the folder from Zoe. She flipped to the first page, and Zoe watched her scan the document.

"There is good news and bad news in that file. DCS already has a copy, and they are doing what they need to do. But Olivia's mother is in fact dead. She O.Ded around the time we believe Olivia was taken from the park. The reality is the statement you received from Olivia could be possibly true. What Olivia didn't know was her mother had parents who were actively searching for their daughter and when they learned she'd passed, they searched for Olivia."

Dilynn looked up at Alex. "Simone is going to kill me."

"She already knows this is a possibility. I spoke with her after we talked with DCS," Alex stated.

"Who is Simone?" Zoe asked.

"My best friend," Alex said. "She and her wife are fostering Olivia and Henrie, the baby. They will have a hard time letting Olivia go to live with grandparents."

"Oh."

"Thank you for this information," Alex said, extending a hand to Zoe. As they shook, Alex added, "We will consult with Parker and Olivia's foster parents since we are no longer her legal guardians. We'll figure out the best way to provide Olivia with this information."

"Yes. Of course." Zoe got up from her chair as the couple returned to hugging each other. Quieter, Zoe added, "Thank you again."

"So, are you still planning on running for DA?" Dilynn asked again just as Zoe turned to leave.

"Uhhh... yes and then no." Zoe pulled at the back of her neck. "I want to, yes, but everything with this trial... I feel like I may need to reassess how I plan to go about it."

"No one has run against Nia in years," Dilynn stated.

"Yes, I know." Zoe raised her eyebrows. "She has a lot of support."

"Not mine." Dilynn went to her desk, rummaged through her purse, and pulled out a check book. The first pen she tried didn't work and was tossed in the general direction of a trash can. It hit the wall and bounced in. Without looking up, Dilynn pointed at Alex. "You saw that shit! Swish!"

Alex groaned, then rolled their eyes. "A swish means you didn't use a backboard."

"Semantics."

With a crooked grin and another roll of their eyes, Alex said, "I'm not the English teacher, but I am pretty sure that is not what semantics means."

"Always got to troll me," Dilynn mumbled.

Dilynn found another pen, and it scratched against the paper as she quickly signed the bottom. "Here is a contribution for your campaign."

Waving the check in the air, Dilynn walked towards Zoe and closed it in Zoe's hand.

"But I—" Zoe started.

Dilynn squeezed Zoe's fingers tighter around the check. "I have seen you fuck up and I have seen you recognize your fuck ups and try to fix things. I am giving you this with the hope you won't stop correcting your fuck ups."

Zoe shook her head. "I can't take your money."

"You can. And you will."

"I promised you I wouldn't come to you for money."

"And you didn't. We are offering it to you so you can kick that bitch off her pedestal."

"We?" Alex said.

"Yes, we," Dilynn confirmed.

Zoe stared at the check in her hand. She closed her mouth when her pocket started singing.

"I'm sorry. It's my brother," Zoe said. Swiping across the screen, Zoe answered the call. "What's up, Zion."

"Dad had a stroke. Hospital's off the 101 and Bell. Come now."

34

The chain link fence towered over the car. It had the same razor wire spiraling along the top as the fence surrounding Durango Juvenile Detention Center. This was a maximum-security prison for violent female offenders, not the place they sent kids.

Evie's fingers tapped against the steering wheel in the quiet car. "Is there a reason you asked me to bring you?"

There was an hour left for visiting, and Parker couldn't ask Evie to drive her again. With a heavy exhale, Parker rolled her head against the headrest towards Evie. "Because the universe says we're supposed to be in each other's lives."

Evie rubbed at the smile threatening to spread across her face, then looked over at Parker. "Doesn't answer the why me part."

Looking back at the familiar yet different walls, Parker's arm hair rose on end. "Echo has her hands full with the girls. Xio has too many family members inside. Your sister broke up with me. Your parents are... touchy feely.... Shit. I don't honestly know. I ran through the list of who knows... so it was you. Plus, the last three times I tried to go in I chickened out, and I figured you are enough of a bitch that I wouldn't want to stay in the car with you."

"Mom says you're avoiding her."

Rather than lie, Parker chose not to answer.

"Is this why?" Evie probed.

Parker rolled her eyes. "No. She came with a list of Lyra's favorite flowers and candies. She also offered me a rental house on her street, because, and I quote, I live too far away from work. I just need a break from her trying to fix me. Can you not tell her?""

"Yep," Evie answered. But Parker knew better than to believe her.

The radio played through three songs. Other visitors began to file through the heavily guarded gates. Gates similar to the ones Parker said she'd never cross again.

"I never had a visitor in juvie," Parker confessed.

"It's weird," Evie recollected. "Some people are weepy. Some act like it's just a day in the park like Xio's mom did. That woman was cold as stone and, I swear, it was like talking to Xio in jail was just part of her life plan for Xio."

Parker felt the heaviness lift momentarily. "Your mom was the park person, huh?"

Evie shook her head as she chortled. "She tried to bring in a coloring book the first time she came.”

The snake of humans slinking through the gate had come to the tail end. Evie reached over and pushed the button to release Parker's seatbelt.

“You're as ready as you'll ever be, so get the fuck out of my car because your stress is pissing off my pregnancy nose.”

“I don't stink,” Parker stated.

“Your deodorant failed twenty minutes ago. Now get the fuck out of my car. I'm going to CVS because I will puke if I have to drive back with you like this, and I'll be back with a pitstick.”

The silver table edge pressed indents into Parker's forearms as she leaned against the surface. She stared at it, unable to see her own reflection. Fear crept up her spine when the navy prison garb came into view.

Janice Carter still moved like a ghost, and the hairs on Parker's arm rose at the correlation between her mother and ghosts. Twelve ghosts were released into her childhood home.

Eleven locks of red hair found in a memory book each tagged with a year. A book Parker had found once, assuming they were from her haircuts throughout her childhood. She'd wondered why the book didn't have pictures in it at the time. Now she knew.

She'd come hoping to get answers to when it started, and more importantly the why. Not just why it began though. She had so many questions beginning in why. She'd even written them on her hand, most too sweaty to read. One still remained un-smudged though.

‘Why did he need to kill twelve women with red hair?

She'd had an assumption based on her studies. Believed it might be linked to hating women who looked like him.

Her gaze remained on the table that refused to reflect back her face, even though it might need to be fixed before she looked at her mother. The worry hovering in the air just over the back of her neck wasn't new, but it was bigger. For years she'd wondered if there would be a point she understood why he did it. A hint to whether she would wake one day needing to murder too.

“Your hair is the same red as your father's. I thought it would lighten, but it's still red.”

Her mother could have led with a million different greetings, yet she'd managed to tap into the one thought in Parker's head. The one thought that had kept her sleep from hitting the REM cycle for what felt like weeks when she learned they'd all been redheads. Then she realized her hand was lying open on the table. The question easily read from across the space she'd not looked up from.

Parker's eyes rose to meet the same shade of brown as her own. Janice Carter's greasy blonde hair hung in clumps around the weathered pale skin. The navy uniform looked like scrubs a nurse would wear, so civilized for someone who watched her husband butcher redheads.

The smile was the same it had always been. Just a hint of teeth no longer well cared for. Her canines still forced the minor incisors further into her mouth, and the bottom row still looked a little like a zipper.

"How have you been?" Janice asked, not breaking her smile.

Her fingers twitched to reach across the table like her mother used to during dinner. A simple urge to pat the woman's hand to see if she was real.

If Parker was dreaming though, she wouldn't know. She'd had this dream before. Woken up occasionally, compelled to sketch out the woman's face from various angles to see if she could find the fear her mother held for her murderous father. She'd smiled at him like this though, whenever Parker was around. Always the same smile, occasionally sticking to the prominent canines.

Picking at the cuticle on her thumb, Parker shrugged. "Fine. I guess."

"It's been so long." The even timbre of her mother's voice was so familiar. Same voice she'd asked about school or dance class.

Parker could hear a small celebration of a pending parole at the table next to them. A conversation they would never have, but they could have had this if she hadn't been so angry. Glancing around the room at the other inmates and their visitors conversing, Parker wondered if their relationship could have been mended years ago. If she could have helped her mother heal, like she was doing with Olivia. Other families did that, and she should have done it too.

"Why did you come?"

The question pulled Parker back to her mother's gaze. She'd asked herself similar types of questions, but for once she knew the answer was to calm the chaos. She was tired of swirling through life in a twister, wanting it to finally set her down. There would be another storm, but she wished to be done with this one.

"How could you... watch the things you did and then cook breakfast in the morning? Take me to dance class? Just act all normal?"

Janice's head tilted. The smile shifted just enough to not show her teeth any longer, but the corners were still lifted. With a voice as smooth as butter, she said, "Probably the same way people watch Freddy Krueger or Michael Myers."

"That's fake." Parker tapped her head. "Seeing it. Hearing it. It's different when its real."

"You don't like scary movies." Janice nodded once, and her lips parted to recreate her smile.

"You didn't either," Parker reminded her. "Dad did, but you hated them. Is it because they reminded you of what you had to see?"

"The psychologists didn't ask questions like these."

Janice's gaze didn't move around the room, nor did her chin drop to her chest.

She sat still, still scanning Parker's face as a conversation grew heated a few tables away.

"How do you know I won't wake up one day and want to... to... to do what he did?"

The hand reaching across the table was older. It was cold when it rested on Parker's, patting her three times before withdrawing. A little quieter, Janice assured her daughter, "Honey, we would have known. Helped if you showed any signs."

"What signs? To see if I was just like him? If I had a murderous monster hiding in me?" Parker's head tilted to the side. She went through the list of criteria she would use to identify psychopathic behavior. Settling on the most basic, she said, "I didn't kill any puppies. Is that what you looked out for?"

When Parker leaned back from the table, Janice didn't move. She stayed still, watching Parker as invisible bugs crawled under her daughter's skin.

"What did you grow up to become?"

Parker carded her hair from her face. Took a moment to accept her mother still didn't like to answer questions, but also still expected answers to questions she asked.

"I'm an art therapist."

Janice's head dropped to the side. She didn't say anything right away. Just looked at Parker. Moved her hands to be in the same position as Parker's. Adjusted her posture to match Parker's.

"When you were little, I let you paint your own fairytale land on your wall. You used it as a backdrop for your dolls. Always so creative." Janice's unwavering smile didn't change the steadiness of her eyes as she reminisced. "When something bad happened to your doll in the story, you cried. That's when I knew you were not like him."

Parker hadn't thought of her childhood mural in so long. The last time she'd tried to draw, she'd created a self-portrait in her childhood bedroom. Three versions of herself, and the mural lay behind the youngest. She questioned if it was real when she studied her drawing to check if she was losing it. She couldn't be sure if it was another lie to add to her list.

"What do you paint now?"

Parker looked at the table once more. "Reflections of people. Mirror images."

"Interesting. You always wanted to know the other side of stories. You'd ask what made villains so angry." Janice paused just long enough to scan over Parker's face from top to bottom. "There are books about them now. The villains. They make me think of the stories I would tell you about them."

"I remember. You would change the story in the book and talk about how the villain had a good reason for doing what they were doing. Like the witch in Hansel and Gretel. You said she wasn't any different than a lion, and we would never blame a lion for eating a child if it found one."

"You're not like him." Janice's lips rose into a kind smile. "He was a lion. You are a human."

The skin on Parker's thumb split from the picking. She pressed on it, trapping the blood. "Did you even want me?"

"You were a surprise," Janice admitted. "A surprise, but not unwanted."

The brown eyes looking back at her were so familiar, and not because they looked like hers. They were the same as they were in every moment of her life before the screaming. No tears were welling at a lost decade. The smile didn't cause creases in the corners. They were just brown orbs scanning Parker's face like she were a book to be read.

"You're a sociopath." The words fell from Parker's lips as she thought them.

She carefully examined the woman's face to see if the declaration shocked or angered Janice. The eyes studying her didn't faulter for a moment. It was an answer to Parker's silent question of whether or not the woman knew.

She had, and Parker now knew as well.

Shifting just slightly in her seat, Parker had to take a moment to consider this revelation. She'd been mistaken when she'd thought Olivia had Split Personality Disorder. And this was not something she could be wrong about.

The woman's face was the same only older. But she noticed the lines of age were all deep indentation from carrying the same smile at all times. Eyes with nonexistent laugh lines didn't stop looking at her like she was measuring every reaction to determine what Janice should do next. The woman was adjusting moment by moment to remain in control of the conversation, always one step ahead of everyone else.

"Was it all fake?" Parker asked, unsure if Janice had ever been amused when she smiled since it still hadn't wavered.

"I don't understand what you are asking."

Parker looked around the room once more. A child sat alongside another inmate. They leaned over a coloring book together. She'd done it with Janice many times she thought. Maybe she didn't though. It would have been too long ago to be certain, and she didn't believe what she thought she knew.

"Did you ever love me?"

Janice's hand moved slowly across the table once, stopping just short of touching Parker this time. She must have seen something in her scan and was detouring to a different manipulation. Coursework had taught her sociopaths were strategic manipulators. Blended in easier because they were astute observers who would use anything to remain in control of the perception of them.

"Love is exhibited through a variety of behaviors. I studied, along with your father."

The list of sociopathic criteria Parker had memorized for her qualifying exams disappeared as she snapped her attention back to the woman.

"Studied?"

Janice's smile grew enough for her lips to get caught on her canines almost like a snarl, but the smile never reached the creases of her eyes.

"Yes, honey bug. The television shows were a great help. *Full House, Family Matters, Leave it to Beaver,*" she said so sweetly Parker had to hold on to the table to keep some form of calm. "And the books. We read them, and we watched the shows, so we knew how to behave. It was harder for your father, always scatter brained. But once I learned how to look. How to talk to a child. Well, parenting was rather easy."

With a wave of her hand at the mothers in the room talking to their children, Janice added, "The other moms helped. People at the park were always interested in telling me about their kids and how they handled their children if I asked the right question. They provided more examples, and I practiced until I found the ones that fit you and what you needed."

Parker bit into her lip. She could only hear her own heartbeat as she felt the boiling blood spread throughout her limbs. Her father was on death row, but Parker had read about sociopath and psychopath relationships. Her mother had said the right things to not take the full blame, when she was the person who probably planned the murders of twelve redheaded women. She was the one who would have put Parker on the list like the others.

"So, you just pretended to love me." Parker bit into her lip. "You're not even capable of loving someone are you?"

"It is probably easier to believe I pretended," Janice stated.

She lost the ability to school her emotions as though this was a session with a client. Her eyes narrowed, and she didn't care if her mother knew she was angry. The woman should know she was angry because for too many years she'd given her a victim's pass for murder.

"What is that supposed to even mean?"

Janice had to force her lips closed, her teeth too dry from constantly smiling. She must have realized smiling wouldn't work any longer, because Parker wasn't a child and the woman didn't have a TV show to prepare her for her daughter learning she was a murderer of women who looked just like her.

"What does love feel like?" Janice asked.

Parker studied her mother's stoic expression. She watched as the woman looked around the room watching the other women, examining their behaviors. There weren't any models in this room to help though.

"You don't know what anything feels like," Parker answered for her.

Janice leaned back in her chair. Her smile stayed tucked away as she met Parker's gaze. The noticeable facade of happiness lost at Parker's declaration. Sweet honey covered words were gone.

"I don't know what things feel like for you. I know what I feel." Janice's lips pursed, the façade of motherhood dropped for a new demeanor she probably learned from a show with cops and lawyers. "Is that why you finally came to see me? To understand what I feel?"

Parker had come to forgive her mother, like she'd sought for Olivia to be forgiven by everyone and herself. That didn't make sense anymore.

"I thought you had feelings when I came," Parker snapped. Rubbing her hands over her face, she tried to press the anger away. "I just can't make sense of anything. I can't trust anyone, not even myself. It's not normal. Normal people... they trust others. They trust other people, but I'm constantly wondering if they are killers."

"You should be doing that anyways, shouldn't you?"

Parker's gaze snapped up from the table she'd found herself searching for her own reflection once more. "What?"

A single eyebrow rose on Janice's forehead. "To be safe, we must consider the worst a person could be. If someone was a killer, well you wouldn't know until they were caught in the act. I would have failed, if I didn't teach you to not fear other people."

"Gold medal winner for mother of the decade," Parker hissed. "I mean, now I get to live with the fear of me fitting all your boxes of one of your victims."

Two women began arguing on the other side of the visiting room. The visitor was leaving as the inmate screamed at her to get back there. To respect her mother.

"Parker," Janice said, calling Parker back to their conversation. "I cannot explain to you why I did the things I did. There are very talented people in the FBI who try to understand. They conduct their interviews, create their assumptions, and pretend to understand another person. But you will never feel another person's emotions the way they feel them."

"Sociopaths don't feel emotions," Parker spat.

"Yet I studied the emotional patterns of the television characters. I learned to kiss your knees for wounds that didn't exist. I learned how to cry at movies so you would feel it was okay to cry." With a laugh that wasn't funny or warm, the murderess added, "And I opened all of the presents on Christmas and my birthday with smiles and occasionally a few tears."

"You were just pretending though," Parker reminded her. "You didn't feel anything. You don't feel anything."

"You assume to know the emotional capability of another."

She's assumed so much. Believe too much in what other people had told her. Studied psychology to find answers that would lead her to forgiveness of not only herself but the woman who'd ruined her life.

Shaking her head, Parker said, "I shouldn't have come."

"Why did you come?" Janice asked, searching her once more.

"Because I needed to know why you didn't love me enough for us to leave." Parker fought back the tears as she admitted. "To find out why you stood by as he murdered women that looked just like me. But it was you. It was you who didn't love me. Couldn't love me."

Janice reached over to touch Parker, but the daughter withdrew her hands from the table. Tapping the surface, Janice shook her head. "The answer you wanted you can't understand because it doesn't fit in the mold the way you wish it to."

Parker chewed on what tasted like another riddle. Riddles and games this woman had played her entire life. They'd always left her mind swimming in water too dark to see if the monsters were coming for her.

"Why are you always like this?" Parker choked out.

Janice's laughter burst the cobwebs in Parker's deepest memories, sending out echoes from the breakfast nook table the morning before the world fell apart. Reminded her of times when she'd thought she was loved and safe.

"I can only be who I am." Janice tapped her sternum. "I accepted a long time ago, and I did what I did because it tingled and sparked. Just like you do what you do because it gives you the tingles and sparks."

Parker stared at her mother. Carefully, she asked, "Happiness?"

"If that's the word you assign to the sensation, then I guess you would call it that." Janice leaned forward again. "What does love feel like to you?"

Love didn't feel like anything because she'd never let anyone close enough to love her. Zoe thought she'd loved her, but she'd left because she learned Parker kept secrets. So many secrets she'd carried. Sharing them with Lyra had calmed chaos just enough to make her feel falsely safe. Lyra was just another tornado, who'd swept her up though. She'd felt loved by them though for a moment. Felt like the women had loved the parts of her she'd let them see, and now they were just an echo.

Echo. She loved Echo without a single doubt in her heart. So, Parker set out to describe what Echo's love felt like.

"Protecting someone else at the cost of yourself. Helping them be happy. Doing things for them even if it goes against... your nature." Parker's lungs refused to work as she ran through her words. "You knew you were different but wished me the world you didn't understand."

She looked up and found her mother looking back at her.

"It wasn't all a lie."

"I never lied to you." Janice's hands found Parker's. Her mother's thumb soothed away the heaviness that had settled into her thin frame a decade prior.

"If you had the chance, would you change what you did?" Parker asked, needing to know if she was worth fighting for.

The "No," sliced through the single fiber Parker had clung to for so long.

Shaking her head, Parker asked the only question that mattered. "Why?"

Janice patted Parker's hand three times again, and her mother's smile was back on her face.

"The only thing anyone can do is pursue what makes them feel alive. Any other way would be just surviving the numbness."

"Is that what it's like? Just numb?"

"What does numb feel like to you?"

Ripping her hand back, Parker tried to wipe away the woman's touch from her skin on her pants. Anger at not being good enough for anyone bubbled as the temperature rose in the room to the point, she was stripping off her sweatshirt, only to twist it in her hands.

"Why can't you just answer a question?"

"I have known since I was a teenager I didn't see things the way other people did." Janice shrugged. "What I think is numbness may not be numbness to you."

"I can't describe numb." Parker tried to rip the material of the fabric. "I feel hot when I'm angry. Crushed when I'm hurt. Light when I'm happy."

"And loved?"

Parker's stomach fluttered as Zoe and Lyra's faces appeared behind her eye lids. Their smiles fell when the tears she'd locked away inside her mind soaked them through. Eye liner ran down their faces until they were fit for battle. Possible promises were replaced with panic, which caught in Parker's throat. She pushed away another time she'd thought meant love but was... something else.

Hurt?

Disappointment?

She caused both women to feel those things in her. That wasn't love though. It was the aftermath of love like embarrassment was the outcome of being wrong. She shook her head. She was searching for what love felt like, not how her romantic life sucked.

Her fingers played with the pendant, she'd ironically adorned since adolescence when both her childhood and mother had been snatched from her. Her fingers touched the cool metal, measuring all the women she'd thought would love her.

Looking down at the pendent, she realized her thumb had rubbed the rose gold finish off the child. A chunky, booger covered monster in a corrective helmet smiled up at Parker when she blinked. It was a moment. A time Henrie would never remember, but Parker had loved her.

"So warm," she whispered. "My skin was alive on its own, not bugs crawling under it. My heart wasn't trying to escape because it was there with me. And I smelled her, because I didn't want to forget. Like my body knew scent is a greater memory than any visual cues."

"Do you enjoy that feeling?" Janice asked.

"Yes."

"Then you should pursue the things that make you feel that way."

The laughter spilling from Parker's lips tasted sour. Shaking her head, she couldn't stop the tightening of her chest, realizing she'd let her mother turn her into a client. Allowed a sociopath to pretend to be a therapist after studying Parker for twenty minutes.

Janice's smile didn't move. "Is there something in your life that makes you feel that way?"

Throwing up her hands, Parker scoffed. "I don't know."

She knew it was a lie nevertheless. She knew Henrie made her feel that way. Olivia even made her feel that way when she had reached over earlier and they'd locked pinkies. She didn't want to be a mother, but she loved those kids in a way Janice had never loved her.

When she leaned back, she stared across the table at the woman who'd birthed her. Pinned butterflies into her hair as she stared at her own terrified reflection gripping the pink tutu tied to her waist. And in the dark of the night cut women open with her father.

"Whenever I start to feel it, I push it away because I don't want it to be a lie."

"Has it been a lie before?"

"My childhood home had blood soaked into the foundation." Parker searched her mother's face for any hint of remorse. A quivering chin or even a tear she knew wouldn't be there because Janice Carter was built differently. "My whole life was a lie."

Parker's stomach twisted as she considered what she would be saying if Janice was a client instead of her mother. Her searching only lead her to a truth. "I keep trying to balance the monster you are with the mother you were."

"Do you have a new mother?"

Parker tried to find her reflection once more, wishing she could see her deepest desire. Wanting to see herself surrounded by family, but the table gave her nothing just as her mother gave her nothing.

"A person can have more than one mother," Janice offered.

A pathetic laugh caught in Parker's throat. "Which show did you learn that from?"

"I believed you would get a new mother when I came here."

"Well, I didn't."

"That's unfortunate. You were a very pleasant child. You had manners. You were kind." Janice's head tilted slightly to the side, but her smile remained fixed and her eyes unwrinkled. "I believe not having a mother has made you very angry. Not angry like your father was when his sister ran away. You asked about redheads. She left him alone with his mother. It was the chase, and then the need to make sure she didn't leave again. She was like his mother when his mother wasn't a mother at all."

"Like you," Parker said, wanting to erase the association between the title and woman. "You aren't my mother. Just a woman who gave birth to me."

"There is a maternal figure." Janice scanned over Parker, clearly looking for the slightest crack in the younger woman's mask to get a finger under and peel it away. "You came because there is a new mother, but you are afraid of her. Afraid like your father was of losing someone else. What is she like?"

Parker thought of the way Dilynn Greyson's cheeks rose when she smiled, and the tiny crinkles gathered when Alex would catch another f-bomb falling from her lips. She remembered the way her chest felt warm when she forced her into a hug. Examined how her heart hadn't tried to runaway during the embrace. She hadn't known what to do when Dilynn cared for her, but she didn't runaway when the woman touched her.

"I think when she cries, she means it. And when she hugs me, I feel safe."

"That's nice."

Parker leaned against the table, fingers tapping against the metal. "I did ask if she was like you."

"And?" Janice asked.

"I guess if she was, she wouldn't tell me."

"Probably not." Janice matched Parker's stance, clearly learning from every move Parker took. "But would it matter?"

Parker looked over Janice. Her navy scrubs with prisoner ID card might look harmless, but she was a monster with a pretty face. A face with a slight yellowish tint to it and teeth gradually decaying. Looking like her father didn't feel like something to fear anymore since the other option was to be like her mother.

"I think I am done trying to figure it out."

"Five minutes!" a guard called out.

Looking around the room, Parker took in the tense conversations and the light meetings. "If I don't come back, would you be sad?"

"Would you come back if I learned to look sad?"

Parker stood up. Exit was printed in large letters across the floor. She couldn't get a better sign as to which way her life path needed to take.

"No," she said, knowing it wouldn't stab the woman in the chest because Janice Carter wouldn't regret not seeing her again.

Evie hadn't said a word when Parker returned to the car. She drove in silence down the highway, pulling off only to go through a Starbucks drive-thru. They sat in the line of cars, waiting for their turn at the speaker box. Parker stared at the smiling stick family stickers on the back window of the car before them.

"She hasn't changed," Parker said. "She still answers questions with questions.

She still smiles all the time."

"Is that good or bad?" Evie asked.

Parker side-eyed Evie, as the mother-to-be's eyebrows rose and mouth twisted into a knowing smile. Shaking her head, Parker pulled her knee to her chin and looked out the passenger's side window. She chewed on 'good', but it tasted salty. 'Bad' made her scrape her tongue against her teeth. She tried to come up with a way to help Evie understand, but she didn't know Evie well enough to know what she would understand.

Rubbing her hands over her face, she tried to wipe away the exhaustion hitting her like a truck when they had begun to drive.

"It helped... I guess."

"Are you okay?" Evie asked.

"Yeah. I'm fine."

The speaker came to life, interrupting the potential interrogation. Evie ordered, then stared at Parker. "What do you want?"

"Cold brew, the pumpkin one. Big as they make it."

When Evie finished ordering, she followed the stick figure family van forward.

"I think I'm ready to stop avoiding your mom."

35

A hummingbird flitted around one of the many feeders on the patio. Zoe dug dirt from under her nails as she wondered if somewhere a tsunami was being set into action because of the bird's wing flaps.

Giving up on getting the grit out, Zoe leaned back in her chair. She rocked slowly back and forth in the patio chair, then tried to push the wrinkles out of her black pants. When the teenage second cousin moved from the yard to the house where the other mourners had gathered, Zoe pulled out the vape. Each puff inhaled eased some of the tension in her neck. The guilt for not making it to the hospital in time made the autumn air catch in her throat.

When the door opened, she didn't turn. She didn't have the courage to face the person walking out, whether it was the man she couldn't stand, the mother she'd disappointed, or another person who felt the need to play an extravagant game of pretend pity because it turned out her father had more enemies than friends. The chair next to her creaked, then moved in rhythm with her.

"Mom said you found out about me knowing your ex." Zachery adjusted his tie. "She said that's why you haven't returned my texts or my phone calls."

Zoe pressed the vape to her lips, wishing the vapor she inhaled would suffocate her. When it didn't, she exhaled it upward as she stared at the patio awning.

A Daddy Long Legs spider wrapped its captured prey into a silk tomb. She watched the fly struggle against the spider, and the dream of Zachery's hands on Parker resurfaced. Even with her eyes open and the pool shark slurping loudly at the rim of the side, Zoe could see Parker's fear as her brother, her best friend, restrained Parker's helpless body.

"I showed you the ring. You helped me plan my proposal," she said.

Her fingers slapped against the metal arm rest in no coherent rhythm. Her lips stuck to her teeth, a small crack opening. She tasted the iron as she tried to soothe her dry lips, but her sandpaper tongue just caused more damage. She wished she hadn't left her water inside.

"Zoe, it's too late to apologize, but I wi—"

Zoe shook her head. "Don't."

"I was a kid. A stupid..." As the words fell from his mouth, the pounding in her chest began to echo in her ears. He was just as much a monster as Gibson and any other asshole who thought don't, stop, or no didn't apply to them.

She took a long inhale, letting the vapor exit slowly. She pulled at the peeling skin on her lower lip as she ran through all the things she'd tried out in the isolation of her own car. Every string of words twisted into a knot, unable to roll off her tongue.

"Why?" she finally asked.

She heard his sigh, then the chair creaked as he rocked faster. "The truth?"

"Yep."

He wrung his baseball cap between his hands.

"I wanted what you had," he said simply.

Her skin burned in the shade of the patio. She glanced down expecting to see the flesh bubbling on her forearms.

"Everyone is always rooting for you, celebrating you. You had it all. Nothing about me has ever been special, and when I saw her on that stage... you weren't kidding about how beautiful she was. And I wanted her. I wanted for once to not come in second place. I wanted her to want me and choose me over my perfect sister."

Zoe turned to look her brother straight in the eyes. "You put your hands on my girlfriend."

He offered with an awkward smile. "If it makes you feel any better, I'm pretty sure she tried to poison me."

Zoe leaned forward. She flipped the vape between her fingers. "You know, I let you convince me a child should be locked behind bars for the remainder of her life. When you asked me if it was you, what would I do? The thing was, I couldn't imagine letting anyone hurt you."

She took a quick inhale. Vapor exited with the words, "But now I wish Parker had actually poisoned you. I wish she'd sent you to the hospital in organ failure because assholes like you, who think they can just take what they want are no better than the monster who drugged and raped a child."

"Wow, harsh much."

Shaking her head, she shut her eyes. "You ruined my life."

"Bullshit," he barked. "You have everything. The job everyone brags about. All the girls throwing their numbers at you. I'm just your dumb brother who can't get past the second date. The stupid history teacher."

"How many other girls did you put your hands on that asked you to stop? How many other women did you think you had the right to possess?"

Zachery got to his feet. "Possess?" He pointed his finger at her, and growled, "I paid that bitch at least a hundred a week. I paid her to rub her tits all over my face. And you're calling me a rapist because I just wanted to hold her for a second. To know what it's like to be you for once."

She stood up with his finger still pointing in her face. "Get. Your. Finger. Out. Of. My. FACE!" She smacked his hand when he didn't move fast enough.

Spit flew from his mouth as he snarled, "You were the one who called her a piece of trash. You never loved her. You never loved anyone but yourself."

His fingers ran through his floppy hair. Shaking his head, he asked, "Why are you really mad at me? Because I tried to steal your girl, or I showed you the truth about her. That she was nothing but a whore."

Zoe's fist collapsed against the butterfly bandage on his cheek. She heard the crack of her knuckles on his jaw before she felt the pain in her hand.

The bandage released, and blood oozed from the healing wound. Zachery touched his cheek, pulling back fingers covered in blood again. His eyes shot up at her.

His charge started with a flare of his nostrils, but Zoe hadn't expected him to tackle her. Her head hit the damp grass as he smeared her into the ground. He grabbed her hands and tried to force them down, but she landed a knee to his crotch.

Zachery cried out in pain, rolling off the top of her. She rolled with him, her fist coming down on his head again.

"She's not a whore," she screamed as she wildly landed punches on his head and chest.

She didn't stop trying to hit him when Zion's huge hands yanked her body back and tossed her like a rag doll to the side.

Zoe pushed off the ground, charging Zachery again. She couldn't reach him as Zion pushed her back again.

"Stop this shit," Zion demanded. Turning to his younger brother, he yelled, "What the fuck is going on?"

Zachery pushed himself up from the ground. "She's lost her mind over that fucking cunt from college."

She lunged at Zachery, but Zion grabbed her by the waist and slammed her body to the ground. The air in her rushed to escape her. Her chest burned as she choked. Her lungs were begging for oxygen, but she couldn't get enough in before it was coming out again.

"Stay down," Zion ordered Zoe.

Zackery got to his feet. He was standing and coming at her. She tried to get out of his path, but Zion stepped between them.

Zion's bulky body blocked the boyish build of the younger man. The older pushed the younger back with each attempt Zachery made to come after her again.

"Crazy, fucking dyke," Zachery screamed at her as he tried to push through his brother.

Zion's hand wrapped around his brother's throat as he held him back from Zoe now on her knees. He pounded the fat pointer finger between Zachery's eyes as he said, "Never again will you call her that. You understand me?"

Zoe watched Zackery pull at the fingers around his throat. His eyes bulged as he hoarsely said, "Yes."

"Never," Zion repeated, then tossed his brother backwards.

Zoe choked trying to get enough air to yell at the man who wasn't her friend. Wasn't her brother any longer. Tears fell from her eyes when they found her mother on the patio.

Family and friends dressed in pressed black suits and somber knee length dresses spilled from the grieving house. Some whispered, while others shook their heads at the display.

Zion's large hand pulled Zoe to her still unsteady feet. He smacked the grass off her before asking, "You okay?"

"I hate him," she whispered.

"He hates himself," Zion stated. "What he did was fucked, but he was right about one thing."

"If you call her a whore, I'll hit you too," Zoe warned.

"You're the best of us. So, if you really love this girl, go after her."

Zoe looked up to see Cassandra being led back into their family home. She'd accomplished the one thing she'd never thought she'd see. Her mother hadn't said a word.

She'd fix it though.

She'd fix everything.

Starting with fixing things with Parker.

36

Echo's parking lot was unusually crowded for a Thursday night. Parker translated the "I need you" text to mean she was working tonight. Something that had become basically every night since there was no reason to try and save a day for a date with Lyra.

The line at the door was filled with various representations of the Alphabet Mafia. Parker bypassed the line, nodded to the bouncer checking IDs, and walked inside. Protests broke out as the door was held open for her, but the music pushed the words back to their owners.

On the other side of the heavy wooden door, people knocked into each other trying to get through the crowd. Standing on her toes, Parker struggled to see the bar, let alone find Echo in the chaos. Even though she couldn't see the bar, she knew Echo would be there.

Parker fought her way through the crowd. Her size allowed her to duck and squeeze between most of the people until she caught sight of Echo talking to an attractive blonde in a vibrant purple shirt. When the woman turned, Parker's jaw dropped as she recognized her coworker, Charleigh Marshall. She hung back momentarily, watching Charleigh smile sweetly at Echo before making her way towards the dance floor.

A huge cheer broke out, pulling Parker's attention from Charleigh to three giant athletes. Women of all shapes and sizes swarmed the players, leaving a clear path to Echo who was leaning over the bar glaring at one of the women towering over the fangirls.

Parker started to move forward as the path to the bar cleared but was pushed off course into thick arms of an older masc. The woman kept Parker from falling over, and yelled, "Don't worry, beautiful! I got you!"

"Thanks," Parker said. She let the woman hold on to her only long enough to locate the trampling beast.

Making her way over to Echo, she waited just behind the pushy woman. Echo took the woman's order and a credit card. Handing over two long neck bottles, Echo warned, "I mean it. Keep your bitch on a leash tonight, Kayla."

Parker followed Kayla's eyes back to three athletes posing for photos. With a pained voice, she said, "She's only looking for one tonight. Hopefully, she'll choose quickly, and I can get her out of here."

"I'll call the cops this time. I don't care who the fuck she thinks she is." Parker bit her lip, concerned of how Echo's voice dropped an octave lower than normal.

The same voice Echo used to tell the original Henry if she didn't get clean, she would fire her ass.

Parker knocked into the back of the woman as she pushed against the bar. One of the bottles in her hand hit the surface, foaming immediately. The painted face snapped in Parker's direction; her eyes narrowed.

Holding up her hands innocently, Parker called over the music, "Oops. I'm sorry. It's so irritating how people keep pushing everyone out of their way."

Echo popped the top to another long neck and pushed it into Kayla's hand. "Go," she instructed.

The corners of Echo's eyes softened when the woman walked away. She leaned across the bar to Parker, ignoring the other women trying to flag her down to order. "The one in the center is Sylvia Winter's wife and was just named MVP for the NWBA. She comes in just to find someone to fuck while Sylvia's little sister, Kayla is hanging on her arm begging to be the girl that bitchface cheats on Sylvia with. It's sick the way the bitch thinks women are just disposable."

"Kayla? As in OG Henry's Kayla?" Parker asked.

"Yeah. We hate her too, but she's Sylvia's sister, and I'm not looking to get shut down by Sylvia."

Parker glanced back at the cocky woman posing for photos like she was God's gift to the bar. She reached over and touched Echo's hand. Tucking her fingers around Echo's, she said, "You can handle her."

Echo shook her head. "Also not looking to get sued by Sylvia for beating the shit out of her wife."

"Maybe she'll reward you."

"Or maybe she'll try to bury my bar."

Parker followed Echo's gaze to where Charleigh leaned against the railing of the dance floor. She was alone and staring at the basketball player Kayla was hanging on to. The center of Echo's eyebrows furrowed as she looked back and forth between Charleigh and the player now staring each other down.

Tapping Echo's hand, Parker told her, "That's my co-worker, Charleigh."

"Nice girl," Echo said. "Said she needed to dance."

"Yeah. Quiet. Kind of awkward."

"So, she's you." A smirk spread over Echo's face as she continued to watch Charleigh. "Only looks like Dilynn Greyson when she was like 22. Jesus, that's freaky."

Parker reached across the bar, landing a punch on Echo's shoulder. "Fuck you."

"What?!" Echo said. She looked back at Parker and rubbed her shoulder. "If I was going to describe you, those would be the exact words I would use. Except the looking like Dilynn part. You're hot like a 22-year-old Dilynn too, but in an angry sorta way."

"Simone not give you any this week?" Parker asked, confused at having never heard Echo talk of a woman like someone she was attracted to.

"More like six months," Echo confessed. She ran her hands over her face. "I'm pretty sure she's cheating on me, but I don't know. I don't know and... that girl is cute. Not like Sylvia Winters hot but cute. Sweet, and... I need to shut up."

Shaking her head, Parker looked at the other two bartenders filling orders. She adjusted her breasts to look as though they would possibly fall out of the tank top, then twisted the center of the shirt up and tucked it through the neckline until every customer could see her flat stomach. She grabbed a tray from the bar top. "Where do you need me?"

"Take the patio."

Parker's lip curled as she glanced over at the patio door slapping shut. Smoke floated in a haze around the door. But she said, "'Kay."

Echo reached over the bar, pulling Parker back. "And stay away from those players."

Parker rolled her eyes. "Oh-kay."

"I know you're the heir to hell and all, but I don't want you getting hurt."

"I'll be safe," she promised.

Parker made her way through the crowd, pausing as the basketball players crossed her path. The one Echo warned her about stopped in her way. The glassy dark eyes of the MVP landed on her tits, then slid down her torso. The long fingers started to reach for Parker, but Kayla's hand guided them away.

"Those tits belong to Echo," Kayla stated.

Parker stared at the painted pained face and read the lie in the angled eyes. As the MVP took a long swig of her beer and scanned the rest of the bar, Kayla pressed herself between Parker and the woman.

"Go before she wants you and your girl gets into a fight," Kayla instructed. "My sister and Echo are friends. The last thing anyone needs is for Sylvia to find out Lexa and Echo were throwing punches at one another."

Stepping behind Kayla, Parker was able to make it to the patio doors. When Parker looked back to make sure Echo wasn't fuming, she found her friend maneuvering between the clusters of customers until she reached Charleigh. Echo offered the teacher her hand and guided her to the dance floor. Parker shook her head, hoping Echo wasn't self-destructing because of all the new stressors.

Parker watched from where she stood as Echo danced against Charleigh. The dark eyes never looked at the blonde pressing against her but followed the MVP to the back of the bar. Smiling, Parker understood what Echo was doing. She chastised herself for not realizing Echo was pulling the same tricks Echo used to protect Parker when she was prey and to piss Xio off after the barback tried to flirt with her all those years ago.

A hand came to rest on the exposed skin of Parker's lower back. She snapped around; her tray ready to bash the person in the face.

Zoe's hazel eyes crinkled at the corners, and Parker noticed the first hints of Zoe growing older. Her fingers itched for a pen and napkin to sketch the two versions of the woman. See if the change was only surface deep.

"What are you doing here?" Parker asked.

Zoe's hand came up to rest on the back of her neck. "I took a chance you'd be here."

Parker raised an eyebrow at her. "Stalking me now?"

"I heard about what happened with Lyra."

Parker sighed. "Really, Zoe?"

With the slightest shrug of her shoulders, Zoe offered a weak smile.

The beat changed, and more people flooded onto the dance floor. Parker saw an escape route forming. She turned to Zoe whose hand was still setting her skin on fire.

"You know every time you show up at my work, I end up getting told I'm nothing but a loser by some bitch who thinks she's better than me."

Parker clutched her tray tighter to her chest as one of the NWBA players made her way towards them. It wasn't the one Echo was worried about, but still a drunk athlete who could break her if the steroid cocktail was even slightly twisted.

"Hey, little Red Hot," the woman said, leaning closer to Parker.

She smiled up at the woman who looked to be older than the rest of her teammates. Squinting her eyes, Parker's mouth dropped open. "Emma?"

The woman's head bobbed, and her smile grew. "I wasn't sure if you would recognize me since our class was all online that year because of the Covey, but I couldn't forget the partner who kept me from blowing a gasket."

Emma held her arms out as she asked, "May I hug the woman who helped me graduate?"

Nodding, Parker allowed her former classmate to pick her up as they hugged. When she had her feet on the ground, Parker put the tray up once more to cover her chest.

"It's good to see you. I totally forgot you played for the Devils."

Emma smiled, then moved so a group of girls could get past her. "Well, I stopped by because I saw your picture on Echo's insta. I was, like, damn, I gotta say hi to the Red Hot but every time I came in you weren't working."

"I only work a couple of nights. I am working at a school actually. Greyson Academy, it's—"

"Oh shit, that's Sylvia's school. I mean, her ex, like, runs it, but my girl owns the place," Emma said, but her attention turned back to her teammates momentarily. When she looked back at Parker, she held out her phone. "Lemme get your number. I got a season or two left in me, but when I'm done, I'm going to open a clinic, and I want you to come work with me."

Glancing towards the bar, Parker found Echo staring her down. She offered her friend a middle finger, then took Emma's phone. She tapped her phone number into a text, then opened the camera.

"Take a photo with me to piss Echo off," Parker said.

Emma didn't hesitate. She lifted Parker up, and Parker wrapped her legs around Emma's waist before the woman held out her hand and took an almost full body shot of them.

"Send that shit to me," Parker said.

"Echo your girl now?" Emma asked. Then followed up with a glance towards Zoe still hovering over Parker's shoulder. "Or is this mean muggin' chick yours?"

Zoe's shoulders rose, but Parker pushed her away. "No girlfriend for me. This idiot is the one we talked about when we had to role play telling off an ex who broke our hearts."

The dark eyes rose to Zoe, and she sucked her teeth.

"And Echo is my sister. She stuck me on the patio because she apparently didn't want me where the money was falling tonight," Parker stated, batting her eyelashes at Emma.

The ball player glanced over at the fake VIP section where her teammates were all posted. Shaking her head, Emma said, "Your sister is smart. Lexa is trashed and spiraling even though her ego was almost too big to fit through the door. Stay away from her because she a playa who don't know how to work her dick."

"Good to know," Parker said.

Emma nodded towards her seats. "I gotta get back to my babysitting duty for Sylvia. It was good to see you." Her eyes ran over Parker's chest, and she nodded once more. "Real good to see you. I'm gonna text you tomorrow, so maybe we can see some more of each other before I ship out to Italy."

Parker could almost hear Zoe about to explode, and when she turned, she saw the rage etched into the woman's eyes.

"She isn't looking to work with you," Zoe stated, her hands flexing by her sides.

Gesturing to the dance floor, Parker said, "There's hundreds of girls better than me here. Go buy one of them a beer and ask her to dance. And stop worrying about people trying to play me. I already got third degree burns from two rich girls, and I'm not stupid enough to walk into the fire again."

The bar was so busy time felt as though it moved faster. There was a hefty number of tips hanging out of Parker's tits, and she didn't stop the women from pressing fingers against her to add more. She'd have enough to buy the car she wanted soon, maybe even move into one of the nice apartments with a pool she wouldn't have to talk to the crackheads through the gate.

Parker made her way with the tray of drinks through the crowds of women still ogling the athletes on the dance floor. Each of the basketball players had a girl on their arm or grinding against their crotch as they swayed to the hip hop music. Parker sighed as she saw Charleigh sandwiched between the MVP and Kayla.

She paused, considering if she should get involved. Charleigh pressed against the toxic woman completely transfixed by the attention she was getting. Parker knew this wasn't a good situation for her co-worker, but she also didn't know the woman well enough to convince her she was in possible danger.

Parker turned to the mostly vacant patio. Only three of the plastic tables and chairs were occupied by small groups of regulars. Smoke hung in a thick haze, trapped between the patio and the covered fence. Parker fought her urge to cough, reminding herself hacking lowered her tips.

Zoe leaned back at a table. She puffed on the vape, smiling at a blonde who'd taken the vacant seat across from her. Parker watched Zoe scanning over the tight space. She tried to ignore the perfectly soft smile spreading to Zoe's eyes when they landed on Parker.

Moving from table to table, Parker delivered drinks, dropped off two credit cards, and took three orders. Having serviced all of the other tables, she forced a broad smile on her face and approached Zoe's table.

"Y'all need another drink?"

The blonde's eyes turned up and widened in recognition. "Michelle! Is that you?"

"Ashley." Parker's fake smile faded into a real grin. "I haven't seen you in forever."

Pushing the weak chair back, Ashley stood. She pulled Parker into a tight hug with a white girl squeal. When she took a step back, the woman asked, "How have you been?"

"Good." Parker tucked the tray under her arm. Sheepishly, she felt the blush creep up her cheeks, "Well, great really. I finished school. I'm a therapist now. I'm here tonight helping my sister, Echo. What about you?"

"Oh, you know. Still at the club. And I've started my own business. I teach people now."

Parker laughed. "That's a thing?"

"Oh my God, yes! Gurl, you have no idea. I host lessons and all these soccer moms pay more than their husbands to learn what we do." Ashley pulled a card from her clutch, handing it to Parker. "If you have any soccer mom friends, send them my way."

"Look at you moving up in the world," Parker said, not sure how to end the conversation as Zoe watched.

Ashley reached over, tucking a lock of red hair behind Parker's ear. "You look beautiful, as always."

Parker felt the blush spread down her neck, and prayed she'd not turned herself into a giant tomato.

Ashley turned when someone called the blonde's name out. Three thin women were gesturing to Ashley to come inside from the doorway.

"I have to go, but it was great to see you." Ashley grabbed the pen from Parker's pocket and took the redhead's hand. On Parker's wrist, the woman wrote her phone number and a little heart. "Save the card for your friends. You call my cell. Maybe we can get dinner, and you can be dessert."

"Okay," Parker said as Ashley left her with Zoe.

Zoe puffed out a series of o's, then set the vape atop the table. She fiddled with the beer as Parker took the open seat across from her.

Parker leaned back until the chair creaked in protest. She still had drinks to fill, but she wanted the chance to see Zoe's full reaction when she said, "Hundreds of lesbians here, and you flirt with the blonde stripper I got under to get over you."

Hazel eyes shot to the doorway Ashley had left through, then back to Parker. Parker's fingers pressed the smirk on her lips to keep the laughter from breaking out.

"Your face is as pale as my ass," Parker said when Zoe's head fell back. She couldn't contain the laughter any longer. She covered her mouth, but it felt good to watch Zoe turn her own shade of pink.

Parker was so lost in her amusement at Zoe's predicament, she almost missed the crash of a table inside. She'd jumped up from the chair, but Zoe's hands collapsed around her arms. They pulled Parker backwards, then pushed her into the corner of the patio fence.

The back of Zoe's body trapped Parker. Chain-link diamonds pressed into Parker's flesh as Zoe kept her in place. The long dark hair tickled her nose while Zoe guarded her from the fight inside. Parker pushed at Zoe and tried to move her, but the taller woman didn't budge. Zoe's hand rested on the side of Parker's thigh, keeping her pinned from squeezing out the only opening.

Sirens screamed their way towards the bar. The lights flashed through the fence, where Zoe kept Parker secured. Parker pushed her again, but Zoe didn't move until uniformed officers walked past the patio doors.

Zoe's eyes scanned over Parker when she finally stepped aside. From inside, Parker heard Echo's voice boom, "You're a fucking rapist!" Zoe flipped around, again holding Parker against the fence when Echo stormed through the patio.

Echo wiped away the blood from the split in her already swollen lower lip. Parker had witnessed Echo's involvement in fights. She'd seen Echo take out a number of tatted teens in juvie, and even more trying to start trouble in her bar. Especially when a few customers got a little handsy with the barmaids. But as her eyes fell on Zoe, Parker saw a new level of rage surface.

"What the fuck are you doing here?!" Echo yelled. The other occupants of the space quickly cleared as Echo stormed toward them. She tossed a plastic chair. The leg splintered and soared through the air.

Parker pushed Zoe out of the way and took over the space between her sister and the assistant district attorney. She held up her hands to stop Echo. The bigger body halted as Parker pressed against Echo's chest, holding her in place.

"What happened to your face?" Parker asked.

Echo's wild eyes turned to Parker, and she gestured inside. "That NWBA rapist just tried to assault your co-worker. I told her to get her hands off her and then she hit me. Then I come out here and that bitch has her hands on you." Echo raised her arm in the air, pointing at Zoe over Parker's shoulder. "You don't get to touch her. You fucking hear me? You don't get to touch her after what you said to her."

"She was trying to protect me," Parker said. "We are not... There's nothing there. We heard the crash, and I swear, she wasn't trying to do anything besides keep me safe."

Echo's arm dropped, but the flush in her cheeks didn't fade. She folded her arms over her chest. Looking Zoe straight in the eyes, Echo barked, "Stay the fuck away from her. Do you fucking hear me?"

Zoe's shoulders straightened, and her head tilted as she studied Echo. Her eyes narrowed when her set mouth parted. "If you're looking for another fight, then I would suggest someone besides a state prosecutor."

"You think I'm scared of you?' Echo snapped. Parker was forced to step back as Echo moved forward. "Oooo, the big shot lawyer that calls women trash. Belittles child rape victims. You ain't shit!"

Parker watched Zoe's face shift from angry to confused, then back to angry. She took a step forward, causing Echo to step up as well. Parker pushed on both their chests, her own bubble crushed as they sandwiched her between them.

"Stop it!" Parker pleaded. "Both of you! Stop it!"

"What's the problem?" The question boomed from the doorway.

Parker focused all her strength on Echo, pushing her friend a few steps back. Echo's defense didn't drop, but Parker felt better when her sister was no longer within arm's reach of Zoe.

Evie stepped out from behind Echo with her hand resting at the neck of her vest. Never in her life did Parker think Evie's presence would make her feel more comfortable, but this time it had.

"Stay away from my sister," Echo warned again, but Parker had had enough.

She reached up with two hands, shoving the only family she had with all her strength. Then she shoved her again. She shoved her a third time, planning to do it until Echo looked at her.

As the dark eyes dropped from over Parker's head, the redhead hissed, "Knock it the fuck off. You're pissed. I get it. You couldn't stop what happened to Charleigh, so you're trying to stop it from happening to me."

Evie whispered behind Parker, "What happened?"

"Nothing," Parker snapped with a side glance. "Nothing happened besides Zoe trying to pick up a new blonde stripper and Echo trying to protect a girl from someone getting handsy."

With a single brow raised, Evie looked at Zoe. "Dude?"

"I wasn't flirting!" Zoe protested. She held her hands up as she explained, "I was just sitting here, waiting to order another drink. She came up to me and asked me to dance. I was polite when I turned her down."

Echo ran her hands through her hair as she exhaled heavily. Her eyes scanned the completely vacant patio besides the four of them. She reached down and picked up the broken chair and the busted off leg. Walking away with the pieces, she left Parker with Zoe and Evie.

Parker turned to Zoe. "You should go. She's going to be closing up for the night."

Zoe reached into her back pocket, pulling her wallet out. She held up the credit card, but Parker shook her head. "I got it."

"I can pay for my beers," Zoe protested.

"No one said you couldn't, asshat," Evie stated with a dramatic eye roll. "She's being nice, so don't be a dick."

"Sorry," Zoe mumbled. She put the plastic card away and pulled out a different card. Waving it in the air, she said, "That's my number. Since you're going to call Emma and may call Ashley back, why not give me a chance?"

With shoulders slumped, Zoe walked past Evie and out of Parker's sight. Parker looked at the handwritten phone number on the bottom of the card. A part of her said throw it away. Another part said call Zoe. Talk to Zoe. Give Zoe a chance, since apparently even the nicest women end up leaving her in the end. At least Zoe was trying, while Lyra hadn't shown up, messaged, or called.

Evie pulled the card from Parker's fingers. She gripped it in her hand against her vest and studied Parker.

"You're thinking about calling her."

Parker picked up one of the toppled chairs and sat down. She rested her elbows on her knees as she held her head. Evie sat across from her.

Glass scraped against the floor inside where Xio swept up the mess. The sound broke up the unspoken words spinning around Parker's head. She felt the ground start to tilt, so she closed her eyes. She only opened them when the handset on Evie's shoulder screamed to life.

Evie twisted a nob on the radio attached to her belt, lowering the volume. Her head tilted, moving her ear closer to the letters and numbers being read off. She didn't respond, and shortly after the dispatcher's voice ended, an older man's voice answered. When the call ended, Evie pressed the button on her handset and said, "Dispatch, 3Paul9."

"3Paul9, go ahead."

"Can show me at Code 7."

"Copy that."

Parker looked at her in confusion. Evie shrugged, "I told them I was taking my lunch."

The quiet didn't have a chance to settle as a loud truck beeped in front of the bar. Echo walked back through the patio doors, a triumphant smile plastered on her tired face and a Coors Lite in her hand. "I'm getting the bitch's car towed." She raised her fist in the air, then pranced around like she was riding a bull.

Evie's eyebrows disappeared into her hairline as her eyes tried to look everywhere but at Echo. She whispered to Parker, "Make it stop."

Parker narrowed her eyes at Echo. "You're talking about the rapist and not the lawyer, right?"

Echo's hand dropped. "Shit. I should have done hers first." The smile gradually returned to Echo's face. "No, I didn't tow your ex's car. I scared her enough with my 'Don't come near my sister again.'"

Parker's eye roll was accompanied by Evie's unfiltered laughter.

The smile on Echo's face dropped. "What are you laughing at?" she demanded.

"She's not scared of you. She's pissed you are trying to run some clitoference, but she's not scared of you," Evie said.

Echo's hands tapped her broad chest. "I'm scary."

Parker's eyebrows scrunched together. She tapped lightly on plastic armrests before saying, "To most people yes, but Zoe's not scared of anything."

With a single finger up, Evie interjected, "I call bullshit. She's terrified of you."

"Me?" Parker shook her head. "No one is scared of me. I mean, look at me." She gestured to her mostly nude torso. "Zoe could bend me in half if she wanted to."

Evie's lips crinkled in disgust. "We don't need to know about what the two of you used to do."

Echo spit her beer out, choking on the drink she was trying to take. She waved at Evie as she regained her breath. Between the coughs, she said, "No. No. You see the quiet innocent little girl over there is all a game."

"What are you talking about?" Parker asked.

Echo stood up to her full height, raising her chin to be parallel with the ground. With a hardened face, she growled, "I'm an alpha bitch!"

Parker's head fell back against the plastic, and she laughed at herself. She didn't correct Echo though. The corners of her mouth pulled up in a slight smile as she remembered hearing people refer to Zoe as the Commander, since she'd given Zoe the name for Parker's own ironic amusement.

"So," Evie said. "Let's talk about this phone number."

Echo took a sip of her beer, looked between the two seated women, and slowly backed her way out of the patio. "Have fun with girl talk," she said before turning to slow motion run back into the bar.

"So," Evie said again.

"What do you want from me?"

"I want to know what you are thinking about this whole Zoe-Lyra situation. We're not even going to talk about who Emma and Ashley are because I know you care about my sister and my friend."

Parker leaned back in the chair. She unraveled the twisted portion of her shirt and pulled it down to cover the front of her body. She started counting at ten, slowly making her way to zero. Each number she said she thought of how everything had suddenly spiraled out of control.

She licked her dry lips and glanced at the still mostly full beer on the table. Resisting the urge to take a drink of the previously owned bottle, she looked at Evie.

"Lyra broke down all of my defenses. She didn't waiver when she found out I was a stripper. She didn't make me feel less than her. She just chipped away at all the things I told myself made me not good enough, and as she learned more about me, she wanted me more."

"You felt safe," Evie contributed.

A tear broke free when she nodded. She quickly wiped it away, praying the rest would stay put.

"She told me—"

The tears fell, despite her prayers.

She started again, "She told me we had to flush the baggage together. But she didn't."

Parker wiped the tears with the back of her hand.

"She didn't flush hers and when shit hit the fan, I couldn't support her because she just locked me out. She locked me out of her life. Took back the safety she'd promised. She closed the door of your mother's house in my face, and it was like I was standing in that parking lot all over again."

She tried to swallow the pain.

Stifle the tears.

Stop feeling.

"The girl. The family. The not being alone anymore," she cried. "Gone."

She wiped her hands up and down her face. Her fingers came back covered in pitch colored eyeliner.

Parker whispered, "Every time I think I have a chance of being a part of a family, it's just gone."

When Parker looked up from the ground, she watched Evie staring at Zoe's card. She spun it between her fingers, before holding it out to Parker. When Parker went to take it from her, Evie pulled it back just enough Parker would have to get up to take it from her.

"One, the door to the Greyson-Trikru house is always open. Literally always unlocked and open. Lyra or no Lyra, you can at any point in time walk through the door, raid the pantry, sleep on the couch, really anything. I wouldn't walk into my parents' bedroom of nightmares, but you get the point."

Evie held the card again but pulled it back once more.

"Two, Lyra and my mom are the nicest people alive, but when something breaks them... it's bad. So bad. They snap, and they say mean shit, and they mean that mean shit. But it doesn't mean they don't love you. Lyra does love you; however, right now she has to figure out how not to hate herself."

When she held the card out for the third time, she didn't pull it back because Parker didn't reach for it. With a flick of her wrist, she shot the card at Parker, striking the redhead in the boob with the sharp corner.

"Three, you should call Zoe. You should let her try to get you back, because she broke your heart; and I bet you have always wondered what could have been if you'd just told her everything. If she'd known, would she'd have been more careful with your heart. If you could fit in her world."

Parker went to wipe her face again but stopped when she saw the streaked boogers over the back of her hand. Instead, she let the tears fall as she stared at the tin awning above them.

"Mom says the answers aren't in the sky," Evie said. "I should know, I have searched for them over and over again."

Parker looked at Evie and found her staring back at her. "We should write the answers up there."

Evie quirked her eyebrow. "What answers?"

With a shrug of her shoulders, Parker answered, "All of them."

"Like, the answer is not in the darkness but in the moment?" Evie offered.

"Perfect," Parker said, pushing whether or not to call Zoe out of her mind. She got up from the chair and moved to the doorway. She looked around until she found Echo, Xio, and one of the bartenders sitting at the high tops in front of the dart boards.

She called out, "Hey Echo, can I use your ladder?"

"What for?" Echo asked. "And what the fuck is wrong with your face?"

Parker wiped her face with her hands roughly, hoping to dislodge the tear tracks from her skin. Then she said, "Need to write the answers to life's secrets on your patio ceiling."

When Echo's forehead crease deepened, Parker lowered her chin and looked up at Echo with her wide eyes. She forced an innocent smile on her face. "Please," she said, and jutted her lower lip out.

Echo stared at her for what felt like a full minute, then got up from the stool. She retrieved a tall ladder from a room behind the bar. As the large woman made her way over, she stopped at the bar and grabbed a handful of black Sharpies. Xio and the bartender followed Echo to where Parker and Evie waited.

With the ladder set up in the middle of the room, Parker handed Evie a marker and told her, "Write it."

Evie maneuvered up the ladder while Echo and Parker held it steady. In careful cursive, she wrote her truth. When she was finished, she handed the marker to Echo.

Echo moved the ladder to a different area. In bold block letters, she wrote, "Hatred is only heavy for the holder."

Xio and the bartender took their turns, picking a place on the ceiling at some point they'd stared at for answers. Xio wrote, "Today is the first day of the rest of your life," while the bartender contributed, "Coming out is just a moment, the ones that follow are the ones you'll remember more."

Parker twirled the marker between her fingers. Each of their words hit her differently. She stared at the ceiling of the blank space, where the bartenders had moved the ladder for her. She tapped her finger to her lips as she waited for the ceiling to tell her what to write.

She nodded when she knew what it needed to say and carefully stepped up the ladder. Placing the marker between her teeth, she climbed. The metal creaked as the legs wobbled momentarily. She held on tightly as she straddled the top. Echo and one of the other women steadied the ladder, allowing her to reach up to the awning.

In careful print, Parker wrote, "No matter what beliefs you hold about an afterlife, this is one opportunity to live this life as you."

Parker didn't know who she was as she took each shaky step down the ladder. Didn't know why those were the words she'd chosen. Didn't know how they would help her decide what to do about Zoe and Lyra.

But they felt right.

37

'Meet me at the top of terminal 4 parking garage in 30 -P'

Zoe reread the text four times, once for each of the days that had gone by since she'd left Parker at the bar. After day two, she didn't expect to hear from the other woman. But her lowered expectations didn't stop her from checking to make sure the volume was up on the ringer and the internet connection was working.

She put the Xbox controller down, and stood up, staring at the message once more. Three dots appeared on the screen, then disappeared. Parker was texting her again. She waited as the three dots appeared again.

'Your messages are set to read'

'So I know you got this.'

'Don't leave me hanging.'

Zoe swallowed her nerves, and typed back, 'See you soon.' Then, 'Thank you'.

She waited to see if Parker also had her messages on 'read', but the 'delivered', never changed. She looked down at the tank top and baggy sweats she'd been wearing since Thursday night. On one leg the pizza sauce was beginning to peel off. Lifting her arm, she did a quick smell test, which was a mistake.

Dropping the phone, she raced to the bathroom. Ten minutes wasn't even long enough to do something with her hair, let alone pick out an outfit that said: I'm the one.

With the short timeline, she was barely able to take a whore bath, pull on a clean pair of baggy jeans and cut off shirt, and run down the stairwell to her car.

She arrived ahead of time, thanks to the I-10 for once being open to full capacity on a weekend. As she made the last turn to the top of the airport parking garage, she saw Parker already waiting for her.

Zoe's fingers shook as she put the car into park. Her stomach twisted into a knot. Even though she'd practically begged Parker to call her, the idea of seeing her on Parker's terms became suddenly terrifying.

The redhead didn't turn from the landing planes when Zoe approached her. Zoe noticed how the woman's knuckles were white from her grip on the railing.

"You came," Parker said on the roar of the plane passed them.

"I told you I would."

A large plane touched the ground causing the air around them to whip Parker's hair in a crazy frenzy around her head. Zoe appreciated the magic of the moment, remembering how she used to think Parker sparkled because she'd been made for Zoe to find.

"Why'd you come to the bar?" Parker asked, still studying the tarmac.

Zoe leaned against the railing. "I told you I went to see you."

Parker turned, her hand still holding the railing but her whole-body facing Zoe. Her bralette hung out of the cut off shirt draping over her like a dress, which made the lawyer less self-conscious of her lack of time to properly get ready.

"Why, Zoe? Why did you come to see me? Why keep coming to see when you threw me away like I was nothing? Because not a lot has changed. I'm still using my body to make money, and I still don't trust anyone enough to tell them anything about me." Parker managed to get all of her sentences out before another plane touched the ground.

Again, the wind ripped around them. Red locks danced around her head as though to illustrate Parker's point. The plane passing them gave her time to think. Every three minutes she'd have a minute to consider what she would say since Parker hadn't given her notice to script out her opening statement or find evidence to present. It wasn't enough time though.

"Because..." Zoe huffed out a heavy breath as she pulled at the back of her neck again. "Because I wanted to talk to you. I wanted to apologize—"

Parker's shoulders slumped and she shook her head. "We already played this game. We did the apologies, and the secrets were revealed. If you just want to apologize, then it's happened. It's done. You need me to tell you I forgive you?" Parker raised her hand in the air and made the sign of the cross. "I absolve you of your sins. There the game is over. You win."

Zoe waited for another plane to land. She imagined it was coming from Ireland. Pictured Parker holding her hand as the plane brought them home from their latest adventure. When the air settled momentarily, she said, "I heard Lyra and you broke up. I saw you. I saw you and Lyra on your first date, and it was because I was too late because I was stubborn and stupid. And I didn't want to lose another chance, which was wise since that night two women literally gave you their numbers."

"So, you went to see me to be the rebound. To get a redo."

"I'm not who I used to be."

"But I'll never forget, Zoe. Never."

Parker turned back to the runway as a plane cut off all conversation. Zoe watched the way she stared into the distance. The way her hands gripped, released, and regripped the railing. Zoe wondered if Parker was imagining ringing Zoe's neck.

"Why can't you just leave me alone?" Parker whispered.

"You never said to leave you alone," Zoe stated. "You just keep asking why. And I think it means you do want to give me a chance to prove to you I'm different. Because I can be the woman you fell in love with all those years ago."

Parker looked Zoe dead in the eye. "You're not the woman I fell in love with all those years ago. That woman didn't actually exist then, and she still doesn't exist today."

Parker gestured up and down Zoe's body. "You're still the same self-absorbed asshole you were then. That whole spiel was about you. You wanting the girl I used to be. The one that was awestruck by you and your perfect life."

Holding her hands in the air, Parker cried out, "I'm not her!"

A plane engine silenced her as it rushed by them. They both stared at the ground, waiting for another imaginary dream vacation to end.

"No where did you say you loved me." Parker sighed. "That you wanted me."

"Look, Parker—"

"No, you look, Zoe—"

But Zoe was done looking at Parker trying to run. She was done letting the woman push her away. She closed the distance between them and collapsed her lips against Parker's. Her arms wrapped around the thin waist, pulling their bodies together.

When Parker's lips parted, Zoe deepened the kiss. Their mouths pushing against each other, then Zoe's teeth pulled Parker's lower lip closer. Only releasing it when Parker moaned softly. She soothed the bite with her tongue until Parker's tongue joined hers in a dance to the familiar beating of their hearts. They kissed through two planes landing. A kiss that could have mended things years ago, if only one of them had taken the chance.

As they separated for air, Zoe pressed her lips to Parker's head. Her arms tightened around the woman she felt was hers once more.

Parker's fingers tapped Zoe's clavicle. Traced the protruding bone, until it rested on the toned bicep. Pulling back, Parker looked at Zoe. She licked her kiss swollen lips, then bit down.

"I love you," Zoe whispered.

Parker pushed the rest of the way out of Zoe's embrace.

"I wish I could believe that," Parker said.

Zoe held Parker's hand for as long as she could until the space between them grew too great.

"You and me; we're bleach and ammonia. We're toxic together. I remind you you're not perfect. You remind me I'm disposable."

Zoe felt the plane landing in her whole body as she tried to process how their kiss turned into Parker telling her how she felt. She looked over at the woman walking away.

Calling out over the roar of the plane, Zoe asked, "Why couldn't you have said that over the phone?!"

Parker stopped. She stopped where she stood but she didn't turn around.

It was a chance Zoe couldn't give up. She closed the distance. Her arm pulling Parker back to her, being the commander Parker had always joked she wasn't.

She put her lips just past Parker's ear. "You're not over me. You came out here because you still want me."

Under her hand, Zoe felt Parker's breathing stutter. The redhead wrapped her fingers around Zoe's fingers.

Zoe pressed a kiss to Parker's temple, whispering again, "I have made so many mistakes in my life. I have done many hurtful things. The worst choice I ever made though, was hurting you. Was thinking any part of my life could be better without you. We could have an amazing life together."

She pointed at the plane landing like they'd used to do when they came up here at the end of their dates. "Where's that one coming from? Where did we just go visit?"

"You went—"

Zoe whispered, "Not me, we. Us."

Parker pulled Zoe's hand from around her middle. She turned to Zoe only when she was out of the lawyer's reach.

"I came here to give you a chance." She shook her head. "If you'd said those words... asked that question... put me in a world with you, instead of the past. Maybe... Fuck, probably..."

Backing up to the car, Parker rested her hand against the chipped paint. She looked over her shoulder. "I would have been thinking about flying away with you if you had started that way. I wouldn't have been thinking about Lyra while you kissed me. I wouldn't have been thinking about how I need to get out of here and fix things."

Parker opened the door to the car. Her finger ran along the open window. "We're push and pull but never settle. I don't want to be pushed and pulled. I want peace. I found peace with Lyra. We're good together."

Zoe's eyes hardened. She tried to fix the crack in her heart with another layer of superglue. She felt the poison bubble, turning into a gas coating the words falling from her bitter mouth.

"She won't want you if she finds out we kissed."

Parker's fingers tapped on the car door. She licked the rest of Zoe's kiss from her lips, then shrugged. "If that's the truth, then it is what it is."

The car started even though Zoe willed the battery to die. Begged it to stop the woman from leaving her again. But the reverse lights worked with ease, and then shifted into drive without an issue.

Zoe searched for Parker's eyes to find her in the rearview mirror as she drove away from the second chance. But the brown eyes never looked back. She left Zoe with the same words ricocheting off each memory and hopeful dream her tortured mind could locate.

38

One of the lightbulbs in Echo's master bathroom flickered before going out. Echo rummaged through the shoe box, pulling out the match to the earring Parker had already fixed to one ear.

Parker pressed the retrieved diamond stud through the bottom hole in her ear lobe. She dropped the back as she fumbled with it on the dressing table.

"Are you sure you want to go?" Echo asked, bending down to retrieve it once more.

Scraping her fingers against her scalp to get the hair out of her face, Parker said, "I have to. Everyone from work is going. Plus, it's my chance to see her."

Parker jumped when a shadow moved in her periphery. "Shit. You scared me, Olivia."

The girl blinked several times, frozen in place.

Parker instantly felt her stomach tighten in knots at Olivia's frozen position. "Sorry. I'm just... nervous."

Olivia softly said, "You look really pretty." Then she handed an iPad to Echo.

"How did it go with your grandparents?" Echo asked, fixing the back of the earring for Parker.

Parker watched in the mirror as Olivia pressed herself against the closet door. She cataloged the detail as something she still needed to address at their next session.

"They said they spoke with you about coming to visit over Thanksgiving," Olivia said. "They said they are getting a hotel, and they want to go shopping."

Echo nodded. "Yeah, we are going to work out the details."

The teen's eyes were locked on the floor. Her thumbs rubbed against her fingertips back and forth before she asked, "I don't have to go with them, right?"

"Correct. They are coming to visit and that is it. You are staying here with us."

Moving towards Olivia, Echo held open her arms but did not embrace the teen. She stood, waiting for the girl to decide if she wanted a hug.

Olivia stepped into Echo's arms. She didn't reciprocate the embrace, but she let Echo wrap her long arms around her. Echo said, "Thank you," then released the girl.

Parker smiled and watched Olivia retreat around the corner. The door down the hallway closed quietly, and Henrie could be heard babbling with the babysitter on the first story of the house.

Turning from the mirror, Parker closed the distance between Echo and herself. She smoothed the corners of Echo's shirt collar, then straightened the black and silver tie she'd picked up for Echo. It was something Parker knew she wanted to wear, but Simone would be less than thrilled with. She wanted Echo to have it though, in hopes she could get the baseball cap off the woman's head with little fight. As Echo dipped her chin to look at the tie in place, Parker tore the cap from the woman's head and held it behind her back.

"You're not wearing this to a black-tie party."

Echo reached her arms all the way around Parker, trapping her against the closet door. There was no real way for Parker to keep the faded purple from the other woman who grabbed the cap and shoved it back on her head.

With a grunt, Echo turned her attention back to the mirror. She pushed her hair back, as she carefully placed it on her head. She growled, "You're not my wife," when she turned back to Parker with the hat sitting just as it had every other day.

"Should I call her up here and ask her opinion on it?" Parker challenged, even though she wouldn't. She just wanted to know why Echo wouldn't take it off. "Or is there a reason you're still supporting the Phoenix Devils after one of them busted up your bar?"

"I just need it, okay?" Echo looked in the mirror once more "There's just a lot of change, and this doesn't have to change. I don't think anyone would even recognize me if I wasn't wearing it."

Parker hummed, and decided one day she would get the story behind Echo's refusal to take off the ancient NWBA championship hat. Especially since the woman hated NWBA players even more once Sylvia Winters came to pay for the damages to Echo's bar.

"Olivia said she thinks she wants to change her name to something like Spruce or Willow," Echo said, changing the subject. "The girl loves trees."

"How do you feel about it?"

"I mean, I want her to change her name, but can't she come up with something a little more cool. Like, I always thought I would name my kid, like, Elliot or Gemma or—"

"You should tell her she should call herself Parker," Parker interjected. "Henry got a namesake, but I'm the coolest cellmate so naturally a cool kid like her would want to be named after the coolest person you know."

Echo's eyes rolled, and she shook her head. "Not gonna happen."

"Rude."

"What kinda mom would I be if I told her what her name had to be?"

"You've always been a great mom."

The corners of Echo's lips curled up ever so slightly. "Thanks."

Stepping back, Parker turned slowly. The tightly fitted black dress glittered subtly in the remaining bathroom light. "So, does this dress say I want you back?"

"I don't know if it says I want you back." Echo's eyebrows rose as her lips squished into a ridiculous looking duck face. "But it definitely says I want you to dick me down atop a table and fuck up your sister's night."

Parker turned back to the mirror. Pressing the dress against her ass, she twisted just enough to check she had no panty lines showing. Then, she adjusted each breast until a little more cleavage squeezed out from the top.

"Well, that will work too."

She counted on her fingers, and a smile spread over her face. If Lyra spoke to her tonight, it would be date three. The other times they'd gotten together had still not ended the teasing as something always came up, causing them to call it short. She would make sure the woman understood she was all in by going on an all-night marathon between Lyra's thighs.

The elevator music rolled along the path lined with twinkly white lights around the Greyson family home. White linen cocktail tables were already filled with her coworkers and other people she'd seen at Echo and Simone's parties. Parker paused between the familiarity of her current position and the warmth of possibility.

A soft breeze fluffed her curls and tickled the skin on her arms. Goosebumps spread over the flesh as a shiver ran down her back. Parker traced the shadow line just before her toes. Everyone who mattered was on the other side.

She glanced down at the shimmering dress, pulling the length to a more respectable position.

Heels clicked along the pathway behind her. Parker turned in time to see Zoe lose her footing and catch herself on the bush.

"Shit," the lawyer hissed.

Parker put her hand to her lips to muffle the escaping laughter.

Zoe fixed her footing and adjusted the emerald tie at her throat. She fiddled with the clip as she mumbled under her breath. When Zoe looked up, she clutched her chest.

"You scared the shit out of me."

Taking in the full suit with heels, Parker smiled. "You look good in a suit, Ms. Asst. District Attorney."

Zoe took another step, but the same heel twisted on an uneven brick. Parker caught Zoe's flailing arm.

"When are you going to give up on Jimmy Choo's?" Parker asked.

"Never," Zoe growled. Straightening herself again, Zoe held out an arm to Parker. "May I walk you in?"

Parker glanced over her shoulder at the backs of people all facing the dance floor. The voices and music had silenced, only to be reawakened with a rolling roar of laughter from the crowd surrounding the voice of Dilynn Greyson.

"I'm sorry but it wouldn't look right."

Parker's gaze paused momentarily on the hurt in Zoe's eyes looking her up and down. She offered her ex an apologetic smile, then moved into the space of people who mattered. Her eyes scanned the backs of hes, shes, and thems moving away from the dance floor.

Evie was the easiest to find in the crowd. Her gravelly voice scraped over the now resumed music. Parker watched Evie try to get Lyra's attention as she limped off the dance floor to the bar.

When Parker moved towards Lyra, she noticed the gift table. She tightened her grip around the strings of the gift bag, imagining the look on Evie's face when she opened the nipple tassels, fishnet stockings, and two passes to Ashley's pole dancing classes. Parker set the gift down on the table with the attendant before she made her way around the dance floor.

When she passed, Charleigh Marshall waved quietly from a table wrapped in a cardigan that looked to be borrowed from Dilynn Greyson's own closet. The tiny blonde stood almost as tall as the table she shared with Echo and Simone. Then Evie caught her hand and pulled her onto the dance floor for a brief moment before she became distracted by someone else, she found more interesting.

Just as Parker's feet made it to the grass, her path was blocked by her blonde boss. "You've been avoiding me."

Parker nodded, "I was."

"Was is past tense. Does that mean you are no longer avoiding me?" Dilynn demanded.

Parker smiled, glancing over Dilynn's shoulder to ensure Lyra hadn't moved. She snapped back to Dilynn once she realized Dilynn was waiting for a response. "I... I don't... I mean, I'm not avoiding you anymore. I just... there was something I needed to deal with."

"Evie said you saw your mom."

Parker's head fell back. She didn't even bother to school the frustrated sigh leaving her body. "Of course, she did."

Dilynn laughed, "The kid doesn't keep secrets and I think you can understand why."

"Yeah."

"I was worried you wouldn't come."

Parker bit her lip. "Honestly, I almost didn't. I had to sort through some traumas. But I've made some important decisions."

Dilynn's brows cinched in the middle. "You're not leaving, are you?"

"No," Parker said with a soft chortle. "But I really do think you need to talk to someone about that."

Swatting away the words, Dilynn rolled her eyes. "Hire a therapist Alex said.

Fan-fucking-tastic idea that was." A smile spread to Dilynn's eyes though. "It was the best idea honestly."

Parker released the breath she didn't know she'd been holding.

"Tell me about these important decisions," Dilynn commanded, locking her arm around Parker's as she led her to a small table. She flagged down a server, handing Parker a glass of white wine and getting one for herself.

Parker checked to make sure she didn't lose track of Lyra, then decided talking to Dilynn would be the fastest way to move on with her plan.

"So, I, uh... I actually enrolled in a teaching program. It will take two years, but it will get me certified and next semester I could teach a class on how to paint. I was planning on coming in to talk about it next week because I have to have a certified teacher oversee my internship—"

Dilynn clapped her hands together and bounced softly on her toes. "Say no more. I would happily do it."

Folding her arms over her chest, Parker said, "Actually, I was hoping Alex would agree to be my mentor."

Dilynn's eyes fell from Parker's face to her dress, but the smile remained plastered on. Parker glanced down, regretting the extra cleavage now Dilynn was close enough to be practically eye level with her breasts.

"It's not that I don't... you know... I like working with you," Parker stammered.

"Don't apologize," Dilynn huffed out. "You and Alex really bonded that night. And I know I'm just insecure about not being the favorite. I mean, I'm always the favorite. But the things you said really resonated with them, and I'm pretty sure the conversation will end up having a very positive outcome for not only our relationship but the girls as well."

Dilynn rubbed her hands over the goosebumps spreading over Parker's exposed arms. "We should have been seeing a counselor a long time ago, and it's a good thing."

"Uh... good," Parker said.

The smile returned to the ocean eyes. Dilynn squeezed Parker's arm lightly. "I'm glad you came. I was worried you wouldn't feel like you were welcome."

"Pretty accurate," Parker said. She glanced over Dilynn's head to find Lyra still leaning against the bar with her back to the party. "I'm actually here to do what I should have done instead of pulling away. Actually, let's start here."

Parker's arms wrapped around Dilynn. She held on tightly as her angles and sharp edges were met with the soft body of a mother who knew what it felt like to love someone. Parker bit into her lip, willing the tears away.

Dilynn didn't release Parker until the younger woman began to shift back. With a smile, Dilynn took two steps with Parker towards the bar. The bodies shifted leaving a clear path to the onyx waves cascading across Lyra's slumped form.

Leaning in close, Dilynn whispered, "Take care with her heart and she'll take care with yours."

Parker squeezed Dilynn's hand once more. "Thank you."

The old-fashioned stool next to Lyra creaked when Parker turned on it. She didn't look at the woman she wished to woo, just said, "Oh, they have Cold Snack. I heard that was a good one."

The bartender smiled, pulling the tap. The amber colored liquid filled the glass as the foam gathered along the top. With a light sip, she hummed in approval.

"I love when I try something new and its truly amazing, don't you?" Parker asked without turning.

Lyra picked a piece of lint from the sleeve of her dress shirt. "Doing something new is like a gateway to doing other things new. Sounds kind of dangerous to me."

Parker felt the smile grow on her face. Turning her body just enough to use her dress to her advantage, she waited for Lyra to look up. She watched as the chocolate eyes fixated on her chest before shaking her head.

Pleased with Lyra's response, Parker said, "Someone once told me talking to a beautiful woman at a bar could be deemed a dangerous act."

Lyra's lip curled in a smile as she sipped her own drink. "I would have to agree. Women are terrifying and complicated. I should know, I am one."

Tilting the glass so the bubbles within changed direction, Parker realized her plan was short lived. She'd gotten Lyra to notice her and speak to her, but her mind was now rolling the credits of their happily ever after that seemed like fiction.

"I didn't think you'd come," Lyra stated.

"Your mom said the same thing."

Lyra turned in her stool. Her thin back leaned against the bar as she watched the dance floor. "I didn't think you'd come back. I thought... I shouldn't have—"

Parker ran her finger over the top of the glass. "I wanted to respect your wishes. I wanted you to know you could say what you needed, and I would give you what you need."

"I didn't know what I needed. I thought I did. I thought telling you to go would help me move forward, but I haven't moved," Lyra confessed.

"What do you mean when you say you haven't moved," Parker probed.

Lyra's throat bobbed as she drained half of the liquid in her glass. She chugged silently, and Parker watched the world moving around them.

Setting the glass back on the bar, Lyra met Parker's eyes. "I honestly don't know what I expected to happen. But it's been weeks. Weeks of staring at the stupid heart next to your name in my phone. Weeks of my mother whining you won't talk to her. Weeks of waiting for Zoe to show up at pizza night with you by her side."

"There's nothing between Zoe and me," Parker promised.

"She's in love with you." Lyra rubbed her face. "And Evie said Zoe tried to kiss you, but you left her on top of an airport parking garage. I couldn't just call you to verify, but I was angry. This time not with you. I was angry with me. I know she only got a chance to kiss you because I told you to leave when I shoulda asked you to stay."

Parker followed Lyra's eyes to the hazel eyes constantly glancing in their direction. Zoe tried to appear uninterested, but her subtlety was on par with her ability to walk in heels. Especially when Lyra's little sister stood by clearly trying to make conversation with Zoe.

She pressed her shoulders back and lifted her chin up. Her muscles strained under her skin as she braced herself for the answer she needed.

"Why do you care if she loves me?"

Lyra's hands rubbed at her face. With a heavy sigh, she said, "Because she's everything I'm not."

Parker watched as Zoe's mother pushed Zoe towards a woman with an outstretched hand.

"We both know Zoe is all the things you are not. Self-absorbed. Possessive. Entitled. Honestly, I think we both were infatuated by her because she had one thing we both wished for."

"And what's that?"

"Confidence."

"I'm confident." Lyra's shoulders raised as she sat up on the stool. The metal of her brace clicked as it bent in tune with the protest from Parker's stool.

Lyra's eyes rested on Parker's bust spilling from the front of the dress. She swallowed. "You look—"

"Like she wants your dick," Echo said. She plopped down in the stool Parker had vacated.

Blood rushed up Parker's chest to her face. Freckles peaked out from under the foundation, she'd layered on. She searched for a smooth quip, but the searching took time, which defeated the purpose of a quip, and she was left with, "Fucker!" bursting from her lips.

Echo ordered a Coors Lite with a lime as she danced on the stool. She tapped the table, then glanced over her shoulder at them.

"You two have been over here too long staring at your mutual ex."

"We weren't—" Parker started.

"— staring the whole time," Lyra finished.

Placing a hand on Lyra's knee, Parker searched the crowd.

"What are you looking for?" Lyra asked.

Parker shot her hand up and waved Simone over. "Simone. She must not realize Echo is running around off leash."

"Okay, Princess." Echo choked though. Holding up her hands in surrender, she gave a subtle bow, "Sorry. I meant Alpha Queen."

Lyra's eyebrow rose at Parker.

"I said it one time to scare off a bully from picking on you!" Parker cried out. She lunged at Echo, but her body was stopped short with Lyra's arms pulling her backwards. Red lips spread into a smile as Lyra pulled Parker between her legs. Leaning forward, Lyra whispered, "You know if you have to say you're an alpha, you're definitely not an alpha."

Head back, Parker searched for a single star to wish this moment away. She mapped the path of a light flashing from the bottom of an airplane.

"Yes, I know," Parker whined. "I know, okay? I am probably a fucking omega, but omegas can be badass."

Lyra's hands rested on Parker's hips, holding her in place. Her thumbs traced circles over Parker's bone.

Parker lowered her chin and found her eyes at equal height to Lyra's. Stepping further into Parker's space, Lyra rested her forehead against Parker's. They breathed in together. Exhaling warm air in the space between each other.

"This feels dangerous," Parker whispered.

"Dangerous is kind of harsh. Let's go with adventurous," Lyra offered with a broad smile.

As the older guests performed their long-lost high school dance routines in a large circle to the pop hits of the early 2000s, Lyra and Parker swayed from side to side. Lyra twisted her arm, sending Parker back then pulling her close enough to land an elbow in Lyra's gut. Holding her stomach, Lyra coughed out curse words.

Only when Lyra was able to breathe again did they resume a classic middle school slow dance. Parker leaned her head against Lyra's chest as they moved in a slow circle.

The group on the dance floor split down the middle, revealing Dilynn facing off to Alex in a poorly choreographed dance battle. Through the division, Parker caught Zoe's stare.

She held it just long enough for Zoe to bow her head. Then each turned away from the other, unraveling the knot they tied around the other.

"So, about this you're an alph—"

"If you want to see what I have on under this dress, you won't finish ffethat sentence."

"Okay, I just—"

Parker pressed a finger to Lyra's lips, then replaced it with her own lips.

"But I think we need to address I am definitely more—" With a raise of Parker's eyebrow, Lyra stopped talking.

They moved in a slow circle. Occasionally, they stopped to smile and greet whoever wished them well. They turned quickly when Evie and Landon moved alongside them, just long enough for Evie to tell them it was about time they stopped being stupid.

After two songs, Parker guided Lyra back to the bar. They ordered another round of beers, holding their pinkies together like a promise to take this adventure together.

"One was Pizza Bianco. Two was dancing at Echo's," Parker said. She leaned in close to Lyra's lips. "This is three."

Lyra's eyebrows scrunched together. "Three?"

"Three dates," Parker whispered while pressing herself against Lyra. "And you said after three dates, I could," her finger just slightly grazed Lyra's breast, "invite you to not sleep at my house."

"See," Echo said, walking by with her beer. "I told you she wants your dick."

There wasn't a chance to hit her sister. Her hand was taken, and the party and fresh beers were abandoned as they slipped through the crowd. Parker's car was left down the street from the Greyson-Trikru house when Lyra pulled Parker to her own truck, parked right out front.

Parker reached for the door but was shoved back. Confused, her head snapped to the woman now holding her gut laughing.

With a hand in the air, Lyra laughed out, "Sorry. I was going to... I was... open the door for you. But you were—"

"You shoved me!" Parker hissed.

Lyra pushed the button on the handle and jerked the door open. "I was trying to be romantic."

"I'm not a freak like your parents," Parker stated, folding her arms over her chest. "Pushing me around isn't going to get me wet."

"I promise to get you good and wet," Lyra whispered, pulling Parker back into her arms.

With their bodies flush together, Lyra pulled at a necklace hidden within her partially buttoned up shirt. A quarter dangled from the silver chain, and Lyra smiled. She pulled it over her head and placed it on Parker.

"For finding me when I thought I was lost," Lyra offered.

39

Monday morning came quicker than Zoe could handle. For the first time since taking the job as a prosecutor, she had to drag herself to the office. Once there, she went about the room, collecting the photos of Gibson's house and putting away Olivia's mugshot. When Zoe placed the last file on Vincent Gibson in the white box, she closed the case with its lid, praying she'd trapped the nightmare of Gibson within.

She rested her arms on the box and stared out the window. When she caught sight of the plane descending to the airport, she held her breath and made a wish one day she'd fly away from here.

The door to her office slammed open. Zoe jumped up and around to find Nia scowling at her. The woman looked her head to toe and stopped at Zoe's naked toes peeking out from the suit trousers.

Tisking in disapproval, Nia walked to Zoe's desk and slapped a folder on it. "Here's the next one," she said.

Zoe made her way over to the desk and plopped down in her chair. She picked up the dense file and looked at Nia. Her eyebrows furrowed in the center. "I'm just about to start trial for the trafficking case."

"And?" Nia said dismissively.

Zoe looked at the file again. "Isn't there someone else who could—"

Nia cut her off. "No. It's yours."

"Why?" Zoe asked. "You never assign a case to someone just starting a trial.

"Top priority. All over the news," Nia said. She turned to leave but stopped. With her back still to Zoe, she said, "Perfect case for your career."

Zoe watched the spiteful woman leave. Listened as the other lawyers silenced their conversations and shuffled out of Nia's way. Zoe huffed at the still open door but turned her attention back to the file.

The first page had a photograph paperclipped to it. A stumpy dark-haired woman stared back up at Zoe. She'd barely made it through the basic information on page one when a legal aid stomped into her office with a new box of nightmares. She nodded to the young man as he left. Before she could return to the file though, several other legal aides paraded through her office, setting five boxes in a line on the floor, then four more boxes on top of the first row. The last legal aid shut the door behind himself as he left.

Eyes wide, Zoe went back to the file. She flipped through the pages, scanning each to get an overall feel for the case.

Rosie Rodriguez was in custody for murdering six men. The only link between the men was their participation on a local radio program called "Second Date Update." She searched the evidence logs, and found no weapon, no DNA matching, no video. Nothing beyond circumstantial and a questionable confession.

Zoe sighed. "Well at least this one speaks."

She took notes as she read the confession a second time.

- She murdered them to stop them from hurting the girls that the radio station called for the men.
- Claims she had to protect them.
- States she disposed of the weapons after leaving each crime scene.

Zoe picked up the file again. Photos dropped from within. Glancing down, she counted the six different bloody faces. Six new tormentors.

Moving about the office she began taping them to her board. Learned the first murder scene, then constructed the second on the floor of her office. She didn't have enough space here, so she'd take them all home at the end of the night. Spend her evening alone learning each victim in detail. Walking through the scenes as she stared at the blood-soaked bodies.

Checking her watch, she realized Evie would be there in an hour. They would go over the testimony for Caliscpo's trial set next week.

With time to spare, she studied each of the photos for the first murder once more. Held up the woman accused of murdering them next to the bloody remains. Leaning back in her chair, she closed her eyes.

She sits in the backseat of the car where Michael Wells is tapping against the steering wheel. The Lift logo is stickered to his windshield. He waits outside of an apartment complex. The details of the complex are lost in the darkness of the night. Wells rolls down the window and calls to a woman standing alone outside the building.

"Hey are you, Rosie?"

She doesn't smile, but nods.

"Cool. I'm Mike, your driver."

Rosie slides into the car. Her imaginary body glides straight through Zoe. The driver doesn't talk. Zoe watches Rosie fiddle with the taser in her hand. She's never done anything like this before, and she's second guessing her plan.

The car stops outside the Harkin's movie theater. Before Wells can turn around or say a word, Rosie pushed the taser to the back of his neck and pressed the button. This was not where she would kill him. She clicks the buttons on the phone completing the ride. Giving herself an alibi.

Zoe watches as Rosie gets out of the car into the dark parking lot. She pulls the driver side door open and lugs Wells from his seat. He's on the ground, but too heavy for Rosie to move him much more without drawing attention to herself.

She pulls out a box cutter from her pocket, and quickly slices him across the neck. Blood spurts from the wound, and Zoe closes her eyes.

She gives herself a moment to adjust to reality. The photo in her hand is relatively close to what she pictured. Looking over the notes from Rosie's confession, Zoe stopped. She stopped the routine she was so fond of.

Putting the image of the bloody body away, she looked at the woman's cold brown eyes. Searched her face for the answer to the most important question.

"Why did you think you needed to protect those women?"

"No one probably protected whoever you're talking to," came from the doorway. Zoe jumped, holding her chest as Sadie Greyson-Trikru walked into her office.

A brown paper bag with a smiley face drawn in black Sharpie over the Chipotle logo swung between a claw-like grip. The sack was raised, then the bag dropped on the other side of the computer monitor. Sadie gave her a tight-lipped smile and pushed a pair of large-framed glasses up her nose.

"Dinner for two." Sadie pointed to the bag. "Kids tacos for you and a burrito for Evie. You didn't say what kind of salsa, so I got pico, but there's a side of hot in there. I had them put cheese in the kiddy pack and the sour cream on the side. I remember you said no beans also, at least I think you did. The rice is in a little container too." With a soft shrug, Sadie added, "Mom said you two were working late, so I figured I would save you the DoorDash delivery fee and drop off food since I had an emergency hearing at the Downtown Courthouse."

Zoe looked at the bag, and her stomach fluttered. She'd told the girl her order over a week ago at Evie's engagement party. Thought nothing of the conversation because she was busy watching Parker get back together with Lyra, yet Sadie remembered.

"Anyways enjoy," the woman whispered when Zoe just stared at her. She started to turn but stopped at the whiteboard with the pictures from each of the murder scenes Zoe had already begun putting up.

"It's like a real-life episode of Law and Order in here," Sadie mused. Her head turned from one side of the office to the other. "Only messier."

Zoe pushed her hair from her face. The office was a mess. The system she normally had to maintain organization had gone out the window when the legal aides had paraded into her space and dropped the files in unorganized heaps. She hadn't even had a chance to label the boxes beyond taping the victims' photo to a few.

Sadie stepped over a cluster of crime scene photos on the floor to the line of victims. Her finger grazed the picture of the youngest taped to the top of the box like a head. She pointed to the line up staring back at them. "It's like you made the boxes look like people."

Finding her voice, Zoe said, "I have to remember they're not just names. I'm fighting for what their life could have been."

Sadie's head tilted to the side as she looked over the photos of each crime scene taped to the board. Tapping one of the images, Sadie mused, "This is the only one inside."

Zoe nodded and she explained, "It was the last one. Only one not in a public place."

"Why?" Sadie asked the photo.

The question had plagued Zoe since she'd first examined the photos. Sadie had picked up on the obvious difference immediately, but there had been a litany of differences. The privacy yes, but also the fact it was at a gym. A public gym bathroom with plenty of surveillance. The reason Rosie was caught.

Zoe shrugged. She didn't need her best friend's kid sister to know she was stumped.

"I have an idea, but the finer details are still coming together."

Sadie's chin turned in Zoe's direction, causing the lawyer to try to school her expression: fix her face, specifically her eyes; look directly between Sadie's eyebrows, a tactic to gain control. But with the woman staring preposterously at her from the corner of her eye, Zoe's face flushed.

How Sadie was able to tear down her confidence with half a glance worried Zoe. Worried her enough to twist her pen between her fingers. Spun the writing utensil like a baton, until it flew out of her grip and lodged like a dagger in the boxed chest of the youngest victim.

"I thought lawyers were supposed to be good liars," Sadie mused. She wrapped her sweater around her chest and folded her arms over it.

With eyes still studying the scene, Zoe started to back pedal. She could tell the truth without seeming like she was clueless.

"A part of me thinks she wanted to get caught," Zoe said. Her tongue poked the side of her cheek. Stretched it out before working the other side. "Everywhere else was dark. Parking lots. No cameras. Towards the end there was a little more foot traffic, don't get me wrong, but it was like a complete shift."

"Or the urge became too strong," Sadie offered.

Zoe looked at the now black computer screen. She'd watched the interrogation video at some point, which felt like hours ago. However, she could still see the woman rocking in her chair. Whatever control she'd had before her arrest was gone, which made the concept of urges interest Zoe.

"Too strong?" Zoe repeated.

She picked up a plastic water bottle. It scrunched in her hand as she unscrewed the cap and took a sip. Her gaze searched Sadie's face, trying to answer her own question so she could immediately contribute. Prove her worthiness for some reason after being called a liar. Bile rose in her throat and mixed with the water as she forced it down. She hadn't just been a liar but a shit listener in comparison to the other woman as she realized she would have to call the girl to get Sadie's Chipotle order if their places were reversed.

She took another sip when she accepted she never would have thought of the woman's need to eat dinner or cared if she had to order though. Water, already not being her favorite thing, became worse with the way it helped the guilt spread over her tongue and wash away any excuses for herself.

Her mother had been right to call her selfish. Right to tell her to leave Parker and Lyra alone. Right to remind her she'd ruined her chance with both of them. Just like Evie had been right to tell Zoe to keep the hell away from the girl who wasn't selfish.

Sadie looked at her Apple watch. She tapped the screen, answering someone worth her time, while Zoe still waited for the girl's insight. With a heavy sigh, Sadie held up her wrist.

"It's an emergency call," the woman explained. "I have to go to Phoenix Children's Hospital."

"Yeah, I... uh... I get it," Zoe answered.

The straight lipped smile was back. A look making Zoe wonder if Sadie hated her or liked her.

A thumb gestured to the door, and the girl said, "I'll get out before my sister gets here."

Zoe stood up and started to go around the desk. But Sadie was quick. Her feet almost to the door, and Zoe had to stop her because she still needed an answer.

"What did you mean by urges being too strong?" she asked a little louder than was needed for the office.

Sadie paused, turning her head just enough to show a petite nose placed over parted plump lips. When they'd first met, Zoe was struck by how similar Sadie looked to Alex. From this angle, in the fading light of the day, Sadie seemed to almost glow. Her stray curls formed a halo around her head, and the pink blossoms in her cheeks stole Zoe's breath away.

The woman's chin dropped to her chest as her eyes met Zoe's. "Oh... you, like, actually wanted to know?"

The question caught Zoe off guard. She had asked, hadn't she? Her mind rewound the last few moments, and she distinctly remembered asking a question. But maybe it could have been in her head. However, if it was just in her head, then Sadie wouldn't have said the word 'actually'. This led Zoe down a different aisle in her library of memories. Shelves of books on her interactions with the Greyson-Trikrus. She searched for a time one of them didn't care about the question asked. When they'd cast aside something said to them.

She found nothing, but simultaneously drawn into making sure the woman, who listened to something as lame as her high-maintenance food order, knew she cared about what Sadie had to say. That was something she'd failed to do with

Parker, and she needed to change her habits.

"Yes. I think... maybe, you might be on to something I hadn't thought of."

Sadie squeezed the purse over the front of her. Her lip popped out from between her teeth.

"Well... I watch a lot of, like, documentaries and listen to podcasts and stuff on murders. Like "Serial." That one was really good." Sadie waved her words away though. Wiped them from the air like she was cleaning a whiteboard. "You don't care about that. The urges... well... the documentaries all say serial murders escalate. They do a whole thing about it on *Criminal Minds* and *Mindhunters* too, before it went off air."

Sadie took a deep breath. Her words falling out quickly like this was the first time someone had listened to her talk about something she was clearly interested in.

"So, like, the endorphins the killer gets... they constantly are trying to reach the same peak. Like from the first time when they feel that, like, rush. Like a sense of freedom or power. The sociopaths with the muted emotions though, it's, like, a buzz when everything is normally turned, like, way, way down. Killing for them can give them this type of release of what we think of as, like, joy. You know, how normal kids feel on Christmas. I mean, I think of, like, the movies I've seen about kids when they get that big present. I didn't have Christmas's like that, but I bet you did. Your mom seems, like, the big Christmas person."

Sadie shook her head, and Zoe couldn't help but notice how excited she was. Excited, and at the same time trying to remain serious.

"Sorry, rambling. Anyways, the killer is going for that, like, high, but it can't be reached by doing the same thing over and over again." Sadie turned on her heel back to Zoe. Her face bright, like serial killers excited the woman more than anything else.

"It's kinda like sex," the girl said.

Zoe choked on the drink of water she'd just sipped. Luckily it dribbled out her pursed lips rather than spray over the woman. She swallowed quickly, praying not to asphyxiate on the liquid.

"I'm sorry?" Zoe said.

Sadie shrugged as though she hadn't almost killed the ADA with her comparison.

"You know what I mean," Sadie stated. But her eyebrows furrowed and her upper lip tucked below her bottom. She stared at Zoe, then carefully added, "Like the first time you have sex with someone it is crazy and exciting, but if you always do it exactly the same, it... it doesn't feel the same. You have to shake things up. Couples that don't... the ones that just do the sex the way they did it before lose interest and they stop having sex as often because it doesn't do it for them the same way."

The words made sense. The words coming from Sadie's lips though just felt weird. She returned to her chair when she felt the first wobble of her knees. Getting told keeping sex interesting was like a serial killer escalating was weird enough. It was even weirder when Zoe began to imagine a scene where Sadie and her leaned over her kitchen counter as they studied the crime scenes. That they could look up from a photo and for a moment stare into each other's eyes.

No, it wasn't something that would happen with the third Greyson. It couldn't after Zoe had hurt Lyra. Not after Evie had said Sadie was too young for her.

'She is too young,' Zoe reminded herself as she studied the smiley face on the Chipotle bag. Her mouth was watering for the food. Not the girl who seemed as fascinated with murder scenes as she was.

"What is a song that randomly sneaks into your thoughts when you're doing mundane tasks?" Sadie asked, ripping Zoe's mind back from the kitchen scene where she wouldn't be looking at Sadie's lips but tasting them because Sadie was maybe not too young.

Zoe's mouth opened to dismiss the question as being too crazy. Immediately though, she heard the beat pound in her ears. She blamed Evie's obsession with Disney of course, but it was her song. Sure, she'd watched the film recently with Evie, but she couldn't deny having sung it before.

"'Almost There'," Zoe said. "*The Princess and the Frog*. I love that movie. Only princess who works hard."

Sadie's brows crinkled slightly. Her eyes scanned over Zoe's face, making Zoe recall Sadie's confession to not having the type of childhood she did.

"Ain't' got time for messing around. And it's not my style," Zoe sing-spoke the words. She was prepared to continue when Sadie's smile rose from just a hint to her eyes.

"I know exactly where I'm going," the other woman sang. Sang as though the animated character was in the room doing a voice over. "Gettin' closer and closer everyday."

"Yeah, that's it," Zoe whispered in awe when Sadie cut short the verse.

Sadie hummed a few more bars. Her head nodded slightly as she took in the office once more. Then she said, "Makes sense."

Zoe licked her lips. She'd messed up with Parker by not talking about anything besides herself. Sadie was off limits, but she could still practice.

"What's yours?" she asked the younger woman.

Sadie didn't answer though. Her head turned to the doorway even before Evie breached the space. Zoe watched Sadie's smile vanish. The chiseled chin dipped to her chest when Evie barked, "What are you doing here?"

"She brought us dinner," Zoe said. A finger pointed to the bag on her desk. "Chipotle."

Evie's eyes rolled as she said, "You don't even like Chipotle."

Her heavy police belt hit the top of a box. The navy bulletproof vest growled as the Velcro was pulled from the side and shoulder. It hit the chair the sister should have been asked to sit in. Asked to share the meal she'd brought for them.

Evie tugged until the buttons of her uniform shirt popped open. Her body flopping in her self-proclaimed assigned seat.

"Last time I made you eat there you whined the whole time and ordered a fucking kid's plate like a five-year-old because you couldn't handle your food was touching," Evie reminded her.

Zoe watched Sadie's shoulders fall. She didn't have a chance to thank Sadie. Didn't get a moment to tell the girl she appreciated Sadie not only brought them dinner but actually listened to her when she hadn't given the conversation even half a brain cell.

None of those things were possible because Sadie whispered, "Don't work too hard," and disappeared quietly through the door. Her internal song of motivation left unshared, and Zoe understood the shock of someone caring. Understood the question Sadie had asked in a way that made her wonder why she put up with Evie's crass candor.

"I told you she had a crush on you," Evie stated. She pulled the food from within the bag and laid it out on the desk. She wiggled the brown box of tacos at Zoe. "Like a stalker, I tell you. You told her one thing and she rushed out to get it for you."

Zoe opened the lid to the box. Each item contained in its designated place like her lunch had been on the partitioned plates from her childhood. She had said she liked the kid's meals because it kept everything from touching. She told Sadie that, and it had mattered enough for the woman to remember.

"I mean, it is nice she actually remembered my order," Zoe tried. "Clearly she knows your order too."

Evie looked at the burrito already bitten into. She stared at its contents, then said, "She didn't put any hot sauce on it."

Zoe's head fell back. Her frustration building, until she heard her friend add, "She knows I always like hot sauce... but lately... It made me sick last time. We were all out with Mom and I spent the whole meal in the bathroom."

Evie's eyes turned back to the door. The sound of the elevator closing caused the cop to look back at the burrito. Then her narrowed gaze slowly rose to Zoe. A manicured finger pointed across the desk at her.

"Still too young for me," Zoe stated, but a part of her felt like Sadie wouldn't be freaked out by photos of murder scenes acting as accent rugs around her apartment.

Questions for Discussion

Zoe spends a lot of time in her imagination, trying to reconstruct a crime scene. How does this internal struggle between imagination and reality affect her as a character? What does it reveal about her dedication to the case?

How does the story address issues of social inequality and the impact they can have on individuals like Olivia?

How does the setting, such as the party and the room, contribute to the atmosphere and the events of chapter 4? Are there any symbolic elements in the text?

Both Parker and Lyra talk about solving puzzles or pieces of someone's puzzle. How might this concept be significant to the story's development?

How does humor contribute to the character development and overall tone the book?

How did Olivia's art serve as a form of expression and communication, especially when she was initially hesitant to speak about her feelings and experiences?

Olivia mentioned that she jumped off the swing set because her friends were doing it. What does this tell us about peer pressure and the desire to fit in? How can peer pressure impact young people's decision-making?

Olivia's confession about her role in protecting the baby in the past raises moral and ethical questions. Do you believe her actions were justified, given her age and circumstances?

The passage touches on themes of forgiveness and understanding. How might Echo's response to Olivia's confession signal a shift in her feelings towards her?

How do Parker and Alex's past traumas influence their ability to trust others, and in what ways does it affect their relationships? Can you relate to their experiences in any way?

How do Parker and Lyra's experiences with jealousy and insecurity impact their relationship? How might they navigate these emotions in a healthy way?

Alex mentions how they and Dilynn ended up in a parenting role for the young adults they took in. How can this affect a romantic relationship, and what advice or insights would you offer to couples in similar situations?

Parker questions the concept of trust and suggests it might be based on our expectations and experiences. Do you agree with her perspective on trust? How do you define trust in your relationships?

Alex mentions repeatedly leaving Dilynn and coming back, possibly as a response to trauma. How important is it to address and work through past trauma in relationships, and what methods or strategies can be helpful in doing so?

How do you think Parker's perspective has evolved during the conversation with Alex, and how might this impact her relationship with Lyra or her approach to future relationships?

Discuss the motivations and feelings of the two main characters, Zoe and Parker. What drives them to act the way they do in chapter 37?

Zoe claims she's not the same person she used to be. Do you think people can truly change, and can their past actions be forgiven? How does personal growth impact relationships?

Chapter 37 ends with Parker driving away. Do you think this conflict is resolved, or do you see more unresolved issues? How do you predict their relationship will evolve from this point?

Analyze the use of symbolism, such as the planes landing, to convey emotions and themes in the scene.

How does the conflict between Zoe and Parker relate to the theme of seeking closure and resolution in relationships? Do you think they will find the closure they seek?

Acknowledgements

I am deeply grateful to the remarkable individuals who have contributed to the creation of this book in countless ways. Your support, insight, and understanding have been the lifeblood of this endeavor.

First and foremost, to my wife: thank you from the bottom of my heart. Your incredible patience and extraordinary capacity for forgiveness during this turbulent journey have been a priceless gift. Enduring my moments of creative madness and letting me act out scenes to capture the perfect expressions was a testament to your unwavering support. You are the cornerstone of my creative endeavors, and I could not have done this without you.

To Tara, my friend and confidante, your role in this journey has been invaluable. Sitting across the lunch table, engaging deeply with my characters, and reading each chapter after dinner infused life into this book. Your friendship and dedication have been a constant source of motivation, and I am profoundly grateful.

Emilie, your assistance in ensuring the accuracy of the murder case details was crucial. Answering all my cop-related questions with patience and expertise helped shape the narrative's authenticity. Your guidance has been indispensable, and I am deeply thankful for your help.

To everyone who supported me, through sharing experiences, offering guidance, or simply believing in this project, I extend my heartfelt thanks. This book is as much a product of your generosity and understanding as it is of my creativity.

As I send this book out into the world, it is with immense gratitude. I hope it resonates with readers and stands as a testament to the collaboration and support that brought it to life.

About the Author

Chelsey Blue Spicer is a trailblazing author with a deep commitment to amplifying the voices and experiences of the LGBTQ+ community. Born with a storytelling spirit, Chelsey embarked on her writing journey at the age of twelve, inspired by her mother's own published autobiography. From a young age, she understood the power of words to spark conversations, challenge norms, and create positive change.

Chelsey's novels stand out for their fearless exploration of post-coming out narratives within the LGBTQ+ community. Fueled by a deep-seated passion for representation, she confronts and dismantles harmful stereotypes, particularly the "bury your gays" media trope that has plagued LGBTQ+ storytelling for years. Chelsey's stories break free from the shackles of conventional narratives, showcasing everyday life and celebrating the diverse experiences of LGBTQ+ individuals without resorting to violence or relegating characters to stereotypical roles.

Infuriated by the lack of nuanced representation, Chelsey Blue Spicer writes with a mission—to provide models of life for LGBTQ+ individuals after they come out. Her narratives go beyond the struggles, offering glimpses into the joy, resilience, and triumphs that define the everyday lives of the LGBTQ+ community.

Chelsey is not just an author; she is a voice for those whose stories have often been overlooked or misrepresented. Through her work, she aims to create a literary landscape where everyone can see themselves reflected, celebrated, and understood. Chelsey Blue Spicer invites readers to join her in breaking down barriers, fostering understanding, and embracing the diverse and beautiful spectrum of human experiences within the LGBTQ+ community.

www.chelseybluespicer.com

Available October 2024

Meet Charleigh

The almost brawl began because Charleigh deep down had always been a liar. A good enough liar to fool even herself half of the time. Charleigh and Mona were late for tip off because of a tug o' war match over a purple jersey with Lexa Jenson's name on it. Thirty minutes of arguing about whether wearing the jersey was a crime against womanhood.

"Lexa Jenson is a womanizer and a cheater," Mona yelled, her fist tightened around the purple mesh material.

Her evidence was TikTok videos where Jenson was shown holding on to a woman that wasn't her wife. A blonde half Jenson's size had tried her best to keep her face covered as she pulled and pushed her way free from Jenson's drunken grip.

Mona had a very strong argument, and if Charleigh was grading it like one of her student's essays, then she would have to give Mona an A. However, Mona wasn't Charleigh's student. The tattooed taller woman was basically her sister and had once been her girlfriend. A once upon a time type of story that did not end in a happily ever after. Their story was a fractured fairytale, and the almost brawl ended with the blonde's decision that being told what she could not wear by the girl who dumped her was a battle worth winning.

Charleigh jerked the jersey from Mona's hand. She'd worn it to every game since Mona gifted it to her three years earlier. The other woman had to know that. Three years of supporting the Devils and Lexa Jenson in that jersey. And they hadn't lost a home game all season while she wore it. A win streak that brought them to the playoff game the two women were late for.

The real question was: how could she not wear it?

She didn't ask though. It would mean the topic was up for debate.

She pulled it over the top of her. Got her head briefly stuck in the arm hole before she fixed herself. She always fixed herself.

"You stopped being allowed to lecture me when you decided to dump me," Charleigh hissed. "It's supposed to be my birthday present, so I'm going to wear what I want."

They left Charleigh's house without talking to each other. The music played while Mona huffed at every red light on the trip across town. The gravel lot across from the arena was filled, but Mona made her own parking space. She navigated the truck with ease, while Charleigh's mind ran through their argument once more.

With arms folded over Jenson's number on her chest, Charleigh convinced herself she was right to wear the jersey. Reminded herself, Mona didn't even know what happened at the bar the night Lexa Jenson was arrested. Mona didn't even watch basketball enough to care that this was the Devil's shot at the first championship in seven years. Or to care about what Lexa was going through.

Charleigh understood what it was like to have someone come between her and the girl she loved. Mona had just never loved Charleigh enough to understand, which is why Charleigh could forgive Jenson. She had to forgive. After all, she'd done worse things in her life.

The cracked soles of her orange Converse Chucks slapped against the wet concrete. Charleigh dragged Mona through the mostly vacant courtyard outside of the basketball arena's doors. At least there wasn't a line to move through the metal detectors.

The court was visible from the lobby, but the teams looked like ants fighting over a Cheeto crumb. Luckily, the big screen was focused on Lexa Jenson in possession of the ball. Charleigh stopped and stood on her toes. She watched the woman drive toward the center, fake left, then slip around the opponent on the right for an easy lay-up.

The ball sank, but the behemoth in blue hit Jenson's face. Jenson's body twisted while she was still in the air before hitting the wooden floor with a slight bounce. She curled into a ball, holding her nose. Her dark hair came loose from her standard bun.

The footage replayed the thick elbow smashing Jenson in the cheek and nose in slow motion. Then from a different angle.

"About time someone decked her," Mona grumbled. "If I had known you're still obsessed with that bitch, I never would have brought you here for your birthday."

Charleigh swatted Mona for thinking it was a good thing the Devil's MVP and highest scorer lay on the floor.

"We need her," Charleigh explained. "If she's out, then we're fucked. Tanzon is only averaging sixteen points a game and her field goal average has dropped over the last four weeks. She is really only good if she gets a clear shot, and Jenson is the one who clears the lane for her to shoot. So, you know what that means?"

"They lose," Mona stated.

"We lose," Charleigh corrected. Her hands moved in the air but contributed nothing as she explained. "We would have to come from behind in the series, and the blue team has never lost a series where they started out on top. Winning tonight means we take the first round."

Mona laughed at Charleigh bouncing on her toes, trying to see the court where ant-like Lexa Jenson lay surrounded by a few other black ants with miniature red bags. She tugged on Charleigh's arm, but the blonde shook away the grip. Her eyes had returned to the now live action of the medic's prodding Lexa's face. It didn't look like it was bleeding.

Mona called to her, but Charleigh waved her off. "Not now. I need to know if she is okay."

Lips pressed a kiss to Charleigh's cheek. A hand was shoved into Charleigh's front pocket, then the rear one. The right side produced nothing but an old gum wrapper, so Mona tried the other side.

"I need your ID, Princess," Mona said.

Charleigh disregarded the stupid name and pressed her face into Mona's lips to get another kiss. Seven years as sisters instead of lovers still broke Charleigh's heart, but she knew Mona was seeing someone else. She knew she'd never be anything more than what she was, and she was learning to accept that.

She reached down the neck of her shirt. Her ID was a little sweaty when she put it in the other woman's hand. Whether Mona cared or not went unnoticed when the screen switched to a view of the Devils in a huddle. Their coach danced his fingers over the palm of his other hand. His lips curled over his teeth as he snarled at the players. Spittle flew from his lips towards the women not looking at him from the bench.

Charleigh felt something slip over her head and glanced down to see the purple lanyard with a plastic holder in it. The ticket was huge with foiled lettering. Lexa Jenson in 2D went up for a layup across the cardstock.

She held it for a moment, and just looked at the woman. Even after everything that happened, she wished it would have been different. She wished for the woman who'd fumbled through a Shakespeare sonnet in the overcrowded lecture hall they'd shared once upon a time. Or the one who'd stood smiling while she held up the Devil's jersey. Number 1 draft pick for the NWBA before she'd even finished four years of college.

Mona hooked an arm through Charleigh's and pulled her toward the glass doors to a little old man in the oversized orange jersey just as the Devils went back out onto the floor. Without the screen to distract her, Charleigh smiled at him and held out her ticket.

"Hiya, Charleigh." His voice was tired, but Charleigh could hear the happiness in it.

"Hey, Hank," she said. She held up her ticket so he could scan it. The scanner let out the three little beeps of approval.

"VIP tonight. Must be a special occasion," he said with a wink.

Charleigh nodded her head and felt her hair flop side-to-side. "Next week's my birthday."

The old man's bushy gray eyebrows rose. "Your birthday! Well, early happy birthday, Charleigh. How old you gonna be?"

Charleigh ducked her head and smiled, "Twenty-three on Thursday."

"Good for you," Hank offered. He scanned Mona's ticket. "I still remember you coming every summer with your pop. Good man. He'd be proud to see how big you got."

She forced the smile on her face not to waiver. Her father, the one to always make friends with the people he passed by, had brought them to games since Charleigh was a child. Their seats were always too high to see anything, but they'd share a popcorn and a soda as he reminded her to always root for the home team.

"You have a good time. And be safe!" Hank called after her as Mona dragged her from her thoughts and the doorway.

When Charleigh turned back to smile at him once more, Hank waved. He'd been working the door for as long as she could remember. She worried each time he wouldn't be there the next time she came, and the last piece of her life before she was alone would disappear.

Mona abandoned Charleigh without a word in front of another television screen for food fifteen feet later. As play stopped for a commercial break, Charleigh's impatience began to set in. She tapped her foot, watching her sister move like a snail through the line. She'd already missed the first four minutes of the first quarter.

With the screen alongside the concession stand on a commercial, Charleigh glanced down at the ticket around her neck. She checked Mona's position in line, then decided seeing the game was her birthday present and she was done waiting.

She followed the instructions to entry point 101. With step one done, she studied the next set of information. She'd never had a ticket like this before, because the row was a letter, and the letter was A. The first letter in the alphabet, which meant the first row. Her eyes scanned the seats along the floor, landing on the only two open. Two padded folding chairs sat unoccupied, directly next to the Devils' bench.

Her heart beat the air out of her lungs. Mona hadn't just gotten her tickets to a playoff game; she'd gotten her courtside seats. She was going to be right next to the bench. Next to Lexa Jenson and the rest of the Devils.

Watching from the stands was her plan. She would blend in with the crowd. Be far from Jenson's gaze, like in the lecture hall. Squished between older lesbians and soccer moms. Screaming with others where she couldn't be heard, and she wouldn't be seen.

Mona sidled up alongside Charleigh standing at the top of the stairs with her hands overflowing with snacks and a drink in the crook of her arm. She hip-checked Charleigh before leading the way down. Her dark hair swayed, the scarlet red tips peeking out from under the sharp cut.

Charleigh found Jenson on the court. The woman led by a stride, running the ball down the court with two guards in blue closing in around her. She sucked in her lower lip, then chewed on the peeling skin. The ball pounded into the wood with each step she took, but before she was up, she tossed the ball to the left where number 27, Danaya Tanzon had come up. The defenders couldn't redirect the motion to block Lexa, leaving 27 completely open for the corner three.

With hands above her head, Charleigh jumped up and down while yelling, "Yeahhhh!" Her cheers joined the roar of the rest of the crowd, and she felt at ease with her people. Remembering that Jenson had no reason to care she was sitting in the front row of the game. There were hundreds of people there to see the MVP. Plus, she didn't even know Charleigh's name.

Checking the scoreboard, Charleigh noted they were up by six. However, in basketball that was only two three pointers, or three lay-ups, or two shots with fouls for a chance of an extra shot. Really the combinations of scenarios that could lead to her team losing were immeasurable. It didn't stop her from worrying about each one of them.

Mona was already getting comfortable when Charleigh made it down the narrow steps. As she sat, Mona handed over a soda in a red and white cup. It was the perfect combination of syrup and bubbles, and the caramel-colored liquid brought a smile to Charleigh's face with the first sip.

Her sister's arm slung around the back of Charleigh's chair with her legs stretched out. She lounged in comfort of the luxury game seating, while Charleigh sat up on the edge of the cushion as the teams ran toward them. All of the women on the court were so much bigger than Charleigh was used to thinking about them, and so real. With voices that said words rather than the silent play she was used to watching from 20 rows up.

Lexa was at the far end of the court flashing two, then five fingers. She called out "Orange slide!"

The chair wobbled with Charleigh's bouncing legs. Her eyes memorized the details, knowing this was the closest she'd ever be to a professional court. A sweat droplet ran down the center, Emma Delango's face. She watched the guard, Danaya Tanzon, get blocked by the screen, but Lexa Jenson moved past the Stars' forward and stripped the ball away. She passed the ball to Delango. Delango took it back down the court only to fake a shot and bounced it back to Jenson who ran into the key. The ball slapped the board and fell in the net.

When Lexa's feet landed, Charleigh felt her heart rattle against her ribs. The familiar eyes looked directly at Charleigh in her jersey. The corners of her dark lips curled into a smile, and she winked at Charleigh.

Jenson pointed at Charleigh and said, "Don't worry. I got more. Just for you."

Charleigh was breathing too fast because she'd been so wrong. The cavity of her chest refused to fill to capacity when the memories began to creep back to the forefront of her mind.

A colorful tattooed arm wrapped around Charleigh, pulling her back into her chair. She glared at Lexa, whose brows scrunched for a moment before she turned, running back down court.

"Hey, Princess," Mona said. "You okay?"

Charleigh stared at the floor, then up at the game where Emma Delango had recovered a rebound. She knew every stat for number 42, Emma Delango. But none of it mattered as Charleigh tried to will away the last time she'd been this close to the woman. The same memory where number 27, Danaya Tanzon, had stood by.

'They were there when...' Charleigh stopped the thought.

She was supposed to be home. If she had just gone home instead of the bar, Lexa Jenson wouldn't have gotten in a fight and been arrested. It was her fault for even going there.

"Did you cream your chonies?" Mona asked as Charleigh stared blankly at the court.

A part of her wanted to leave, it would be easier that way. However, there was nothing at her little house but her dog. Going home meant being alone because Mona would leave again, and Charleigh had exhausted being alone with Mona off living her new life.

She wanted to be here. Needed to be here so she could feed off the energy of the crowd and leave with the drumming of victory in her ears. It would give her something to think about. A win to cherish between the memories of all the loss.

Charleigh shook her head. "No, just in awe," she said. "Thank you for getting the tickets for my birthday. I know they probably cost you a paycheck."

"You're worth it," Mona said. She went back to eating her snacks, basketball being of no interest to her.

Charleigh's heart was still beating too fast, but it raced in step with the fast break that brought 27 back down the court. Charleigh locked away the memory of 27's eyes on her and created a new memory of the woman in this moment. The smile that spread across the dark face as she smacked a hand to her chest in pride.

"Welcome to the DEVIL's DEN!" Danaya Tanzon yelled. She held her hand up to her ear, calling for the crowd's cheers. "You know who gets it done!"

As the crowd shouted out the 'Get it Devils' chant, Charleigh created a new memory of 42 to replace the way her eyes had run down Charleigh's pinned body. She replaced it with an open-mouthed laugh at 27 when she helped the woman to her feet after the blue behemoth struck again. Her close-cropped hair shook and sweat showered the younger teammate as they celebrated their lead.

Charleigh couldn't create a new memory of Lexa Jenson, though. She couldn't because every time the Devils came back to defend, the woman's eyes fell on her.

Stared at Charleigh as though she could see straight through the jersey hanging off her.

She stopped looking at Jensen. Instead, she spent her one night as a VIP learning the details of the rest of the team and eating the pretzel Mona bought her. She dipped torn chunks of dough into the fake yellow cheese and shoved it into her mouth each time her team played defense on the other end of the court.

Time had moved so quickly with each team seeming to only have a fastbreak offense in their playbook. Charleigh became so engrossed in the game; she didn't even notice halftime was approaching until the fans began to count down the last ten seconds.

As the team headed her way, Charleigh looked up to find the tired brown eyes standing out against the sweat sheened skin. They were locked on her once more, and she remembered when she thought it was because she mattered.

Those important eyes had looked at her...

had chosen her to dance with.

had wanted her over the rest in the room.

had looked her over and decided she existed.

Just like they were doing at this moment. Hundreds of people were watching as Lexa walked directly to her.

She turned her body to face Mona. The familiar warmth of Mona's arm wrapped securely around her. She gazed at a different shade of brown. An earthy brown that flitted down to her lips, however, didn't move forward. Their kissing days had passed with their youth. Now in their twenties, Mona had someone she didn't want to know Charleigh.

And Charleigh had her first house. Her dog, Rexa Pawson. And her job.

Charleigh's eyes closed. She thought of the time kisses were stolen between them in their shared bedroom or between classes. But the past was the past, and the present was not a love story between two foster sisters.

"Well, she can't keep her eyes off you," Mona said. "But that's not unusual. You always are the brightest star in the room. Mainly because you're fluorescent."

Charleigh placed her fingers to the red lips. She closed her eyes and locked the door to the past, then pressed a kiss to the flushed cheek. "Thanks for bringing me, even though you hate basketball."

They cheered for the tiny hip-hop team during halftime, then for the Devils as they made their way back to the court. Charleigh pointed out each of the players, taking warm up shots on their side of the court.

"...and 15 is Denise Forte. She is only 5'6". One of the shortest players in the league so she never really gets to play much."

A ball rolled into Charleigh's feet, and she stooped down to pick it up. She turned to pass the ball back on the court but froze. Lexa Jenson stood in the same spot where she'd missed every attempted shot all season with her hands held out.

With a deep breath, Charleigh thrust the ball back to the woman. A strong chest pass caused Jenson to take a step back. Jenson caught the ball and looked at her. Her eyebrows cinched again. Instead of going back to shooting though, she walked over to Charleigh and Mona. That cocky smile from quarter one was plastered back on her face.

"You want to go out tonight?" Jenson asked with her feet still on the court.

Charleigh swallowed. "Uh, we..."

"Aren't interested in hangin' out with misogynistic assholes like you," Mona snapped. Her arm fell over Charleigh's shoulder. "Anyone ever tell you that you give lesbians a bad rap?"

"Feisty. I like a little fight." Jenson cast her eyes back on Charleigh. Then she asked, "What about you? You busy tonight or is the girlfriend just threatened?"

"I..." Words wouldn't work.

"You know, you could use your hall pass." Jenson's eyebrows rose and fell. "I promise it'll be worth it."

Charleigh studied the way the woman's lips curled at the corners in a self-approved smirk when she spoke this time. And a familiar feeling settled in her chest.

"I... I can't tonight."

Jenson grabbed the Sharpie a fan waved in her face from the row behind them. She scribbled on the ball before handing the marker back to the owner and the ball to Charleigh.

"I'm here all year," Jenson said with another wink.

Charleigh turned to show Mona the birthday prize realizing it was Lexa Jenson's phone number instead of an autograph. There was a point in her life that she would have fought someone over ownership of that ball. However, when the ball came loose from her grasp, Charleigh didn't rush after it. She steadied herself on Mona, then looked back to see what had caused her to lose control of the now lost ball.

"Don't touch her," Mona barked. Her fingers dug into the ball player's wrist. Jenson's bicep flexed as the chemical compounds tattooed over Mona's wrist seemed to give her superhuman strength. "She's too good to end up like the last girl that thought you were something special."

Lexa Jenson's lips formed a straight line, but her eyes widened in surprise. She pulled her wrist back, but Mona didn't release her.

"Let go of me," Lexa rumbled. The surprise was gone, and the frame of her body rose from the slumped position. Her height loomed over Charleigh's back.

"What?" Mona scoffed. "You don't like it when people put their hands on you?"

Charleigh placed her hand on Mona's, and she released Jenson's hand. She glanced up at Lexa and tried to remember the girl she'd seen in college. With a soft shrug, she explained, "She's just worried you're going to hurt me. You and I have a bad history of touching."

Lexa's glare softened when she looked down at Charleigh. Her brows furrowed, and Charleigh awaited a bitchy comment. Waited for Lexa Jenson to snap like she'd done both times she'd been close to Charleigh.

The music in the arena was getting louder. A buzzer rang when the clock hit zero. The sound seemed to flip a switch in Lexa Jenson. The woman's eyes widened; this time not dilated with lust.

The pale seashell brown irises pulled Charleigh's gaze. Even in a state of shock, Charleigh couldn't help but swoon over how beautiful Lexa Jenson was. How her eyes seemed to be just a shade paler than her skin. Her hair in a natural curl set, the bun having come undone in the first quarter.

The woman shut her mouth only to open it again. She did this a few times, but no words came out. Emma Delango came up behind Lexa. She shoved the basketball with the phone number back into Charleigh's hands before pulling at Lexa.

"Jenson, let's go," Delango said, but then she looked at Charleigh. Her eyes grew as wide as Lexa's. They were darker and sadder when they stared down at her.

"You're the girl from the bar," she breathed. "I went after you, but you were gone."

Lexa's posture shrunk once more. Her hands gripped the air like bars separating herself from Charleigh. Words began to fall and fail with each breath she took.

"The next day..."

Fans were screaming around them. Called for their team like sirens.

"I tried to find you..."

Inflatable tubes struck together. Their cracks were as loud as thunder in the cavernous space.

"...to tell you I was...."

Lexa was panicking. She was panicking, but halftime was over.

"I'm so sorry. I wasn't going to..." Lexa's head shook back and forth. Her hand extended to touch Charleigh, but hovered just out of reach. "I didn't mean to...."

Charleigh grabbed the dark hand. She squeezed it like a hug instead of a handshake. She told herself not to stutter, but it was hard. It was hard because she was holding the hand that pushed her into the railing. The hand that tried to push its way into her pants because the woman hadn't cared.

"I forgive you," Charleigh yelled over the people screaming around her.

It wasn't the truth, but Lexa wouldn't know Charleigh looked at people's noses when she lied. The woman would feel better about what happened, and the game would go on. Life would go on, like it always had without the blonde.

Lexa's eyes blinked. In a single breath, she said, "I'll make it up to you. I'm not the monster they say I am. You'll see. I'll show you. I'll see you after the game."

She turned before Charleigh could agree. Ran down the court as the Stars inbounded the ball with only four Devil's defenders in place.

Once Lexa was on the other side, Charleigh felt the weight lift from her chest. She leaned back into Mona with the ball over her middle, cradling it like a proud mom to be. Mona's arms wrapped around her center, pulling the smaller woman flush to her as they waited with the rest of the fans for the Devils to score their first points before taking their seats.

Mona's breath warmed the back of Charleigh's neck. Her chin rested on Charleigh's shoulder as she asked, "Were you the girl in the video at Echo's Escape?"

Charleigh nodded. She nodded because there was no reason left to lie to Mona. There was no reason to try to hide something from Mona she already knew. Because if she tried to deny it was her, then Mona would question the other things she'd said over the years. She'd ask questions Charleigh hoped never to have to answer again.

"Why didn't you tell me?" Mona asked. "Call me to get you? I saw the video. You were scared."

Charleigh lowered her head. Her eyes traced the inconsistent pattern of the floorboards. Taking a deep breath, she confessed, "I shouldn't have been there. I wasn't drinking, but I have said that before... so I figured it was better if no one knew. I just went home and hoped no one would recognize me."

Mona's arms tightened. She pressed another kiss to the honey hair. Her chin made its way to Charleigh's shoulder where she rested the brilliant brain on the smaller woman. The woman had given up so much to stay with Charleigh. The least the blonde could do was not make Mona regret it.

Charleigh could hear the smile in Mona's voice when she said, "Well you have a new ball out of it, and apparently an annoying douche canoe trying to make it up to you. I mean, she could be worse. She could be like Kyle, who used to try and watch you take a shower."

"She could be worse," Charleigh echoed. She tried not to hold her breath when she thought of their oily foster brother. "She could smell like a chicken nugget."

"You really do have the worst taste in women. Even Jenson's sweat smelled better than the culinary chick." Mona leaned into Charleigh. "But before you go calling that phone number. I need you to ask yourself. Do you honestly think she is more than her latest catch phrase?"

Charleigh looked over just enough to scan Mona's face. The woman watched the players on the court closer than she'd ever paid attention to a game before. The rich cognac eyes ran over the team, then fell on Charleigh's face.

"What do you mean?"

Mona's arms released her, and she held up her hands as she pretended to yell, "I'm Lexa Fucking Jenson."

Charleigh snorted loudly, because even though Mona hadn't screamed, she could hear the exclamation points in the words. Her hands shoved Mona back slightly.

As if on cue, number 1 held up an arm. Her bicep caught the Stars' guard just over the chest. The blue uniformed player hit the ground hard as Jenson stood over the woman.

"You're going to have to do better than that!" Jenson taunted the girl, who was still trying to catch the air forced out of her. "I'm Lexa Fucking Jenson, not your little school friend!"

Charleigh leaned down and picked up her drink. The tension she'd felt twisting within her began to unravel, and she smiled at the cup of happiness. Her team was going to win, and they would go on to win a championship.

Just as she took a sip, a body slammed into her. Her lower back hit the chair behind her. The stands of people flipped sideways in slow motion. She knew she was falling, but there was nothing she could do to stop it.